STRANGE ATTRACTION...

"Please forgive my intrusion, Miss Beaufort, but I must speak to you."

Bewilderment marred Monsieur Andrew's tone and etched his handsome features. Fiery flames from the blazing torches that surrounded the courtyard shone in his blue eyes, the reflections haunting in his tortured face. He stared at her as if she were his savior, as if she knew how to repair whatever was wrong with him. Only she didn't. She had too many obligations to fulfill already. Because of them, she didn't know how to fix her own life. She certainly didn't want to take on the responsibility of someone else's once again.

"Monsieur?" Her questioning tone bespoke her own bewilderment. She'd just met him. Why would he seek her out?

"Miss Beaufort ... Marianne, I need your help. I must speak to you now," he repeated.

He seemed different from any other man she'd ever met. Although she didn't know quite what set him apart from other men, it drew her to him in ways that no one else ever had. From the moment she'd seen him, she knew he possessed a kind spirit, but he seemed as if he didn't belong here, as if he were from an entirely different world. It was an impossible thought, but one that couldn't allow her to walk away from him . . . .

A Hitch In Time

Christine Holden

JOVE BOOKS, NEW YORK

TIME PASSAGES is a registered trademark of Penguin Putnam Inc.

A Jove Book / published by arrangement with
the author

PRINTING HISTORY
Jove edition / October 2000

All rights reserved.
Copyright © 2000 by Leslie-Christine Megahey and Shirley-Holden Ferdinand.
Cover illustration by Franco Accornero.
This book may not be reproduced in whole or in part,
by mimeograph or any other means, without permission.
For information address: The Berkley Publishing Group,
a division of Penguin Putnam Inc.,
375 Hudson Street, New York, New York 10014.

The Penguin Putnam Inc. World Wide Web site address is
http://www.penguinputnam.com

ISBN: 0-515-12928-3

A JOVE BOOK®
Jove Books are published by The Berkley Publishing Group,
a division of Penguin Putnam Inc.,
375 Hudson Street, New York, New York 10014.
JOVE and the "J" design
are trademarks belonging to Penguin Putnam Inc.

PRINTED IN THE UNITED STATES OF AMERICA

10 9 8 7 6 5 4 3 2 1

Dedication

We thank God, for His wonders never cease.

Acknowledgments

We send love and thanks to:

Trudy Abrasom, who doesn't know what it means to refuse a request.

Brenda Boettner Borcherdt, for her enthusiasm for Christine Holden and her aid to us in a special quest.

A special acknowledgment to Donald R. Polk, simply because we love him.

Metsy Hingle, fellow author, whose energy and kindness is boundless.

Pete Rhodes, for his generosity.

Chapter 1

THE LOUD SCREECHING of tires, followed by the angry shouts of the wronged driver, didn't halt Andrew's stride as he hurried toward his parents' Esplanade Avenue home. Alaina Rousseau, his daughter's nanny, had arrived nearly an hour late, an explanation his father would consider an excuse to forestall the inevitable confrontation between them.

A few drops of rain hesitantly fell, doing nothing to alleviate the intense heat or Drew's irritation. Thunder rolled, and lightning flashed. Just as the rain started in earnest, he reached the huge wrought-iron gates of the mansion, set far back from the tree-lined street.

Using his key to unlock the gate, then quickly reclosing it behind him, he walked up the pathway, passing the neatly manicured lawns, and finally reached the stately veranda. Anticipating his arrival, the butler opened the door before Drew's feet had touched the third and final step.

"Good afternoon, Webster," Drew drawled, his mood not improving with Webster's disapproving stare.

"Master Cranneck," Webster greeted, his British accent more pronounced in his pique, the use of Drew's first name a small reparation in his father's stead.

C. Andrew Montague III glared at Webster but didn't take the bait. Shouting at Webster would do no good and only serve as fodder for his father's already flaming temper.

The butler had been in the Montagues' employ since Drew was a small child, yet Webster and Drew never got along, partly because of the man's snobbish stoicism, but mostly because of Drew's irreverent ways. Only in the past twenty-four months had Drew begun to mature. The birth of his daughter, directly followed by the breakup of his marriage when his soon-to-be-ex-wife decided motherhood wasn't for her, then the floundering of his grades in law school, facilitated matters in that direction for him.

"Your parents await you in the library, sir," Webster continued, ignoring Drew's growing anger.

Without acknowledging Webster's directions, Drew started down the hallway, his loafered feet silent on the highly polished wooden floors. Several padded benches circa 1850 stood along the satin-covered walls. A gilded mirror hung above a console where a green-potted plant sat on the marble surface.

His parents prided themselves on the old furnishings. Everything in the house had been handed down through the generations. If it had been left up to Drew, he would have refurbished the house long ago, but unfortunately it hadn't been.

Turning his attention away from the hideous decor to the coming meeting, he halted at the end of the hall outside the oak door of the library. No matter what his father said, he would *not* lose his temper.

Drew glanced down the hall and saw Webster return the receiver of the telephone to its cradle. Since Drew hadn't heard the phone ring, he knew Webster had used the intercom to alert Drew's parents to his presence.

Unable to prevent himself from giving Webster an obscene hand gesture, which the butler ignored, Drew swung the door open. He nearly collided with his father as Cranneck headed toward the door.

"Well, I see you've decided to quit skulking outside the door and present yourself to your mother and me," Cranneck bit out as he stepped aside so Drew could fully enter the room.

"Cranneck, please!" Ursula snapped. "Is that any way to greet your son?"

"Don't trouble yourself, darling," Drew said to his mother. She had always been one of his few allies in the household, which at one time included two older brothers. "I'm used to it. A pleasant good afternoon to you, too, Father." In mock deference, Drew gave his father a small bow.

An angry flush settled into Cranneck's ruddy complexion.

Thunder rolled again, and lightning flashed, momentarily illuminating the room, which was already brightly lit by matching table lamps.

Ursula sighed dramatically and rose from her seat on the brocaded settee. An older, female version of Drew, her honey-blond hair was swept up in an elegant style, and her sapphire eyes sparkled with intelligence and contentment.

How anyone could be content living with his father remained a mystery to Drew, but in some strange way Ursula and Cranneck complemented one another, though certainly not in looks. Where his mother had always been tall, reed-slender, and classically beautiful, his father was stocky, a half-inch shorter than his wife, and rugged.

"How's Teal?" Ursula asked, referring to her granddaughter, as she glided up to Drew and placed a kiss on his cheek.

"Perfect," Drew said with pride. "I have never seen a toddler who is as gifted as she is."

Ursula laughed. "A modest father, aren't you?"

"Where Teal is concerned, always," Drew answered without hesitation. "She really enjoyed her visit with you last week. I know she's looking forward to seeing you tomorrow."

"As I am her. She's such a darling child." Ursula walked to the cherrywood liquor cabinet. Pouring herself a sherry, she continued, "I have a surprise for her that I think she's going to love."

Drew raised his hands in supplication. "Please, darling, it's not necessary. If you continue to bring Teal gifts, I'll need a bigger apartment."

"Something I would be more than happy to provide you with."

His mother made it sound as if she supported him, but that wasn't the case. The money she spoke of was his own.

When Teresa walked out on him eighteen months ago, leaving him with total responsibility for the care of six-month-old Teal, he'd had to give up his job as a night auditor at the Holiday Inn on Chartres Street. For a while he'd worked a day job at a busy deli and went to school at night, but his grades had begun to suffer because Teal still hadn't learned to sleep through the night. Then she'd gotten an ear infection, and he had taken several days off to care for her. By the time Drew was able to return, the deli manager, an unsympathetic bachelor, had replaced him.

Finally Ursula had demanded he accept more of his inheritance money, in addition to the money his father had already promised him. The additional amount would see him through Tulane University for another year, outfit him in a modest apartment, buy decent meals for him and Teal, and pay for Teal's nanny while he attended school during the day.

He hadn't wanted to dip into his money again. His preference had been to save it until his graduation; then he would invest the money while he pursued his legal career. But his mother had made him realize that continual profits from Bienvenu, the family's still-active sugar plantation in St. Francisville, would quickly replace any money he took.

Drew would be forever grateful to his mother.

Ursula reseated herself on the settee. "Have you eaten, darling?"

The rain outside fell harder, and thunder rolled again, seemingly an ominous warning for the confrontation to come between him and his father.

As if on cue, Cranneck snorted. "He wasn't invited to eat, Ursula. He was invited here to discuss his continued nonsense about becoming a lawyer when it's obvious he's not cut out for the profession."

"Invited?" Drew growled, ignoring his mother's felicitations. "It sounded more like an order to me."

"If you wish to take my request as such, then who am I to dispel that notion?" Turning away from Drew and Ursula, Cranneck went to his Sheridan desk and took a seat in the matching chair behind it. "Let's dispense with the pleasantries, shall we, Cranneck?"

"What pleasantries?" Drew responded, barely civil, hating the name that linked him to his father a little more than he already was. "But by all means, Father." He stalked to one of the winged chairs sitting in front of the desk and took a seat. "To what do I owe the honor of your . . . 'request'?"

Cranneck pounded his fist on the desk. "You know damned well why you're here. As much as it breaks your mother's heart, I've decided to halt any further withdrawals from your inheritance for you and that child you sired, including your college fees. You've wasted enough of your money—at Ursula's insistence—to see you through law school. And for what? You're a failure at it. If you had taken my suggestion and gone into the family business, your life could have been completely different, but you've never listened to me. You wouldn't have further burdened us with all your legal expenses if you'd listened to me and not married that no-class woman."

Drew stiffened. "Leave Teresa out of this discussion. She's the mother of my child. But for the record, at twenty she was one of the classiest people I knew, much more so than the present company I'm attending, excluding Mother, of course." He worked the muscles in his jaw in an effort to control his anger. "As for *my* legal fees, the Montagues have a lawyer on retainer, and he receives a *set* monthly fee. Unless I am no longer part of this family, I think that umbrella of legal hospitality extends to me."

Drew felt his mother's hand on his shoulder, and he glanced back.

"I'm so sorry, Drew." Ursula sipped her sherry, her manicured hand holding the delicate stem of the glass gracefully. "I've tried everything in my power to change your father's mind, but to no avail. After all, you're entitled to that money, as your brothers were entitled to theirs."

"And they received every penny they deserved," Drew snarled, "because they allowed their strings to be pulled as though they were nothing more than Father's puppets."

"I know how you've always disdained the sugar business and how much you've always dreamed of becoming a lawyer. But if you'll just listen, your father has another proposition."

Drew eyed his mother suspiciously. "One that you agree with?"

"One that was *her* idea," Cranneck cut in, drawing Drew's attention.

"Mine and your brother Sebastian's," Ursula clarified with another sip of sherry.

At thirty-two, Sebastian was two years older than Drew. He was Drew's complete opposite in mannerisms, but Sebastian was the voice of reason for all the Montagues. Drew's other brother, Nolan, was the eldest. At thirty-six, Nolan had been happily married for thirteen years. He and his wife, Lena, along with their four daughters, lived at Bienvenu in St. Francisville, Louisiana.

While planning their family, Ursula and Cranneck had decided not to give any son she bore Cranneck's name, but when their third son had come along—Drew—in a fit of disappointment at not having a girl as their final planned child, Cranneck had gone against Ursula's wishes and named the boy after himself.

Drew sighed against the recollections and focused again on his father. "Let's have it. What proposal would you possibly agree to that would give me and Teal assistance from my own money that you're holding hostage?"

His mother spoke before his father could reply to Drew's acidic question. "Sebastian and I thought if you went to Bienvenu for a year and allowed Nolan to show you the workings of the business, you and your father could work out an agreement."

"Mother—"

"I suggest you hear your mother out, Cranneck," his father interrupted. "Maybe if you had complied with my wishes in the beginning, I would be more lenient with you now."

Drew had no response for his father's acridity. Their animosity had begun years before Drew's decision to spurn the booming Montague business in favor of his own independence. It had a lot to do with the differences in their personalities, as well as the attention Ursula bestowed upon Drew.

For some inexplicable reason, the two men had always been jealous of each other's relationship with Ursula and ruthlessly guarded their time with her. Even after Drew met Teresa and turned the majority of his attention to her, his father hadn't been appeased.

"Drew, at least hear me out," Ursula pleaded. "If you're still set upon going to law school at the end of the year, your father would release your inheritance."

"And if I'm not still 'set' upon becoming a lawyer?"

"Then we would create a position for you at Bienvenu and pay for tuition for Louisiana State's sugar course out of our pocket," Cranneck answered, opening a side drawer on the desk and retrieving a fat cigar. "You should be proud to have such an offer, boy," he went on, biting off the tip of the cigar and spitting it out. "We have a long, distinguished family tradition to continue, in case you've forgotten."

"How can I, when you constantly cram family history down my throat?"

"Enough!" Cranneck roared. "If you were half the man my great-grandfather Rafe Montague was, I'd be blessed! He laid down the South's arms with Lee at Appomattox, and I'm sure he never gave Pierre, his father, a day's grief. Rafe Montague *fought* for our heritage, and you won't even *work* for it. Well, damn me, you'll work at Bienvenu one way or another!"

Glaring at Drew, he placed the cigar in his mouth. After several flicks of his lighter, the spark caught the wick, and a flame appeared. He lit the cigar, flipped the lid on the lighter closed, and again placed it in the drawer, which he then quietly shut. He took in several deep puffs before releasing the smoke from his mouth. Holding the cigar between his teeth, he looked in speculation at Drew.

When Drew remained silent, Cranneck prodded, "Well?"

Drew narrowed his eyes, seething with resentment at his father's tactics. "Are you honestly giving me a choice, Father?"

Knowing he held the upper hand, and therefore unperturbed by Drew's contemptuous query, Cranneck shook his head. "Not in the least," he replied mildly. "Either you agree to my long-standing request or you and your daughter can starve, for all I care."

His demeanor turning dangerous, Drew shot from his chair, but his mother spoke before he responded.

"You will leave that innocent child out of this, Cranneck Montague!" Ursula commanded. "No matter that she is your youngest grandchild, you've never set eyes upon her and don't know what a sweet child she is. But if you believe I would let my son and granddaughter starve because of your despotic disposition, then you're more of an old fool than I thought, and very badly mistaken!"

The force of Ursula's furious words caught both men off guard. Drew and Cranneck merely stared at her without speaking.

Cranneck's shock yielded quickly to rage. His eyes

turned wintry blue, his face an unflattering red. "That's quite enough, Ursula! I have given in to every demand you have ever made concerning your Drew, and how does he repay me? By marrying a money-grabbing little tart, who got herself pregnant, then left him to raise that child."

Drew took a step backward in an attempt to control his scalding anger. Another surprising emotion surfaced also— hurt.

Long ago he'd decided he didn't care what his father thought. Yet there were times when he wished that his father would give him the same guidance and advice he bestowed upon Nolan and Sebastian.

Quickly he tempered the unfamiliar feeling. "I can see that this meeting has come to an end."

He started around his mother, but she halted him.

"Drew, please. Don't leave like this. Stay, and I'll have the cook prepare one of your favorite dishes. We'll talk in private."

"Dammit, woman!" Cranneck sputtered. "Did you hear a word I said?"

"Hush, Cranneck!" Ursula flared. "This is my house as well as it is yours. And as long as I'm living here, 'my' Drew and his daughter are welcome. You may well leave and find one of your friends to golf with you."

By now the rain was lessening to a gentle pitter-patter, indicating that the thundershower was coming to a close.

"I think I may very well do that." Cranneck got up from his chair and walked to the door. "I will see you at supper, Ursula."

"Don't bother. I have another engagement."

Cranneck replied by slamming the door behind him.

Tense and still furious, Drew faced his mother.

"Follow me," she said.

Instead of protesting as he wanted to, Drew obeyed his mother's command and followed behind her as she opened the door on the opposite side of the room. It connected her sitting room with his father's library.

Much the way it probably looked a century ago, the room

was a frilly, feminine affair and one in which Drew felt singularly out of place. It was solely for the use of Ursula and her bridge club. But against the far wall stood a Queen Anne secretaire, which was his mother's destination. She retrieved a check and handed it to him.

"Your monthly allotment, dear," she said quietly. "From my personal funds."

Briefly glimpsing the familiar four figures, he folded the check and stuck it in the pocket of his Polo shirt. "Thanks," he said, embarrassed. He felt like a freeloader, but he needed the money so damned bad. His animosity toward his father increased. His mother shouldn't have had to do this, and he shouldn't have been made a virtual beggar. If Cranneck had released Drew's monthly allotment, this generosity from her personal funds would have been unnecessary. Yet he'd endure embarrassment, humiliation, or anything else he had to for Teal's sake. "I'll pay you back."

"I know, son." Ursula sat in the plush desk chair and looked levelly at Drew. "So what are you going to do?"

"What choice do I have but to go to Bienvenu?" he asked bitterly.

"It shouldn't be that bad, Andrew," Ursula pointed out. "This will give you a chance to get to know Nolan better. It will give Teal a chance to become acquainted with her cousins finally. And with Lena there, she'll have the constant guidance of a woman, something a young girl desperately needs."

"Adding in the benefits to Teal makes this virtually impossible to resist." Drew laughed dryly. "I see you've thought of everything, darling."

"Isn't that what I do best?"

"You needn't fear, Mother. I'm going to accept Father's proposal."

Ursula released a breath of relief. "You'll not regret it, dear. Sebastian and I alone understand your desire to become a lawyer, and until Teal is older and less dependent upon you, we decided this would be the best way for your father to continue releasing small increments of your rightful inheritance."

Drew glowered at his mother. "Remind me to thank Sebastian the next time I see him."

"Oh, hush, Andrew," Ursula said with a smile, waving a dismissing hand at Drew's sarcasm. "Can you stay and have brunch with me?"

Glancing at his watch, Drew saw it was nearing three-thirty. "It's well past brunch time, Mother, but I'd be happy to stay and have an afternoon snack with you."

"Wonderful!"

Without another word, Drew followed when Ursula stood from her seat and headed for the door. He hoped he'd be gone by the time his father returned.

Chapter 2

TWO HOURS LATER, with the afternoon rain long over, Drew returned to his house on Burgundy Street. He lived only eight blocks away from his parents' home, but it could have been a world apart.

He had shared a light meal of poached salmon and steamed asparagus with his mother, genuinely enjoying her company. But, as the hour grew late, he became increasingly uncomfortable and decided to leave before his father returned.

Now he stood in the living room of his four-room apartment, listening to his daughter's squealing laughter.

"Hello?" Drew called. "Come out, come out, wherever you are!"

Before he finished, Teal's small footsteps bounded across the floor as she ran from the back of the house to where Drew stood.

"Dadee!" she said in delight, throwing her tiny arms around Drew's legs.

He picked her up and kissed her chubby little cheek, noticing the chocolate smeared on her fingers and chin. "Hello, princess. Where's Alaina?"

Teal pointed in the direction of the kitchen. "Choc'lat spill."

"I see. Why don't we go and see if we can assist her."

Teal nodded and wriggled to free herself of Drew's hold. Before obliging her, he kissed the tip of her nose. The moment she touched the ground, she was off again, yelling, " 'Lain!"

Walking behind his daughter, Drew marveled at how more and more Teal, with her flaming red hair and bright green eyes, was beginning to resemble Teresa.

Reaching the doorway of the kitchen, he paused. Alaina's shapely backside greeted him as she knelt to clean melted chocolate. The sweet aroma permeated the air; he looked at the table, where a little bit of milk-chocolate morsels still lay in their bag.

"Problems, Alaina?" Drew asked mildly, gazing at his daughter.

"Of course not, Drew," Alaina answered. In one graceful motion, she stood to her full height. She smiled at him, her teeth gleaming against her honey-colored complexion. "Teal and I were going to surprise you with a chocolate cake, but we had a little accident." She tousled Teal's hair affectionately. "Nothing we can't handle. Isn't that right, Teal?"

Teal nodded and placed her small hand in Alaina's larger one.

Drew swallowed hard, wishing that someday a woman would come along and show Teal the same motherly affection that Alaina did, while being happily married to him. "May I help with anything?"

Alaina shrugged. "Not unless you absolutely want to, Drew," she drawled. "We have everything under control. Why don't you just fix yourself a drink and sit at the table while I prepare dinner for you and Teal."

Drew opened a bottle of chardonnay as Alaina quickly cleaned the tiled floor and Teal's hands in turn. Taking a swallow of the wine, he savored its coldness, then returned the bottle to the refrigerator.

"I think I'll go and look over some notes for school." As he was uttering the words, he remembered that instead of

taking a test on Monday, he would have to withdraw from
all of his classes. Suddenly the weight of his problems
didn't compare with his loneliness, and he dropped back
into his seat. Taking another swallow of his wine, he decided to unburden himself on Alaina as he so often did
after he'd had a run-in with his father.

"Up we go," Alaina said to Teal as she lifted the little
girl and sat her on a chair next to Drew. Then, turning to
her task at the counter, Alaina said, "Care to talk about it,
Drew?"

"I do, but not now." He didn't want to discuss Cranneck
in front of Teal. Since she didn't even know he existed,
Drew didn't want to confuse her. "Would you stay and have
dinner with me—us?" he quickly clarified.

Alaina halted her peeling of Irish potatoes. "Uh—"

"I'm sorry, Alaina. I should have asked if you have
plans."

"It's not that, Drew," she said, resuming her task. "I just
wasn't sure if you were inviting me to dinner as a friend
or if you were asking me to work longer."

Drew cleared his throat. "I . . . want you to stay on your
own time. That is, if it won't present any problems with
your boyfriend."

Alaina laughed. "I don't have a boyfriend anymore,
Drew. Don't you remember? We broke up four months ago,
and I'm well rid of the lying weasel."

"I see."

"Does my single status present a problem for you?"

"Of course not." He emptied his glass, then went to the
refrigerator to retrieve the bottle. "Would you care to join
me in a glass of wine?"

Alaina nodded.

"Dadee, wead?" Teal asked, holding up one of her many
books.

"What's the magic word?"

"Me fo'got."

"I forgot," Drew corrected. "And it's 'please.' "

"P'ease, wead?"

"My pleasure, princess."

For the next hour, Drew amused Teal while Alaina prepared parsley potatoes, fresh shredded carrots, and tossed salad for them. Before she cooked the steaks and they ate, however, she fed and bathed Teal in preparation for her bedtime. Finally she did the steaks according to her and Drew's different tastes and sat down at the small table.

They went through dinner in comfortable banter, Teal settled in Drew's lap, Alaina so near to him he could smell the light fragrance she wore.

By the time their meal ended, Teal had fallen asleep. As Alaina removed the dinner dishes, Drew went to place his daughter in her bed in the room next to the kitchen.

"I'll do those later," Drew said when he returned and found Alaina at the sink washing the plates and pots. "Come and sit with me in the living room."

With their glasses of wine and Drew's favorite radio station playing softly in the background, they settled on the sofa, which doubled as Drew's bed, and he told Alaina about his meeting with his father. "Any advice?" he finished.

"No," Alaina responded, regret deep in her voice. "It seems your father has you right where he wants you."

"In the palm of his hand?" The bitterness and anger he'd felt earlier returned with a vengeance.

"Exactly." She emptied her glass of wine.

"Only for a year." Drew stared into her eyes, his attention drifting away from his father. "Would you care for another glass?"

A long second passed before she answered. "I really shouldn't. If this is your attempt to begin a long romantic involvement with me, I have to warn you I'm not ready," she joked.

The wine buzzed in his head, and months of loneliness flashed through his mind. Alaina was only seven years younger than he was, whereas Teresa had been ten; he'd met his almost-ex when she was seventeen. That age difference had been a first for him, because he generally preferred women his own age and older. But Alaina was Teal's nanny, and she'd become a dear friend. He'd never compromise their relationship by making a play for her.

"I'm not looking for *any* involvement," he told her.

Although she looked curiously at him, his answer seemed to satisfy her. She nodded. "One more glass, Drew, and then I have to go."

After two more hours of enjoying Alaina's company, Drew watched as she readied herself to depart. It was close to ten o'clock and he did not want her to walk alone to the bus stop. He telephoned his neighbor, Mrs. Watts, to see if she could come over and keep an eye on Teal while he saw Alaina safely onto the St. Claude bus.

Agreeing without hesitation, Mrs. Watts came over within five minutes. A short, round woman with graying brown hair and a kind disposition, she smiled when she looked in on the sleeping Teal.

"She'll be just fine, Drew," Mrs. Watts said with reassurance. "You just take your time, but be careful out there. You know it's none too safe."

"I'll be sure to stay off the darker streets," Drew responded.

"It would be easier if you just took Alaina home yourself."

"No, ma'am, Miz Watts, it wouldn't be," Alaina asserted. "I'll never set foot on that Harley, or *any* Harley for that matter."

Drew smiled. "Alaina isn't a motorcycle fan, Mrs. Watts."

"Neither am I, child. Those things are none too safe. One of my son's friends lost his leg in a motorcycle accident."

Alaina shivered. "I'm so sorry to hear that. It must have been awful for him."

"Oh, it was. How's school coming along?"

"I graduated in May, Miz Watts. I'm just helping Drew out while he attends summer school. But I've already applied at Touro Infirmary for a position."

"That's wonderful, child. A nurse! What do your parents think?"

Looking to Drew for rescue, Alaina politely answered, "They're very proud of me. I'm the first to graduate from college."

Mrs. Watts frowned in concentration. "Didn't you tell me one of your ancestors was a voodoo healer? Maybe it's in your blood."

Alaina laughed good-naturedly. "No, ma'am, not a healer. An enchantress. She was my great-grandmother several times removed. She wasn't on the scale of Marie Laveau, of course, but it was said Laurinda Toussaint had skin the color of rich coffee and eyes that could pierce you from a distance. She died in 1853. It was the same year all those folks died from Yellow Fever."

"Or Yellow Jack or Bronze John or whatever you'd like to call it," Drew interjected, tired of the inane conversation. "I hate to interrupt, Mrs. Watts, but we need to get down there in time for the bus."

"Of course, Drew. Don't let me hold you up. If you miss one of those buses, they are none too quick about returning. I wonder what those drivers are doing all that time. Personally—"

"We'll talk when I return, Mrs. Watts. I'll even share some of the stories my father pounded into my brothers and me about the Montagues of the nineteenth century. They were something else, passionate Southerners all."

"Certainly, Drew. Just take heed of your surroundings now."

Alone outside, Drew and Alaina laughed and walked toward Esplanade Avenue at a brisk pace. Though it was nighttime, the heat had alleviated by only a few degrees. Mosquitoes buzzed in the air. Once the scourge of New Orleans residents, these carriers of the dreaded Yellow Fever had spread disease that reached epidemic proportions in the nineteenth century.

But his ancestors had thrived through floods, disease, droughts, and war, and some were near legends in the fam-

ily. As a teenager, Drew had resented his father for constantly spouting the place the Montagues held in Louisiana
history, especially Rafe, Drew's great-great-grandfather.
The perfect son, the perfect gentleman, the perfect hero. Yet
Drew realized he wouldn't mind sharing some of those stories with Mrs. Watts. Thinking back, he'd actually enjoyed
them. He was just too pigheaded to ever let his father know.

"Poor woman," Alaina clucked. "She's awful lonely
since Mr. Watts passed away."

"I know. Maybe I could invite her over for dinner tomorrow. What do you think?"

Alaina shrugged. "It's your house, Drew. I can't tell you
whom to invite there."

Drew didn't respond to Alaina's flippancy, but asked instead, "Where do we go from here?"

"How so?"

"I hadn't realized how close you were to leaving Teal
and me."

"One way or another, we're going to go our separate
ways," Alaina said gently. "And you and Teal are also leaving. Or have you forgotten so soon?"

"Only for the evening, but tomorrow morning reality will
come crashing back. Allow me my bliss tonight, will you?"

"Of course."

"You still haven't answered me," Drew prodded as they
took a left turn on Esplanade Avenue, heading away from
the direction of the Mississippi River. The loud whistle of
the *Natchez* steamboat resounded in the distance as the boat
docked for the final time that night.

"Where *can* we go from here, Drew? Even if you weren't
leaving, there would be no chance for us. Would you want
your father to totally disown you? And as liberal as your
mother is in some things, I doubt she would welcome me
into your family."

"There's not a prejudiced bone in my mother's body."

"That's where I think you're wrong. There may not be
a *racist* bone in her body, but everyone has their preju-
dices."

"Is there a difference, Alaina?"

"You're too streetwise and educated to sound so naive, Drew," Alaina snapped. "But let's not end our evening by getting into a debate on race. Tomorrow will be soon enough."

They reached well-lit North Rampart Street in silence, but saw no sign of a bus in the vicinity.

"When are you leaving?" Alaina asked finally.

"I haven't told my father I've accepted his proposal, but tomorrow I will. I guess I'll be leaving in the next week or two."

Alaina lowered her head, but not before Drew caught her despondency.

"What was that look for?" He placed a finger beneath her chin and tipped her head up again. "Dare I hope you're going to miss me and Teal just a little?"

"You know I will," she whispered, then giggled, the sound unlike her usually throaty laughter.

Drew wondered whether it was from the effects of too much wine or her discomfort.

"I'm going to miss our conversations and seeing Teal. I've cared for the two of you for nearly a year now and I've become rather attached."

"As we have to you," Drew responded huskily. "But if you think we're letting you go this easy, think again. We'll come to visit you on Saturdays."

"Yeah, right."

Drew placed a hand over his heart. "Does the fair maiden doubt her knight in shining armor?"

"First of all, there are no more knights in shining armor, neither literally nor figuratively. Secondly, I most definitely doubt a man who would use a phrase like that."

"Then I guess I'll have to prove you wrong," Drew retorted with a laugh.

"I guess you will."

"Had I still been living in New Orleans once you were no longer in my employ, would you have agreed to date me?"

"Yes, I would have, despite the difficulties we would have faced. And not only from your end. My daddy would have taken fits had we started dating."

"Well, there's nothing more exciting than going against our parents' wishes now, is there?"

"Will you still feel that way when Teal starts going against *your* wishes?"

"Touché, darling. Now why would your father object?"

Alaina threw him a severe look. "For pity's sake, Drew! Your family owns a plantation. Need I say more?"

Drew raised a questioning brow. "What does that have to do with anything?"

The sound of pressure being released from a bus's air brakes as the big vehicle halted to a stop in front of them prevented Alaina from responding in detail.

"This is another discussion we'll have to finish tomorrow."

"Call me to let me know you made it home safely."

"Will do." She quickly kissed Drew's cheek and hurried up the steps, stopping at the fare machine as the doors closed behind her.

Drew watched until the bus was out of sight before he turned and headed for his apartment.

Instead of going back down Esplanade, he walked up North Rampart to Dumaine, where he made a left turn. He passed the old Creole cottages, where the wealthy planters had kept their quadroon mistresses. All of the residences had been restored to varying degrees of their former beauty. Iron hitching posts topped with horses' heads stood in front of some.

Passing a hitching post, Drew noticed a gleaming gold pocket watch and chain hanging on the ear of a horse. An admirer of fine things, he remarked to himself on how lovely it was. Someone might have lost it, yet from the way the jewelry hung there, it looked as if it had been deliberately placed on the horse's ear. A strange eeriness saturated the air, drew him closer. Cautiously he picked the watch and chain up, the low-keyed tick growing louder. Looking closely at it, he saw the letters *RM* inscribed in curlicue on the back of the heavy gold watch.

An old chant that one of his nannies had sung to him surfaced in his mind. She'd always warned that under the right circumstances—which included a watch being present—uttering the words might produce dire consequences. Remembering the warning now, Drew thought it all a joke; he didn't believe in such nonsense. Yet the powerful urge to recite the chant overrode all else, and the saying rolled from his tongue at great speed:

"One summer's eve, a clock went tick-tock. Those behind were left to grieve. At that place with horses' teeth, I shall be taken to the fate I meet." The disconnected words didn't make much sense and sounded like an old 45 record stuck on slow speed.

The ticking grew louder, nearly deafening. Drew grew dizzy, and lights danced before his eyes. He staggered a few paces, not sure what was happening and wondering if someone had hit him. He had to release the watch. Something was happening to him because he held it in his hands, which burned with the weight of the gold piece. Suddenly his head pounded, and bile rose in his throat.

A sensation of floating through space surrounded him.

With all the strength he could muster, he pitched the watch, knowing that this insanity would end only after he rid himself of it. He was right. The ticking sound changed to blissful quietness. Whatever battle he'd just faced was over.

Chapter 3

Gas LANTERNS SURROUNDED the magnificent St. Louis Hotel, a stark, glittering jewel where flickering flames cast distorted shadows. A clear, cloudless sky graced the late-spring night, an artless intruder on the nemesis that lurked about, a yearly predator upon the citizenry of New Orleans.

The perfect evening belied the preparations to leave the city that were taking place due to the approach of the Yellow Fever season. It belied the grief and confusion Marianne Beaufort felt as the carriage she and her sister rode in glided to a stop in front of the St. Louis Hotel.

After an eternity, the carriage traffic had become nearly nonexistent, but it seemed as if she and Genevieve were the last to arrive for the ball. She had changed into four different gowns before finally settling on this one, a white muslin with diaphanous skirts. After that delay, when they'd arrived on Rue St. Louis, the traffic was snarled for blocks. Tomas, their driver, ever loyal to Marianne's mother, had refused to allow them to leave the carriage before they reached the hotel entrance.

As a result, she was nearly an hour and a half late.

Sighing deeply, Marianne smiled at Tomas, who held open the door for her as she stepped out of the carriage at a sedate pace. Her heart had never beaten faster. Tonight she had to publicly accept Rafe Montague's proposal of marriage, in a long-anticipated event orchestrated by her mother. Marianne had never questioned her own true motives before now. From the moment she'd said yes to his private proposal, she'd been promised a life locked in a loveless marriage.

The closer the moment came, the more Marianne wondered how important it was for her and her mother and her sister to maintain the lifestyle they'd led before the Fever claimed her father last year. Annoyance added to her discomfiture. Instead of her older sister, Genevieve, Marianne had been chosen to rescue the family by marrying an affluent gentleman.

She had always been the responsible one, the daughter whom her family looked upon because of her rock-solid faith in herself and her extreme loyalty to her family. But at this moment she had only one thought in mind—escape. For several days she'd weighed the consequences of going to the family solicitor, demanding the release of her minute inheritance, and running away to Paris.

But she hadn't. Yet. Instead, she found herself at the very place she didn't want to be, less than an hour away from the formal announcement of her betrothal.

Admittedly, she could do much worse than Rafe Montague. Even after several years of bad crop harvests, his family's plantation, Bienvenu, was one of the finest around.

His mean spirit and bad temper, however, detracted from his otherwise high regard. Yet the Montagues were the wealthiest family in St. Francisville and even wielded power here in New Orleans, where Marianne had become reacquainted with him at one of the balls at the start of the social season last November. Since then, and despite Rafe's supposedly putrid reputation, she found that he held *her* in the highest regard.

She breathed in deeply again, pinpricks of resentment needling her. She could turn and run as fast as her high-heeled feet would carry her—turn and forget that Rafe had already paid off the debts that saved the family's modest plantation just upriver; run and leave her mother and sister to their own destinies.

Wanting to get her thoughts in order, Marianne paused in front of the entrance. Inside the ballroom, her fate awaited.

"Come, *mon chou,*" Genevieve said gently, tugging at her sleeve as she walked up behind her.

Marianne perused the brightly lit surroundings. "I shall be along shortly," she responded, an uncharacteristic tremble in her voice.

Genevieve hugged her. "You are nervous, *oui*?" she asked, squeezing Marianne's silk-gloved hand for reassurance.

Marianne nodded, though unable to explain the true origin of her jitters. "Suppose he does not come?"

"Then he would be a fool, and from what I've gathered about Monsieur Rafe, he is anything but a fool. Besides, it has always been his policy to arrive long after the festivities are under way."

Acknowledging her sister's explanation with a small chuckle, Marianne started forward. When she reached the entrance of the iron gates, she nearly tripped over a man curled on the ground there. A small shiver went down her spine. She was almost certain this spot had been vacant a few moments ago. "*Mon Dieu!*"

"Come." Grabbing Marianne's hand, Genevieve tugged her forward. Her sister seemed unconcerned at the man's sudden appearance. "He is no more than a drunk who needs to sleep off the effects of too much alcohol."

"*Non.* He may have been robbed." Refusing to budge, she started toward the blond-haired man. The need to know that he was flesh and blood urged her forward as much as her worry for him. It was quite possible she'd overlooked him when she'd arrived because she'd been so lost in her thoughts. "He may need our help."

"We are already late, Mari," Genevieve said in exasperation. "Maman is probably worried sick."

"Then hurry in and let her know we're here," Marianne suggested. "I will be along shortly."

"And leave you alone with a stranger?" Genevieve shook her head. "I think not, *mon chou*. For all we know, he could be a criminal."

Pulling her hand out of Genevieve's and ignoring her sister's apprehension, Marianne looked down at the man again. She frowned at the strange clothing he wore. Maybe Genevieve was right. Maybe he was a dangerous criminal.

She studied him for a moment, the gaslights along the street affording her a good view. With a sculptured mouth, perfect nose, straight forehead, and square jaw, he didn't appear in the least dangerous. He was also extraordinarily handsome, his body curled upon the ground like a sleek cat.

Drawn to him, Marianne stepped closer. "Monsieur?" she called.

Not realizing he'd closed them, Drew opened his eyes. A woman's billowing skirts brushed his cheek.

He blinked. Nothing of his surroundings was familiar. He lay in front of an elegant building surrounded by a wrought-iron fence. The clip-clop of horses' hooves on cobblestoned streets sounded in his ears. The gaslights strewn along the way were bright, intrusive.

One woman stood so close over him he could see the chemise and drawers beneath her petticoats. Quickly averting his gaze, he saw another woman a slight distance away, near the open gates.

Head still pounding, he swore that he would forsake alcohol forever once this moment passed. Obviously he was hallucinating, though he didn't think he'd had that much to drink.

Sitting up, Drew noticed how lovely the woman who stood near him was. Smooth and unmarked, her ivory complexion complemented jade eyes and black hair parted down the middle. Long ringlets fell softly on each side of her face. Her small nose sat between high, delicate cheekbones. As he gazed at her lips, pale pink and pouty, he ached to taste them. She nearly took his breath away.

Had he been murdered? Was she his guardian angel come to walk him through the Pearly Gates?

Preposterous! He would have felt some kind of pain. Then Drew remembered the intense headache, the blinding light, and the sensation of floating through air.

Tentatively he pressed his hand to his head, checking for bullet wounds. He found none. Then again, he wouldn't arrive in heaven all torn and bloody, would he?

Still, the idea that he was dead didn't make sense. Maybe he was just dreaming, yet he didn't remember going to bed. He clung to the idea anyway and took consolation in it. He wanted to believe that the whole day, including the meeting with his father, had been only a bad dream.

Drew squinted up at the figment of his imagination, applauding his fanciful side. Her costume looked quite authentic. But then, in dreams, he reminded himself, everything from emotions to surroundings usually appeared authentic. Upon closer inspection, his dream weaver looked incredibly young. "Who in the hell are you?"

"Marianne Beaufort, *monsieur*," she answered.

At least his dream would end on a pleasant note, even if his mind had somehow brought him to nineteenth-century New Orleans in front of the St. Louis Hotel, where the finest Creole families socialized.

Marianne frowned as she gazed at his denim-covered legs. She glanced over her shoulder at the other woman, who appeared just as confused by his clothes.

"They're jeans," Drew explained as he stood up to find himself a head and a half taller than Marianne. "Levi's."

"*Pardonnez-moi?*"

The accent in her genteel voice struck him. A dream, huh? There was something rotten in Denmark. He knew not a lick of French, and certainly his mind wouldn't conjure up a woman who spoke a language he wouldn't understand.

His heart pounding, he checked his surroundings again. The magnificent building sitting in front of him pulsed with life. Music and laughter mingled and floated on the night breeze. A delicately sweet scent rose from Marianne, the warmth of her nearness suffusing him with a growing realization.

It wasn't a dream. He wasn't asleep and he most definitely wasn't drunk, although if he'd had an option he'd have settled for one of the above. A flesh-and-blood woman stood before him, looking as confused and frightened as he felt.

Desperately he searched for answers, his mind reeling. He replayed the events of the past couple of hours. He'd done nothing out of the ordinary. Arguments with his father occurred whenever they saw one another. Enjoying his mother's company was also a frequent event. Entertaining and caring for Teal . . . walking Alaina to the bus stop.

He paused as he remembered what happened next, and his blood turned cold. He'd found a gold pocket watch and chain and recited that silly chant. The watch! That goddamn watch had somehow thrown him back in time!

He barely remembered the nanny who'd sung the words to him; the warning she'd given to him that something dire might happen if he ever repeated the saying under the wrong circumstances seemed almost a distant dream. Certainly she hadn't been telling the truth, had only told him such nonsense as a way to frighten a misbehaving boy into obeying her.

"Monsieur?"

"Oh, hell, what's the use?" Drew said in exasperation. The sound of her soft voice brought his predicament into sharp focus. "Denims won't be invented for another twenty or thirty years, I guess. I just thought maybe since you are a figment of my imagination you would know what jeans were."

Marianne started to back away.

"I'm . . . uh . . . from out of town," he added, noting her alarmed look and catching her wrist.

The other woman advanced upon him. "Do not harm her, monsieur," she said in a rush. "She merely wanted to see if you needed assistance."

"Harm her?" Drew asked with incredulity. "Miss, I assure you I don't have a violent bone in my body. I just want some questions answered."

"'Mericain, *oui*?" Marianne asked, her voice musical, her eyes sparkling.

Instead of answering her question, Drew asked one of his own. "What year are we supposedly in?"

"M-May, 1853," Marianne stammered in surprise.

"Damn! Have I really been jettisoned back to the year eleven thousand people died from Yellow Fever?"

Both women released frightened cries. Marianne attempted to pull herself free, but he held her fast as the other girl made the sign of the cross.

"Don't be afraid," Drew soothed. "I promise I'm not going to harm you." He knew he'd better refrain from blurting out other pertinent facts of the day. Scaring the hell out of people wasn't the way to make friends. And if he wasn't dreaming, he'd need all the friends he could get.

His mind kept insisting that time travel was impossible, even though on occasion, just for the hell of it, he read those romances where women went back in time, met their dream lover, and lived happily ever after.

But they didn't leave behind a little girl with fiery red hair and adoring green eyes. A little girl who expected his imminent return.

Could he really be dreaming? He remembered that earlier in the day, while he'd gazed at his parents' period furnishings, he'd been thinking about nineteenth-century New Orleans and its Yellow Jack victims. He frowned. If that had only been a dream, how could he remember it so well?

He desperately wanted to cling to the idea of the dream, but suspected that in reality, nineteenth-century reality, he was fully awake.

He smiled at the beautiful girl. "Marianne, my name's C. Andrew Montague III."

Though he still held on to her, she took a step back, her look turning suspicious, wary. "Are you related to the Montagues of Bienvenu?"

Nearly speechless, Drew went rigid. He'd forgotten the position of the Montagues during this time. What were the chances of his landing in an era in which his ancestors were reaching the pinnacle of their prominence and power? The question made him uneasy, and he wondered, if he had indeed traveled through time, whether it was mere coincidence that he'd landed in this era or an occurrence manipulated by some deeper force.

"Bienvenu? The plantation in St. Francisville?"

"*Oui,* monsieur," Marianne answered. "One and the same. Are you related to the Montagues of Bienvenu?"

"Yes," Drew responded with some relief. "That's my family's plantation." At least she knew something about his family, which meant he wouldn't appear so weird to her. Not with the Montague name.

"Is Monsieur Rafe your cousin?"

"Rafe Montague is my great-great-grandfather," Drew said with a laugh.

This was insane! He *had* to be dreaming. Facing the most dire circumstances of his life wouldn't allow for this nonchalant, cavalier attitude. He'd be in a fit of panic by now because, from all accounts in the books on local history that his father forced upon him, 1853 was one of the worst years to be alive in New Orleans. Chances of survival were rather slim. No, he wouldn't be so calm after being thrown back to this time.

Marianne released a laugh. Drew liked the infectious sound. Until he awakened he'd just let nature take its course.

"You make sport of me, *non*?" she said with humor. "Monsieur Rafe is only thirty."

"Marianne, *petite,* I think I see Monsieur Rafe's carriage coming," the other woman inserted before Drew could re-

spond to Marianne's statement. "We'd best hurry in before
he spots us."

"Monsieur Montague, I've been remiss." Marianne indicated the other woman with a touch of her gloved hand.
"This is my sister, Genevieve."

Genevieve curtsied, her dark curls done in the same style
as Marianne's and bouncing becomingly. She had a slightly
darker complexion than Marianne, was taller, and had a
fuller figure. Looking closer at her, Drew found no obvious
family resemblance. Where Genevieve was merely pretty,
Marianne was strikingly beautiful.

With a smile, Marianne pulled away from him. "Monsieur, it was a pleasure to meet you."

She curtsied and allowed her sister to guide her through
the gates and into the ballroom beyond, leaving Drew to
stare after what all reason insisted was a figment of his
fantasy.

Chapter 4

IMMEDIATELY DREW FELT abandoned. But a carriage stopped and pulled Drew's attention from the sway of Marianne's hips as she departed.

If the occupant of the vehicle was indeed his great-great-grandfather at thirty years old, he wanted a glimpse of him.

A man, finely dressed in a light gray waistcoat, white shirt with lace cuffs and collar, and dark trousers, stepped from the coach. Not as tall as Drew, Rafe resembled Cranneck more than the old painting at Bienvenu suggested.

Giving Drew a cursory glance as he passed, Rafe clamped his lips together in a tight line, his disapproving sneer obvious. Resisting his baser instincts to respond in some way to the blatant snobbery, Drew turned his head away. He was unimpressed by the man his father touted as a true gentleman and Confederate hero.

He had seen the illustrious Rafe Montague live and in person. The man was nothing to write home about, even if his father would have been inclined to welcome a letter from him.

Thinking of home, Drew realized he was now a homeless person. He needed to get his bearings. Maybe he'd find some answers on Burgundy Street, where his home is . . . was . . . or whatever.

Drew started in that direction, the warm night air not in the least comforting. He walked quickly, wanting the feeling of normalcy to return. The cobblestones soon gave way to dirt roads littered with sewage and horse offal, their stench overpowering.

Finding some streets dark and deserted, as dangerous-looking in 1853 as they appeared in the year 2000, Drew wished he hadn't sold his .38-caliber handgun. He most definitely would have been carrying it for protection, as he once did. But when Alaina had first started working for him, he hadn't known how reliable she was. With Teal walking and curious about everything, Drew thought it best to get rid of the deadly weapon.

Hurrying his steps even more, he soon reached the place where his house *should* have been, and found an empty lot.

"Dammit!"

Releasing a frustrated sigh, Drew started for Esplanade Avenue. Although he knew his parents' house hadn't been built until after the Civil War, he was desperate to find something familiar.

Unable to contain his growing dread, he began to run, frantic now and truly afraid for the first time in his life.

When he came to the familiar spot on Esplanade, he stopped dead in his tracks, his blood turning cold. Though he knew he would find the lot empty, confronting reality head-on chilled him. The watch and chain had truly brought him here. It seemed time travel *was* possible after all. That was the only explanation. There was no other way he could have been pulled from his precious Teal.

What had become of her? Did she even exist? Was there anything left of his former life?

He glanced at his digital watch. Pressing a button on the side to illuminate the dial, he saw the time in large numbers, the day of the week and date of the year above in smaller letters and numbers: 12:30 A.M., SUN., JUL 20.

If this was still the year 2000, it had been two and a half hours since he'd left his house to bring Alaina to the bus stop.

But Marianne had said it was May 1853.

Feeling alone and confused and ashamed of himself for being so, having no choice, he headed once again in the direction of the St. Louis Hotel.

Marianne attempted to concentrate on Monsieur Rafe's conversation, but her thoughts continually drifted to the man who claimed to be C. Andrew Montague III and Rafe's great-great-grandson.

Monsieur Andrew was surely jesting. Otherwise, he was addled. There could be no other conclusion for his strange mutterings. And what of his prediction of the number of Yellow Jack victims there'd be this year? Was he a sorcerer? Her tante Helene spoke of odd occurrences involving people who practiced the black arts, but Marianne had never known anyone who predicted the future with such precise numbers.

A small amount of people died from Yellow Fever every year; her dear father was claimed within days of getting the disease. She was thankful she was immune to it, having already had a bout of it eight years ago at the age of ten.

"Mari, where is your mind wandering to?" Rafe broke in, his query laced with annoyance.

Her mother's careful instructions on social graces abandoning her in the wake of her musings, Marianne's cheeks heated, and she released a small, embarrassed laugh. "*Pardonnez-moi,* Monsieur Rafe. I was just thinking how gallant you are to choose the ball to make public our engagement." Her blush deepened over the tiny lie.

Rafe chortled, an overstuffed peacock who believed such nonsense. "My pleasure, mademoiselle," he responded, some of his humor restored at her statement. "As long as you do not make such wanderings a habit." He rubbed her cheek, his thick fingers sending an involuntary shudder of disgust through her. "You are the most beautiful woman in attendance. I have a twofold motive for announcing our engagement in such a prestigious and public place."

"And they are?" Marianne asked with forced lightness, his glacial look daunting her.

"To let it be known that I've claimed one of the great beauties of New Orleans," Rafe whispered, his hot breath fanning her neck. "And to make it clear that from this night forward, every man must distance himself from you or reckon with me."

Marianne snapped open the delicate fan her mother had given to her when she arrived and began fanning herself furiously. "You honor me," she replied in ambiguous tones. Had she mistaken his regard for her? It sounded as if he intended to make her his prize mare to trot out for show and envy.

"As honor you I should, *cherie*," Rafe agreed. He took two glasses of champagne from a tray a waiter held out to them and passed one to Marianne.

"Marianne, I must speak to you!" Without waiting for a response, Genevieve pulled Marianne in the direction of the courtyard. Once they were away from the surprised Rafe, Genevieve released her sister's hand. "Follow me."

If not for the frantic note in Genevieve's voice, Marianne would have been furious at her rudeness. Instead she asked, "What is it?"

"You'll see, *mon chou*," Genevieve answered nervously.

Looking over her shoulder, Marianne saw that Rafe was following close behind, not in the least amused. "Please, Genevieve," she whispered, a disconcerting tingle creeping down her spine. "Rafe is following us. He does not look pleased. Where are we going?"

There was no time for a reply, because they'd reached the courtyard and the reason for Genevieve's alarm.

C. Andrew Montague III apparently awaited Marianne's presence.

Chapter 5

"PLEASE FORGIVE MY intrusion, Miss Beaufort, but I must speak to you."

Bewilderment marred Monsieur Andrew's tone and etched his handsome features. Fiery flames from the blazing torches that surrounded the courtyard shone in his blue eyes, the reflections haunting in his tortured face. He stared at her as if she were his savior, as if she knew how to repair whatever was wrong with him. Only she didn't. She had too many obligations to fulfill already. Because of them, she didn't know how to fix her own life. She certainly didn't want to take on the responsibility of someone else's once again.

"Monsieur?" Her questioning tone bespoke her own bewilderment. She'd just met him. Why would he seek her out?

"Miss Beaufort . . . Marianne, I need your help. I must speak to you now," he repeated.

He seemed different from any other man she'd ever met. Although she didn't know quite what set him apart from other men, it drew her to him in ways that no one else ever had. From the moment she'd seen him, she knew he possessed a kind spirit, but he seemed as if he didn't belong here, as if he were from an entirely different world. It was an impossible thought, but one that couldn't allow her to walk away from him.

Concern and curiosity coursing through her, Marianne stepped closer to him.

Just as she thought to speak again, Rafe made himself known. Marianne had all but forgotten he existed. Part of the anger mottling his complexion, she felt sure, stemmed from her neglect of his presence.

"How dare you, sir!" Rafe thundered. In a high state of fury, he roughly pushed her aside. "The only speaking you'll do is to me. You've summoned my bride-to-be, a lady of high quality and good standards, to your presence as though she were a common tart. Without regard to my presence, you insult her character. Such insolence cannot go unchallenged. I demand satisfaction here and now!"

"Rafe!" Marianne gasped, horrified. It was a daily fact of life that a duel could be called at any given time for the least little infraction. While Monsieur Andrew's request of her time was no small slight to Rafe's honor, she didn't want any blood shed on her account.

Glancing around at the small contingent of onlookers that had already gathered upon hearing Rafe's tirade, Marianne hoped to find someone to reason with him. But seeing the dislike directed toward Monsieur Andrew, she knew her battle was already lost.

She grabbed Rafe's arm. "Monsieur, please."

Snatching his arm out of her grasp, Rafe stung her with a reproving look. "*Never* contradict me, *ma cherie*." The underlying venom in his words made their meaning crystal clear. He turned to a fancily dressed man standing by his side. "See to a pair of weapons, brought out posthaste, Emmett."

Like every other man there, Rafe had left his pistol in the small armory adjacent to the ballroom. Because of the distance from their homes to the city, most planters carried a sword or pistol along the route toward their destination.

As a matter of courtesy, they checked them in the weapons room at big functions such as this one.

Before Emmett could move a muscle, someone rushed up to Rafe, carrying two menacing-looking swords. Frightened, Marianne stepped back and threw a pleading look to Rafe. He ignored her as he glowered at the helpful newcomer.

"Here you are, Rafe. The moment I heard that insolent good-for-nothin' nobody speak to Marianne, I ran to the armory and just picked the first weapons I saw."

"Pistols are my choice, Fred," Rafe said with a sneer, "but these will serve my purpose." He grabbed them from his friend, bloodlust in his eyes as he started forward.

"Remember, first blood, Rafe," Emmett reminded him, then released a nasty chuckle. "Whether he lives or dies depends on where you strike him."

Nodding in agreement and removing his topcoat and waistcoat, Rafe looked at Marianne and Genevieve. "You ladies go inside," he ordered as he opened the top two buttons of his lacy shirt. "This is not the place for you at this time. Marianne, the moment to announce our betrothal has passed. We'll discuss this later."

Rooted to the spot where he stood, Drew watched in horrified fascination as the scene unfolded before him. The man who would become his great-great-grandfather was preparing to annihilate him. The knowledge that the duel would end with first blood relieved him slightly. First blood probably meant his own. Drew couldn't take the risk of injuring the old devil, who might die of his wounds. Then where would Drew be?

Rafe swung his sword above his head. It swished through the air with deadly intent. Drew wasn't a coward by any means, but sword-fighting? Learning the art had never been amongst his top priorities. He had to talk some sense into Great-Great-Granddaddy.

"Prepare to defend yourself, vagabond!"

"I would rather discuss this in a civilized manner, sir," Drew said with confidence. Surely the bugger could be reasonable. "I am truly sorry for any offense I caused to the lady. And to you," he added quickly when Rafe narrowed his eyes to mere slits.

"Your apology is unacceptable at this time, monsieur," Rafe said in a most *un*reasonable manner. "Arm yourself." He thrust the hilt of the spare sword at Drew.

He wouldn't have put it past Rafe to cut him down, armed or not. In frustration, Drew grabbed the weapon, hardly fathoming the situation he faced. A duel! And with his ornery ancestor yet. What the hell did he know about sword-fighting? Did he look like Zorro to the jerk?

As if the jerk would know who Zorro was.

"En garde!"

Rafe's cold voice cut through the warm air. This was a night to have Teal in his arms as they walked through the Quarter enjoying the sweet smells of the flowers, the whispery caresses of the breezes, the bright buzzing of the fireflies. This wasn't a night to die.

"Look, I don't want to do this," Drew said, desperate now, his shaky voice betraying him. Rafe swung the blade, and Drew ducked backward. "There has to be a better way."

"Defend yourself now, sir, or die like the sniveling coward you are!" Rafe thrust the point of his sword forward. "There can be no retreat!"

In the nick of time, Drew sidestepped the blow and raised his sword defensively.

"Ahh, so you do have a backbone after all," Rafe goaded. "For all the good it will do you."

With the skill and litheness of a night predator, he thrust forward, catching Drew's sword arm. A small gash opened up; bright red spread over his shirtsleeve.

"You bastard!" Drew angrily yelled. "You have your first blood. Now put down that goddamn sword, and I'll show you what backbone is."

Eyes gleaming with hatred, Rafe went on the offensive, slashing determinedly at his quarry.

Stumbling in his effort to escape his sure-as-shooting mad ancestor, Drew lost his sword. Sword-fighting required skillful maneuvers: a parry there; a riposte here. Drew could do it—he just needed to know how.

This was a deadly serious situation, he reminded himself, one that couldn't be taken lightly. Yet for all the good his sword had done him, he might as well get rid of it. But how could he, when despite the fact that first blood had been drawn, this lunatic was still coming after him.

"Enough!" Drew yelled, knocking over a potted plant in his bid to escape. His heart was pounding, his mouth dry. Never had he known such fear. If he could only get inside and find the entrance, he might be able to make his escape. After all, there was no way to reach the iron gates that stood only yards away. The crowd was too thick, their jeers and disapproval of him and his tactics maudlin.

"First blood, Rafe!" a spectator yelled, a faceless voice of fairness and sanity. "You won, sir! It's over. Let him be."

Great-Great-Grandpa gave no indication that he heard or was even aware of the rules. Drew knew now that he should've taken off at the beginning of this fiasco. He should never have come back to the hotel, but he'd had no one but the sweet Marianne to turn to for help. Because of that, Rafe Montague was bound and determined to kill him.

The sword sliced through the night air.

"Enough, Rafe!"

Drew recognized the voice as belonging to Fred, the idiot with the long sideburns and balding head who'd started this by handing Rafe the swords. Pistols would've resulted in a fairer fight, although Drew probably would've ended up dead in a split second. He'd underestimated Rafe's intent.

"Monsieur Rafe, *non!*"

Marianne's scream intruded upon the male voices now debating whether Rafe was going too far or not. At the sound of her voice, the crowd parted, opening a way for Drew to escape. But he wasn't quick enough.

The blade cut across his upper right shoulder and chest. Gut-wrenching pain brought him to his knees. A wet, red stain spread across his shirtfront, now sticky with the flow of his blood.

Staring down at himself in amazement, he held his hands over his slashed chest, hoping to stem the flow of blood.

"Mon Dieu!"

Drew looked up at the shocked sound and glimpsed the face of his ancestor. The hatred that was there moments ago had given way to surprise, as though he couldn't believe what he'd done.

The sword dropped from Rafe's hand, and he gazed at Drew. Other than revealing surprise, his expression was fathomless.

Sheer willpower helped Drew to his feet. Blood soaked his clothes and still seeped from the long wound, but no one made the slightest attempt to aid him.

"Monsieur, what have you done?" Marianne cried.

"It is no concern of yours, Marianne," Rafe responded tightly.

"But it is my concern," she replied, staring at Drew with worry, tears glistening in her eyes. "A man has been hurt because of me."

"Come, Marianne." Rafe took her by the arm and steered her back into the ballroom. Everyone followed behind them.

In mere moments, Drew was left alone—alone and bleeding, with no one to turn to. The garden began to spin. A carousel of torches, flowers, and wrought-iron gates raced about him in dizzying madness.

He didn't dare move, for he would surely have fallen. An eternity passed while he tried to regain his balance. Instead his vision blurred, and heat spread the length of his wound.

As Drew blinked rapidly to steady himself, the lights of the ballroom beckoned him, and he turned in that direction. Marianne stood in the doorway, the flickering flames of the torches turning her billowy white gown into a flimsy gossamer that silhouetted her perfect figure.

Genevieve was there, too. With them was a man and

another woman. Drew smiled, glad that he was still standing. But why did he feel as if he were floating?

Everyone converged on him at once. An arm went around his shoulder, and he flinched at the pain as his feet left the ground. He was being carried. Or maybe he'd fallen. At the moment he didn't care. He felt himself losing consciousness, and just before he drifted into darkness he thought of Teal, his precious daughter. Maybe these people had come to bring him back to his beautiful little girl.

Chapter 6

A SMALL MOSS bed and ladder-back chair were the only pieces of furniture in the room located in the servants' quarters of the house on Rue Dumaine. The French doors stood open, inviting fresh air and sunshine inside to ward away the bad humors and restore vigor to the unmoving man lying on the bed.

Moments ago Marianne had come in to gaze at C. Andrew Montague III. She hadn't even dressed for the day. In her nightwrap and gown, she'd crossed the courtyard in her bare feet, her hair trailing down her back in loose waves.

Her worry made her state of dishabille irrelevant to her. They only had four servants, and none of them would ever gossip about her, so her momentary lapse would remain a secret. It wouldn't have mattered to her if it didn't. She only wanted to assure herself that Andrew would get better, and piddle to everyone else.

But he was so silent, so still, that she feared he'd never get up again. It was all because of Rafe's jealousy. Now more than ever, she wanted to flee to Paris. She didn't want to subject herself to a life of hell with Rafe. Last night she'd seen firsthand the truth of his bad temper. He didn't have a loving bone in his body, and the high regard she'd thought he felt for her had been nothing but a ploy to win her over.

A simmering anger at the unfairness of it all began to boil within Marianne. Somehow she had to come up with a way to get out of the betrothal. Her change of heart might not be so bad, since they hadn't had the chance to announce their engagement to the public yet.

The duel had prevented that.

Sitting on the chair, Marianne leaned over and trailed her fingers across Andrew's forehead. Finding it cool to the touch, she breathed a sigh of relief.

Dr. Oubre's healing touch of last night was now working. He'd cleansed the wound with burnt alum, then applied a primrose salve to the angry red slash and covered it with cool cloths before tightly wrapping it. For nearly an hour the doctor had ministered to Andrew. Just after the doctor departed, Andrew had awakened in unbearable pain.

Marianne had ordered a glass of claret mixed with powder from the bistort plant to be brought up. Holding his head in her hands, she'd coaxed the drink down his throat. When he'd depleted every last drop from the glass, she'd hummed a lullaby to him, rocking him as gently as a babe.

Now she touched him again, remembering the feel of his rippling muscles beneath her fingertips when she'd carefully settled her arms around him. He had a powerful chest, a smooth bronze mold of sculptured perfection that was now irreparably scarred, and a washboard-flat stomach. The counterpane shielded his legs from her view, but she'd seen enough of him to know that he possessed a beautiful body from head to heel.

A shadow of hair stubbled his cheek. If she had been in a better frame of mind, she would've shaved him. Then she would have had a legitimate excuse to touch him again. As it was, she was supposed to be a lady of the highest quality. Ladies didn't possess such scandalous thoughts about men, strange men at that.

Last evening, Genevieve had suggested that Andrew

might be dangerous. It turned out that Rafe had proven himself to be the more dangerous of the two. But her sister and mother would never see that. Or if they did, they'd never admit it.

"Marianne?"

Genevieve's voice startled Marianne out of her thoughts. Turning away from Andrew, she stared at her sister, meeting her disapproving stare with an unrepentant smile.

"Bon matin, cherie."

"Maman insists you come immediately," Genevieve instructed, folding her arms in annoyance.

Marianne turned to Andrew again. She brushed her fingers through his thick, golden hair, ignoring her sister's indignant gasp. "I cannot leave him, Gen," she said softly. "He is still unconscious."

"But the servants will see to him, Mari. He is but a stranger. You should not concern yourself with him so. I summoned you to him last evening because I feared he would create a scene. He was going to find you with or without my help. It seems my judgment might have been faulty. You are a betrothed woman attending the wrong man."

Marianne ignored Genevieve's goading. Genevieve, as much as she loved her sister, was rather envious of Marianne. Marianne always tried to diffuse any situations that might put them at odds, but that seemed impossible now, when she suspected that Genevieve carried a tendresse for Rafe, who hardly noticed her.

Was it any wonder that Genevieve wasn't the least bit sympathetic that Marianne was worried over another man?

With a sigh Marianne got up from her chair and smoothed out the covering on Andrew's bed. Before Dr. Oubre came last night, she had ordered clean white linen to be put over the moss mattress.

"How is your head, *mon chou*?"

"My head?" Marianne repeated.

"Oui. Last evening you claimed your head pained you. How is it?"

"Fine," Marianne answered, waving a hand in dismissal. She hurried to the door, her sister trailing behind her. Closing the French doors, Marianne rushed away.

When Rafe had pulled her inside and away from a wounded Andrew, she'd immediately faked a headache and asked to be brought home by her family. He wanted to see her safely to the carriage, but Maman had convinced him that she and Tomas would take care of her two daughters. Besides, Rafe needed to clean the sword of blood and put it back in the weapons room.

Promising to call on her within the week, he'd walked stiffly away. Then Marianne insisted they get Andrew and bring him home with them. Maman and Genevieve put up a small, useless argument, but finally agreed to let the stranger come home with them. Her mother did insist, however, that he be housed with their servants lest there be any surprise visits by Rafe.

Genevieve caught up to Marianne halfway across the long gallery and placed a hand on her arm. "Do not worry, Mari. The stranger seems only to be sleeping."

"I know. I only wanted to reassure him when he wakes up that he's safe here."

"Henry will summon you when the stranger awakens. You must come now and dress yourself properly."

"You're right, of course," Marianne said with a sigh. Henry was an intelligent, trusted servant, and he would most certainly come for her when Andrew awakened.

Crossing the courtyard and then climbing the stairs that led to their apartment, they headed for Marianne's bedchamber. Quickly she donned a mousseline home dress of stone color trimmed with corded crimson silk. A brown silk apron and crimson ribbon at her neck completed the outfit. She twisted her hair into a simple chignon, then headed for the parlor, where she knew her mother always passed the morning away.

Opening the French doors, she stepped into the chamber. Marianne especially loved this room. It was beautiful, with the furniture of the local craftsman, Belter, dominating throughout. Sea green walls complemented the jasper-colored settee and wing chairs. Light, airy draperies pooled at the wooden floor.

Despite the fact of her father's unexpected death last year, they'd managed to retain their wealth of belongings in New Orleans. But it was their cotton plantation that gave them the prestige of belonging to New Orleans' aristocracy. Rafe had seen to its survival in the Beaufort family, indebting them to him forever.

A bright smile wreathed Marianne's face, and she kissed her mother's cheek. At forty, only dark hair streaked with fine gray hairs gave signs of her age. She had smooth, unlined skin and clear eyes, though only months ago she had been devastated by the loss of her husband and hadn't had a clue as to how they would survive.

"*Ma cherie,*" Clarisse greeted, laying aside the newspaper she had been reading and returning Marianne's kiss. A grave look settled across her features as Marianne sat next to her. "You have been at the bedside of the stranger most of the morning. I do not think that is wise."

"What can it harm, Maman?" Marianne asked, knowing that if Rafe were to call on her and find her in Andrew's presence, he wouldn't be pleased. "He seems so lost. And it is because of me that he lies so wounded."

"Because of you? How can that be so? He sought you out without your permission or knowledge. You cannot hold yourself responsible for that," Clarisse chastised.

"Yet I do."

"Oh, Mari, you need something to refresh you." With the enthusiasm of a child, Genevieve pulled the bellcord. Not long after, their housemaid, Luella, came in. "We need sweet biscuits and lemonade, please, Luella."

"Of course, mademoiselle," Luella said, nodding to Marianne and Clarisse before departing.

"I read a most interesting article," Clarisse began. She picked up the newspaper, the bilingual *Bee/L'Abeille,* and read the headline: "*Disease an Obsolete Idea.*"

Genevieve and Marianne exchanged glances. Neither of

them cared to talk about disease. One of the most dreaded, Bronze John, had forever altered their family. While Genevieve had grieved right along with Clarisse, Marianne had had to hold everything together. She hadn't been given the privilege of openly mourning her father, other than wearing black for the requisite period of time.

She should have worn black for a year, but in order for Marianne to win a wealthy suitor, Clarisse had declared otherwise. Since February, a mere six months after her father's death, Marianne had dressed in her normal clothes. Two months ago, Genevieve had followed suit. Clarisse, however, still wore heavy mourning attire.

"Honestly, Maman, do you think disease is a topic we should like to hear about?" Genevieve asked peevishly. "It is not a happy subject, *non*?"

"Let Maman finish," Marianne said. It seemed as if her mother was searching for answers to her father's death, when there were none. Yellow Fever had been around for decades; there was nothing to be done about it. And at least her mother was beginning to open up and let some of her grief out. She was also speaking of something other than Rafe Montague. "We're listening, Maman."

"*Merci*, Marianne. It isn't anything terrible. In fact, it should brighten your day." Placing her spectacles on the bridge of her nose for in-depth reading, Clarisse bent her head. *"The future is glorious. Imagination can scarcely conceive a more brilliant destiny for the City of New Orleans!"*

Clarisse's voice droned on as she read the editorialist's opinion. Marianne wholeheartedly agreed with the piece. The winter had been a prosperous one. Instead of being the squalid port town it once was and being known as the pesthole of the world, New Orleans was now a bustling city with a joie de vivre unmatched anywhere else.

Luella returned with their snack and sat the tray on the table in front of the settee. After handing out a serving to each of them, the maid started for the door.

Marianne halted her. "Has Monsieur Andrew awakened?"

"Not to my knowledge, mademoiselle," she said. At Marianne's nod, she left them alone.

"Try to relax, Mari," Genevieve urged, taking a huge bite out of the sweet biscuit and slowly chewing it. Once she swallowed it, she said, "The stranger will survive."

"Are you aware that the stranger has a name?" Marianne snapped, exasperated that both her mother and sister refused to refer to him as anything other than "the stranger."

"Enough!" Clarisse declared, laying aside the newspaper once again. "We have bigger problems than the stranger. *My* question, *enfante cheries,* is will we survive?" Her look demanding an answer, she raised the glass of lemonade to her lips and tasted.

"I don't understand, Maman," Marianne said, not in the least hungry. "I have seen to it that our future is secured by accepting Rafe's suit. Of course we will survive."

"Not if Monsieur Rafe gets wind of your deception," Clarisse said heavily. "He will call off the engagement and foreclose on Baywood," she predicted, referring to the family's plantation in Roseland.

"Do not fret, Maman," Marianne said with a nerveless chuckle. "That will never happen. We will keep our plantation, and I shall remain engaged to Rafe. Andrew will be on his way the moment he is well enough to travel."

She couldn't allow Andrew to interfere with her future. If she succeeded in escaping the marriage, she couldn't do so because of someone else. It would have to be her own decision completely. As it was, Rafe's fury would be great. If she bowed out of the betrothal because of another man, she'd disgrace her family and add humiliation to Rafe's rage. But listening to Clarisse, she felt much more than just her usual guilt at the direction of her thoughts—she felt trapped. She was bound by responsibility and loyalty to accept a man she didn't love. Yet as Rafe Montague's wife, she'd continue to live in the manner in which she'd grown up, the manner in which her father would want her and her mother and sister to live.

"I only want your happiness," Clarisse said softly, close to tears as she was so frequently. "Both your happiness."

"*Oui,* Maman, we know," Genevieve put in, uncomfortable with Clarisse's fragile emotions. "But somehow I feel Mari is the sacrificial lamb for our jaded appetites."

Glaring at Genevieve and heaving a deep sigh for patience, Marianne laughed. "Gen, do not go on so. It's what *I* want, too," she lied for her mother's sake, although she did feel like a sacrificial lamb. "I can endure Rafe to reap the rewards of our union for us all—"

"Miss Mari!" Henry stopped when he saw the surprised looks on their faces. "Pardon me, Miz Clarisse, Miss Gen, but that young man is 'bout to come to."

"Oh! *Merci,* Henry." Marianne jumped from her seat. "I'll see to him right away."

"We'll go with you," Genevieve said, starting behind her.

"*Non!*" In an attempt to allay their fears, Marianne smiled serenely. "*Non,*" she said with more aplomb. "Gen, Maman, Henry will come along. I promise I'll be safe."

Clarisse and Genevieve exchanged unreadable glances.

"Please?" Marianne said softly.

Clearing her throat, Clarisse inclined her head. "Very well. But make yourself heard if the need arises, *cherie.*"

"*Merci,* Maman," Marianne said, and rushed through the doorway, urging Henry to quicken his pace once she was out of earshot of her mother and sister.

The room was dimly lit and small.

Beams of sunlight shone through the cracks in the wall, making the daylight hour known to Drew. Yet the cracks were not sufficient to give full light to the room.

It had been one hell of a night for him. Weird dreams had dogged him the whole night through. Now, in the light of day, he couldn't wait to feel Teal's small arms about his neck and hear her childish laughter. He couldn't wait to take his Harley out for a spin and feel the wind in his hair as he rode along the highway. Afterward, he'd tell his mother and Alaina of his wild night.

He couldn't even wait to start out for Bienvenu so he could stomp on the portrait of Rafe Montague.

"Teal?"

He heard nothing. Not the pitter-patter of her little feet and her happy giggling as she called out to him.

Not fully aware of his surroundings, he tried to sit up. Pain sluiced through his being, almost taking his breath away. A loud moan escaped his lips, and he fell back on the uncomfortable bed.

Oh, no! His bed was an uncomfortable strip, suspended in the air, held up by leather straps tied around metal posts. Oh, no! Swallowing hard, he attempted to move again.

"*Non, non,* monsieur. You must lie quiet."

A gentle hand stilled his movements; Drew turned to gaze at the owner of that soft hand. It was Marianne, and she was smiling at him.

Would he see that beautiful face every time he awoke from a nightmare? That would be fine, as long as his daughter was with her. For him, Teal was like the blood that pumped to his heart. She was his everything. Some said he spoiled her a little too much, and maybe he did. But he would do everything he possibly could to make up for her mother's abandoning her.

He couldn't have her thinking she'd lost him, too.

He swallowed deeply, his very soul aching at the thought that she might not even exist. Who knew what had occurred during his breach of time.

"Where am I?" he asked hoarsely, his voice weak.

Marianne clasped her hands around one of his. "You have been brought to my family's home on Rue Dumaine. You have been wounded, monsieur."

The circumstances of the night before flooded back in waves. "Yes, I remember."

"I am very sorry, monsieur, about what happened," she whispered, sitting in the chair next to the bed. A man stood near the closed door, a silent watchdog to their conversation. "It was because you sought me out."

"Yes, I know."

He tried to keep his rising anger at his ancestor in check, but the bastard had tried to kill him. Had there been a time on this earth when one could feel safe? Gingerly he touched the wound with his free hand, not wanting Marianne to stop the gentle rubbing she was providing to the other one. He flinched at his examination. He needed to get this properly attended to, and the only way he could do that was to get modern-day help. But he had thrown the watch away.

"One summer's eve, a clock went tick-tock. Those behind were left to grieve. At that place with horses' teeth, I shall be taken to the fate I meet."

The chant ran through his mind again. Perhaps any watch would do.

"I need to ask you about a watch."

"A watch, monsieur?" Her lovely features screwed up into a frown. She would have made a perfect supermodel if she'd been born a century later, he thought.

"Yes," Drew answered, ignoring the jade eyes brimming with wistfulness and longing. "A pocket watch with a gold fob chain—"

"That sounds like my father's watch. How could you know of it?"

"I . . . Lucky guess." Hope and fear twisted his insides. Would he so easily find the means to return to the year 2000? "May I see it, please?" he asked, flinching at the puzzled look Marianne gave him. "Please," he repeated.

He was in pain, hungry, and terribly worried about Teal. He only wanted to get back home and saw no reason to explain his request.

"I'll get it," Marianne announced, abruptly releasing his hand and standing. A few minutes passed before she returned and handed him the watch.

"Please be careful," she said, her voice catching. "It was my father's favorite."

"Was?" Drew asked, curious despite himself, her small, sad voice touching him. "Is he . . . ?"

"*Oui,* monsieur," she answered. "Claimed by the Fever last year."

"I'm sorry to hear that, Marianne. It sounds as if you miss him greatly."

She smiled bravely but didn't confirm or deny his assumption. All animation left her features. Sorry he'd probed, he turned his attention to the watch.

He knew immediately that it wasn't the watch that had brought him here. It didn't have the eerie force the other one had. Nevertheless, he enclosed the watch in his fist and shut his eyes tightly. Knowing that Marianne was watching his every move, he repeated the chant in a whisper.

Nothing happened, no loud, deafening ticking or lights dancing before his eyes. Opening his eyes to find that Marianne had lost some of her color and her eyes had widened with alarm, he felt the complete nut. Considering her look, that seemed to be Marianne's sentiment as well.

His disappointment, however, was keen. Then he remembered that the chant mentioned something about a summer's eve. Well, the present season was spring. Summer wouldn't arrive for another several weeks; perhaps at the right time of year, with the right watch, he could successfully return to 2000.

Somehow he had to find the watch that had brought him here, then wait for summer to make an appearance. Once he was well enough to get around, he'd return to Rue Dumaine and walk the length of it in an attempt to find it. If he didn't, he wasn't sure what he would do to recover it, but at least he had a purpose, something to keep his mind from constantly straying to his daughter.

He handed Marianne her father's watch. "Thank you," he said, indicating with his hand that she reseat herself. Since he couldn't explain his strange behavior, he thought it best to change the subject. "How did I get here?"

After she sat on the ladder-back chair, Marianne explained that Tomas, their driver, and her family had brought him to Rue Dumaine. Tomas and Henry had put him to bed, then Dr. Oubre cleaned him up and saw to the wound.

"Thank you," Drew said again, denying his urge to touch her, his gaze locking with hers. The first chance he got, he knew, he'd be on his way. If the warmth and passion brimming in her eyes were any indication, he could easily break her heart.

No, he told himself, he must be mistaken. That passion couldn't be for him. She belonged to Rafe Montague. And he wouldn't appreciate Marianne's attitude one bit, unless it was directed at him.

Lowering her eyelids, she caressed Drew's arm, leaving a trail of burning desire wherever she touched. Her passion was definitely there. For him. Uncomfortable, he cleared his throat.

Long, thick lashes framed her eyes as she met his gaze again. "A-are you hungry, monsieur?" she asked in a throaty whisper.

The spell was broken, and relief swirled through him. Wounded or not, he wasn't sure how long he could have resisted Marianne's flirtations. He would have at least attempted to kiss her.

As if on cue, his stomach began protesting. He was bandaged so tightly he wondered if he could maneuver himself to eat, but he needed to concentrate on nourishing himself back to health and putting Marianne in the proper perspective.

"Yes, Marianne, I'm famished."

"Then—"

A knock on the door interrupted her.

"Marianne? Are you in there?"

The sound of Rafe Montague's voice was unmistakable. It was also unamused. Helpless, Drew could only stare at the door.

Chapter 7

"MON DIEU!" MARIANNE exclaimed in a whisper, her hand flying to her breast. She gazed at the servant. "Henry!"

"Yes, Miss Mari, I'll fix it."

Heart racing and head pounding, Drew watched Henry open the door and step outside. But it was Marianne's reaction that stunned him as Henry spoke, his words carrying through the slightly open door.

"Good afternoon, Mr. Rafe, suh," the servant said jovially.

A tremble seized Marianne, and she grabbed the side of the bed, grasping it so tightly her fingers quickly became bloodless.

"Henry," Rafe responded stiffly. "I was told Mistress Marianne was here tending one of the sick slaves. I have no desire to enter your dwelling."

Rafe sniffed with disdain, and Marianne wrinkled her nose. Drew smiled covertly at her pert little nose, straight and charming.

"Please inform your mistress of my presence."

Nervous fingers fidgeted with the scarlet ribbon around her throat when Marianne heard Rafe's command.

"Can't, suh. I heard Miss Chloe was ailing. There ain't nobody *here* I know of is sick."

Marianne sat motionless, anxiously waiting to hear Rafe's response. Drew thought her expectation matched his. They both thought Rafe would burst through the door at any moment. If that happened, it was all over—Rafe would certainly kill him.

"Miss Chloe?" Rafe asked after a few moments.

Releasing a breath, Marianne sagged with relief, using her small hand to fan herself.

"Yes, suh. Miss Mari's friend. She lives on Rue St. Ann."

"Really? All this solicitude will certainly cease upon our marriage. There are doctors to tend to the infirmed," he grumbled. "Tell your mistress I will call on her on Friday."

"Yes, suh," Henry replied.

Retreating footsteps pounded down the gallery before silence descended. After several minutes Henry reentered the room.

Marianne rushed to Henry and embraced him. "*Merci,* Henry," she said with utter relief.

Drew cursed Rafe's black soul. Watching the tension leave Marianne's body, he wondered what motivated her to consider marrying such a snake. Related to him or not, the man was sewer scum who wrought fear with his mere presence.

How could Drew have defended Marianne against Rafe if he'd burst through the door, when he couldn't even defend himself at the moment?

"Monsieur Drew?"

"Yes, Marianne," he responded huskily, his gratitude to his lovely benefactor acute. His appreciative glance soaked in her beauty. The scarlet ribbon at her throat was feminine, but quite sexy against the backdrop of her stylishly combed black hair. "Are you all right?"

Sweeping lashes lowered, and her eyelids covered her jade eyes. Managing a tremulous smile as she opened her eyes again, she fixed her fathomless gaze on him. "I must leave you now. Monsieur Rafe is unpredictable. He might very well return."

Disappointment soared through Drew. He didn't want her to go. Yet what could he expect? She wasn't his nurse. As it was, she'd exceeded kindness in helping him. But, hell, she was the only bright spot in his existence right now. When she left, he'd be alone with nothing but his dark, scary thoughts and the pain he was trying so hard to ignore.

She kissed his cheek, her lips warm and soft upon his skin. It was awfully familiar of her, he reflected, given the era they were in, but Drew wouldn't question her behavior, and he'd try not to take advantage of how smitten she seemed with him. An unknown scent imprinted itself in his brain, and he inhaled deeply as Marianne spoke again.

"I will have Luella prepare a dish to nurture you. Henry will bring it in shortly."

Drew smiled. He wouldn't burden her further by asking her to stay. "Thank you, lovely lady. For everything."

With a last smile at him, Marianne departed the small chamber. Empty of her presence, the room grew lonely, oppressive. Contemplating his reaction to her absence, he realized that he felt an affinity toward her, a strange pull. In the few short minutes she'd been gone, he missed her terribly.

Drew knew that it often took only a matter of moments for a man and woman to recognize a chemistry between them. Wishing he could learn more about her, he knew, too, that he and Marianne shared this instinctive attraction for one another. People in this era, however, didn't date. Gentlemen *called* on ladies. They sat in parlors, engaging in mundane conversation, while the ladies batted their eyelashes flirtatiously behind an unfolded fan.

In this era, such old-fashioned ideas were pounded into boys and girls from birth. But Drew had been taught differently. He'd been taught to express himself in whatever way he thought best to a woman who interested him. Twenty-first-century culture demanded intimacy, equality, and communication between men and women. Marriages were no longer arranged to align families, nor was marriage a necessity anymore for a woman's life to be complete. But Marianne wouldn't understand this, and if he ever called upon her, he'd have her and her family swooning with a straightforwardness that would be considered indelicate in 1853. Besides, he might tolerate mundane conversation for a short while, but a constant stream of it wasn't his strong suit.

A stinging pain shot through his shoulder.

Neither was sword-fighting.

Wondering just how badly he'd been wounded, he swore softly. The next time Marianne came by, he'd have to ask her about his prognosis. It couldn't be too bad, he thought. Even with the lack of proper medication, he wasn't raging with fever. Either a very good doctor had seen to him, or he wasn't as severely wounded as he thought . . . as it had felt.

But the next time he saw Marianne, she might bring tidings he didn't want to hear. With Rafe lurking about, he wasn't sure how long he'd be able to stay at the Beaufort house.

What place could he go to that would keep him out of his ancestor's vicious grasp? He sighed. Who could have known the true character of Rafe Montague when Drew or Sebastian or Nolan listened to their father's stories about the man?

Drew frowned at the ceiling. Marianne was engaged to the man who would be his great-great-grandfather. On the wood-framed family tree that hung in the foyer of Bienvenu, Rafe's wife was listed as Genevieve. Every birth, marriage, and death that had ever occurred in the Montague family was listed on the heavy parchment, but there was no record of Marianne. Only of . . . of her sister, Genevieve Sophie Beaufort, married to Rafe in October 1853.

So what had happened to Marianne?

Now that it had dawned on Drew that Marianne was destined to be his great-great-aunt, he'd be more inclined to put her into perspective. Altering history didn't sit well with him.

As for Genevieve, he mused, he'd like to get to know her better. Perhaps in her he'd find the missing link that would bridge the gap between him and his father once he returned to the year 2000.

He had questions galore, the least of which had to do with his unassuming great-great-grandmother. He wanted to discover why Marianne hadn't become a Montague.

Knowing that the answer was elusive as long as he remained in bed, he sat up with some effort and swung his legs over the side of the low bed. His entire body protested with stiffness.

What the hell had he been lying on?

He kneaded the mattress like dough, and it made the rustling sound of dry leaves. He drew his brows together in perplexity. "Straw?" he said aloud.

"No, suh. Moss," Henry volunteered.

Drew nearly sprang from his seat. "Wha . . . ?"

"Didn't mean to scare you, suh."

"You damn sure did a good job, though, Henry," Drew said with a chuckle. "I thought I was alone."

"Miss Mari wouldn't allow you to be alone now, suh."

Trying to conceal his pleasure at hearing that, he kept his face passive. "Oh?"

"Well, suh, you wasn't cut too deep, but you lost a lot of blood. Miss Mari was afraid you was too weak to do anything."

"So she asked you to look after me?"

"Yes, suh."

"How long have I been here?"

"Just since last night," Henry answered, confirming Drew's calculations.

He perused his surroundings again. "Whose room is this?"

"Mine, suh."

"But there's only one bed. Where did you sleep last night?"

Pointing to the pallet on the floor, Henry said, "Over there, suh."

Drew inhaled deeply. "God, Henry, I'm sorry. You shouldn't be displaced because of me. Take back your bed, and *I'll* take the pallet."

Henry stared in disbelief at him, puzzlement and respect shining from the dark brown eyes in the chocolate face. Henry didn't know that Drew had come from a different time, a time in which men were learning to respect the rights of others. Although that concept wasn't yet fully perfected, it was working. And as a man from the future, Drew would do his part in the era he now found himself in.

Unsteadily he got to his feet, refusing to acknowledge the hot pain of the cut.

"Suh, I thanks you, really I do. But Miss Mari won't hear of it. And neither will I," Henry added proudly. "You needs your rest."

He smiled at the man's determined tone. In fact, Drew told himself, there couldn't be much difference between the pallet and the mattress, except that the bed was about a foot off the floor.

"You're a good man, Henry," he said, not wanting to insult the man by refusing his offer. "For the time being, I *will* keep the bed. The added height will make it easier for me to maneuver with my injury."

"Yes, suh," Henry agreed with a grin. "You sit over there at the little table, and I'll go and get your food."

"Sounds good to me."

The question of why Clarisse and Genevieve had been careless enough to send Rafe to the room where Drew was lying helpless plagued Marianne. But she wanted to avoid their questions about Andrew for the time being, so she skirted the parlor when she heard their laughing chatter trailing out into the hallway.

Escaping to the foyer, Marianne rushed up the steep staircase to the privacy of her bedchamber. Her heart raced in her chest. She should have been more concerned with her relationship with Rafe than she was, she knew. But until she'd heard his voice, she hadn't thought of the consequences of what would occur between them if he discovered her with Drew.

And what would Rafe have done to Drew? *Non,* that wasn't the question. The true question was what *wouldn't* Rafe have done to him.

She realized that her loyalties were somewhat misguided, yet she felt overwhelmingly protective of Drew. He was in a helpless state, with no one to turn to and apparently no place to stay.

He might even be a little addled. He'd sung to her father's watch, almost worshiping it as he gripped it in his hand, eyes tightly shut. The incident could be attributed to his infirmed condition, and she sincerely hoped that was it. She'd hate to be attracted to a deranged man.

Sacre bleu! Of course, there could be no other explanation for her strange behavior. She was attracted to a man who was little more than a stranger.

What kind of wanton was she? A woman of her station— her *engaged* station—shouldn't have had such thoughts of other men. *Mon Dieu.* She must take hold of her emotions, she told herself. C. Andrew Montague III appeared penniless. He'd never do for her. There was no other choice for her but marriage to Rafe.

She'd simply stay away from Andrew. Henry could keep her apprised of his condition, and Dr. Oubre would return in a week. Perhaps he'd pronounce Andrew well, and then he'd be on his way; she could get on with her life as planned.

Yet Marianne knew her life would never be the same again, that her planned and ordered life was only wishful thinking. The pull of this man was too strong. She wanted to see to his condition herself. To gaze into his deep blue eyes. To see his smile. To feel his hands on her.

And she'd risk all for it.

Chapter 8

DR. OUBRE METICULOUSLY REMOVED
Drew's bandages, placing them on the bed. The robust doctor glided his meaty fingers across the thin red slash that
was sure to leave a scar on Drew's chest when it healed.

As still as stone during the examination, Drew fought
hard to control the anger he felt for Rafe. Until now, he'd
been proud of his unblemished body. He was a real stud
when he wore his swimming trunks, drawing stares from
old and young alike. But now people would stare at him
for a different reason, if he ever wore his trunks again.
They'd be looking at his scar.

"Monsieur Montague, I'd say you were a lucky man,"
Dr. Oubre said, stepping back from the bed. "Your wounds
are not deep. You lost a fair amount of blood, though. That
was due to the slicing of some small veins and blood ves-
sels."

"Thanks, Doc," Drew responded wearily. He hadn't seen
Marianne for seven days, not since Rafe's unexpected visit.
She'd abandoned him, leaving his welfare to the servants—
and now to the doctor.

Not that he hadn't been taken care of. He was well fed
and watched over—in fact, he'd been told to venture out

onto the gallery or down into the courtyard only at night, if at all. They couldn't have Rafe surprising him.

While Drew appreciated the aid, he wanted Marianne. She, at least, would keep his mind off his predicament. He hated to think that he might be stuck in 1853. As long as he remained in bed, cooped up in the stifling little room, anxiety would continue to plague Drew. But the worry he felt for Teal, his complete sense of helplessness, would remain at bay while he talked to Marianne.

But she wasn't his keeper. Marianne's interest in him went only as far as the kindness she'd already shown him.

"Raise your arm, monsieur," Dr. Oubre instructed.

Drew did as he was told, and felt a slight discomfort. Flinching, he brought his arm back to his side.

"Was that bothersome in any way, monsieur?"

"Just minuscule unpleasantness. Somewhat stiff," Drew answered. If it had been worse, he wouldn't have told the doctor. He was anxious to go and explore the city in order to get some leads on the watch he needed.

Dr. Oubre began packing away his lethal-looking instruments, which to Drew's relief he hadn't had to use. "The stiffness will gradually recede. I don't believe that slash will leave a very noticeable scar. It is very thin."

Wondering if the doctor had read his mind a moment ago, Drew smiled. "That's good to hear."

Dr. Oubre nodded and walked to the door. He paused. "Unless there's a setback, monsieur, you won't need to see me again. Mademoiselle Marianne will know how to reach me if the need arises. *Bonjour*." With that, he stepped out into the morning sunlight, leaving the door ajar.

Sitting on the only chair in the tiny room, Drew relished the sunlight streaming through the door. A magnolia tree stood within his range of vision. Big white flowers bloomed in the midst of waxy green leaves. Whenever the breeze blew, the lemony scent of the flowers filled the air.

For a solid week he'd remained inside, deciding caution was the better part of valor. But he was becoming claustrophobic. He needed stimulation and activity.

Unseen birds were singing outside his window. He'd never had much time for nature. Before he married, he'd been a wild child, into all things fast. That included women and motorcycles. Then he'd met Teresa, and she'd settled him down. Or maybe he'd just realized it was past time he grew up.

Ironically she'd been the one to bail, deciding marriage and motherhood were just too much for her to handle at such a young age.

Way before that happened, *he'd* gotten some direction to his life and decided to go to law school. Not that his father supported him. Whether it was good or bad, Cranneck always managed to find fault with Drew's behavior. His father questioned his aspirations, disparaged his wife, and spurned his own granddaughter.

Drew cursed. He'd already been gone for nearly nine days. Knowing Cranneck's propensity for thinking the worst of him, he figured his father undoubtedly believed he'd run off because he wanted to renege on the deal they'd made. He only hoped Teal's sweet disposition had finally won her ornery grandfather over and that Cranneck wouldn't make Drew's daughter suffer because of her father's perceived infractions.

The fluttering of wings drowned out the chirping noises. Silence followed as the birds flew off and took away Drew's sole source of company. What injustice had he committed to deserve this?

He would give anything, *do* anything, to see his daughter again. And Ursula was probably worried sick. His mother withstood adversity extremely well, but he knew what it meant to be a parent, and her family meant everything to her. She carried an unsurpassed pride for each of her sons, and for her to think that she'd lost one of them would be almost unbearable.

He had to get home.

But where would he go from here? Now that he was on the mend, he'd be left to fend for himself more than he had this past week. Even Henry had made himself scarce, coming in only to serve him his meals and then to bed down for the night.

Just as the last thought rumbled through Drew's mind, the servant walked through the open door. Male garments were slung across his arm.

"Mr. Andrew," he said with a wide grin, "Miss Mari asked me to give you these clothes. They were her papa's."

Drew straightened in his seat, his mood lightening at the mention of Marianne. "Really?"

"Yes, suh. She said you be about his size."

"Well, thank you, Henry, and thank the lady for me."

"You can do that yourself, suh. She wants you to join her and her maman and sister for breakfast when you gets dressed."

Well, she hadn't abandoned him after all. And he'd have a chance to talk to Genevieve and get a true measure of her character. He'd watch her reactions closely and perhaps discover a clue as to why *she'd* married Rafe, when Marianne was presently engaged to him.

Had it been her choice or someone's treachery that prevented the union?

"It'll be my pleasure to join them," Drew said, happy to have something else to wear. For the past few days, he'd worn only a long, loose nightshirt over a pair of trousers. He wondered what became of his original clothing, including his briefs. "Is it possible to have a shower . . . uh, bath before I dress? Even a cold one?"

"Yes, suh. You can takes a shower, too, iffen you wants."

"How?" Drew asked suspiciously. He hadn't realized showers were in use in pre–Civil War New Orleans.

"Luella told me Miss Mari come up with a way to get water to rain down on her through a long pipe at the plantation upriver. When Masta Jean had the manor outfitted with running water, Miss Mari came up with her idea."

"I take it this cottage doesn't have running water?" Drew asked mildly, all the more intrigued with Marianne because she seemed so *advanced* to be living in the era in which she did.

"No, suh."

"So how can I take a shower here?"

"Why, I'll be happy to stand and pour water over you after you get through with your bath. Or, if you'd prefer, Luella can do it—"

"No," Drew said, more sharply than he'd intended, knowing that Henry was serious and hating that the man would have no choice but to do any task Drew asked of him. That included pouring water over a grown and competent man if the whim had hit him. "I'll just take the bath, thank you."

Within thirty minutes, Drew had completed his wash in a frigid bath. The weather had been unseasonably cool and damp this year, Henry explained. On another occasion, the water might have been slightly less chilled, or could have been heated over the fire first, but they were pressed for time.

Once the chillbumps were gone from his skin, it really didn't matter to Drew. His body was clean again, as were his clothes. Even if he did feel outdated in loose-fitting blue trousers with a button fly, a frilly, long-sleeved white shirt, a blue vest shot through with silver, and a gray waistcoat. The highly polished boots that completed the outfit were a bit snug, but his loafers just wouldn't do.

"How do I look, Henry?"

"Like a gent'man planter, suh. I expect now I'll be getting my bed back."

Henry's grumble surprised him. He was comfortable enough with Drew to express his displeasure.

Drew burst out laughing. "You certainly will, my friend. I am most grateful for the use of it and I thank you very much. Now, which way do we go?"

"I been told to bring you to the parlor, Mr. Andrew."

"In that case, Henry, my good man, lead the way."

As Drew followed Henry across the gallery, the lushness of the courtyard surprised him. Thick honeysuckle vines grew along trellises at the far side. Huge potted plants stood in strategic places along the inner walls. A marble fountain sat in the middle of the courtyard. Sturdy iron chairs and tables offered seating amidst the floral beauty.

They reached the stairs on the other side. They went up, then he followed Henry through the foyer and to the parlor. His breath caught. Marianne sat there, alone and deep in thought. An air of isolation and loneliness surrounded her.

He wanted to dispel it but knew he should keep his distance.

"Here he be, Miss Mari," Henry announced, beaming in Drew's direction with fatherly pride. "Don't he make a fine-looking gent'man?"

Drew stared at Marianne, hardly digesting Henry's compliment. Maybe he was dreaming after all. No one could be so beautiful and be real.

Her black hair sported long curls that fell on each side of her face, framing skin as delicate as porcelain. Eyes like liquid jade brightened with pleasure upon seeing him; small, pale pink lips curved into an intimate smile.

She had the most exquisite features of any woman he'd ever seen: finely carved facial bones and high, exotic cheekbones with wide-set, slightly slanted eyes. And from what little he knew of her, she had inner beauty to match.

She couldn't seriously be thinking of throwing herself into a marriage with a devil like Rafe, Drew told himself.

"Ain't he handsome, Miss Mari?" Henry repeated.

Unsure of what to do in the face of Henry's question, Marianne stood up and extended her hand. "It is good to see you again, monsieur," she said, unsuccessfully trying to ward off a blush at his appreciative look and ignoring Henry's question at the same time. "I hope I did not offend you with my father's clothes?"

Dieu! How magnificent he looked! She hadn't realized how handsome he was—or how tall. His long, sinewy form stood inches from her, his self-confidence and vitality drawing her in. Brilliant blue eyes smoldered with interest as they danced beneath thick, tawny eyebrows.

She'd only wanted to show him an extra kindness by inviting him to breakfast. She'd given no thought to the bewildering emotions she'd experience when she saw him again. She knew she mustn't let Andrew know how his presence affected her. Or how only sheer determination had kept her from going to his bedside during the week. After vowing to herself that she'd risk all for him, she realized the tendresse she felt for him wasn't wise.

But he intrigued her. Mystery enveloped his mere presence, and Marianne wanted to know more about him. Where had he come from and how did he end up in front of the St. Louis Hotel? She wanted to spend hours with him, discovering every secret he was willing to share with her. Maybe then she could enter the union with Rafe without the feeling of not having experienced love and desire with a man she admired.

Yet she knew there could be consequences from her dangerous attraction. Dire consequences.

Even if she didn't go through with this marriage to a man who couldn't love anyone but himself, she couldn't risk giving in to a temptation that might produce a bastard child.

"No, Marianne," Drew said, breaking her wicked thoughts. "You don't offend me. You are very kind to even consider letting me wear your father's clothes."

Marianne drew in a steadying breath. His voice was crisp and clear, one that she'd gladly listen to for hours. "*Merci*, monsieur," she said softly.

Andrew indicated the settee with a wave of his hand. "Please, sit down," he said with a ring of authority, as though it were his home he stood so regally in.

Not taking offense, Marianne seated herself and smoothed out her white embroidery-edged cambric dress. She hid a smile as he sat across from her on the wingback chair. Anticipating his acceptance of her breakfast invitation, she'd agonized over her choice of attire this morning. But he wasn't Rafe. What she wore didn't matter one whit to Andrew.

Clearing his throat, he captured her attention. "Thank

you for all you've done for me, Marianne. I may never be able to repay you."

Marianne smiled. He was so unlike Rafe in every way, yet the two men shared a faint resemblance. She wanted to know if he was an outcast of the Montague family—but didn't dare ask. Maybe he was a bastard born to Rafe's father.

His impossible jest that he was Rafe's great-great-grandson suggested he didn't want to share his true connection to the family.

"Marianne?"

"Oui?"

He leaned forward in a casual pose. "I don't want to cause any trouble for you. Or for myself, for that matter. Is it safe to be here?"

"Oui. Rafe is at Bienvenu in St. Francisville. I saw him last evening just before his departure. He says he will be indisposed for the next week or so."

Drew nodded. It pleased him that they could converse so easily. Without further explanation, she had understood his question of safety. "Henry said there would be others here."

"My maman and sister are already in the dining room. We will join them shortly."

Suddenly her features clouded with sadness, taking on a distant, faraway look. Deep in thought, she was the very picture of grief and despair.

Unable to bear seeing her beautiful face marred by such emotion, Drew was beside her on the settee in an instant. "Marianne," he whispered, taking her hand in his, "what are you thinking to cause you to look so sad? Is it your father? Or is it your upcoming marriage?"

"Monsieur, please," Marianne murmured, her voice quavering. "You . . . I do not wish to burden you with my problems."

"No, never," Drew reassured her. "Tell me. When I came in, you seemed so lonely, as if you needed someone to listen to you."

She stared at him a brief moment more, and then the

words came pouring out. "My father was claimed by the Fever nearly a year ago. It will be a year in August, and now the swamp miasma is again sending its vaporous waves over the city. Several have already lost their lives this year. It frightens me. The season is starting unusually early. What if I lose someone else dear to me?"

"Like Rafe?" he asked, sounding like a jealous paramour, which she certainly didn't need at the moment. "Do you love Rafe?"

She inhaled deeply. "Monsieur, how would you know beforehand the number of lives claimed by the Fever?" she asked, pointedly ignoring his question. "Can you see into the future?"

"No, Marianne, I cannot," he answered, unwilling to share his source of information: history books. "But you haven't answered my question."

"Andrew, please!" she implored. "You must not—"

"I must not what, Marianne?" Drew asked, drawing her slim body closer to his, his attraction overtaking his reason. "I must not do this?"

Releasing her hand, he slipped his arm around her waist. His gaze caught hers. Finding the encouragement he sought, he croaked, "Marianne," before lowering his lips to hers.

She gasped in surprised pleasure as he sealed his mouth to hers in a searing kiss. The feel of his warm tongue was even more persuasive than she'd imagined. Her body started to react. Warm wine seemed to run along her veins. Heat rushed into her cheeks as Andrew probed the recesses of her mouth. His hands roamed over her, igniting tiny flames that burned through her entire body.

His strong arms tightened around her, holding her with firm gentleness. Even knowing the folly of this act, she couldn't resist. Nor did she want to. He was everything she'd ever dreamed of and more. He was tender and seductive, bold and mysterious.

Responding to the feelings he wrought, she kissed him

with wild recklessness. She'd never shared this kind of kiss and had no desire to have this one end.

His lips trailed hot kisses along the column of her throat as his hands invaded her bodice. In an instant, he'd freed one of her breasts and bent his head to the strawberry tip, then enclosed the hardened bud within his mouth. She shuddered at the wanton touch and buried her hands in the thick silkiness of his golden hair. Her heart pounded, and her pulse raced.

Throwing her head back, she released a small, heated cry, her hands tightening in his hair as his tongue explored her nipple.

Somewhere in the back of her mind, she remembered they were not alone, that at any moment her indiscretion could be discovered. But her belly was tight, and moisture soaked her loins. She needed succor. She needed him to carry her to some secret place and make her his.

"Drew, *mon* monsieur," she whispered through the fog of her want.

He was as hard as the Rock of Gibraltar and as hot as molten lava. He wanted to make love to Marianne right then and there. He'd thought simply to kiss away her turmoil and confusion; to halt any more questions she had about his knowledge of the future; to show her the difference between him and Rafe. She'd surprised him and proven a most willing participant, catching him at his own game and sending blood rushing to his loins.

But instead of romancing the past, he needed to find a corridor to the future.

He could easily fall in love with Marianne, yet he could never remain with her. He knew he must return to his own place in time, if for no other reason than his baby girl.

Besides, he told himself, Marianne had her own place in the past that he must not infringe upon.

But he needed release. He needed the one thing he would never have—her.

He tore his mouth away from her breasts, swollen from his kisses. He trailed his lips along her neck, over her eyes and cheeks. Finally he found her lips again, for one last sweet kiss.

"Marianne," he said in a husky voice, putting her disheveled clothes to rights, her flushed, heated skin making the task almost impossible. "Forgive me. You're irresistible. I hope I haven't offended you." His breathing was still somewhat uneven, and sweat beaded his brow.

"*Non,* Drew, I am not offended," Marianne said, passing her hand over his forehead. Offended? How could she be offended when all she wanted was to feel his arms around her again? "I had dark thoughts, but they are gone out of my head now."

Forcing herself to push out of his arms, she straightened in her seat. She ran her fingers through her hair but found most of it still intact. What wasn't intact seemed purposely out of place.

Her lips felt swollen from his kisses, however, her breasts tender. Her entire body tingled, and she fought for control. If she felt like this from a mere kiss, she asked herself, how would it be if he made love to her?

"Drew," she began, barely steady, "when I asked Maman and Genevieve for a moment of privacy with you, it was because I wanted to tell you myself of our decision regarding you."

Drew hung his head, contrite. "Instead, I took advantage of that privacy."

"*Non,* Drew," Marianne amended quickly, grasping his hand and squeezing it gently. "I am as guilty as you are. I didn't mind it. So it's all right. I promise you."

Drew knew she'd said something else, something about a decision, one that he knew could see him out on the street. But he'd already been through much worse. Perhaps because of that, the only thing he'd really heard Marianne say was, "I didn't mind it." It confirmed that she was as attracted to him as he was to her.

"Do you have a place to stay, Drew?"

His eyes widened in surprise at her question. Was she

offering him a place? Her place? "In all honesty, Marianne, I have nothing. I am penniless."

"Then we will help," she said quickly. "We have a guest room at your disposal. And you may have use of my father's garments."

What happened to the sheltered, conservative, nineteenth-century woman he'd read so much about? he wondered. Having a stranger without a nickel to his name beneath an aristocratic roof wasn't a normal, everyday occurrence. With Rafe lurking about, it mightn't be such a good idea, either. But then, Marianne wasn't a fool, Drew knew, figuring she must have a plan to offset Rafe's anger if he discovered Drew's residency.

Blessing his good fortune at having dropped into the path of such a forward thinker, he stood. He gazed into Marianne's expressive eyes, shook his head, and released an amused laugh. "Why do I feel this was entirely your idea?"

Her creamy complexion turned a very becoming pink.

"Did you have a hard time convincing them?" he added, grinning.

Totally at ease with him, Marianne chuckled. "*Oui,* monsieur. But I can be very persuasive when need be."

Bowing chivalrously, Drew kissed the top of her head. "Thank you, sweet lady. I will accept your offer."

"*Excusez-moi,* mademoiselle," Luella said as she appeared in the doorway. "Madame summons you to breakfast."

"*Merci,* Luella. We'll be right there," Marianne said, standing. "Come, Drew. We must not keep Maman waiting."

"Not on my account," Drew said, a little nervous at the prospect of meeting Marianne's mother. But with a daughter like Marianne, he reassured himself, the woman had to be at least halfway decent. He touched Marianne on the arm, stopping her as she began to walk past. "I promise that in due time I will try to explain everything about myself to you."

"I would like that, Drew," she said with a blinding smile.

He held out his arm, and Marianne slid her hand through the crook at his elbow. He was beginning to relax again, but she had to have seen the evidence of his arousal bulging in his pants. He certainly didn't want anyone else to see, especially her mother—his great-great-great-grandmother, whose daughter he'd just kissed until they were both senseless. What kind of a pervert—or whatever aroused men were called in the here and now—would she think he was? She surely wouldn't allow him to sleep under the same roof with them.

He sucked in a ragged breath, thinking it unwise to continue forward. "Marianne," he began, "perhaps—"

"It is all right, Drew. I assure you," she said. She looked up at him and smiled knowingly.

Drew grinned sheepishly at her, amazed. So she *had* noticed. How liberated she seemed. Perhaps she'd believe his story after all, he mused. He felt a small tug on his arm. Walking beside her, he let her guide him to the dining room, where two of his grandmothers, several times removed, awaited him.

Chapter 9

As THEY ENTERED the dining room, Marianne slipped her arm from his, and Drew allowed his own to drop to his side. Sunshine bounced off the rose-colored linen walls, and cool, fresh air streamed through the open French doors, which led to an outside balcony.

Genevieve and a woman dressed in black mourning attire were already seated at the modest-sized table. A heavy silver bowl stood in the middle, filled with fresh fruit. Beneath it lay a Battenberg lace table runner.

The woman in black—Marianne's mother, he knew—scrutinized him with a suspicious eye. Genevieve, on the other hand, savored him with pleasure gleaming from her pretty features.

Marianne scowled at her sister, and Drew surmised she didn't like the flirtatious looks Genevieve threw his way. Warmed at the thought, he chuckled to himself as Marianne glided to her seat.

"Maman, Gen, I do not believe you have had the pleasure of formally meeting Monsieur Andrew Montague. Drew, may I present my mother, Clarisse Beaufort. You've met Genevieve already," she said mulishly.

Drew nodded to Genevieve. "A pleasure to see you

again, ma'am." Walking over to the head of the table where Clarisse sat, he bowed low at the waist. "Good morning, Mrs. Beaufort," he said, taking her hand and pressing his lips to it. Ignoring her stiff resistance, he charged on. "I owe you and your daughters a great debt of gratitude for your charity. I will not forget it." He smiled rakishly. "Never admit to being the mother of two grown daughters, madame. No one would believe you. If I hadn't been told who you are, I would think you are a beautiful sister to these equally beautiful ladies."

In that he wasn't lying. She was still quite a beautiful woman.

Clarisse's hand fluttered to her breast as a blush stained her pale cheeks. "Why, *merci*, monsieur. You are most charming, sir. You are indeed welcome to lodge here until your matters of affairs are set right."

"I'm grateful, madame," Drew said, glancing at Rafe's future wife. "To you, too, Mademoiselle Genevieve."

Genevieve blushed. "My pleasure, monsieur," she said softly.

Drew winked at Marianne, and she smiled at him.

Genevieve seemed so unassuming, without the passion that defined Marianne. But she was a sweet young lady, easily flustered in his presence. He surmised Rafe had constantly taken advantage of her over the course of their long marriage.

"Please seat yourself, Monsieur Montague," Clarisse said sweetly, "and Luella will begin serving us."

Three days later, Drew stood on the balcony at the cottage on Rue Dumaine. Clouds blocked the sun, and the threat of rain hung in the air, but he welcomed the fresh air while the women took an afternoon nap. His days had been filled with the company of the three Beaufort women. Constantly. The attention had been tiring. While he enjoyed being near Marianne, he saw the pains she went through to keep her distance from him in the presence of her mother and sister.

This morning Clarisse told him she intended for a tailor

to come and fit him for some new clothes, which forced
Drew to come to a decision. He was being "kept" by three
women, and he didn't like that one little bit.

He had always been too independent to allow even his
father to do such a thing. It had only been due to his desperation that Teal be well cared for that he'd finally capit-
ulated and accepted his mother's offer to give him part of
his rightful inheritance in small, monthly increments. Otherwise, his father could have burned the money for all he
cared.

Now these women were determined to trample upon the
self-esteem that his disastrous first meeting with Great-
Great-Granddaddy had already weakened.

He had no money, no job, no prospects, and he was
constantly aroused in Marianne's presence, which wasn't
good at all. She vied for attention with Teal in his mind.

He had to leave.

Recalling the history he'd learned of Bienvenu, he remembered a great-uncle, thrice removed, who'd left the
plantation in 1820, never to be heard from again. Rumor
had it he had been killed in a duel. Nothing more was
known of him. The man in question was Pierre's brother
and Rafe's uncle, which would make Drew Rafe's cousin
in this little lie.

It didn't matter. The lie could turn Rafe into Drew's aunt
for all he cared. He wanted only to be productive and to
be able to support himself until summer arrived. Then he
could try again to get back to the twenty-first century.

He hoped going to St. Francisville and posing as the
man's son would be easy. He knew the workings of a plantation firsthand, since in his own time Bienvenu was still
in operation—although with employees and thankfully not
slaves. He had been taught how to run the place, as had
Nolan and Sebastian, from the time they were all toddlers.

If only he could remember the name of his supposed
father. He racked his brain, but to no avail. What was that
fool's name? Nathan? No, that didn't sound right. Noah?

The guy's name began with an *N.* Perhaps it would come to him along the way.

"*Bonjour,* monsieur," Marianne said, gliding onto the balcony in billowing skirts of green and floral patterns. "I hope I am not intruding."

Drew cleared his throat. How could he leave her? Since his arrival, she'd become his link to sanity. To sunshine. If he left and was accepted into the fold at St. Francisville, he mightn't ever see her again. Then again, it would be too dangerous to both of them to share a flirtation right beneath Rafe's nose. As it was, if Rafe ever discovered the kiss they'd shared, he'd want to castrate and then disembowel Drew.

He shivered at the thought. Seeing Marianne's eyes widen, he smiled. "Not at all, lovely lady," he said, caressing her cheek. "You could never intrude on anything I do."

"I'm glad." She glanced down onto the street. It was a residential section, and relatively quiet. At the moment, not even a carriage intruded upon the peaceful cloudiness of the day. "You seem lackadaisical of late, Drew. Are you not satisfied here?"

Taking her delicate hand in his, he planted a kiss on the back of it. "Seeing you every day is the closest I've been to paradise, Marianne, and you could never bore me. But I cannot tolerate my inactivity."

Marianne gripped the railing, staring straight ahead. "What are you trying to tell me, Drew?"

He didn't miss the dread in her voice, the tenseness in the clear-cut lines of her profile. For whatever reason she'd consented to marry Rafe, it obviously wasn't love. But Drew refused to come between them. For, as bad as things might seem, at least he was alive and *breathing.* Something old Rafe would surely try to put a stop to if he thought anything was happening between him and Marianne.

He joined her at the railing. "I must leave," he told her softly, hoping she understood his reasons without his having to go into detail. "But I'm afraid I must impose on your generosity yet again, Marianne."

"What is it, Drew?"

"I'll need the use of your carriage and horse to transport me to Bienvenu."

"*Mais non!* Bienvenu? Such folly will cause your demise. Monsieur Rafe will surely kill you, Drew!" Marianne exclaimed, anxiously grabbing his shoulders. "You must not go there!"

Unable to resist, Drew pulled her into his embrace. "Shhh!" he soothed. "I'm not looking for revenge, Marianne. Only gainful employment—"

"But there are other places—"

"Bienvenu is my family's business. I'll ask my uncle Pierre for work."

"Monsieur Pierre is your uncle?"

"Yes. He and my father are brothers," Drew lied.

"Then why did Rafe try to kill you, his own cousin?"

"He doesn't know I'm his cousin. My father left Bienvenu long before I was born."

"Then you've never seen your family?" Marianne asked, amazed.

"I'm afraid not, Marianne," Drew said, hoping to convince Pierre Montague as easily as he seemed to be convincing Marianne. "I don't even know if Uncle Pierre will take me in."

"Oh, of that you have nothing to fear, Drew. Monsieur Pierre is one of the kindest gentlemen I know," Marianne said.

"Really?" Drew asked in disbelief, thinking of Rafe. "If that's so, I wonder why your betrothed turned out to be such a scoundrel."

Stepping out of his embrace, Marianne faced the courtyard once again.

"Forgive me, Marianne. That was unworthy of me. I'm sorry."

When she turned to him again, her eyes brimmed with tears. "I hate to think that you might be right about him, Drew. But I feel there is good in Rafe Montague. Otherwise, I wouldn't have consented to a union with him."

Going behind her, Drew slipped his arms around her slender waist in a tender embrace.

"Please, Drew, someone may see us," Marianne half protested, sniffling.

Drew frowned as he rested his chin on her soft hair. "Why are you crying, sweetheart? Surely it isn't because of what I said about Rafe?"

"I-I'm confused. I do not know why I am crying. I only know I do not want to lose you—I-I mean your friendship."

Drew turned her around, slanted his mouth over hers, and kissed her deeply, the only outlet he had for his own jumbled emotions. He could almost hear the thud of his heartbeat as she slipped her arms around his neck and returned his kiss with fiery passion. Her mouth was like a taste of heaven, a dangerous inferno that sent his spirits soaring and had the power to crescendo out of control.

For he'd only be here a short while, a brief murmur in time that would be over as soon as he found that watch. It was good that he was leaving the temptation of Marianne; she would bring about his downfall if he didn't flee to Bienvenu.

Besides, he needed to go there and confront his dislike for the place head-on. Maybe when he returned to the twenty-first century he'd have a better understanding of why his father loved the plantation so much.

Marianne stood on tiptoe, losing herself to the pounding cadence of her heart, to the kisses that wreaked havoc on her senses. Heat consumed her, urged her closer to Drew, made her respond with all the passion in her. Drew pulled her up against his raging arousal as his big hands cupped her bottom. Instinctively, she began gyrating, unable to control the maelstrom gathering in her body, fog and mist clouding her senses.

"Drew, my Drew."

Inflamed with desire, Drew kissed her long and deep. He left her mouth and kissed her small, delicate nose, then gulped in a huge breath. His body afire, his penis engorged, he held her trembling body close to his, never wanting to release her, but knowing he must.

Yet for endless seconds they lingered, until the sound of a carriage and the clip-clopping of horses intruded upon their moment. He pulled away from her.

"Mari, sweet Mari," he finally croaked. "I think my decision to leave is a good one. I am beginning to forget caution and common sense. Among other reasons, you're the most important one why I must leave. You do understand, don't you?"

Marianne sighed. "Yes," she said in a small voice. "I am ashamed of my wanton behavior. I have not acted like a betrothed woman. What must you think of me?"

"I think you're a wonder, Marianne. A wonder to whom I could lose my heart." Gently he pushed her away from him, refusing to say more. He'd spilled too much information as it was. He didn't want to give her any hope that there could be a future for them. If she broke her engagement to Rafe for him, she would still end up with her heart broken. Either he'd have to leave her, or she'd be wrenched away from all things familiar to her, never to return again. He wouldn't allow that to happen. "May I see that horse and buggy now?"

Chapter 10

MARIANNE SEEMED TO share Drew's need to stretch the ride to Bienvenu out for as long as possible. At his urging, she happily instructed Tomas to show Drew a little of the city. He was only prolonging their inevitable parting, but he couldn't seem to help himself.

She enthralled him. He enjoyed watching the display of emotions across her lovely face as she explained something she found interesting. Jade eyes, already sparkling with life, brightened even further. Laughter bubbled up from her more often than not, a contagious sound that he couldn't help but respond to. Excitement flushed her features and pinkened her lips to a deep rose.

The carriage rumbled through the French section as the clouds that had darkened the sky earlier gave way to a burst of sunshine. Rays of light illuminated newly built structures that were still standing in the twenty-first century. In Jackson Square, changed from the Place d'Armes in January 1851, the mansard roofs of the Cabildo and Presbytere pointed proudly toward the clear blue sky.

The architecturally amazing St. Louis Cathedral of 1853, flanked by the Cabildo and Presbytere, was the third church built on that spot.

Until that moment, he'd never really appreciated the history the buildings represented. To see the beginnings of architecture that would endure for well over a century was phenomenal. Regrettably, he'd been living on the fast track, attempting to make a life for himself and his daughter. Not only had he been unable to enjoy the world around him, but also he hadn't been inclined to do so. Now the very sight of the buildings awed him.

Marianne had long since fallen silent, lost in thoughts of her own, her underlying sadness returning. He kept telling himself to leave matters as they were, to let her be, but he knew deep down that he couldn't. He'd suggested they take this ride through the city so she might open up to him. He knew she was still grieving for her father; he'd glimpsed it several days ago. But watching her together with her mother and sister, he got the feeling that she was the one who was expected to carry the brunt of the responsibilities; that she was the one who'd been *chosen* to marry Rafe.

In short, that it hadn't been her choice—it had been her duty.

But she hadn't married Rafe. Genevieve had.

Tomas gently guided the team down a narrow passageway, then clicked his tongue to encourage the horses on. Colorful awnings lined the way, preventing the sun from glittering on the long, cramped street. The stench of human waste assaulted his nostrils and made his eyes water. Seeing Marianne discreetly pull a perfumed handkerchief from her reticule and place it beneath her nose, Drew followed suit and held his own nose. It hardly helped. The unholy scent crept between the crevices of his fingers.

The carriage rolled passed a dog, dead and bloated, lying in the gutters and surrounded by refuse of unknown origins.

"It's a miracle this city survived at all," Drew commented testily.

"Pardonnez-moi?" Marianne said from behind the handkerchief she still held to her nose. That she was unaffected by the sight of the dead animal attested to the commonplace nature of it.

"The filth, Marianne. It's a disgrace."

"*Oui,* Drew, I agree." Marianne shrugged her delicate shoulders. "But what are we to do? We are at the mercy of the city planners."

"You could protest against this sewage," Drew argued, noting the rise and fall of her breasts, round and straining against the light fabric of her gown.

"We do, Andrew," she said wearily. "And each time the Fever comes, the government vows to clean up the mess. But when the crisis is past, they do nothing."

"And you go on as before?"

"*Oui.*" The single word sounded so lost and vulnerable. Grief and anger drew her pretty mouth into a tight line. She had gone on, but not as before. Never again as before. She had lost her father.

Drew struggled not to take her into his arms and comfort her, to soothe away her pain, there in the clear light of day. For all to see and her reputation to get shredded to pieces.

No, he would never subject her to such disgrace. And then, of course, there was Rafe to consider.

"How is it across Canal Street?" he asked, deciding to drop the subject of how filthy the city was.

"Canal Street? In the American section?" Marianne asked with incredulity.

They emerged from the dank street, and Marianne removed the handkerchief from beneath her nose. Drew stretched his arm out, allowing it to rest on the carriage seat behind Marianne. Long, silky curls of hair escaped her bonnet and brushed his arm. He tempered the urge to remove the frilly bonnet and run his fingers through the inky mass.

"Yes, Marianne, the American sector," Drew replied, annoyed. He knew the animosity that existed between the two cultures in this time period. Especially from the French. They thought of Americans as uncouth barbarians.

But his annoyance stemmed from more than just that. He was annoyed with himself for noticing every small detail of the woman who sat next to him. The flawless skin that reminded him of white velvet. The layers of lace and taffeta

skirts that curled around his leg and gave rise to his wildest
fantasies.

"I do not know how it is on that side of the neutral
ground, monsieur, since I have not had the occasion to go
there," Marianne replied in vexation.

Drew laughed at her pique, her nimble mind her most
attractive feature of all. He knew the term *neutral ground*
in 1853 terminology had a literal meaning. In this century,
the median on Canal Street had become the dividing line
between the Creoles and Americans. Many on the French
side absolutely refused to cross it, and it seemed Marianne
was in that number. Some, however, did meet on the median, and it became known as the neutral ground, a term
that was still in use in twenty-first-century New Orleans to
describe any median dividing the city streets. "I'm sorry,
sweetheart. I shouldn't have brought the subject up, but I've
always been interested in this city's history."

"You have?" she asked, surprised.

"Yes. And I know the hostility that exists between the
French and Americans. But nonetheless, I would still like
to see the other side."

Marianne gave him a curiously puzzling look. "Very
well," she said, and instructed Tomas to cross the neutral
ground to the American sector.

Along St. Charles Avenue, Drew noted a fair amount of
construction going on. Some homes were ostentatiously
completed; others were shells that showed promise of being
palatial estates. All were surrounded by stretches of lawn
that reminded Drew of an emerald carpet.

"What are they trying to prove with the pretentiousness?"
Marianne huffed, her slim body stiffening in outrage.

"I beg your pardon," Drew said with a chuckle. "You
don't think those huge French homes and plantation manors
are pretentious?"

"I never said they weren't, Drew," she answered. "But
the French don't need visual effects to prove how cultured
and mannered we are."

"And the Americans do?"

Marianne swept her hand before her, indicating the mansions. "Is it not obvious? They are naught but brawlers, fighting with sticks, clubs, and bottles. They would not think of dueling like civilized people."

Drew burst out laughing. "Yes. If one has to die, what better way to go than with a bullet between the eyes or the blade of a sword piercing the heart, the cultured, *civilized* way."

"You know what I mean, Drew," Marianne said, her luscious mouth curving into the hint of a smile.

"Yes, I do. Dueling is less messy than having one's brains clubbed out of one's head." Drew shook his head. "Tsk, tsk, not at all civilized."

Marianne laughed. "You're silly."

Drew wanted to keep talking, just to get his mind off the fine heart shape of her face, the inviting curve of her mouth. He just wanted to bring her someplace and make love to her until the barriers between them were torn down, until he discovered what her future was and why her marriage to Rafe didn't take place. But mostly until she accepted what he knew he must tell her about himself.

Until there were no secrets between them.

Sitting so close to her, her gown still teasing his leg, heat coursed through him. A fresh scent clung to her, surrounded them, shimmied through his veins. He moved restlessly, ever closer to her. Amazing eyes, slightly slanted, searched his face, touched his soul.

He felt a disturbance between his thighs. Blood engorged his manhood, and all he wanted to do was sink into her warmth. He wanted her desperately; he couldn't have her at all.

A delicate pink stained her face. Her small tongue wet her lips. Desire darkened her gaze. She had seen his arousal and wasn't embarrassed by it. Instead, her body responded in kind. Shame marring her features, she bowed her head.

"Marianne," he whispered, finally giving in and reaching for her.

"*Non,* monsieur," Marianne said softly, her voice thick. "We mustn't."

Of course they mustn't, he knew. Not now. Not here. Not ever.

Drew removed his arm from behind her. "You're right, of course," he said in agitation. "I've seen enough. Let's start out for Bienvenu." Bringing her hand to his lips, he kissed it, then slid to the other side of the seat. He put as much space between them as he could without sitting on the bench across from her, and refocused on his surroundings.

He noticed it wasn't as filthy here as it was in the *Vieux Carrè*, figuring it was probably due to the wide-open spaces that still existed in this section. Even so, every now and then a dead animal littered the ground.

"Drew?"

His name, spoken so softly, tightened his loins all over again. "Yes, Marianne?"

She hesitated briefly. "Luella prepared a picnic basket for us. Are you hungry?"

"Let's get out the city first, Mari," Drew responded gently. "I'm sure diseases and germs are airborne. Won't do to have them landing on the food."

A mass of tangled emotions, Marianne merely nodded. She'd hardly be able to endure Rafe's touch after the way Drew had made her feel. She knew what it took to become a man's woman, and she wanted Drew to show her the way. But if she allowed him to take her virginity, Rafe would spurn her and once again demand satisfaction from Drew. Perhaps he'd even insist on a duel and kill him.

There was something different about Drew. Something vulnerable and strange. He wasn't the least concerned about the mores of the day and was most concerned about her. He was attentive to her every thought, her every need. Her every desire.

Maybe that's what drew her to him so quickly. From the moment she'd seen him on the ground, he had a power over her she found impossible to resist.

It seemed as if from the moment she'd seen him, she'd fallen just a little bit in love with him. The very notion made her tremble. But no other man had ever made her private parts throb for attention as Drew had. Or caused her bloomers to become soaked with moisture as they now were.

The obvious press of his shaft against the buttons of his trousers hadn't embarrassed her as much as her own desire did. She probably knew more than she should have about the facts of life, but then, she had a thirst for knowledge that her father had never discouraged.

He'd hired the best tutors for both her and Genevieve, but her sister had shown no interest. He'd fed Marianne's thirst with weekly forays to bookshops, where she'd purchased whatever volumes caught her fancy. Worlds had opened up to her, and she'd craved more, wanting to experience life to the fullest, to have love inspired by Shakespeare's sonnets, passion ignited by Eros.

When she'd gone to Europe with her papa, she'd been awestruck. While Maman and Gen traversed the boutiques, couturiers, and milliners of Paris and London, managing to coax Marianne along sometimes, she lived to visit Westminster Abbey, ride through Hyde Park, share a discussion with a stranger at a café in Montmartre.

She liked London and Edinburgh and Florence, but Paris she absolutely adored. It was where they had stayed the longest and where she vowed to run away to escape her engagement to Rafe.

But the idea seemed a distant dream in comparison to her thoughts of Drew. He made her heart flutter maddeningly and tiny flames spiral through her entire being. The only reaction Rafe ever caused within her was abstract boredom. There was no pounding heart, no racing pulse, no flushed skin.

She would just have to focus on something other than Drew. He was dangerous to her objectives. For her, they couldn't reach Bienvenu quickly enough, although deep down she wished they'd never arrive.

At least Monsieur Pierre would welcome her at the plantation. And since Drew was a Montague, although Rafe would be angry, he would probably understand her wanting to introduce his father to the nephew he didn't know he had.

She focused on the state of Drew's body and the feeling of her own. They couldn't hide their attraction for each other, and it showed physically on both of them. She was flushed with agitation, and Drew was very much aroused.

She scooted to the corner, almost hugging it.

Dark blue eyes, shadowed with secrets, imprisoned her.

"Am I making you uncomfortable, Mari?" Drew asked in a husky voice.

Marianne forced a grin, refusing to acknowledge the well-defined planes of his face, refusing to remember the feel of his lips upon her own. "Not half as uncomfortable as I've probably made you."

Drew laughed at her candor. A large hand raked through his thick, golden hair, leaving pieces slightly askew, which she ached to smooth back into place.

"I must say you've been very observant of that particular part of my anatomy."

Her eyes strayed to *that* particular part of his anatomy, and she didn't even flinch. Or blush, for that matter. Yet discussing such subjects with a man was not permitted. It was considered offensive and objectionable. Certainly she wouldn't have dreamed of broaching such a subject with Rafe. Nor did she have the slightest desire to. She dreaded the time to come when she'd have to submit to him.

She raised her gaze to Drew's face, and her heart thumped even faster. He was so impossibly handsome, with a sculptured mouth that was an artist's dream and a square jaw that gave him a raw, masculine beauty.

She sucked in a calming breath. Changing the subject, she decided, would be a discretion well worth observing. And what better subject than their imminent visit to Bienvenu to bring sobriety to their moods?

"Tell me, Drew, what will you do if Monsieur Pierre cannot give you employment?"

His massive shoulders straightened for a moment, then he smiled slowly, his air of calmness suggesting he had every confidence that he'd win the master of Bienvenu over.

"A very good question, Mari," he answered. "I suppose I'll have to look elsewhere for employment if that happens."

Marianne lowered her eyelids. "You'll always have a place with me and my family, Andrew," she murmured softly.

"Thank you, Mari," he said, neither accepting nor refusing her offer. "You and your family have gone beyond the expectations of goodwill."

"It's the least we could do, monsieur." She smiled to lighten the mood. "Would you care to eat now?"

"Eat? Not at all, Marianne. I am totally void of an appetite at the moment. But, please, you go ahead."

"Non," Marianne responded. "My appetite has deserted me also."

Drew nodded and turned toward the window, but not before Marianne glimpsed the same naked need in his eyes that she felt, the need that had dogged them this entire journey.

Indeed, they *were* hungry. But unfortunately that hunger had nothing to do with food.

Chapter 11

AFTER TRAVELING MOST of the day over barely passable roads, all-but-deserted ferries, and near the outskirts of small towns, twilight found Marianne and Drew at last standing on the long porch at the double oak doors of Bienvenu.

He missed the faster interstates. St. Francisville was north of Baton Rouge, and on his Harley, at breakneck speed, he would have reached the town in two hours. In a car, going the legal limit, it usually took an additional half hour. If he'd intended to go there with Teal, he would've had to find a car. Whenever she was with him, he took taxicabs.

He wondered how his daughter was faring. Did she understand that though Daddy was gone, he loved her still and missed her terribly? No, of course she wouldn't—she was only two. But, he thought ruefully, in her young life she'd been through so much heartbreak already, with her mother having abandoned her.

His arms ached to hold her warm little body again as she drifted off to sleep the way she sometimes did when she refused to get in her own bed fully awake. His worry for Teal and his desire for Marianne, coupled with the suspense of what kind of reception he'd receive from Pierre Montague, had his gut twisting.

He'd sacrifice his life for Teal. Now it seemed he'd also have to sacrifice his feelings for Marianne, once he found a way to return. But how would he ever be able to leave her?

His question went unanswered as the door was finally swung open. He'd been so lost in his thoughts, he hadn't realized Marianne had banged the brass knocker until then.

"Mam'zelle!"

"Hello, Ralph," Marianne responded with a smile.

The old gentleman at the door had skin the color of burnished wood. Long white sideburns ran into his thick beard and matched his hair. The gray and white livery outfit brought to Drew's mind the uniforms that people wore at the Bienvenu of his own time. Though the styles were different, the colors were the same.

But the people who served at the big functions Nolan hosted were paid to do their jobs. The man standing before him wasn't as lucky. He was a slave.

Drew breathed in heavily. Marianne's family owned slaves as well—Tomas, Henry, Luella—and even more at their plantation upriver. Yet he couldn't sit in judgment of her. When before his eyes, the evidence of the people his ancestors owned still worked the fields.

"Come right on in, Mam'zelle." Ralph gazed at Drew and nodded deeply as they walked inside and Ralph closed the door behind them. "Hello there, suh. I can tell you's some weary trav'lers. Welcome to Bienvenu."

Suspense eating at him, Drew gave the man a half-smile. "Thank you, Ralph. You're quite right. We are both weary."

"Would you's please follow me. I'll—"

"No," Drew interrupted. "Would you mind if we waited here in the foyer? Rafe mightn't be that happy to see me." He might demand a duel right then and there, in fact. But there was no way Drew would allow Rafe to take up a sword or gun against him again. He'd just have to beat the shit out of the arrogant, self-absorbed bastard. Using nothing but his fists.

"Of course, suh. I'll be a moment. Mam'zelle, would you like to freshen up?"

"Uh, *non, merci beaucoup,* Ralph. I shall remain here with . . . Monsieur Andrew." When Ralph departed, Marianne turned to Drew, concern in her lovely eyes. "It's all right, Drew," she whispered. "It might be a while before Rafe or Monsieur Pierre is located. You should've allowed Ralph to situate us in the parlor."

He should have, but he was decidedly uncomfortable. He'd hated Bienvenu in his own time, and he detested it even more now. Always he'd felt out of place, even out of sorts there. It could be an agricultural nightmare in time of droughts or freezes. The work there might have stimulated the muscles, but for him it did nothing to stimulate the mind.

Now it would be even worse, because he couldn't imagine what place he had there—that's if he was accepted into the fold.

A caramel-complexioned young woman, dressed in a drab gray dress covered with a white pinafore, made her way toward them from down the hallway. When she reached them, her pretty face lit up as her lips split into a wide grin.

"Missus Mari," the girl said happily. "Master Rafe and Master Pierre didn't know you were comin'. They would have made us fix somethin' special for you."

"Which would have been unnecessary, Eve," Marianne responded pleasantly.

Considering the reception she was receiving, she was obviously a frequent guest here at Bienvenu, a thought that didn't sit well with Drew. Even slaves whom they'd passed along the long tree-lined driveway recognized her carriage and called out a greeting to her.

"Please inform Monsieur Pierre that I am here. We'll be in the parlor."

Eve curtsied. "Yes, missus."

"She's very pretty," Drew commented once the girl was out of sight.

Marianne raised her eyebrows in surprise, then laughed knowingly. *"Oui,"* she agreed, "but she's already spoken for. Come, the parlor is this way."

"Yes, dear," Drew said, chuckling. She'd misunderstood his remark, thinking his interest focused on Eve. It didn't. Only one woman had captured his fancy so quickly and so completely. Marianne. "Or is it *'Oui, cherie'?*"

Marianne started down the hallway, and he automatically followed. "Do you speak French?" she asked, tilting her face toward him.

He heard her, but it was his surroundings that captured his attention. He realized he was viewing everything almost at its inception. The mansion, only a few years old at this point, was magnificent. Everything gleamed with freshness, with newness.

Light-colored linen wallpaper lined walls crowned with cornices and elaborate dentils. High ceilings with ornate medallions and Baccarat crystal chandeliers and *faux-bois* interior doors decorated with hand-painted knobs were only a few things the manor possessed. Now, however, everything wasn't gilded by time. The furnishings were not antique, but the height of modern fashion. The rusty attic pipes that had cost Nolan thousands to replace hadn't yet been installed.

He felt an odd pulling, a sudden strange fascination as he reached the parlor and stopped in his tracks. The very secretaire that sat in his mother's bridge room stood near one of the windows. A red-and-white-striped settee and matching benches were situated over an Oriental carpet and surrounded by rosewood tables and elaborate oil lamps. It was the same furniture that had sailed through the decades, remaining at Bienvenu in excellent condition.

He knew it was known as the Red Parlor, so called because of the red satin wallpaper and matching decor that would be softened up quite a bit years from now.

"Well?"

Through his daze, he heard Marianne's soft voice. He gazed at her and swallowed visibly, his heart pounding. Slowly, with legs made of lead, he walked to where the secretaire sat and ran his fingers across the smooth, unmarred wood. "Well, what?"

"Do you speak French?"

Before he could answer, a tall, broad-shouldered, distinguished-looking man entered. Dressed in riding attire, his white hair windblown, he appeared as if he'd just returned from the fields. His face was clean-shaven and sharply defined. The friendly look in his eyes encouraged Drew to relax ever so slightly.

"Marianne, my dear!" the man greeted in a booming voice. Bowing low, he took her hand in his, placing a kiss on it. "You never cease to amaze me. Coming unannounced and traveling unchaperoned." His words held only a vague hint of disapproval, the smile removing any trace of censure. "None of that simpering, helpless-female nonsense."

"I do not wish to burden anyone with my female frailty," Marianne said with a smile.

"I wonder if that scoundrel son of mine knows what a lucky man he is. . . ." Pierre's voice trailed off as he glanced in Drew's direction for the first time. Disbelief clouding his features, he gasped. "Emory?" he whispered, his healthy complexion going pale, as if he was staring at a ghost.

"I beg your pardon?" Drew frowned at the unexpected reaction. "Emory?"

Marianne's smiled faltered only slightly as she took in her host's ashen features. "Monsieur Pierre, judging by your reaction to your nephew, you obviously see the family resemblance."

Pierre looked from Drew to Marianne and back again. His eyes watered. "My nephew? Emory's boy?" His voice cracked.

Emory? Way to go, Drew. He had always thought the name of Pierre's long-lost brother began with an N. Nonplussed over Pierre Montague's discomfiture, Drew stepped

forward, his hand outstretched. It was also a little disconcerting to discover that he bore the resemblance of a great-
great-great-uncle that the man's brother mistook him for.
Drew always thought his looks came from his mother's
side. "Yes, Uncle Pierre. I'm your brother's son, Andrew."

"I know that now," Pierre answered, some of his composure returning. He hastened to his liquor table and poured
a measure of gin into a glass and drank from it deeply. "I
thought I was seeing a ghost, boy. You are the image of
him when I last saw him thirty-three years ago."

Not knowing what to say, Drew merely nodded. He was
an intruder on the grief Pierre still carried, an imposter of
the worse sort. But unfortunately, he didn't have a choice.

"We got word that he'd been killed in a duel down in
New Orleans, but we could never really be sure, since no
one produced his body," Pierre continued, finishing off his
drink and heading for the settee.

In many ways, his mannerisms reminded Drew of his
own father. The hostility toward him was missing, however.
No flames of battle lay in Pierre's eyes in an effort to control Drew's life, no jockeying for Ursula's attention. There
was only expectation and gratitude there, which turned into
confusion at Drew's continued silence.

"Er, Papa died dueling in South Carolina, Uncle. Two
years after I was born," Drew lied. Except for the fact that
Pierre's brother had struck out on his own in 1820, leaving
Bienvenu behind forever, he had no other history about
him. So who would challenge Drew if he made up one for
the man?

"I'm sorry to hear that, son," Pierre said, chastened. He
cleared his throat and eyed the liquor table again, but didn't
move. "Did your maman come with you?"

"No, sir," Drew responded. "She died when I was born."
At both Pierre's and Marianne's questioning looks, he felt
compelled to continue. "I was raised by my mother's sister.
The only family I had. Until I decided to seek you out after
her passing. She always spoke highly of you," he added,
remembering Marianne's words about Pierre Montague.

"Oh, Andrew," Marianne said sympathetically, her delicate features filled with anguish for him. She looked as if she wanted to run to him and throw her arms around his neck. She remained where she was. "In spite of what you had to go through to get here, you are where you belong."

Pierre's bushy brows furrowed. "Go through? What do you mean, my dear?"

Marianne volunteered the information, explaining how she'd first found Drew, dazed and disoriented in front of the St. Louis Hotel, and how Rafe had tried to kill him in a duel after Drew sought her aid.

"That son of mine will never learn," Pierre said around a dry cough. "Did you make yourself known to him, Andrew?"

"I . . . er . . . never got the chance, sir," Drew replied quietly, his mind on Marianne. What had prompted her to divulge such information about Rafe to the man's own father? Undoubtedly Pierre already knew what a wallowing swine his son was, but Rafe wouldn't be pleased that his bride-to-be was spreading tales about him.

"So," Pierre said after an interminable silence, "why were you lying out of your head in front of the St. Louis Hotel?"

"I . . . er . . . I was attacked on the waterfront, Uncle Pierre." *God, forgive me.* "Some sailors tried to shanghai me, but I fought them off. When I came to my senses, however, I had no money and no identification on my person."

"Mon Dieu!" Marianne gasped, her hand flying to her breasts. "You never told me this, Andrew."

"I know, Marianne," Drew said with as much calm as possible, when her concern for him was so obvious. Concern that he knew was genuine and deep and intimate. His gaze captured hers. "I didn't want to further burden you with my problems."

"It's no burden, son," Pierre said kindly. "I'm glad Marianne had the good sense to bring you here, a place you can always call home."

"Like hell he can!" Rafe stormed, stalking into the parlor, as windswept as Pierre had appeared. Wild eyes focused on Drew. "This man is an opportunist, Father. And he will *not* stay in this house!"

"Rafe!" Marianne began in protest, rushing up to him and laying tentative fingers on his arm. "Andrew is your cousin. Your uncle's son. How could you in good conscience turn him out?"

A deceptively vapid look crossed Rafe's features as he studied Marianne. Drew wondered what Rafe saw when he looked at her. Was it the earnest intelligence in her slightly slanted, long-lashed, jade eyes? Or the high, delicate cheekbones that gave her an exotic look? The midnight silk that was her hair?

Drew doubted it. Rafe only saw Marianne as his prize, not his pride. He was sure she knew as much. Yet she was still going to marry him.

Suddenly Rafe jerked his arm away from her. "How can you and my father believe this . . . this person's story? And you, Marianne, had the audacity to bring him here. How dare you! Have you forgotten you're my betrothed? You've been travelling around unescorted with this man," he raged.

Marianne stepped away from him. Slippered feet splayed, she glared at him, hands on hips. "How could you, monsieur?" she snapped angrily. "You question my virtue with your unfounded accusation."

Drew fought to control his temper. He'd already decided he wouldn't allow Rafe to bully him, though it might mean risking another duel. But insulting Marianne was not to be tolerated. The man needed to be punched in the mouth.

"Why don't you think before you open your biased mouth?" Drew suggested in stinging tones, moving himself closer to Marianne and Rafe. "But judging from our first meeting, you seem lacking in such ability."

"I'll show you 'lacking,' monsieur," Rafe snarled, taking a step toward Drew, his hand going to the pistol at his hip.

"Goddammit, Rafe!" Pierre snapped, coming to his feet. "Restrain your foul temper, boy!"

"Father—"

"I've heard enough. Andrew is Emory's boy, and *I* am most happy to meet him. You don't have to accept him. I know kin when I see one, and this *is* my brother's son!"

Rafe sucked in an angry breath but remained where he was, his hand falling to his side. "Believe what you want, Father," he protested, "but Bienvenu is also my home, *my* inheritance, and I should have a say in who stays in this house."

"Yes, you should," Pierre agreed with fairness, "but I haven't died yet, and Andrew came seeking his family's help, son. Where do you suggest he live?"

Well, he was done for, Drew thought with a sigh. Rafe probably felt Drew's place was a graveyard.

Rafe glared at Drew, and Drew stiffened. They hated each other and didn't hesitate to show it.

"Not in this house, Father."

"Oh?" Pierre asked. "Do you suggest he live in one of the outbuildings surrounding the fields?"

"No, Father," Rafe answered with a feral grin. "Not out in the fields. The *garçonnière*. I'm sure 'Cousin' Andrew wants to avoid me as much as I him. It's unlikely that we will see each other with such an arrangement. As much time as I spend in the fields and surrounding buildings, that would just do."

Nodding thoughtfully, Pierre looked at Drew. "Andrew, you are more than welcome to share my house if you so desire."

Garçonnière? If he remembered correctly, that was the French name for bachelors' quarters. A place for young men of the family to reside once they reached a certain age. In other words, a motel for young guys graduating from puberty. Drew chuckled to himself. How appropriate.

"I'll take the *garçonnière,* Uncle Pierre," he said. He bared his teeth to Rafe in a semblance of a smile. "Thank you, Cousin Rafe, you're more generous than you pretend to be."

"Stay out of my way," Rafe warned in lethal tones. He

held out his hand to Marianne. "Come, we must talk."

Folding her arms, Marianne raised her chin, refusing to budge. Drew silently applauded her grit, while Pierre chuckled with approval.

Rafe flushed, sweeping an unreadable gaze over her, a hint of a smile on his lips. "I'm sorry, *cherie*," he gritted. "It was anger speaking earlier. Please? Accompany me to the study."

Marianne stiffened her shoulders but nodded. "Certainly," she said coolly, taking his hand.

Drew watched them depart, jealousy overtaking him. He hated that Marianne would probably allow the rat to kiss her as *they* had kissed. But she was a passionate woman, and Rafe was her betrothed.

Living at Bienvenu, he feared, was going to be worse than living on Rue Dumaine beneath the same roof with Marianne. At least there, no matter how many times Rafe visited, Drew wouldn't have seen the man go off alone with Marianne.

He could barely accept what had just happened and knew he'd taken on an unsolvable problem that had nothing to do with him and everything to do with her. Under the circumstances, he cared about her much more than he should have.

She was betrothed.

Chapter 12

MARIANNE STOOD IN the open doorway of the parlor in her family's house on Rue Dumaine, looking out over the balcony to the street below. At mid-morning, the Vieux Carrè was overcast and damp. It was almost as if the clouds that hung over her were affecting the entire city.

Rafe's words from the night before, after he'd demanded her company alone, kept echoing in her brain.

"I must tolerate this so-called cousin of mine because of my father's misguided sense of family. But the scoundrel has been reckless and inconsiderate of your reputation. Therefore, I forbid you his company."

With that declaration, he'd informed her that he was leaving for New Orleans immediately, in anticipation of a business appointment in the morning.

"Even with Andrew over five hundred feet away from the main house, his proximity to you is still too close. Therefore, *cherie,* I insist you make the trip back to New Orleans with me. I'll deposit you at the cottage and be on my way."

But Marianne had refused. She didn't want to leave Drew yet. She'd expected to have at least one day with him before she and Tomas started the long journey home. Besides, she and Rafe would be traveling half the night on dark, dangerous stretches of land inhabited by criminals, runaway slaves, and wild animals.

She'd dug her heels in and shook her head. "*Non,* monsieur. I cannot possibly leave with you tonight."

Rafe's brow arched. "And why is that, Marianne? You show no signs of fatigue. As a matter of note, you seemed as sharp as ever when you stood up to me in Andrew's favor. Dare I surmise that perhaps I was right, that maybe your virtue should be questioned?" He'd studied his fingertips casually, as if his vicious words were a mere discussion of an afternoon shower. His cold gaze had fastened onto hers. "Maybe I should even forget about our marriage, *oui*?"

"Of course not, Monsieur Rafe," Marianne had whispered, deflated. "I—I will just go and tell them good-bye."

"You will do nothing of the kind. They will simply be apprised of your departure when they discover us gone."

And so she'd left with him, having absolutely no choice, unable to see Drew a final time. If she'd insisted on remaining, he would've called off their unannounced engagement, throwing her family into financial peril.

Thankfully she'd seen Tomas on her way to the stables with Rafe, and told him that she was going back to New Orleans; she hadn't wanted Drew to worry unnecessarily. But it had taken half the night to reach home again, and when she did she was exhausted and stiff from bouncing about on the back of that demon horse with his wild master.

Not asking any questions, Luella prepared a hot bath for Marianne and brought her some leftover beef and hard bread. But once she'd completed her bath, she hadn't been able to sleep, so she'd come to the parlor hours ago, only to discover that her mother and sister weren't even in residence.

Maman and Gen had left for Baywood yesterday afternoon. Knowing she'd accompanied Drew to Bienvenu, they'd expected her to remain a guest there for the week that they would be at the family plantation. Everyone knew of the old man's fondness for her.

In the family's absence, the servants had stayed behind to thoroughly clean and polish, which was a considerable relief to Marianne. She would not be alone in the house.

She wasn't sure how long she'd been gazing outside, not focusing on anything in particular, a light shawl wrapped around her shoulders, when a knock sounded on the door. Knowing it was one of the servants, she didn't bother to respond. Whoever it was was only alerting her to the fact that someone was coming in, not asking permission to do so. After a moment the door quietly opened, and Luella stepped into the room.

"Mademoiselle?"

Marianne smiled at her, glad for the company. "*Oui,* Luella?"

"Is there something I can do for you, mademoiselle?"

"*Non.* I'll be fine." There wasn't anything anyone could do for her. Not even Drew. He'd valiantly stood up for her, and had it not been for Monsieur Pierre, Rafe would have shot him down. She shivered just to think about it.

"You wasn't expected back here, Miss Mari," Luella said, reminding Marianne of her whereabouts: home, a place she didn't really want to be just now, because Drew wasn't here.

"I know, Luella. But . . . I . . ." She paused, cursing Rafe. "I came back. I'll try and stay out of your way."

"I didn't mean that, Miss Mari. I was jus' wonderin' if somethin' was wrong, is all. There is a different kind of sadness, one that has nothin' to do with you missin' your papa."

"*Merci,* Luella, for your kind concern. But I am truly all right. Drew is settled in at Bienvenu. That was my purpose for going, to make the introductions to Monsieur Pierre easier."

"Monsieur mus' have been happy to meet his nephew, mademoiselle," Luella speculated.

"Very happy," Marianne said, recalling just how happy

the man actually was and bringing to mind Rafe's wrath once again.

Marianne didn't believe Drew was safe being so close to Rafe. He was hell-bent on hating Drew, and nothing, not even Drew's inherent charm, would break through Rafe's wall of revenge.

"If you need me for anything, mademoiselle, I'll be cleaning your bedchamber," Luella said into the stretch of silence.

"Merci," Marianne responded. Watching as the house-maid departed, she went and sat on the settee, then picked up the piece of needlework she and her maman and sister all worked on at one time or another.

She found it all but impossible to concentrate on her stitching. It was during times like this that she missed her father dreadfully. When he was alive, she'd rarely become melancholy, instead enjoying her responsibilities, the social season, their discussions.

One of their discussions had even been about Rafe, four years ago, after her debut into society. He'd been enthralled by her beauty, amazed at her quick wit. Clarisse had pressed for an immediate engagement, but Jean-Louis had listened to Marianne express her hesitation and conceded to her wishes. She'd had many suitors since her spectacular introduction, but none had come close to being the type of dashing man she wanted to wed. None except Rafe.

That's why it had been so easy to reacquaint herself with him last year. That's why she'd hesitated only slightly when Clarisse devised her plan, which consisted of Marianne and Rafe's marrying if Rafe would be kind enough to rescue them financially.

But the scene from last night was casting serious doubts upon her judgment. She could hardly fathom Rafe's intense dislike for Drew, a man he'd never met until a few days ago. Why wouldn't he welcome his own kin into his family?

Rafe's behavior gave her pause. She had never been one to take orders well, and to think he'd ordered her back home was incredibly upsetting. Like an obedient child, she allowed him to bring her back to New Orleans. Like an obedient, *frightened* child, his threats all too clear.

What had happened to him? He had always been kind to her, and at the beginning of their relationship had been positively charming. Yet, since Drew's arrival, all that had changed. It seemed he'd gone mad.

She wrinkled her nose as the thought crossed her mind. Had he changed toward her? Or had she changed toward him?

He was a very discerning man. He might have noticed her attraction for Drew. Yet how could that be? Other than last night, Rafe had only seen them together briefly at the St. Louis Hotel. He didn't know to what extent she and Drew knew each other. And he certainly didn't know Drew had been a guest in her house for nearly two weeks.

Her guilty feelings for Drew made her paranoid. She knew Rafe was only being protective of her, but she didn't want that kind of protection. Especially not from what he perceived Drew to be. Drew was an honorable man, a fact which Rafe didn't care about one way or the other. He only wanted Drew out of her life.

Well, C. Andrew Montague III would become part of her family when she and Rafe married, and she would *not* ignore his presence. She only hoped she could gentle Rafe into accepting his newfound cousin.

"Miz Mari?" Tomas called from the open doorway.

Thinking she was alone, Marianne turned with a jolt. "T-Tomas," she got out.

"Yes, ma'am," Tomas replied. "I didn't mean to cause you a start."

Marianne smiled. "No harm done, Tomas. That was rather silly of me." She looked at the wiry little man with surprise. "I thought you were still in St. Francisville with Drew."

"Well, Miz Mari—," Tomas began before a familiar voice halted his words.

"I'm afraid I'm guilty of 'directional influence,' Miz

Mari," Drew said with a chuckle. "I must look that up. Directional Influence. I wonder if that could be used as a legal term one day."

Marianne gasped and got up from her seat. She'd never been so glad to see someone in her life. "*Mon Dieu!* Andrew! What are you doing here?" Her heart beat a rapid tattoo, and her pulse pounded frantically as Drew advanced toward her.

Chapter 13

"DON'T BE ALARMED at my presence, Marianne," he said, his voice sending waves of heat washing over her. "I know my cousin is conducting business at this time."

She faltered, wanting nothing more than to rush into his arms, knowing she couldn't. "*Oui,* but—"

Tumultuous, dark blue eyes gazed into her own. "I must speak to you alone, Mari."

Her skin tingling, Marianne contemplated that statement a moment. Drew wanted to be alone with her, and she almost said yes. She almost did exactly what she ached to do since he'd first walked into the room—run straight into his arms. But an image of her mother and sister rose up in her mind's eye. They expected her to keep Baywood in the family. Going to Drew might destroy everything.

Unfortunately Rafe might have been right. Perhaps she should have been indignant, at the least, over such a blatant intrusion. Drew took her for granted by taking so many liberties. A gentleman would never interrupt a lady's life as he was doing.

Neither would he make her feel such hot desire.

She'd done her duty toward Drew. She owed him nothing more. The man was a virtual stranger, and she would not, *could* not, allow him to jeopardize her planned marriage to Rafe. After she married Rafe, Drew would become kin, and she wouldn't ignore him then; it might cause a scandal. Rumors would undoubtedly circulate about why Marianne was ignoring Rafe's handsome newfound cousin, especially since Pierre so readily accepted him. The ensuing speculation might do more harm than good. But if she wanted to be a Montague, Madame *Rafe* Montague, it was imperative that she ignore him now. Which meant she'd just have to ask him to leave.

Suddenly Paris was becoming more and more appealing. By running away, she wouldn't have to face her muddled thoughts. She wouldn't have to sacrifice her life for the sake of her family's comfort. She could book passage tomorrow and never let any of them hear from her again.

"It's very important, Marianne," Drew said in a hoarse whisper.

He was suddenly standing in front of her, filling the space with his broad shoulders and long, lean body. He slid the back of his hand across her cheeks ever so slightly. At the brief contact, fire tightened the pit of her belly, flames fanning out into her nether regions.

"T-Tomas, I'll call you. Please close the door behind you," she instructed the quiet servant, who looked straight ahead, as if he had no awareness of her and Drew's display.

"Yes, Miz Mari."

After Tomas departed, an uncomfortable silence descended on her and Drew, one that they'd never experienced in their brief acquaintance. But last night they'd reached a turning point. He'd been accepted into his long-lost family, the very family that Marianne would soon marry into. Her position should have been made quite clear when she'd given in to Rafe's demands and departed with him.

She'd hear what was so urgent that he'd left Bienvenu to seek her out again, and then she'd ask him to leave. It was as simple as that. She couldn't ask him to leave any sooner, not when she'd heard the distress in his voice.

Resentment toward Drew pricked her, toward his beautiful face and perfect body. If she hadn't been staring into his very blue eyes, she would've been listening to her own advice and insisting he leave.

Even being alone with him for a brief time was dangerous. He might have come to seduce her, to put his own claim upon her. She hadn't missed his angry flush last night as she'd left the drawing room with Rafe, and could only imagine what he thought of her departing with Rafe without even a by-your-leave.

Drawing in a calming breath, she reseated herself. "Please, do sit down, Drew." Applauding herself for her serene tone, she indicated the wing chair facing her.

With a slight dip of his head, Drew sat. He studied her lovely features. She seemed withdrawn, even somewhat hostile. For an instant, when he'd first walked in, he'd seen her undisguised joy. But it had only been a brief flicker in her jade eyes, a tiny spark of happiness on her features. Then the look had disappeared from her face. She'd grown silent, her stance rigid.

He'd realized then why he'd really taken such a chance to come and see her again. He'd feared Rafe would turn her against him. Besides, she'd seemed so reluctant to leave the room with the stupid jerk, Drew had worried for her. So he'd asked Tomas to take him back to New Orleans to assure himself of her well-being and to discover if she was even still willing to see him.

At first Tomas had steadfastly refused, being unwilling to anger Rafe Montague and firmly believing he'd be severely punished if he brought Drew back to New Orleans to see Marianne. But Drew promised he wouldn't let any harm come to Tomas at Rafe's hand. After three hours, Tomas finally agreed to return to the house on Rue Dumaine.

Now Drew wondered at the wisdom of his impulse. Not because of Tomas: Drew had meant what he said, and wouldn't allow any harm to befall the man. Upon discovering she'd left with Rafe, he'd decided to tell Marianne how he'd come to find himself in the year 1853. Yet glimpsing her as he'd walked in, he knew that that hadn't been his true purpose for coming, that *she* was the sole reason.

The jealousy he'd felt when she'd left with Rafe still gnawed at him. Wild images had plagued Drew the entire ride back to New Orleans. Once she was out of his sight, he'd reasoned, her pique toward Rafe couldn't have lasted too long, since she'd consented to journey back with him. Though Drew had worried about her, he had to admit to himself that she and Rafe might very well have ended up in bed together.

The thought sickened Drew, but he knew it really wasn't his concern what they did. Her fate had been determined long before he'd dropped into this place—a fate that hadn't included marrying Rafe Montague, despite her present engagement to him.

He'd tell her about himself and ask for her help. That's all! If she refused, he'd leave and never bother her again.

Not knowing where to begin, he cleared his throat. Since meeting Marianne he did that a lot. She seemed as uncomfortable as he felt at the moment. Clearing his throat let her know that he was about to speak—and made her that much more uneasy about what he had to say.

"Er, Marianne, there's something I must tell you about myself." If only he weren't so concerned with telling her the truth. She might be his only chance to return to his own time, however, and the lie he'd told last night to explain his origins didn't sit well with him. The only person he ever dissembled to was his father. She was looking at him expectantly, waiting for him to continue. Doubt and reservations tore at him. "First, I owe you an apology for barging in on you like this. If my unexpected visit has caused you any anxiety, I'll be happy to do this some other time." He hoped she'd allow him to stay, because he needed to know if she'd agree to help him. But once he broached the subject, would she think him a ghost?

"Andrew," Marianne said, sounding impatient with his

long pauses, "I am not offended by your visit, just surprised to see you so soon. Please go on with what you must tell me."

Her voice was restrained, without any evidence of the warmth he was used to. "Yes, of course," he said. Agitated, he stood and walked to the open French doors.

Deciding how to begin his incredible story weighed him down. To come here had been an unwise decision, brought on by sheer, helpless jealousy. He would tell her some lame story and be on his way. She had problems of her own. She didn't need his as well.

"Is it so bad, monsieur?"

The words floated to him, laced with sympathy. For the first time since his arrival here today, he heard something other than distant cordiality. While he would've preferred it not be sympathy, it seemed as if he was breaking through the barriers she'd erected around herself. She probably thought he was in some kind of trouble. Well, damn if he wasn't! Her assumption would be right on the money. He was in *big* trouble!

Drew turned and faced her, his decision made. "Yes, Marianne. It's very bad. Something beyond your wildest imagination. Something only you can help me with. Will you?"

Her hand flew to her breast. "*Mon Dieu!* I do not know what trouble you're in, but if it's within my power, I vow I will help you." There was no hesitation, just staunch determination.

Encouraged, Drew rushed to her side on the settee and took her soft, delicate hands into his own. "Mari," he said, caressing her smooth skin. "I-I have a little girl—"

Teal would be the perfect place to begin, since he was so incredibly worried about her.

Marianne's brows shot up in surprise, her eyes widening at the news. "*Mais non,*" she whispered. "You are married."

"I . . . No, not anymore. But I was once," he answered, deciding not to complicate matters and mention the divorce he was getting—the divorce that should be final by now.

He felt the pull on his hands as she tried to reclaim her own. Desperation consuming him, he held on to them. Whether it was real or imagined, he felt she was his lifeline to the future, and he wouldn't allow her to pull away from him. "Please," he implored, "hear me out."

Marianne searched his face, his eyes, her gaze inscrutable. He waited with bated breath for her answer, knowing that at any time she could decide she wanted nothing more to do with him.

Apparently satisfied with what she saw in his features, she moved her small hands farther into his. "Where is your little girl, Andrew?"

Images of a frightened Teal being handed back to a mother who didn't really want her flashed before him. Knowing of his father's dislike for her, Teresa would take the child out of spite. He wasn't sure what would be worse—living with a grandfather who'd refused to know her or with a mother who'd spurned her. "She's in New Orleans," he replied, tormented.

"Oh, how wonderful!" Marianne responded, her face lighting up. "Why isn't she here with you? I want to meet her. How old is she?"

Still holding her now-relaxed hands in his, Drew chuckled at Marianne's enthusiasm. "To answer your last question first, Teal is two years old."

"Teal?"

"Yes. Her mother named her. I'm not sure what it means."

"It's a lovely name," Marianne reassured him. "Does she live with her mother?"

"No, Mari. At least, I hope not. I'm her legal guardian and I'm terribly worried about her. I want to be with her." *But I also want to be with you.* He was unable to speak the words aloud.

"I don't understand, Drew," Marianne said in confusion. "Why don't you just go and get her? We're right here in New Orleans."

Finally releasing her hand in order for her to be able to accept or reject what he had to say without coercion, Drew stood in agitation. "It isn't that simple," he began, pacing like a caged lion. "What I have to say will be hard to understand, Marianne. I only ask that you listen with an open mind before you comment. Fair enough?"

She gave the barest of nods, her hesitation and worry obvious. "Fair enough."

"The night I met you, I told you I was from out of town. Well, that wasn't entirely true."

Her body was tense, her breath coming in short bursts that underscored her growing agitation. "What are you saying? Where exactly are you from?"

"New Orleans," Drew replied, pausing in front of her. He swallowed hard, then added, "In the twenty-first century."

Shock, disbelief, anguish, and outrage all crossed her features in a matter of moments. Her emotions collided, draining the color from her face and leaving her visibly shaken.

Although the silence lasted for only a few moments as Marianne digested the news, it seemed to stretch into forever.

"Mari—"

"*Non!* This cannot be so!" She bolted from her seat and hurried to the open doors of the balcony.

Catching her arm, Drew prevented her from rushing outside. "Mari, please!"

"*Non!* It is as Rafe said. You are riffraff. And you are a madman! Release me this instant!" Tears of anger, of anguish, burned the back of her eyes.

She attempted to loosen his hold, but his hand tightened ever so slightly upon her arm. "Marianne, please! I swear I won't hurt you. I need you. Without your help, I'll never see my little girl again. Please help me!" Mist gathered in his eyes at the thought of not seeing Teal again and being unable to watch her grow from a precocious toddler to an accomplished woman. He blinked to clear the blur.

Suddenly a smooth hand was caressing his stubbled

cheek. "Tell me about it, Andrew," she softly coaxed, done in by his passionate plea.

"Thank you," Drew murmured, his relief knowing no bounds. She would listen. She would help him. "Tell me truthfully, Marianne. Are you frightened of me? Is that why—"

"Should I be?" she interrupted.

"No, not at all."

"Then I'm not. Not anymore. You will tell me all about it, and about your little girl," Marianne said, giving him a reassuring smile. "But first things first. You must be hungry. I'll have Luella fix something and serve us in the dining room. We shouldn't face whatever awaits us on an empty stomach."

Drew nodded in agreement, his mood considerably lightened now that he'd shared his terrible secret with Marianne. "You're right. Let's eat, and then we'll talk."

Chapter 14

"IT'S EARLY, DREW ," Marianne said as they made their way past deserted Congo Square an hour later. Sycamores lined a large green grassland, which was enclosed by a picket fence with four iron gates. They were heading toward Grand Route St. John and the cabin of the old voodoo enchantress Laurinda Toussaint. "And a weekday. The servants usually meet at Congo Square on Sunday afternoons after church service—"

"I know. Where I came from, all this is already history to me. Remember?"

"*Oui*. So you've said. It is something so hard to believe. Yet I do."

"I'm glad."

Marianne's heart was still pounding in response to Drew's incredible story, but she pretended to have regained control for his sake. His impassioned plea that she listen to him touched the core of her. Although she could hardly credit what he'd told her, she couldn't readily deny it either. His sudden appearance that night. His strange attire and attitude. He seemed a man lost and out of his realm. But how could such a thing be true? *Time travel?*

She knew she should have been afraid of him and his

incredible story. At first, when Drew revealed his origins,
apprehension had almost caused her to quake out of her
skin. As she listened further, however, the prospect of helping him—in secret, of course—began to excite her.

The very first person they needed to see, the one person
who could confirm or reject his story, was the voodoo enchantress Laurinda Toussaint. Some said she was well past
her one hundredth birthday. Others claimed she was actually a granddaughter of the original Laurinda. Whatever the
case might be, Marianne hoped Laurinda could help Drew.

If his story proved true, then in all likelihood he'd return
to his own time, and she'd never see him again. The
thought disturbed her. She didn't like to think of the day
Drew would leave her life, which was the reason she so
readily agreed to help him, even at the cost of her reputation.

They were completely alone, without even the presence
of Tomas, their carriage driver. These circumstances were
more of a necessity than a choice. Most of the slaves were
afraid of Laurinda. Even if she'd gotten down on her knees
and begged Tomas, he would have refused to bring her to
the woman. So she'd saved her breath and taken the carriage herself, briefly explaining to Luella that she and Drew
had an urgent matter to attend to.

But as the cobblestoned streets and paved sidewalks gave
way to dirt roads and thick stands of trees, she wondered
at the soundness of her plan. She was away from everything
she held dear and familiar, away from civilization, with a
man who claimed to be from the future. The fact that it
was the same man who'd held her in his arms with such
tender regard eased her nerves slightly, even as she realized
that it would never be the same between them again. He
had to return to his daughter, just as she had to marry Rafe.

Colorful wildflowers and perfumed air filled with the
sounds of a dense wilderness: the song of an unseen bird;
the flapping of wings, just beyond the blanket of foliage;
the rustling of grass as an animal moved on the forest floor.
For the next half hour, Marianne maneuvered the horse

and buggy along the winding road of the Grand Route, until
they came to a hut at the edge of Bayou St. John. White-
wash saved the tiny structure from being completely prim-
itive. She pulled the gelding to a stop and looked
expectantly at Drew.

He smiled at her. "Are we here?"

"*Oui,*" she answered. When she saw the hope kindling
in his eyes, she wondered how she could ever doubt him.
"All will be well."

Without responding, he got off the buggy, then helped
her down. Together they went to the open door and peeked
in.

A woman sat at a small table with her eyes closed, making a strange chanting noise. Her leathery skin was the
color of rich coffee, and her long, straight hair was as black
as a raven's wing.

Oil lamps, their wicks turned high, brightened the room
with a smoky light. Glass jars filled with herbs and liquids
lined the back wall, which was covered with alligator hides.
A table laden with religious artifacts, an open Bible with a
pair of rosary beads flung across the pages, a scented candle, and a crucifix lay near the chanting woman.

Marianne shivered as Drew placed his hands on her
shoulders and caressed them lightly.

As Laurinda Toussaint's body shook, she raised her spidery hand high above her head and made the sign of the
cross. "Who comes to Laurinda?" she asked in a whispery,
gravelly voice. Lowering her hand, she opened her eyes . . .
and blinked. "Oh, it's you, Mam'zelle Mari."

She stood with the gracefulness of a woman less than
half her age and fixed her piercing, gray regard on Drew.
She seemed to be looking right through him, to the depths
of his heart and the essence of his soul.

Grabbing a staff topped with the head of a cobra, its open
mouth underscoring the lethal fangs, she staggered back,
her breath coming in rapid bursts. "Lawdy! Somethin' ain't
right 'bout this boy, Mam'zelle Mari. Why you brought him
here?"

Stepping away from Drew's caresses, Marianne stole a glance at him, wondering what Laurinda had seen that made her know something wasn't right about him. Marianne gaped in surprise. Indeed, something wasn't right. His chalky complexion and rapid breathing told her that immediately. His gaze was wide, and his lips were parted in surprise.

"Drew!"

"Mam'zelle!" Laurinda snapped at the same time, rapping her staff against the floor. "Who this be?"

Forcing her thoughts back to Laurinda, Marianne swallowed hard. "This is C. Andrew Montague III. Drew is my friend, and he needs your help."

Laurinda quickly lit two candles on the table in front of her. "Close the door," she ordered, then indicated the two empty chairs near her. "Sit."

Like obedient children, Marianne and Drew did as they were told. He sat as still as stone, staring at Laurinda with fear and awe.

"There's something I must tell you about Drew, Laurinda," she began urgently. Leaning forward and resting her elbows on the creaky table, she met the enchantress's depthless gaze, trying not to be intimidated by it. "Something that might frighten you."

Those penetrating eyes narrowed, and her hand tightened on the cobra's head. "Nuthin' frightens Laurinda!" the old woman scolded. She jabbed a long-nailed, bony finger in his direction. "Laurinda saw this boy in a vision that flashed like a lightning bolt before my eyes. It jus' took the strength from my mortal bones."

Drew moved his body ever so slightly, then cleared his throat. "What did you see?" A mixture of perplexity, exhilaration, and curiosity resounded in his voice.

Leaning on her staff, she walked to her chair and reseated herself. "I saw you flying through space, boy."

"His name is Andrew," Marianne reminded her, not wanting Drew to take offense.

Laurinda drew her staff closer and raised her chin. "You

done already tol' me his name, Mam'zelle Mari."

Drew squeezed Marianne's hand in an effort to assure her it was all right. He didn't mind the label, especially if the frightful old hag would help him travel back to his own time.

If Marianne had warned him where they were going, he might have been prepared to meet Laurinda Toussaint, Alaina's great-great-grandmother. Instead it shocked him to see her. More and more, it seemed that his being brought here hadn't been a mere twist of fate, but rather a design of destiny.

"Now, boy," Laurinda went on, "tell me what happened to you. I done got strong feelin's you ain't from 'round here, that you from some far, distant place."

"Well . . . er . . . Laur—" Drew stopped in mid-sentence. He suddenly realized it would be a wise move to give this lady all due respect. Not because she was probably older than dirt and deserved it, but because she looked as though she had the power to turn him into a mudbug if she so desired. "I-I mean, *Miss* Laurinda, ma'am. You're right. I'm not from here. At least not of this era."

Her gaze fastened to his, holding him captive. "Tell me where you's from, boy." That whispery, gravelly voice mesmerized, encouraging him to comply. The spidery hand lifted again, and the smoke in the room thickened, turning it into a foggy dreamworld. "And how you came to be here."

His voice sounding far away, his body almost weightless, Drew told her about the watch, and the chant, and how right after reciting it he woke up at the St. Louis Hotel in this time period.

"Give me your hand." Laurinda reached across the table. "Yours too, Mam'zelle Mari. Seems this boy had a purpose in coming here."

Holding one of their hands in each of her own, Laurinda closed her eyes and began the watch chant. Three times she recited the poem, her voice growing with intensity each time. Afterward, the chant gave way to humming, loud and eerie and echoing around them.

A bony hand tightened around Drew's stronger one. Trembles racked his body, pulsated through his veins and along his nerve endings. Sweat beaded Laurinda's face, wet his brow, flushed Marianne's cheeks. But he saw Marianne's fear and the vibrating movements of her body.

Heat overwhelmed the tiny room as the three of them began to shake violently, Laurinda's humming deepening, rising, cresting.

Then silence. Just when he'd thought something drastic would occur, everything stilled abruptly. Eyes closed, Laurinda sat as if she'd been fashioned from granite, holding on to their hands. The hairs on his nape stood on end, shivers crawling along his spine.

For an eternity they remained still, the silence unsettling. Finally she released them and stared at Drew. "You must fin' the very same watch that done brought you here," she said, her demeanor changing from fearless to concerned.

The change didn't sit well with Drew. Perhaps she'd realized how impossible a task finding that watch would be.

"And then what?" Marianne asked.

"And then Monsieur Montague must go to the hitchin' post no later than summer's end, Mam'zelle Mari, and recite the chant. It will bring him back home. If he can't find it in time, he stuck back here forever."

The words struck Drew like the bolt of lightning Laurinda had spoken of earlier. "Stuck back here forever," without ever again seeing his daughter or knowing of her fate. Without ever being able to reassure his mother that he was well or making peace with his father.

Impossible, simply impossible. Finding that watch would be as impossible as figuring out the mystery that had brought him here.

Bitter defeat threatened to consume him, but he knew better than to give in to the feeling. It would only interfere with the search that he needed to initiate, immediately.

Regaining his composure somewhat, he asked, "Why did that watch pull me back to this era?"

A mysterious smile wreathed the wise old features. "You'll find out in time, boy."

Having heard enough, Drew stood and pushed his chair under the table. He inclined his head. "Thank you, Miss Laurinda."

"*Oui, merci,*" Marianne said, standing also. She glanced at Drew, worry knitting her brow, then smiled at him with encouragement.

"You shouldn't have left Bienvenu, boy. Monsieur Pierre be mighty concerned about your whereabouts."

"God! I didn't think of that." He'd only thought to get to Marianne. Chiding himself for his foolish jealousy, he turned to her. "I need a lift back to St. Francisville, and I'd better get there, pronto."

"Of course, monsieur," Marianne said with a laugh. "I'll have Tomas bring you there when we return to the city." She reached inside her reticule and took out some coins, which she handed to Laurinda.

"You have many weeks to go 'fore summer's end," the enchantress said quietly, standing in her doorway after Drew and Marianne stepped outside. Her palm rested on her snake's-head staff. She wasn't a tall woman, but she had a commanding presence that made it hard for anyone to ignore her.

Marianne nodded. "*Oui.* Time enough to find Drew's watch."

"Maybe a slave found it," Drew speculated, realizing at the same moment that he'd taken a liking to Laurinda. "Perhaps we can let it be known we'll offer a reward for its return."

"It mus' be somethin' of value in return, boy," Laurinda cautioned, "for seldom does my people have anythin' worthwhile. They won't easily give up the watch you describe."

"I understand," Drew said, knowing well what she meant. "They'll get whatever they consider fair."

Approval straightened Laurinda's shoulders. "Good. Then I'll get the word out myself. *Bonjour,* boy, Mam'zelle Mari."

"*Bonjour,* Laurinda. *Merci* again."

"G'bye, ma'am," Drew said. "Take care."

"No, boy. It is *you* who must beware."

Drew arched his brows in surprise. "Me?"

"Yes. I see a shadow, an evil omen, standing between you and your bid to escape this era."

"*Mon Dieu!*" Marianne blurted, her hand flying to her chest.

Laurinda walked closer to Drew and rubbed her bony fingers across his cheek. Hands that had been warm during her chanting session were now ice cold. Timeless gray eyes searched his face. Only sheer willpower prevented him from stepping away from her.

"Remain alert at all times, boy. Your life is in grave peril."

Before Drew could respond, she ambled inside her hut and closed the door, leaving him to stare after her.

Chapter 15

SITTING WITH RIGID control on the blue silk recamier in the receiving room at Baywood, the Beaufort plantation, Rafe wondered where Marianne could be. When
he'd demanded she return to New Orleans with him, he'd
had no idea that her mother and sister had left the city.

Clarisse usually went a week or two to her plantation to
oversee the servants as they spruced it up before the family's summer move to escape the humors of the city. It was
because of this cursed plantation that Marianne had decided
to accept his proposal, he knew. He might have been many
things, but a fool he was not.

Years ago, when she'd made her debut, he'd pursued her,
but she refused him. Now, as then, she was the loveliest
creature he'd ever seen. Yet she was unconventional and
headstrong. She didn't mind sharing her opinions with others. She had a passion for art and travel, and *compassion*
for everyone she met.

It was what drew Rafe to her, and what turned him away
from her as well. While he could never quite understand
his driving need for control or his hair-trigger temper,
which could quickly turn dislike into bloodthirsty hate,
she'd reached out to him. Still, he knew she always held a
tiny part of herself back from him.

He hadn't known quite what that part was until he saw her with Drew. Sparks of eroticism entered her gaze every time she looked at the man. Rafe was beyond incensed. He was maddened with rage, itching to slit Drew from neck to navel.

He had Marianne right where he wanted her, however. She had no choice but to wed him if she wanted to keep the family's beloved Baywood in their possession. And she had no choice but to come to his bed pure if she wanted to keep Drew alive.

Pulling his mouth into a tight line, Rafe barely noticed a slave setting the silver tea service on the table. Had Marianne been aware of her family's plans to come to Baywood? If so, why hadn't she told him? Suddenly she'd become the obedient betrothed and with a minimum of protest allowed him to escort her to the cottage on Rue Dumaine and see her to her door.

Had she planned a rendezvous with his despicable newfound cousin?

Immediately Rafe rejected that idea. She might be headstrong and willful, but she was a lady first. She was smart enough to know the consequences of sullying her reputation with such riffraff. He snorted. Having the Montague name didn't change Drew. He was still riffraff.

Just to be sure, however, Rafe would query Marianne about her reasons for not coming to Baywood with her mother and sister. They were her family, and she should have remained with them. Instead she'd traveled the long distance with Drew to St. Francisville, when Tomas could have easily deposited the man at Bienvenu. If Rafe hadn't decided to come to oversee matters today, he never would have known she was apparently still alone in New Orleans.

Clarisse's black skirts fluttered about her as she stood and poured coffee into a cup. Smiling sweetly, she handed it to him. "Your concern about Baywood is most charitable, monsieur."

Rafe tasted the piping-hot coffee and chicory, thick and black, the way he liked it. He smiled politely. "My concern, madam, has nothing to do with charity," he retorted. "I merely wish to keep an eye on my investment."

"As it should be," the lady replied, her body stiffening at his reply. "Because of you, Baywood is free of debt, but it is still Beaufort property."

Her sharp tone rankled Rafe, and he arched a dark brow. She was right. But it was his duty as a gentleman to remind her that unless Marianne wedded him, and soon, the consequences to the Beaufort properties—*especially* Baywood, with its modest holdings—might be dire. His gaze fastened to hers, but before he warned her to take care, Marianne's sister spoke.

"Maman, please," Genevieve said softly from where she sat in a laminated rosewood armchair, quietly observing. "I do not think Monsieur Rafe meant any harm by his remarks."

Setting his cup on the table, he inclined his head to the girl. "My dear Genevieve," he said sardonically, "I had no idea you possessed such astuteness. Of course I meant no offense, Clarisse. After all, in a few short weeks, when Marianne and I are married, the whole question of ownership of Baywood will become moot."

"*Oui,* Monsieur Rafe," Clarisse responded, returning to her seat. Pursing her mouth, she folded her hands in her lap. "As is stipulated in our agreement."

The smile pasted on his mouth in the company of the two insipid Beauforts turned into a smirk. "As for the object of that agreement, I find her absence . . . distressing," he admitted. "Therefore, I will take it upon myself to retrieve her from New Orleans and bring her here."

"*Mais non,* monsieur," Genevieve said in surprise. "M-Marianne is at Bienvenu to visit with Monsieur Pierre."

"Indeed?" Rafe asked mildly, picking up his cup and sipping from it again. "I thought she made the journey for other reasons."

Clarisse and Genevieve exchanged uneasy glances. So they knew the real reason Marianne went to St. Francisville, he concluded. Possibly they'd even hurried here to Baywood to pretend the three of them had gone to their plantation to cover up Marianne's lack of prudence, thinking that Rafe was still in New Orleans.

"At any rate," he bit out, angered at the thought that they had tried to deceive him, "I escorted Marianne back to New Orleans last night."

Clarisse frowned. "But why, monsieur?"

He felt the urge to crush the delicate cup between his hands, the consequences of having hot coffee spill on him be damned. "It seems I have a cousin I didn't know about," he snarled. "A vagabond I had dealings with several weeks ago."

Again the women exchanged glances. Silly females! They'd never be any good at poker. Their expressions were too easily discerned. "Do you know of whom I speak?"

"*Oui,* we know *of* him," Genevieve quickly answered. Clarisse seemed at a loss for words. "If he is the man at the ball at the St. Louis Hotel, I was a witness to your . . . your dealings."

"He is one and the same," Rafe clarified. "I should have killed him that night."

Clarisse's hand flew to her mouth. Taking in the hard set of his features, she cleared her throat. "But why?"

"Because he has duped my father into believing his story," Rafe answered, refusing to bring Marianne into this conversation. Thinking further, he realized he might very well have to worry about Drew's relationship with Pierre as well. Until Drew's appearance, Rafe had had no reason to worry that when the old man died, he wouldn't become the sole owner of the family's vast wealth and power; he alone would finally be in complete control of everything. But as long as his father didn't learn about the financial ruin they might be facing if Rafe didn't somehow turn his bad investments around, he'd place his concerns aside. He couldn't allow an event that mightn't ever happen to consume his attention when he had to bring his errant bride-to-be back under his control. "My father has allowed Drew to take up residency at Bienvenu."

"Which is the reason you spirited Marianne back to New Orleans?" Genevieve asked, her brown eyes bright with flirtatious admiration. Her hand fluttered to her abundant breasts, drawing his attention there.

Rafe stared at her in surprise, then released a genuine chuckle. Maybe he'd underestimated her. She was pretty, although she didn't share a family resemblance to any of the Beauforts, and her personality had always been so unassuming. Which was the reason he'd refused Clarisse's offer to marry her instead of Marianne. There was no question she was flirting with him. He was more than willing to take her up on her offer and bed her whenever and wherever she liked, as often as she liked. But he wouldn't give up the prize he'd craved for so long—Marianne. Not for anyone.

"You continue to amaze me, Genevieve. You have a quick understanding of complicated matters."

Clarisse glared at Genevieve when she beamed a bright smile in Rafe's direction. He wondered if Genevieve mightn't be a little jealous of Marianne, after all.

"Monsieur," Clarisse began, still glowering at her oldest daughter, "it will serve no purpose to bring Marianne here. Genevieve and I plan to leave tomorrow."

"And when do you plan to return?" he asked, setting his now-cold coffee down once and for all. He felt sure Baywood would be the safest place to keep Marianne away from Drew. Especially since he didn't think his cousin knew of the plantation's existence.

"The last spring ball occurs in two weeks," Clarisse answered. "As usual, we will depart the city right afterward."

Pretending indifference, Rafe shrugged. "If you wish it, madam," he said, resuming his stiff tone. "I feel it is my duty, however, to look in on her to assure myself of her well-being." He stood from his seat, anxious to see Marianne, anxious to take her in his arms and make her respond to his kisses. Although he'd do no more than kiss her. He wanted a pure wife at the altar and on his wedding night. "Thank you for the coffee."

Clarisse got up from her seat, one of the black gowns she continually wore to remind her of her lost husband framing her voluptuous body. "*Bonjour*, Monsieur Rafe. Inform Marianne that we will see her tomorrow."

"As you wish, madam," Rafe offered, taking her hand into his and chivalrously kissing it.

"*Bonjour,* monsieur."

Genevieve's voice floated to him, and he turned and bowed. He smiled at her. The first chance he got he'd test Genevieve's loyalty to Marianne and her desire for him. "So long, my dear Genevieve."

Hearing Rafe's carriage take off and being assured of his departure, Clarisse turned to her daughter with a stern look. For years Genevieve had been a combination of protective older sister and jealous sibling. And it had to stop. Lately Genevieve seemed to be leaning more toward jealousy. First she'd flirted with Andrew Montague, who seemed interested in Marianne, and now she'd shown interest in Marianne's affianced.

"How can you dare be so familiar with your sister's betrothed?"

"Maman! I resent your implication. I did nothing to encourage Monsieur Rafe's attention."

Hands on her hips, Clarisse said, "Didn't you? Either by word or by gesture, Genevieve? He smiled at you. *Twice* in a matter of minutes. An expression he rarely accords Marianne."

"Or anyone else," Genevieve said with a mischievous laugh.

Her daughter's lack of remorse concerned her. Something of a regrettable nature might happen if she didn't get Marianne and Rafe wedded soon. She had offered the man Genevieve's hand first, but he'd stoutly refused, insisting if he couldn't take Marianne to wife, then Baywood and everything else the Beauforts owned could rot.

Now he seemed willing to wed one daughter and bed the other. Clarisse knew that if Marianne discovered Rafe's flirtations with Genevieve, she'd call the wedding off, and all would be lost. "A smile from Rafe Montague is indeed rare. I would prefer that Marianne be the one to evoke such an extraordinary response from him, however."

"So would I, Maman." She stared at the recamier Rafe had so recently vacated. "Maybe he was just trying to . . . to . . . well, to belong."

"Don't be naive, child," Clarisse snapped, rubbing her temples at the myriad complications forming. If only Jean-Louis were there, everything would be fine. " 'Belonging,' as you put it, is not what Rafe has in mind. Just remember, our agreement is for *Marianne*—not Marianne *and* you."

"Oh, Maman, what must you think of me?"

A glance in Genevieve's direction told Clarisse her daughter was embarrassed, if not entirely sorry, about Rafe's attention. "*Ma cherie,* I think you are wonderful. It is Rafe I am beginning to doubt."

"Mari is very beautiful. Perhaps Rafe is unsure of her. Maybe even jealous."

"Maybe."

"If that is true, it would explain his odd behavior—he's trying to get her away from the stranger."

"*Oui,*" Clarisse said thoughtfully. "And he is already en route to New Orleans to ensure that distance is put between the stranger and Mari."

"Mari is probably feeling abandoned at home with no one but the servants to talk to."

"Rafe will change that. Won't she be surprised to see him?" Clarisse smiled with a cheer she didn't feel. She hoped all was as it should be in New Orleans when Rafe arrived at their cottage. "Come. We must prepare for tomorrow's trip to the city also."

Once there, she'd start making preparations for Marianne's wedding.

Chapter 16

UPON HIS RETURN to Bienvenu, Drew acquainted himself with his bachelor digs. The two-story, elegant little structure housed a sitting room on the first level and a bedroom on the second. Heavy walnut furniture and royal blue decor bespoke a masculine domain.

He supposed he could tolerate the place for the time being, but he missed the shower in his apartment on Burgundy Street, which usually washed away his antagonism, as well as the grime from his body. Frowning at the big, brass tub—which was still in occasional use at the plantation, he knew—Drew decided to content himself with it for the time being.

Surprisingly, the bath proved very relaxing. Although he felt pangs of guilt and sympathy for the servants who had to fill it, he was able to wash away some of the soul-deep weariness and aggravation he was experiencing.

He refused to focus too long upon his daughter's well-being. To do so would only distract him from taking the necessary actions to get back to her. So he'd trust that she was being well cared for by his parents and that, by hook or crook, he'd get back to her.

He wished he could be as optimistic about Marianne.

During the journey back to her cottage, she'd been quiet, lost in thoughts of her own, seemingly hesitant to speak about Laurinda's predictions. Concern had creased her brow when her thoughts deepened, but still she hadn't divulged anything. Drew had sincerely wanted to tell her that all was well, that she really had nothing to worry about. Yet he'd remained as silent as she.

Maybe she was afraid of him, if only slightly, and needed to work through her reservations in her own mind, without interference from him.

Drew realized he should have been more concerned than he was over Laurinda's warnings, but as she and Marianne had pointed out, there was plenty of time before the end of summer. He knew, however, that Rafe must be watched day in and day out. At any moment, Great-Great-Grandpa could decide to do away with him.

Yet now that Drew knew he indeed had a purpose in coming here and that all hope wasn't lost for returning to the twenty-first century, his mind seemed less consumed with worry. Even if he still didn't know what that purpose was, he thought wryly, he could focus a little more on the people around him. Especially Marianne.

Marianne. Her beautiful, proud image floated through his mind, taunting him with her unattainability.

It was only when Tomas was pulling away, with Marianne standing on her step, that Drew had dared to take note of how lovely she looked in the simple summer gown she wore, her hair freshly washed and twisted in a knot.

They hadn't said much in parting, just the barest of nods on Marianne's part and a brief smile on his. It had taken all of his strength to turn away when she remained standing there as the carriage departed, but he'd had to. Otherwise, he would have leaped from the vehicle, hauled her against him, and kissed her until she begged for more. Until she realized her mistake in marrying Rafe.

"Hell." Disgusted with his thoughts, Drew grabbed his dark brown topcoat from the back of the sofa and headed to the manor to talk to Pierre.

It didn't take long to find him. The older man was in the study, a half-full bottle of gin in front of him. Hesitantly Drew gazed around and, finding no sign of Rafe, walked into the room.

"Andrew, my boy! You're back!" A happy smile wreathed Pierre's face.

"I'm sorry for leaving, Uncle Pierre," Drew said, grateful that Rafe hadn't returned and somewhat chastened by Pierre's joy in having him back. He stared at the man, noted his unkempt, unshaven appearance. For a brief instant, a picture of his father flashed in his mind's eye. While Pierre seemed plagued by the fires of hell, Cranneck, to Drew's memory, usually looked only vaguely concerned. He smiled at Pierre, torn between happiness that the man seemed to have missed him and bitterness that his father had never looked at him with such regard. "I didn't want to come between you and Rafe, sir."

Taking a sip from his nearly empty glass, Pierre scowled and waved a dismissing hand. "*I'm* master of Bienvenu, not Rafe," he scoffed with a cough. "You're welcome here any-time, boy." He got up from the seat behind his big desk, his clothes rumpled and his eyes bloodshot. Looking down at what Drew realized were financial records, Pierre closed the book with a definitive thump. "Join me?"

"Of course," Drew said, not daring to refuse when Pierre appeared a wounded bear, ready to retreat to a cave and wait for the inevitable.

Somehow he knew Rafe was at the root of the man's problems.

For the next two weeks, Drew made his visits with Pierre a daily routine. By the time he went to Pierre's study, Rafe would be long gone, for which Drew was eternally grateful. During the day, he explored the grounds of Bienvenu, lands that were even more vast at that time than they were in his own. He visited the slave quarters and roamed the outskirts of the cane fields. Lands that should have been left to lie fallow for two years to rejuvenate the soil from which the cane sprouted had been overplanted and overtilled. Outbuildings and slave cabins were in disrepair. Equipment was broken and outdated.

Certainly planters of the day knew what needed to be done to keep their crops productive. While he'd always refused to have anything to do with the running of Bienvenu, it angered him that it was in jeopardy. He'd always thought these years for the Montagues had been among Bienvenu's most prosperous, but it seemed the family had once again been misinformed.

The plantation was on the verge of ruin. He saw it before his very eyes. Pierre knew it to the marrow of his bones. But the only thing the man did was gaze out the window of his study with a wistful look.

At the moment, Drew was sitting in the drawing room, the light summer curtains Eve had recently hung open to allow the early-evening sun in. Oaks and magnolias stood on the grounds, just beyond the white banisters of the veranda, in stately elegance. In the distance, thick smoke streamed from the huge chimney stack of the smokehouse. He listened as Pierre expounded on the decline of his beloved Bienvenu.

"My son takes me for a fool, Andrew," Pierre said, sober for the time being.

"In what way, Uncle Pierre?" Drew didn't wish to get in the middle of a feud between Pierre and Rafe, but the old man needed someone to listen to him. He needed humoring.

Pierre sighed and picked up the fat cigar that had gone virtually untouched since he'd lit it five minutes ago. He took a long drag. "Don't misunderstand me, Andrew," he finally said. "Rafe is a good man, but he's been in a foul mood of late."

"How so?" Swallowing the remainder of his brandy, then placing the glass on the table, Drew didn't believe for one minute that Rafe's mood was something new. He was just a foul human being. "Are you trying to tell me Cousin Rafe has a . . . gentler side?" He almost choked on the question.

A bushy eyebrow lifted, then Pierre burst out laughing. "Well, compared to a wild boar with a thorn in his side, yes."

Drew chuckled, admiring Pierre's straightforwardness. The man indeed knew his son. "What makes you think Rafe is—to use your words—taking you for a fool?"

Pierre's glance returned to the window, then he sighed again. "He's made some bad investments, son. The chances he took with Bienvenu were unwise. He doesn't know *I* know, however."

Drew noted the sag in Pierre's shoulders, the weariness in his voice. Did his own father ever contemplate their relationship with such despair? Pierre and Rafe's relationship appeared as fiercely explosive as his and Cranneck's. Yet it was obvious the man loved his son, and just as obvious that Rafe acted like a jackass where Pierre was concerned. Uncomfortable at how close to home that hit, Drew asked, "Why don't you confront him?"

"Because I don't think he did it maliciously. He loves Bienvenu as much as I do, and he only wants to see it prosper."

Indeed? Then why was Rafe killing good fields? Drew wondered. And why was he allowing the value of the lands to further depreciate because of the state of ruin some of the buildings were falling into?

Rafe was born into the family of a rich planter, and as such was reared and raised on what it took to make himself a *fabulously wealthy* planter. Unnecessary risks aside, he was making unwise decisions.

Drew straightened in his seat. "Maybe I can help," he offered.

He was, after all, a Montague born and bred, and he'd taken an agriculture course in high school. Although he'd stayed away from Bienvenu as much as he could, Drew knew the workings of the place like the back of his hand. His father had badgered him enough about it.

A glimmer of hope flickered across Pierre's features as

he turned to Drew. "You know about cane?"

"A little," Drew replied quietly, not willing to reveal just how much he knew. His knowledge would only raise more questions; more questions would result in more lies. Besides, it was quite ironic that he'd resisted his father's wishes to go to Bienvenu and work for as long as he could remember, but that now he was volunteering to do just that. Cranneck had used manipulation, however, and Drew had resisted largely because of that. "I'd like to help if I may."

"Boy, if you can turn this place around, I'll give you a share in it. You're Emory's boy. By right you should have his share."

"Over my dead body," Rafe snarled, stalking into the drawing room. "Father, how dare you entertain such traitorous notions."

Rafe had the most annoying habit of overhearing the tail end of conversations and bursting in like a madman.

"Traitorous? Traitorous!" Pierre boomed, his face reddening in outrage. He sat the cigar back in the ashtray, then pointed in Drew's direction. "This boy is Emory's son. My own flesh and blood, as well as yours."

Rafe glowered at Drew, his hand resting on the pistol at his side. "What's that got to do with anything?" he snapped.

Drew felt as if he were watching himself in an unfolding scene from a bad drama. Ol' "Cousin" Rafe had an unhealthy disregard for him. The man was a psycho, although Drew couldn't remember having ever heard of any psychos in his family when his father spouted the sterling Montague history during Drew's childhood. Maybe Rafe was a family secret that wasn't destined to be revealed until the twenty-first century and Cranneck's confinement.

The idea of his father in a loony bin struck Drew as funny, and he burst out laughing.

"What's so funny?" Rafe continued, his gaze boring into Drew before he turned his attention back to Pierre. "I don't care if he's Emory himself, Father. He gets not an inch of soil from Bienvenu. All those years we worked to keep

Bienvenu solvent, Emory and Cousin Andrew were no-where to be found."

"Rafe—," Pierre began in warning tones.

Drew rose to his full height, tired of the bickering. "It's all right, Uncle Pierre," he interrupted. "Rafe's right. I don't want a piece of your hard-earned labor. I don't deserve it."

And maybe he truly didn't, he reflected, considering how indifferent he'd been toward it.

"How gallant you are, Cousin," Rafe sneered. "Now that it's clear what you *don't* want, what exactly *are* you after? Could it be Marianne?"

Drew's body tensed at Rafe's angry smugness. *He* was the better man for Marianne, but she was engaged to Rafe. He'd thought he'd affected her as much as she had him, but in the last two weeks she'd made her position quite clear—not once had she attempted to contact him. "You give me no credit at all for restraint . . . Cousin," he added.

"Restraint?" Rafe clenched his fists at his side. "So you *are* after her?"

"Get control of that temper, Rafe!" Pierre ordered harshly. "Andrew hardly knows the woman."

"Besides," Drew pointed out, "you and Marianne are be-trothed. I would be less than a gentleman if I attempted to come between you."

"Harumph!" Rafe said, whatever that meant. "But I haven't got time to argue the point, Cousin. I must meet the beautiful mademoiselle at the last ball of the season in New Orleans. You and Father have a pleasant evening." He bowed formally. "By the way, Andrew, Marianne's mother has set our wedding for the end of summer. Thought you might like to know."

Hot jealousy spread through Drew as he pictured Mar-ianne turning a pretty smile to Rafe before suffusing the man with her gaiety and intelligence; her features softening in desire as she allowed Rafe to join bodies with her, part-ing her lips for his kisses as passionately as she parted her legs for his lovemaking.

He had to find a way to see her and tell her that Rafe

wasn't the man for her. He was all wrong. *This* was all wrong. But how could he, when Pierre had come to expect his company and when Rafe would probably turn it into an excuse to slaughter him?

Twisting his lips into a smirk at Drew's dark look, Rafe began walking away.

"You can't just sit here and amuse me forever, Andrew," Pierre said, as if Divinity itself had put the thought in his head. "Rafe, what do you say to letting Drew tag along?"

Rafe stopped in his tracks, then spun on his heels. Wide, angry eyes nearly popped from his head. "Are you losing your mental faculties, Father?" he spat through clenched teeth. "Do you want me to be a laughingstock amongst my peers?"

Pierre frowned. "Why in heaven's name would anyone laugh at you, son?"

Rafe stiffened, then sniffed disdainfully. Remaining silent, and looking like a guilty little boy instead of a grown, maniacal man, he focused his gaze on a huge painting of his grandfather.

"Lost your hearing, boy?" Pierre demanded.

"Uncle Pierre," Drew inserted, unable to keep quiet. He didn't want to get involved in Rafe and Pierre's relationship, but by his offer to help with Bienvenu, he already had. "Rafe and I had a little . . . er . . . altercation, shall we say, in front of his friends at our first meeting."

"And you bested him in a fight?"

Drew laughed at Pierre's assumption. "Not exactly. Just suffice it to say he would have a lot of explaining to do if he were seen with me. I'll just go my own—"

"That bad, huh?" Pierre interrupted, torn between amusement and annoyance. "Well, go in separate carriages. Can't have you two boys riding together and coming to blows."

"I'm against it!" Rafe loudly protested.

"Is there anything you're *for*?" Drew snapped. His whiny relative was beginning to bug him. He had to see Marianne, and he'd be damned if he'd let Rafe stop him from going to the ball.

Rafe took a step toward him, his eyes black with hatred. "I'm 'for' throttling you!" he spat sharply.

His temper rising, Drew glinted narrowly at him. He couldn't quite relate to 'throttling,' but he was more than ready to beat the shit out of Rafe, and Rafe could call it what he wanted to. Drew was tired of the man goading him.

"Care to step outside?"

"Stop!" Pierre fairly screamed, raising his hands in protest. "There'll be none of that. Rafe, if Drew wants to go to that ball, then that's his prerogative. Simon will bring him."

Rafe looked from Pierre to Drew and then back again, his anger becoming more defined by the stiffening of his body, the tightening of his jaw. "He's free to go wherever he pleases, Father," he replied furiously, his lips thin. "But he'll do well to stay away from me and Marianne."

"If any altercation ensues, Rafe, you'll have me to reckon with," Pierre said, his voice like bits of ice. "So I'm advising you to control yourself."

Drew and Rafe exchanged angry glances. As he had, Drew knew Rafe had detected a resolve behind the warning. Pierre was fed up with his son.

Rafe glared at his father a moment longer before turning angrily away and stalking out of the room.

"He'll recover," Pierre told Drew. "You'd best get ready to go. I'll send Simon to the *garçonnière* to fetch you to the ball in the buggy in forty-five minutes. That should be time enough for you to change into proper attire."

"Thanks," Drew said, and followed in Rafe's wake.

His need to see Marianne, he realized, had forced this foolishly desperate act. He told himself his only motive in wanting to see her was so she could help him return to his own time, but he knew that wasn't entirely true. He wanted to talk some sense into her.

Since nothing was as it should be, he couldn't be certain that it was no longer Marianne's destiny *not* to marry Rafe. His breach of time might have caused his family history to go haywire. Rafe's behavior was one example. Could the man Cranneck admired more than any other of his lauded ancestors be the same man who had no regard for women, for life, for his father, or for his heritage?

He had to save Marianne. But the Rafe Montague he was acquainted with, the son-of-a-bitch with the lethal temper, had henchmen. Despite Pierre's warning to his son, Drew wouldn't know until he got to the ball if his life would be in jeopardy at the hands of Rafe and his cohorts, the men who'd surrounded them at their first altercation.

Chapter 17

FOLLOWING ALL THE rules of protocol, Drew made his way through the rotunda of the St. Louis Hotel, marveling at the building's circular center and high domed ceiling. Soon he was mingling with the privileged Creoles in one of the second-floor ballrooms. Most of them were cordial to him, but the polite responses to his conversation annoyed him. After three attempts to engage a group of men in conversation, Drew excused himself and stood alone to observe the goings-on.

An abundance of prim and proper beauties glided around the elegant room. Yet none there could compare with Marianne, whom Drew had yet to see. He hadn't seen Rafe, either, for that matter, so he couldn't blame the jerk for his cold reception. Maybe his horse and carriage had gotten mired in some swampy muck.

The thought bringing a smile to his face, Drew admired the huge crystal chandeliers ablaze with light, hanging from the center of intricately carved friezework. Handsomely appointed furnishings lined the rich paneled walls and left a huge space for dancing. Slaves and wage-earning white servants, liveried in black and white, attended thick crowds of guests. French doors stood open to allow warm breezes to circulate inside.

"Monsieur?" A petite girl, eyes walnut brown and wide as a doe's, touched his arm.

He smiled at her. "Yes . . . er, *oui*?"

"Monsieur is alone, *oui*?"

"Louise!" A stern male voice broke in from a few feet away. "Are you being bothered by this . . . this American?"

"*Non, non,* Papa," Louise quickly answered, twisting her hands in agitation. "Monsieur appeared lost—"

"He most probably is," another man interrupted. "He's on the wrong side of the neutral ground. Quite away from the 'Mericain side."

"Maybe we should just point him in the right direction," a third man interjected. "We don't want his kind around our women anyway."

Damn! Not again. Lord, don't let these fools challenge me to a duel. On the other hand, I might win in a fistfight.

Perusing his surroundings, Drew realized he might lose, too. Four big, dressed-up, hairy apes waited to take a swing at him. Yeah, losing was a distinct possibility.

Just then the noticed Rafe standing in a corner. A satisfied smirk on his face, Rafe lifted his champagne glass in salute.

Rafe's work. Drew had been foolishly cheering his kin's absence, but it seemed as if Rafe had been skulking around doing his dirty work from behind the scenes. Drew should have known that Rafe was behind the Goon Squad. Although he could try to talk himself out of this situation, Rafe's henchmen were out for blood. Namely *his* very own precious blood. He couldn't let that happen twice.

Stroking his chin, Drew grinned at Rafe, arching his eyebrows up and down. Accomplished in a few karate moves, he'd aim some well-placed kicks here and there, just to clear a path so he could make a beeline for the door.

Seeing Drew's dark humor, Rafe's smirk turned to a frown, and he nodded to the men.

Drew brushed aside an attempt by one of the men to punch him in the jaw. Spinning around, in rapid succession he connected three hard kicks to three hard heads. He sent one man toppling into a passing waiter. In turn, the waiter fell onto several young ladies, who fell to the floor, entangled in satin and lace.

Serving dishes crashed to the floor, and a loud clattering of glass followed. Cries of dismay mingled with giggles, and shrill outbursts shattered the sedate environment. Immediately gentlemen broke rank to assist the giggling, gasping, and crying young women off the floor.

Fists balled at his side, Rafe advanced toward Drew. "You uncouth heathen!" he raged when he reached him. "You'll not walk away from here this time!"

"What do you intend to do, son? Carry him on your back?" Pierre broke in as he got between Rafe and an astonished but grateful Drew.

"Father!" Rafe's surprise registered in his voice. "What are you doing here?"

"I'm here for the same reason you are, son," Pierre said. "To enjoy the last ball of the season before we retire to the country. Or are you here for a different reason?"

Rafe glared at Pierre, his eyes turning black with anger. "You followed me here," he accused.

Pierre nodded; surprisingly, he was still stone sober. "No doubt," he said. "How fortunate that I did."

"Monsieur Pierre," Marianne said, her soft voice interrupting the angry male voices. She glided to a stop next to Drew, so close to him that he saw the frantic pulse at the base of her throat. "I did not know you had come."

Vaguely aware of more guests arriving to assist in the fiasco and restore order, Drew wondered if there was something special about women in this time period. Marianne was . . . *fresh*. She was exquisite. Ringlets of her upswept black hair dangled on her neck and over her ears. A hint of color touched her pale pink lips and creamy cheeks. Diamond-and-pearl earrings glinted from her delicate lobes, and her compelling jade eyes blazed with good humor. A perfectly beautiful invention, her evening dress of pale violet silk trimmed with slender puffs of ribbon and double lace undersleeves complemented the perfectly beautiful creation that was Marianne.

Pierre bowed and kissed her hand. "Marianne, *ma cherie*. I could not let the last ball go by without a dance with my favorite almost-daughter-in-law."

Marianne's joyful laugh warmed Drew's heart.

"*Merci*. You're very kind," she said, then turned to Drew and curtsied. "*Bonsoir*, Monsieur Andrew. How nice that you could come," she said in a restrained voice. Realizing how close she was standing to Drew, she moved slightly away. Though it was settling down quite a bit, she could not miss the commotion going on around them. "It seems you have a knack for attracting misrule."

His three opponents were being dragged by their feet toward the entrance door by some of the paid servants, wary slave attendants watching in astonishment. The several young women who had fallen were all being ushered into an adjoining room.

With a chuckle, Drew bowed. "Hello, Marianne. It's good to see you again. I'm afraid I must plead guilty to this chaos. With extenuating circumstances, of course."

Pierre indicated Rafe with a nod. "This hotheaded son of mine is the 'extenuating circumstances,' " he bit out.

"Father—"

"Shut up!" Pierre snapped. "I warned you, boy. Marianne, make an old man happy. Andrew doesn't know anyone here. Be kind enough to dance with him while I escort my son to the courtyard for a talk and cooling-off."

Rafe bristled. "Marianne, I forbid it!"

"I said *shut up*, Rafe. And I mean just that," Pierre snapped again, pushing his son toward the door. "Now get out of here! She's in the hands of a gentleman. Besides, you can't forbid Marianne anything, since you aren't married to her yet."

Shrugging off his father's hold, Rafe glared at Drew and disappeared through an archway.

For a brief second, Drew saw himself at odds with Cranneck as Rafe and Pierre were at odds now, and he didn't like how it made him feel. Pierre wanted what he thought was best for Rafe—as Cranneck did for him. When he returned to his own time, maybe he would try patience with his father. He would try to see things the way Cranneck saw them. Bickering wouldn't be the only option anymore.

He shook his head at the myriad servants scurrying to right the mess he'd caused. Looking around at the accusing stares, he grinned devilishly at Marianne. "I guess this means I won't get invited back."

Marianne smiled and entwined her arm in his. "Maybe we'd better find another spot," she suggested as they started forward.

Feeling the heat of her touch through his waistcoat, Drew nodded. "Good idea. The folks at this end don't seem pleased."

"Shall we go to the refreshment stand? We can sip champagne while you tell me why you're here risking your life."

Again Drew nodded. "Fair enough," he said, his tone more subdued. Reaching the ornately decorated table, which was laden with tea cakes, hors d'oeuvres, sugar-covered fruit, petit fours, and wine, he took two glasses of champagne from a tray and passed one to Marianne.

"Would you like to go to the garden?"

Hesitation flickered in Marianne's jade eyes, and she chuckled nervously. "*Oui.* But perhaps we shouldn't. I am certain Rafe and Monsieur Pierre are still out there."

"Then why don't we sit down." Drew pointed to a few unoccupied chairs against the wall.

"*Oui.* I'd like that."

Sitting next to her, Drew felt awkward. He wanted to tell her about his great-great-grandmother and inform her that it wasn't *her*—at least, as far as he knew. Yet Marianne was under the impression that she'd definitely marry Rafe at the end of the summer. So he kept his mouth shut about the Montague heritage according to the family tree at the Bienvenu of the twenty-first century. He wouldn't have Marianne thinking he made up the story to get her away from Rafe and into his arms.

He cleared his throat. "I missed you, Mari," he said huskily. "Why did you stay away?"

When Marianne cleared *her* throat, they both laughed.

"Catching," Drew said.

"*Oui.*" She gazed at him a long moment, the emotions written on her face having a thousand different meanings. "I . . . have obligations to fulfill," she said softly. "I forget them when I'm near you."

Drew squeezed her hand, waiting to hear from her lips the words Rafe had uttered to him earlier. Besides Marianne telling him that a wedding date had been set, he also wanted her to finally admit that she had no deep feelings for Rafe. "Those obligations include marriage to Rafe, don't they?"

"*Oui.*"

"Do you love him?"

Marianne stiffened, and a small tremor passed through her fingers. "Don't. Please don't," she began, her voice cracking. "You won't understand."

"I already do, Marianne," Drew said urgently. "In the future, where I came from, Baywood, your plantation, once belonged to my family. The Montagues. When Rafe married into the Beaufort family, he automatically acquired the property."

Marianne lowered her head, confirming his suspicions. The Beaufort-Montague union had indeed taken place because of financial woes. From what Drew saw, the Beauforts were pretty well-to-do—a lot better off than what he'd been led to believe of his own family of this time. Had Rafe actually married to save the *Montague* fortune?

"You must not think too harshly of me, Andrew," she whispered, misery bathing her beautiful features. "Without Papa, Maman and Genevieve and I almost lost Baywood. I cannot abandon them by not marrying Rafe."

Bringing her hand to his lips, Drew placed a kiss on the inside of her palm, just as the orchestra struck a waltz. He stood and bowed. "May I have this dance, mademoiselle?"

After glancing briefly toward the archway that led to the

garden, Marianne perked, and the frown marring her features faded. She smiled. "It is my pleasure."

One hand holding her slim waist, the other her delicately soft hand, Drew glided effortlessly across the dance floor with her. She was a feather in his arms, her graceful moves encouraging, enticing, and enchanting.

"Rest your fears, Mari," he whispered, his heart pounding at the feel of her in his arms. "What I think of you is anything but harsh. My admiration for you knows no bounds." He wanted to pull her closer and smother her with hot kisses and passionate words.

But he dared not. Not there. Probably not ever. Even if he had been her intended, it was against the mores of good breeding to do such a thing. Yet he had one consoling thought: If he couldn't have her, at least neither would Rafe. But why? What had become of her that Rafe married Genevieve instead?

A horrible thought crossed Drew's mind. Had Marianne succumbed to the Yellow Fever epidemic that would take place this year? What other reason could there be?

"My God!" he exclaimed, so lost in dread that he released the words before he could stop himself.

Marianne slowed her movements, concern wreathing her expression. "What is it, Andrew? Your face is as ashen as a ghost's. Are you ill?"

"N-no," Drew managed, sick with despair. Gathering speed, he waltzed her to the outside door. A servant opened it, and he and Marianne stepped into the humid atmosphere, where a small group had already gathered. The scent of sweet olive and night-blooming jasmine filled the warm, sticky air.

He pulled Marianne close, tightening his arms around her. Sucking in a ragged breath, he gathered her face between his hands. "Mari, there's so much I must tell you."

"Drew, please!" Marianne said, pushing away from him. "People are staring."

Drew's hands fell to his side, and he closed his eyes. He wanted to tell her to leave, to flee, that she was in as much danger from an unseen foe as he was from Rafe. But he couldn't. He knew better than to alter history more than he already had.

If he didn't think he'd frighten her, he'd ask if she'd ever had Yellow Fever. Then he'd know she was safe—from that disease, at least. As it was, he suspected she'd stayed away from him as much because of her obligations as because of the slight fear she harbored of him.

His intense gaze burned into her. "God, what am I thinking? Forgive me, Mari. I certainly didn't mean to make you an object of the curious."

What the hell was he thinking, overstepping the bounds of protocol and good taste? A sure way to prick Rafe's hair-trigger temper.

"Marianne, I must see Laurinda again," he said urgently. "Will she see me alone?" Maybe Laurinda could unravel the mystery of Rafe's marriage and Marianne's fate. For the same reason that he didn't want to ask about the Yellow Fever, he didn't want Marianne to know why he needed to see the old voodoo woman. But he had to find out what happened to Marianne.

"*Oui,* Drew," Marianne answered, puzzled. "When would you like to see her?"

"Tomorrow. I'll just see her before I go back to Bienvenu."

"All right, Drew. I'll send Teddy to tell her to expect you."

Surprised, Drew arched an eyebrow. "I thought they were afraid of her."

Marianne laughed. "They are, but Teddy is adventuresome. He likes to see if he can escape her without having his head shrunk."

"Tell me *my* head is safe, Mari," he said, joining her in laughter.

"Safe from what, Andrew?" Pierre asked, strolling to where they sat, holding a highball glass in his hand.

"Safe from harm, Uncle Pierre," Drew answered, watching as Rafe advanced toward them. "If I make myself clear," he added.

Tasting his drink, Pierre glanced at Rafe. "You needn't fear your cousin, boy. He knows you're not after Marianne. Don't you, Rafe?"

"Of course, Father," Rafe answered stiffly. "I've been remiss, Andrew. Allow me to welcome you into the family." He held out his hand to Drew.

When Drew accepted the proffered hand, a round of applause ensued. Until then, Drew had forgotten that he and Marianne were being observed by the curious creme of society.

"Thank you, Rafe," Drew said, covertly using his pants leg to wipe the hand that had shaken Rafe's. Who would he tell when he got back home that he'd shaken his ancestor's sweaty hand?

Searching Rafe's features for sincerity, Drew saw that the smile was there but that the eyes spoke volumes, and every volume had a murderous ending. Rafe's performance was for the old man's benefit. Well, Drew told himself, two could play at that game.

"Marianne, my dear, before I turn you over to your betrothed, would you do me the honor of one last dance?"

Surprise registered in Marianne's features. Nonetheless, she remained cool and in control, betraying no more of her thoughts. She turned to Rafe. "Would you object, monsieur?"

Rafe forced a chortle from his throat. "As long as it's only, 'one last dance,'" he got out, the smile frozen on his face.

Drew raised his right hand and placed his left on his heart. "On my honor," he vowed. Without awaiting a response, he took Marianne's arm and led her back to the dance floor.

"Andrew!" Marianne exclaimed as they began dancing. "You do not want to provoke Rafe. He did not look pleased!"

"I know. But I want to know when I'll see you again. I

couldn't very well ask in front of him, could I?"

"You know that's impossible, Drew. I cannot see you anymore. I am going to marry Rafe. And even if I wasn't, I could never breach time with you and travel forward. My family needs me. It isn't as if I'd be able to jump into a horse and buggy to visit them."

With grace and style, Drew whirled her around the floor, pretending he hadn't heard her vehement responses, ignoring their merit. She was right: If it was that easy, he would have gone back for Teal in a heartbeat and then returned to pursue Marianne.

He decided to focus on the time they had together now and deal with everything else later. "Tomorrow, after I meet with Laurinda, I'll be going back to Bienvenu. I intend to help Uncle Pierre with the plantation, so I won't be coming back here anytime soon. Unless you promise to see me during that time, I will have to commit suicide by kissing you here and now—"

"W-what do you mean? S-suicide?"

"If I kiss you here, you know your betrothed will kill me on the spot. My death will be on your delicate little hands."

"Andrew, you wouldn't—"

Lowering his head slightly, Drew's gaze fell to her lips, his intention all too clear. "Wouldn't I?"

"All right, monsieur!" Marianne agreed grudgingly, treading purposely upon his foot. "I'll see you."

"Ow!" Undeterred by her action, Drew tightened his hold on her. "When?"

"Soon. Next week."

The music tapered to a stop, and Drew returned Marianne to Rafe and Pierre. He bowed lavishly. "Thank you, Marianne. Uncle Pierre. Cousin Rafe. It's really been a pleasure, but being without an escort, I feel displaced. So I'll say good night."

"Good night, Cousin," Rafe said, the words dripping venom.

Drew knew that despite Pierre's warning, he was still the object of Rafe's unreasonable hate. He would have to be diligent, lest Rafe act on that hate.

Chapter 18

EARLY THE NEXT day, Tomas guided the horse and buggy toward Grand Route St. John and Laurinda's cabin.

Passing Congo Square again, Drew marveled at the place. It was the site of present-day Armstrong Park, but the huge, concrete edifice known as the Mahalia Jackson Theatre of Performing Arts was only a distant dream. He wanted to see Congo Square in all its glory. He wanted to be there one Sunday when the slaves danced the bamboula.

Soon they'd passed the Square, leaving behind all signs of civilization. Sunshine brightened the passing greenery and made for a warm, breezy ride inside the slow-moving vehicle.

Thinking just how little he knew about Marianne, he shook his head. He doubted she would willingly answer his questions, and had taken up this mad quest in order to discover more about her.

Placing his hands behind his head, Drew sighed. He hadn't a clue to her age or to why she had so readily come to his aid all those days ago, even at the risk of what seemed a tenuous betrothal at that time. Already he'd discerned that her engagement was more complicated than mere love. And marrying for any reason other than love, he felt, wasn't a wise decision.

He still couldn't comprehend the jealousy he experienced, the things he imagined when she was alone with Rafe. But he knew he didn't like it, which was part of the reason he'd left early last night. He hadn't been able to bear watching her depart with Rafe, as she surely had. He'd secured a room in the hotel and then remained awake for most of the night.

Bright and early, at eight in the morning, a knock had sounded on his door. The bellman had informed Drew that the Beaufort carriage awaited him to bring him to his destination.

Rambling toward that place now, Drew sighed and settled in for the wait. Although last night he'd brushed off the fact that she swore she couldn't leave with him, come what might, her words dogged him. It wouldn't be fair to her if he insisted she think it over. He'd put undue pressure on her and perhaps succeed in changing her mind. Then, suppose she regretted her decision once she was ensconced in the twenty-first century? Suppose she grieved for her family as he grieved for Teal? There would be no turning back.

No, he wouldn't pressure her to do anything she didn't want to. And although *she* had brought up the subject of her returning with him, he now knew her sentiments and wouldn't bring it up again. No matter how much he'd regret leaving her behind.

Maybe, however, Laurinda would help him to put things into perspective. He wouldn't give up hope completely until after he'd spoken to her.

Half an hour later, the buggy rolled to a stop in front of Laurinda's hut.

As soon as he stepped down the door swung open, and the straight, wizened figure of the enchantress stood just inside the house. Her bony hand gripped the head of the cobra sitting on her ever-present staff. Swallowing hard, Drew made his way inside and quietly sat at the same table he had before.

One curtain, drawn against the lone window, prevented

the bright sunlight from filtering through. The score of candles lighting the small cabin flickered high and low. Drew sat straighter in his seat as Laurinda settled across from him, in her usual spot, holding on to her staff tightly. A shudder passed through him, and he wondered why, since the room appeared well sealed against any breeze that might occur.

Acridity from the candle smoke stung his eyes, and he blinked constantly. Laurinda's frown deepened every time he did, so he supposed blinking wasn't an option. How she was able to sit unblinking and unmoving in the smoky room mystified him. *He* was ready for an oxygen mask.

Abruptly Laurinda slammed her snake's-head staff with the viperous pose on the wooden floor. Her movement startled him, and he jumped.

"Reveal your reason for comin' here, Andrew Montague," she said in her gravelly voice.

"I-I need more answers, Miss Laurinda, ma'am. I also want to know of Teal, my—"

"Your *bebe* be fine. It ain't gonna do you no good to keep worryin' about her!" Depthless gray eyes fastened onto him, piercing him with a savage fire. "As for more answers, there ain't no more I can tell you about returnin' to your own time."

"I know, ma'am," Drew answered, unnerved by her overwhelming presence. "There's something else I want to ask you about."

She leaned back in her chair, the candles around her flaring brighter. "You's smitten with Marianne Beaufort and you be wantin' to know the outcome."

"Why, yes," Drew answered in surprise as he felt himself being drawn to the light, the fire. He watched in fascination as the flames grew brighter, hotter, burning the air around them. But he experienced no worry or fear, only calmness. Then Laurinda shifted in her seat again, and the flame lowered to a tiny light. Suddenly discomfited, he watched as a smile wreathed her rich, coffee-colored, leathery skin. "That, among other things."

She knew the exact reasons for his visit, and Drew stiffened in annoyance even as fear gripped him tighter. It seemed the old harridan was always one up on him. Since she already knew his reasons for being there, he thought, she could save them both some time by providing all the answers at once.

"And what be the other things, boy?"

Heartened by her conciliatory tone, Drew leaned forward. "I want to know why Rafe ended up married to Genevieve. Did something happen to Marianne?"

Before laying her staff in front of her, Laurinda gazed into his eyes for a moment and placed both his hands in one of hers. She closed her eyes, then began rocking back and forth and humming.

"Yes!" she screamed suddenly. "Yes, somethin' will happen to Mam'zelle Mari!"

Drew's heart skipped a beat, and tension knotted his insides. "Is . . . is it bad?" he managed to ask.

"All will reveal itself in time, boy. It is unwise for you to know anyone's fate but your own."

Shifting in his seat, Drew nodded, not knowing what else to do but concede to Laurinda's words. "Will . . . will I end up with the woman I love?" he asked, aware that Laurinda knew of his feelings for Marianne. If the old woman answered that question, he reasoned, all others would be moot.

Laurinda released a cackle, revealing several missing teeth. Those still in her gums were unnaturally white. "You's a smart boy, Andrew Montague. True love is like this bright flickering flame," she said, indicating the candles, which were once again flaring high, with a nod of her head. "When you find it, it guides the way. But like a flickering flame, true love might sparkle for the briefest of times before it's gone forever. Just be lucky, boy, that you had it at all. Some things ain't meant to last a lifetime."

"The bigger the fire, the more intense the heat, Miss Laurinda, and the more you're drawn to its brilliance." An overwhelming sadness pervaded him. He hated to think that he and Marianne weren't meant to be together as she'd suggested, that the brilliant fire Laurinda compared them to would burn itself out. But he supposed some things were only meant to last one shining moment before you lost it.

"Take heart, boy. Even if your love ain't returned, you will still go back to your own time, if you find the watch by the end of the summer."

Having every confidence that he'd get back to his daughter, even if it would undoubtedly be without Marianne, Drew lowered his head. Maybe he was as smart as she'd said, but Laurinda was smarter. How *could* Marianne return his love if something happened to her? he wanted to know. "Isn't there anything else you can tell me, Miss Laurinda?"

Releasing his hands, Laurinda stood, indicating the end of the meeting. "Only this," she said. "Marianne has something planned for the near future that only you can prevent her from doing—"

"Me?"

"Yes, boy, you!" She grabbed her hideous staff and guided Drew to the door. "And one more thing, Andrew Montague. Monsieur Rafe is planning to kill you the first chance he gets. Be on your guard!" The whispery, gravelly voice floated on the air around them like a separate life force. Opening the door and holding it open, she said, "*Bonjour*, Andrew Montague. I'm lookin' to see you again soon."

As confused and worried as ever, Drew stepped into the clean air and took in several big gulps. Laurinda had only made clear what she'd told him the first time he'd visited her—that Rafe intended to kill him.

But he still didn't know Marianne's fate.

Chapter 19

"Is THERE ANYTHIN' else you be needin', suh?" To-mas asked just after he stopped the horse and buggy in front of the St. Louis Hotel. "Miss Mari, her say bring you wherever you wants to go."

"Thank your mistress for me," Drew said quietly. "But I have a few errands to attend to before I head back to St. Francisville. I'll send word to Simon. I'm sure he went to my uncle's apartments on St. Ann Street."

"Yes, suh, but if there's anythin' you need, we'll be at the cottage until tomorrow."

Tomas's statement caught Drew's interest. "And then?"

"Why, in Roseland, at Baywood, suh. We leave every summer to escape the Yellow Fever. You should make haste yo'self."

"Fleeing the city still isn't an absolute guarantee that you won't catch the Fever, Tomas. The death of Jean-Louis is proof."

"Masta Jean, he comed to New Orleans ever week or so on business. Sooner or later, he was bound to get sick, 'cause he wouldn't caution Mistress Clarisse's words."

"It's a wonder the entire household didn't become ill," Drew speculated.

"No, suh. Masta Jean stayed here in the city when he caught it, and Miz Mari came and tended him. Ever'body else stayed in Baywood under the mistress's orders."

A sliver of knowledge about the Yellow Fever epidemic popped into Drew's mind, and his relief knew no bounds. "Then Marianne already had the disease?"

"Yes, suh. 'Bout ten years ago."

Drew smiled brightly, but just as abruptly became serious. Laurinda had sworn something would happen to Marianne. Thankfully it wasn't Yellow Fever, but it only increased Drew's fears. Perhaps it had something to do with the plans that Laurinda claimed only he could prevent Marianne from carrying out. More than likely, the old woman was referring to the wedding. Yet Marianne's mind was already made up, and if he hadn't weaseled a promise from her to visit him, she would have married Rafe and forgotten Drew existed.

He sighed. "Tomas, thank you. If I should need anything, I'll let you know."

"Yes, suh. But you should see Miz Mari soon enough. She always at Bienvenu 'cause Masta Pierre be so lonely all the time."

The words were meant to hearten Drew, but they didn't. Instead, they only saddened him. They meant that if Marianne kept the promise she'd so rashly made to him last night, it wouldn't be for him. "Very good, Tomas," he said, his expression rigidly composed.

He watched until the horse and buggy were out of sight before starting down the street. His destination were the Royal Street shops. He meant to purchase a pocket watch and chain of his own. Drew had come to the decision during the journey from Laurinda's.

As much as he pretended otherwise and as much as Laurinda told him not to, he worried terribly about his daughter. He'd deliberately pushed her to the back of his mind, determined to calmly believe that he'd return to her. But he wasn't doing anything about it. Instead, he was pining for a woman who'd never be his, even if she wouldn't be Rafe's either.

Marianne's duty to her family was too strong for her to desert them and return with him. He would have to leave alone. It was painful to admit and even more painful to act on. Yet he would. The beginning of summer was just ten days away. He would find a watch and chain, then go to a hitching post and try his luck.

Drew welcomed the unseasonably cool mid-morning, with its damp breeze. The sweet olive, cape jasmine, honeysuckle, and other odoriferous flowers, which bloomed in almost every garden along the way, prevented the smell of manure and night soil from overpowering him. Cart-pushing and basket-carrying vendors plying their trades walked amongst the well-to-do citizens. Gentlemen on fine horses and ladies in well-appointed carriages vied for space in the streets of the Quarter.

When Drew saw the faded sign with the words "Roudin's Fine Jewels and Pure Metals" announcing the first jewelry shop on Royal Street, he entered the dimly lit interior. Discovering a treasure trove of sparkling jewels, gleaming gold, and shiny silver, he stopped in his tracks. A huge diamond ring caught his attention, and immediately Marianne came to mind. Just as quickly, he forced the thought away. The ring she accepted wouldn't be from him.

"May I be of some service, sir?" the clerk asked from behind Drew.

Drew turned and smiled. A tall gentleman, curly hair framing a bald crown and converging upon his long sideburns, watched him with uncertainty. He sat behind a display case Drew had failed to notice upon entering, since it was in a far corner—a glass-enclosed case with watches and fobs.

"My good fellow," Drew began, walking forward with purpose, "if you'd be so kind as to assist in my purchase of a watch and fob, I'd greatly appreciate it."

The shopkeeper's trepidation increased. Eyeing Drew from head to heel, he said, "Certainly."

Undeterred by the man's tight civility, Drew leaned against the counter. His being a stranger in this shop that obviously catered to aristocrats was probably the cause of the man's attitude. But Pierre had lent Drew a fair amount of money and insisted he properly attire himself.

Removing the velvet-lined box holding the jewelry, the shopkeeper laid it on top of the glass case. "You from these parts?" he asked casually.

"In a roundabout way, yes," Drew answered, closely studying the watches and fobs. Choosing the largest one with the most intricate design on its back, he clasped it tightly in his hand. "I'm the long-lost nephew of Pierre Montague."

"Are you now?" the man asked. "You're Rafe's cousin?"

Not feeling that same pull from this watch, Drew nodded. A part of him knew that finding a hitching post and attempting his breach through time was a fool's journey. Still, he held on to the shred of hope that had driven him to undertake this mission in the first place.

"I suppose I am," Drew said, releasing a deep breath, tempering his disappointment over the watch. He looked up at the man. "Unfortunately," he added.

The shopkeeper laughed and extended his hand. "Name's Roudin. Hebert Roudin, and I'd like to welcome you to my shop."

"C. Andrew Montague III," Drew said, accepting the proffered hand. "Mr. Roudin, the pleasure is all mine. I take it you've met Rafe?" He hoped the man had only heard him say "Montague." After all, C. Andrew Montague II hadn't been born yet.

"On more than one occasion," Hebert replied, rubbing a hand across his eyes. "He was in here a couple of days ago with Madame Beaufort to choose a ring for his intended. He's to marry Marianne Beaufort—"

"I know, Mr. Roudin," Drew cut in curtly, a cold knot forming in his middle at the proprietor's words. "A more lucky bastard never lived. He doesn't deserve her."

At the surprised look on Hebert Roudin's face, Drew

cleared his throat. He had to remember he was amongst a *civilized* population where manners and a code of honor that begged for bloodshed at the smallest infraction, ruled. "Pardon my rude outburst, Mr. Roudin. I'd like to purchase this." He held out the watch and fob he'd selected.

Hebert Roudin met his gaze. "Of course, monsieur." Quietly he wrote the ticket out and then asked for the twenty dollars to pay for the purchase. "Follow me," he said after the transaction was complete.

"Where to?"

"Just follow me, please," Hebert said calmly, already heading to the other side of the shop.

Drew remained where he stood as he watched Roudin stop at the case loaded with earrings.

"As you're a new customer, I'd like to offer you a lagniappe, a little something extra at no charge. You never know when a pair of diamond earbobs might come in handy to impress a woman who's caught your fancy, monsieur."

Not wanting to offend Roudin by refusing his generosity, Drew complied. He got the impression that the shopkeeper understood what he felt for Marianne and didn't hold it against him. But Drew doubted he'd ever get the chance to see Marianne wear the earrings. If he didn't save them for Teal, he'd give them to his mother.

Standing next to Roudin, Drew skimmed his gaze over the selection. He focused on a pair clustered with black pearls and glittering diamonds, but quickly looked elsewhere. Those probably were amongst the most expensive in the store, and Drew refused to take advantage of Roudin. He pointed to a simple pair of pearls. "I'll take those."

"Non, non, non!" Roudin protested, going to the other side of the case and swinging open the door. He grabbed the ones Drew wanted and set them on the counter. "Choose your heart's desire, monsieur! Settle for nothing less."

"Only if you allow me to pay half the price—"

"You offend me, monsieur, but I understand and insist

you take these as lagniappe. I hope you are not *always* so reluctant to accept a person's kindness?"

Drew didn't respond to the remark. He'd always had the utmost trouble accepting anything that wasn't rightfully his or that he hadn't worked for. Knowing this, his father had turned Drew into a virtual beggar for his own inheritance in an attempt to bend his son to his will. Drew had squandered away the chance to remain with Marianne because he hadn't wanted to feel like a freeloader. Maybe Roudin was right, he mused now. Maybe he needed to look past his insecurities and learn to take what people offered at face value.

"Thank you, sir," he said as Roudin handed him the parcel containing the earrings, which he'd quickly and efficiently wrapped. "Have a good day."

"*Bonjour,* monsieur."

Stepping out into the balmy day again, Drew quickly headed for Rue Dumaine. It seemed he reached the street in record time. Once there, he passed a number of well-kept quadroon cottages along the way to the hitching post that he remembered stopping at in his own time. Finally he was there, standing in front of the black wrought-iron post that had changed the course of his life forever.

He stared at it, saying a silent prayer that shortly he would return to everything familiar to him. Taking the watch and chain from his pocket, he placed it around the hitching post for a moment before taking it into his hands and holding it tightly.

Closing his eyes, he recited the chant. "One summer's eve, a clock went tick-tock. Those behind were left to grieve. At that place with horses' teeth, I shall be taken to the fate I meet."

An image of Alaina pushing Teal on a tricycle, with Ursula looking on, rose in Drew's mind and vied with a picture of Marianne running through a deserted street on a foggy night. A slow buzzing started in his brain and spread into his body. He squeezed his eyes tighter and held on to the watch for dear life, grasping at the impossible, torn by the pull of the future and the lure of the past.

He repeated the chant and remained motionless, until he swayed from the intensity of his emotion, until the sound of horses' hooves intruded upon his quest.

"God, no," he said, overwhelmed with defeat as he opened his eyes and found the same scene he had minutes ago. Minutes that had seemed like an eternity.

The carriage rumbled past, and Drew leaned against the hitching post, holding his head in his hands.

The search for the watch had to commence with all due haste. Before he knew it the end of summer would be upon him, and if he hadn't returned to the twenty-first century by then, he'd be stuck here forever.

In the meantime, he'd do everything he could to put Bienvenu to rights and forget the bitter defeat he'd experienced today.

Chapter 20

MARIANNE STOOD ALONE on the downstairs veranda at Baywood.

In the early-morning hours, mist from the river just over the levee swirled about the stately oaks, acacias, and magnolia trees, a vaporous specter casting its spell across the grounds. Dew clung to the waxy leaves, green grass, and numerous flowers. Birds chirped a melodious tune as they dove into the birdbath in the garden below.

Marianne grasped the banister, thinking of Drew and the wedding plans, now in full swing, for the ceremony that would take place at the end of September. Only she was set to marry the wrong man.

A week had gone by since the ball, but she'd arrived at Baywood just yesterday, although she'd been due six days ago. She'd lingered in New Orleans, torn between her need to see Drew and her duty to wed Rafe.

She'd even contemplated taking her jewelry to a pawnshop and getting as much cash as possible. Surely she could get enough money to repay Rafe's investment in the plantation that had paid off their debts. Then she'd be free to marry whomever she wanted and still keep the family's plantation in her possession.

But then she remembered Drew's telling her that Baywood once belonged to the Montagues, *his* family, which at the moment it certainly did. Rafe had promised to return it to the Beauforts only when she married him.

Marianne knew Rafe wouldn't accept her offer. The only reason her jewels remained in her possession was because Rafe had resolved the Beauforts' debt. He would laugh in her face if she told him she now sought to buy him off with money those same jewels yielded.

Still, the plan might work if she got the money, left it and a note explaining everything to her mother, and fled. Rafe might be more inclined to take the money from Clarisse, who'd undoubtedly be distraught over Marianne's disappearance.

But where would she disappear to? Paris? That had been her plan at first, until she'd halfheartedly decided she couldn't desert her obligations. With Drew and wherever he came from? It was as she'd told him, however: She'd be going into an unknown place and forever leaving behind a family who depended upon her greatly. Besides, he'd never invited her to return to "his time" with him.

He'd only awakened her body to want and desire and wrested a foolish promise from her. How would she ever be able to keep it and seek him out at Bienvenu?

Before Drew's appearance, she'd visit Bienvenu to see Monsieur Pierre whenever the notion captured her fancy. Now, however, Rafe would be suspicious of her visits. Yet even if her true intention *was* to see Drew as much as it was to call on Pierre, she told herself, Rafe's assumptions would be terribly unfair. His father was a lonely man, and Drew's presence was merely coincidental.

Walking along the length of the veranda, she settled herself on the wicker swing. Her head was pounding. The plans Maman were making for the nuptials distressed her. The ring had been chosen, the St. Louis Cathedral secured. Several hundred invitations had been ordered, and the materials for the wedding gown were already en route from Paris.

Before meeting Drew, her desire had been to save Bay-wood. Marriage to Rafe had seemed the only means to that end. But she hadn't been aware of what a truly mean-spirited disposition he possessed. Rumors about his formidable temper had circulated for years, but he'd always shown her the utmost kindness. Lately, however, he'd become controlling, spiteful, and just plain nasty. How could she align herself with a man like that, for any reason?

If Drew didn't want her, she had a small dowry that would allow her to make a good start in Paris. If Rafe refused the money her jewelry would generate, perhaps Maman could renegotiate with him for Gen's hand in marriage.

Such wishful thinking, Marianne thought with a sigh. Rafe had made his choice quite clear. He'd chosen her.

"Mari?"

Genevieve's voice floated toward Marianne from behind as her sister gave the swing a gentle push.

"*Oui*, Gen?" Marianne answered. "Are you and Maman done eating breakfast and discussing final plans for my wedding day?" Her resentment resounded in her tone. Sliding her foot on the porch, she halted the swing's movements, then patted the space beside her. "Come and sit with me."

Genevieve joined her on the swing, her blue silk skirts spilling across Marianne's lap.

"Mari," her sister began softly. Dark brown eyes observed her as Genevieve patted her arm. "Shouldn't you be involved in your wedding plans? After all, you're the one who'll be marrying Rafe."

Marianne smiled serenely, something about the way Gen murmured Rafe's name striking a curious chord within her. Since Marianne had arrived yesterday afternoon, Genevieve's attitude appeared to seesaw between mockery and misery. Yet she doubted that misery was for her. It seemed as if the slight envy Genevieve had always felt for Marianne had turned into deep, abiding hostility. "It's only a wedding, Gen. Anybody can plan one. Besides, I trust you and Maman's proficiency to oversee everything."

Genevieve brought a hand to her breast, her accusing eyes sniping at Marianne. "I can't believe you said that," she said with a gasp. "Only a wedding! It's *your* wedding, after all."

"So I am constantly reminded."

"Oh, Mari," Genevieve said with concern, pushing stray tendrils of hair behind her ear. She searched Marianne's face. "If it distresses you so to marry Rafe, you must not. Do not sacrifice yourself for me and Maman."

Marianne hugged Genevieve and, hesitantly, her sister returned the gesture. "*Merci, cherie,* for the advice, but I will be all right. The arrangements have been made. Within weeks, I will be mistress of Bienvenu."

A sadness creeping into her features, Genevieve straightened herself. The hands that couldn't seem to remain still flattened upon her belly before she nodded and let them fall away. "*Oui,*" she said in a small voice, "you will be all right. Rafe can be won over if you are gentle with him and try to understand him just a little better."

Eyebrows arched in surprise, Marianne looked at her sister. "Were you the one marrying him, Gen, is that how you would approach it?"

Genevieve sighed elaborately. "Oh, *oui,* Mari," she said dreamily. "A woman can always bring out the best in a man, if she but applies herself."

"And you would apply yourself, of course?"

"Of course, Marianne," Genevieve snapped, staring at her as if she were a stranger. "It is a wife's duty, *mon chou.* I can see that Rafe has good qualities. He only hides them for some masculine reason. If you would stop pining over the stranger, you would see Rafe for the gentleman that he is."

Marianne bristled but saw her sister in a whole new light. Genevieve was obviously smitten with Marianne's erstwhile suitor; only someone with romantic inclinations toward Rafe would imagine he possessed such qualities. "How interesting, Genevieve. I must confess I never looked at the situation in that manner. But since you seem so knowledgeable about Rafe, why don't you wed him?"

A smile pasted on her face, Genevieve narrowed her eyes. "Because he didn't ask me," she gritted. "He only had eyes for you, *ma petite.*"

Clarisse's voice prevented Marianne from responding, but she didn't miss the emphasis Genevieve placed on the word "had."

"Well, *enfante cheries,* there you are!" Clarisse said as she walked onto the veranda and joined them by the swing. "What conspiracies are you planning?"

"No conspiracy, Maman," Genevieve said with a high-pitched laugh.

"Gen is right, Maman," Marianne agreed, seething with anger. She wasn't jealous that her sister had hinted that she and Rafe had become something to one another. She was furious that Rafe could be so boorish and hypocritical as to believe he could bed down with Genevieve and still wed her. She worried that Genevieve couldn't see Rafe for the man he truly was because she was blinded by the man she thought him to be. If in fact they had shared intimacies, didn't her sister realize that Rafe still intended to wed Marianne? That his flirtations were possibly a vengeful act upon Marianne to repay her for her attentions to Drew? She slid her gaze in Genevieve's direction. "She only gave me a little sisterly advice."

Clarisse smiled. In a swirl of black skirts, she seated herself in a wicker chair at the table. If any other good besides Baywood's remaining in their care had come out of Rafe's proposal, it was the girlish anticipation that had replaced the grief which had claimed her mother for almost a year.

"How generous of Genevieve," Clarisse said. "Now, you must decide where you want to hold the wedding, here or at Bienvenu."

"Oh!" Marianne said. Before this moment, she hadn't known she had a choice. Nor had she cared. Saving Baywood for Maman and Gen had been her only priority, but now . . .

"Mari, have it at Bienvenu," Genevieve said sweetly.

Clarisse glowered at Genevieve.

A flush staining her cheeks, Genevieve bowed her head and shifted in her seat. "Um . . . I-I mean Monsieur Rafe would be very appreciative of such a gesture. He might even reward you with a beautiful bauble."

"Why, Genevieve!" Clarisse said, traces of annoyance tightening her face, her tone one of grudging agreement. "How wonderfully . . . *devious* you are, *ma cherie*. I am proud of you. You will make some man a wonderful wife."

Marianne laughed at the irony of it all. "I have no doubt that she will, Maman," she said, wishing, as much as she believed Genevieve did, that Rafe might be that man. "As for the wedding, Bienvenu it will be. I think Gen is right: It might take away some of the edge in Rafe's disposition."

Not to mention provide the excuse she needed to visit Bienvenu in order to see Drew without Rafe's suspicions being aroused.

She'd leave for Bienvenu immediately. The servants there needed to be instructed in the preparations for the nuptials, although she would see to it that it was Genevieve's. And since she planned to stay, she'd bring her trunk.

"Maman, Gen, would you help me pack? Perhaps if things settle down here, you can join me in a week or two," she said, springing from her seat. "I can't wait to get to Bienvenu to inform Rafe of my plans. Won't he be surprised?"

Suddenly she didn't feel so weighted down. She insisted to herself it wasn't because she'd see Drew again as much as it was that she'd be keeping her promise to him. She didn't like to break promises—although once she found a way out of her present dilemma, she intended to break her promise of marriage in a flash. It might be as simple as reaching Rafe's heart and directing its attention to Genevieve.

Once, long ago, she and Rafe had shared a camaraderie. If she presented him with high spirits instead of indifference, he might take her into his confidence and confess any indiscretions he'd engaged in with Genevieve. Then she could bow out of the betrothal gracefully and pave the way for Genevieve's marriage to him.

In the meantime, with her attentions so obviously focused on him, Rafe would never suspect any rendezvous with Drew.

It was a sound plan, but one that might be hard to execute with the inimitably unpredictable Rafe involved.

Chapter 21

IN THE EARLY dawn, the sun appeared over the horizon, casting its light across the vast fields in brilliant shades of red and gold against the black earth. The pungent smell of the soil awakened Drew's senses, made him feel a kinship with the land. It gave him a sense of purpose, of being. It also gave him a better understanding of what drove his father and older brothers in their love for Bienvenu.

Having risen before sunup, Drew worked alongside the dozens of servants, helping to clear the fields for replanting. Although slaves populated Bienvenu, Drew refused to label them as such in his mind. The fact that they would gain their freedom in about ten years with Lincoln's Emancipation Proclamation was small consolation. In his time, good men tried desperately to rectify such follies . . . while trying desperately to forget it had ever happened.

In the past two weeks, he'd been working furiously, knowing the time for the spring planting was drawing to a close. That's what he told himself. Actually his energy came from worry and anxiety. He needed to see Marianne, but didn't expect her any longer, since a full fortnight had passed already without a sign of her.

She'd probably agreed to come to Bienvenu to see him

out of fear. What a stupid jerk he'd been to threaten to kiss her in front of Rafe. She was probably so angry with him she wouldn't consider seeing him alone, even if she did come to the plantation.

Not that he would know if she had. She might very well have come and declined to see him. For two weeks he'd worked like a man possessed, wanting to forget his disastrous attempt to return to his daughter and his fever-pitch desire for Marianne. He hadn't even been to the manor house to visit Pierre, partaking of his meals in his sitting room after Eve brought them to him.

He plunged the shovel deeper into the dirt and came up with a pile of soil, which he turned over before starting the process over again. His muscles had never had such an intense workout. No gym in the world compared with arduous labor day in and day out.

"Masta Drew, I s'pose we can start the plantin' 'bout next week," a big servant named Nat said, stopping to mop his brow.

The sun was barely out yet, but the work quickly generated sweat, despite the river breezes from the nearby Mississippi blowing over the fields.

Drew had taken quite a liking to the man and was always telling Nat *not* to call him "master." *"Mister,"* he repeated for the umpteenth time. It was an unfortunate fact of life that Nat had to put some title before his name. "And you're right. I suppose we can start the planting then. The sooner the better. We'll work here for another two hours, then take a break."

"Yessuh," Nat responded. "We have one last east field left. Maybe we can turn the soil there when we commence the plantin'."

"Good idea," Drew said. "It'll save time." He slapped Nat on the back. "It's a big job, my friend, but we'll turn this place around."

Nat grinned a toothy grin. "Yessuh, we sho' will."

Drew didn't feel half as confident as he sounded. Pierre had allowed Rafe to bring Bienvenu to near ruin, and it would take not only hard work to save it, but a hefty bank loan as well. He hoped the Montague word would be good enough to secure a loan, but he had a feeling the family's credit was less than perfect.

Still, he hoped that the word of a Montague was good enough to get what he needed. The family still held sway and prominence, and undoubtedly that would account for something. Besides, for all Rafe's irresponsibilities, he kept secret the family's financial instability.

Now it was up to Drew to put to rights Rafe's damage. Rafe had allowed four thousand acres, a third of the fields, to lie fallow, while setting every able-bodied man and woman to work on the rest of the lands. Pierre ordered Rafe to work with Drew and not against him, and with that in mind, Drew helped in the east and west fields while Rafe oversaw the south and north. He suspected that the reason Pierre made Rafe work was not only to have him fulfill his duty as a Montague, but to keep him from keeling over in a jealous rage because Drew was taking over.

But all their efforts were hardly enough. They needed cash for seed and more modern equipment, and Drew would do everything possible to see that they got it.

More than six hours later, nearing the noon hour, three servants from the manor brought baskets laden with food to Drew. He'd chosen five foremen to oversee the other workers as they cleared and planted his fields. While there wasn't a lot he could do about providing decent food to the forty or so workers in the fields, he saw to it that Nat and the other four foremen ate what he ate. It lessened his feelings of helplessness toward them. But such were the strictures of the time. He couldn't fix them.

"Thank you, ladies," he said, wearily throwing down the shovel. He wiped his blistered hands on his pants. "Just set everything on the ground. This couldn't be more welcome." He'd had a light breakfast of grits and sausage, but after being active for nearly seven hours, he was famished.

He settled on the ground where he was, his mouth watering and his stomach grumbling in response to the tasty aromas filtering through the baskets. In the middle of the fields there was no shade to be found. Although there were shade trees a few hundred feet away, he was just too tired to walk the distance. This spot would do just fine.

Drew instructed his foremen to tell their workers to take off a couple of hours to eat and rest. Then Nat and the other foremen joined Drew in a lunch of mustard greens, corn bread, fried chicken, and apple pie.

When lunch ended, he stretched out on the soil, which was still cool and somewhat damp from the irrigation of the day before, despite the heat of the sun. Closing his eyes, he shielded his face from the glare with his hat.

A few lazy minutes passed before the pounding of horse's hooves caused a slight tremble on the ground where he lay and disturbed this rare moment of serenity.

"Well, well, I see you've found your calling, Cousin," Rafe sneered.

Cursing roundly, Drew removed his hat from his face and sat up. Astride his beautiful, showy palomino, Rafe smirked down at Drew.

Grinning nastily, Drew narrowed his eyes. He really wasn't in the mood for Rafe's vicious sarcasm. "Why, Cousin, whatever do you mean?"

Rafe's horse pranced restlessly. With skill and a gentleness that surprised Drew, he quieted the big animal down. "Just that you're wallowing in the dirt with the rest of the pigs," he said, nodding toward Nat and the other men.

Jumping to his feet, Drew lunged, but Rafe urged his horse on, just out of his grasp. "You son-of-a-bitch!" Drew snarled. "Get off that goddamn horse, and I'll show you what a pig can do!"

Rafe shook his head in mock severity. "Tsk, tsk, Cousin. My father thinks you're a saint. He might change his opinion of you if he knew you wanted to brawl. Besides, I'm only here to deliver his message. He said he hasn't seen you in days and wants you to have dinner with him tonight." Anxious to get going, the high-spirited horse began dancing around again. Rafe's gauntleted hands tightened on the reins. "I won't be dining with you, Cousin. My tastes are a little more discriminating than my father's."

Drew watched in helpless rage as Rafe galloped away on the path along the fields. He hadn't planned to see Pierre today, but a visit was past due. At least he knew he wouldn't have to suffer an evening of watching Marianne and Rafe together.

He had no right to feel the way he did about her or to interfere with her life. They were from different worlds. *Vastly* different. It wasn't as if she was from Timbuktu and he from a small town in Arkansas. It wasn't a matter of catching a plane to bridge the miles between them. Their worlds could only be bridged by time.

Working the kinks from his muscles, Drew stretched.

"Masta—," Nat began.

Annoyed at Rafe's visit and the turn his thoughts had taken, Drew glared at Nat. "I'm *not* your master," he growled impatiently. " 'Mister' will do just fine, Nat. How many times do I have to tell you that?"

Nat bowed his head. "Yessuh."

Drew inhaled sharply, guilt slapping him. He hadn't meant to sound so harsh. Nat was a good man and just acting as he'd been taught to act; it was Drew who couldn't adjust to *his* world. "Look," he said, calmer. "I'm sorry. There's not much left to be done. Why don't we just call it a day. We can start out before sunup again tomorrow."

"There's lots left to do, *Mista* Andrew," Nat said. "We's all appreciating your kindness, suh. But we can't stop workin' 'til sundown."

Hands at his side, Drew regarded his crew, his gaze sweeping the perimeter of the land and the other field hands, who had ignored his order to rest and already returned to work. He shoved a hand through his hair. "I know," he said softly.

"We knows what to do, Mista Andrew," Nat continued. "Masta Pierre's expectin' you—"

"Thanks, Nat, but I guess I can work a while longer, too," he said, and picked up his shovel again.

Chapter 22

LONG AFTER DARK, Drew left his quarters and started out for the manor down the gravel road, perfumed with night-blooming flowers. In the distance, the big house rose against the star-studded, indigo sky in austerity, gray and imposing, beneath the full white moon. Its light softened the rough edges of Bienvenu. Huge, Ionic columns framed the mansion on three sides and supported the double verandas.

Traces of the untamed, raw beauty of Bienvenu that he saw now had filtered down through the ages. Still, nothing could compare with the nineteenth-century paradise, unfettered by the ravages of time and pollution. He had absolutely hated Bienvenu in his own time, and he understood better why in this time. The work was extremely arduous, but it wasn't the kind of challenge Drew thrived on. These past weeks had proved he could do the work, but he preferred the law profession. He preferred using his brain to discover a shred of evidence that would help him prosecute a criminal over looking for ways to secure a bank loan for the plantation. Yet, despite everything, Bienvenu had earned his everlasting respect, and he realized it was the heart and soul of his family's livelihood and existence.

Like the servants, he'd worked 'til the last rays of sunlight faded. Returning to the *garçonnière*, he was exhausted, and all he'd wanted to do was collapse in bed. Even the warm bath hadn't helped. To the contrary, it only served to make him more tired.

But he'd been neglecting the old man. As much as he wanted to put it off, he owed Pierre a visit. Besides ordering Rafe to assist in the work, the old man had left Drew to his own devices these past days. For that, Drew was grateful. If he was going to help, then it had to be done his way.

His troubling thoughts gave him no peace. Would Pierre be sotted again? Would he have to deal with Rafe and still keep his cool to keep the old man happy? He'd never done much to keep his father happy. Why should it matter whether or not Pierre was appeased?

Having no answers to his disturbing questions, Drew remembered Rafe saying he wouldn't be there. If only Marianne would be. But then, he realized he'd have to suffer Rafe's presence as well. Surely his dear "cousin" wouldn't allow Mari out of his sight with Drew around.

The time grew ever nearer to her wedding. From all indications, it was truly going to take place. What in the hell would prevent it? Nothing short of death, it seemed. The decidedly morbid thought refused to go away, even after Tomas explained that Marianne had already had Yellow Fever. Drew knew that there were many other things that could cause her demise.

God, please don't let it be that she didn't marry Rafe because of her death. Swallowing convulsively, Drew nearly choked on the thought of Marianne dying.

Reaching the manor, he determined to push the morbid thought aside as he walked up the steps. He stopped on the wide veranda to restore his composure, then turned and gazed out over his surroundings, taking in the horizon. No slaves headed for the fields on the levee that snaked its way along the curving road just beyond the gates of the plantation. The colorful flora in the gardens just below the veranda filled the brisk air with an even sweeter fragrance than had the flowers along the way. The whirring of cicadas, the chirping of the crickets, and singing of the night birds filled him with an odd peace.

Bienvenu *was* quite beautiful. *His* family's land. A pride in his heritage that he'd never felt before surfaced in him. Once he returned to the twenty-first century, he'd do what Cranneck asked without objection and go spend the year at the Bienvenu of his time. And he'd look—*really* look—at Bienvenu. The way he was doing tonight. When he finished law school, he'd be a better man for his experiences at the plantation.

He walked to the banister and leaned on it, then rubbed his tired eyes. The Bienvenu of his time was "new and improved." The wild beauty that he'd noticed on the road had long ago disappeared; modern buildings that housed equipment to turn raw cane into sugar had supplanted it. Then there were the big trucks that hauled the cane to the buildings after it had been cut by the machinery. Because of the need for more pathways for the vehicles, roads had replaced a lot of the gardens.

Whatever his reasons for being in the nineteenth century, he felt damn lucky to be able to witness the things he had. No other man from his time ever had.

Glancing over the land a few moments longer, he finally went to the door. Just as he lifted the knocker, the door opened suddenly.

Almost plowing into Drew as he started forward, Simon smiled in surprise. "Mista Andrew, suh. I was jus' on my way to fetch you. Masta Pierre say he gettin' hungry."

"Well, looks like I just saved you a trip, Simon," Drew said, stepping into the foyer.

Simon closed the door. "You sho'ly did, suh. They's in the parla."

"They?" Drew echoed, looking down the deserted hallway. "Is Rafe with my uncle?" He knew his evening was ruined. He'd thought Rafe sincere about not wanting to dine with him, but it was just like that jerk to give him false hope.

"Yessuh, he's in there."

"So what else is new?" Without waiting for a reply, he went the remaining distance to the parlor, cursing Rafe with vicious epithets. Wondering how he'd ever make it through the evening, he started through the open door but stopped in his tracks, waves of shock crashing down on him.

There she was! Marianne. Sitting next to Rafe on the settee.

He released a noisy breath, unable to do anything other than stare at her. Her gown was the most beautiful shade of turquoise or aquamarine he'd ever seen; since he'd never paid that much attention to those colors, he couldn't tell which it was, but the shade did wonders for her beautiful jade eyes, giving them a vivid intensity that burned into his very being. Her jet black hair, fixed in the usual style, and smooth, creamy complexion enhanced her exquisite features.

Drew's gaze traveled lower, to the rounded breasts molded against the watered silk and the tiny waist he could easily span with both hands, to . . . the delicate hand entwined with Rafe's larger one.

He felt sick as he met Rafe's mocking gleam. Glancing back to Marianne's face, Drew saw that she looked happy! They both did. God! How would he ever be able to get through this evening? He hadn't known Rafe possessed any expression except hateful. But the bastard had the nerve to look happy and contented.

Hell, and why shouldn't he? He was engaged to one of the great beauties of the era.

"Andrew!" Pierre rose from his seat in the wingback chair near the empty tea cart. "Come in, son. We thought you'd forgotten about us."

"Me? Forget? Never!" Drew said with as much levity as he could manage. He walked into the room and took a seat in the chair across from Rafe and Marianne. He took in Pierre's well-groomed appearance, the clear, observant eyes, the complexion ruddied from sunlight instead of mottled with excessive drink, and blinked. The man was as sober as a judge! What was going on? He hoped no one noticed his surprise. Certainly Marianne and Rafe wouldn't—they were too engrossed in each other to notice anything. "Well, good evening, everyone." Nodding his head, he gave Marianne and Rafe a passing glance. "Thanks for thinking of me, Uncle Pierre."

Pierre smiled. "As I said, you're family, son. And you need to know that."

Resting an ankle on his knee, Drew inclined his head, then looked at Marianne, unable to ignore her any longer. "It's good to see you again, Marianne."

The hand Rafe wasn't holding fluttered across a hanging curl. Ever so slightly, she moved closer to Rafe. "*Merci*, monsieur," she replied, her voice sounding more husky and sexy than Drew remembered.

It took every effort for Drew to remain calm. To underscore his casual nonchalance, he brought his hands behind his head and sprawled his long legs carelessly before him. "Did you arrive tonight?" he asked, knowing full well she must have. She was the only thing that would have changed Rafe's mind about dining with him. It might have been just like the jerk to toy with Drew about certain things, but Drew realized it wasn't pretense when Rafe said he didn't wish to dine with him, unless there was a very good reason. And what better reason than Marianne?

"Tonight?" Pierre boomed. "Hell no, Andrew! Marianne's been here a full week already. She came to set in motion the preparations for her wedding."

Pierre's words struck Drew like a lightning bolt, and he drilled her with a brutal and unfriendly stare. Marianne had been there a week, and he hadn't known about it?

A muscle ticking in Drew's jaw, it pleased him to see the flush spreading across Marianne's face and the slight trembling of her lips. Straightening in his seat, he folded his arms. "Well, Marianne, had I known you were here I would have stopped by to say hello. And congratulations," he added coolly.

"You needn't have bothered yourself, Cousin," Rafe put

in, preventing any reply from Marianne. "Knowing how busy the help is, Marianne understands fully."

Drew chuckled nastily. "I'll bet she does."

Clearing her throat, Marianne pulled her hand free of Rafe's hold. "Everyone knows how important it is to get planting done, monsieur."

Wide, misty eyes seemed to beg for understanding, but he must have been mistaken. She was too giddy with wedding plans to give a rat's ass about the relative whom Rafe relegated to mere "help."

Disappointment rode him hard. Yet to say he was merely disappointed would have been an understatement. He was furious and hurt as well. Even if she hadn't chosen him, he'd sworn she'd shared his feelings. But maybe that was all in the realm of his wishful thinking. Maybe the kisses they shared had never happened the way he thought they did.

No, she hadn't responded with the conflagrant passion he thought she had. She hadn't set his very soul on fire with her scintillating touch. *All* of that had been sheer imagination. It had to have been. This woman appeared entirely different from the one he'd held in his arms.

He got up from his seat and forced a cordial grin. "At the risk of appearing ill-mannered and impolite, Uncle Pierre, when's dinner? I'm starved." He wanted the evening over and done with.

Rising to his feet, Pierre laughed. "I thought you'd never ask, Andrew. I'm hungry, too! Eve!"

A minute passed before the girl appeared in the doorway. "Yes, Master Pierre?"

"We're coming in to dinner now, so you and Hortenzia can commence serving," Pierre instructed, then reached for Marianne's hand.

She stood and placed her hand in his.

"Rafe's my son, *cherie,* but frankly I don't see what attraction he has for you," Pierre continued in a teasing manner, shifting positions so Marianne could walk by his side.

"Father," Rafe began with a short laugh, stepping to Marianne's side to place her in between him and Pierre, "perhaps you're at an age when you're beyond passion and have forgotten the reasons people are attracted to one another." He pulled Marianne's arm through the crook of his own. "Isn't that right, sweetheart?" he said, after throwing a smug glance over his shoulder to Drew.

Marianne chuckled nervously. "I do not believe I am qualified to answer a question about anyone's passion, monsieur. Least of all your father's."

"*Touché, ma cherie,*" Pierre said with another hearty laugh. "That scalawag betrothed of yours will never in his life know the passion I felt in my youth. Or will again if the right woman is ever presented to me."

Drew heard a genuine laugh from Rafe for the first time since he'd met him.

"Father, you're incorrigible," he said.

Dinner was a long, tedious affair that consisted of braised rabbit with pearl onions, caramelized carrots, boiled potatoes seasoned with fennel, and blueberry tartlets with heavy cream. While the food was delicious, Drew endured veiled taunts from Rafe throughout the evening as Pierre and Marianne hung on to the man's every word and laughed at his attempts at humor. The change in Rafe was nothing short of miraculous, but unfortunately that change hadn't affected his feelings for Drew. Rafe's amiability toward him, such as it was, was clearly all for show.

Drew told himself he was glad to see Marianne so happy. But he felt as if a knife had been driven into his heart. When they finally retired to Pierre's office for coffee, he decided to end his torture and excuse himself, pleading exhaustion.

As a matter of habit, Rafe and Pierre stood and shook his hand. He chanced a glance at Marianne as she remained regally seated, and she smiled at him, her look intimate, just for him.

A stunning realization hit him and, on its heels, so did the hot desire his disappointment and anger had tempered all evening. Like Rafe's, *her* display toward him had been all for show.

But walking along the path to his quarters, a question surfaced.

Was the show from Marianne for him, Rafe, or Pierre?

Chapter 23

LEANING AGAINST THE fireplace mantel, Rafe contentedly watched Marianne for the ten minutes that followed Andrew's departure.

"Contented" had never been a word Rafe associated with himself, yet the foreign feeling was undeniable. But it did nothing to decrease his hatred of his cousin. He threatened Rafe's relationships with both his father and Marianne. He'd never been as aware of that fact as he was tonight.

For the entire week that Marianne had been there, Rafe had led an absolutely blissful existence with her. She was everything she'd been upon their initial acquaintance—charming, demure, humorous—and for once most of her attention had been directed toward *him*. She hadn't even asked about Andrew, but then she'd *seen* him, and suddenly every wistful desire she'd apparently worked so hard to hide showed in her exquisite features.

Then it hit him: the realization that as much as he preferred not to care about her, he did. He wanted her to pine for him as she now pined for his cousin. Rafe wanted her to *want* to marry him. But he wasn't a fool. It would never happen.

The completely out-of-character thought went against his

grain, and he knew he must counteract his feelings in some way. His only consolation was that she *would* become his wife. She would bear his sons and daughters.

She would share *his* bed, not dear Andrew's. He smirked at the thought, just as Marianne released a deep sigh.

"I fear I am overcome with exhaustion, messieurs," she said as she stood. "You must excuse me for the rest of the evening."

Pierre came to his feet immediately. "Of course, my dear. You had a long day, and from what I gather tomorrow will be as hectic."

She curtsied, the perfect lady, prim and proper and delicate. "*Merci* for understanding." Her jade gaze fastened onto Rafe, and his heartbeat quickened. "Forgive me for bowing out of our walk?"

"Always, mademoiselle." By sheer willpower, he refrained from offering to escort her to her bedchamber. She wasn't that distant, untouchable creature she'd turned into just after Andrew's arrival several weeks ago. If he escorted her he was afraid he'd forget his honor and seduce her tonight because of the enticing woman she'd turned into for him. "Tomorrow, perhaps?"

"*Oui,* monsieur."

Rafe watched her retreating back, his hatred for his cousin increasing tenfold. Andrew tempted Marianne at every turn. As an inexperienced young lady of good breeding, she couldn't help but be fascinated by the cad's flirtations. But this week had proven her loyalty, if not her devotion, to *him,* and he wouldn't let anyone come between them, especially Andrew Montague.

With a sigh, he went to the liquor table and poured himself a brandy. "Father, would you care to join me?"

"No," Pierre answered. "Thank you anyway, Rafe."

He gritted his teeth at his father's clipped tones. He couldn't exactly blame Andrew for Pierre's attitude, but the rift between them had widened since the appearance of his cousin. Admittedly, at times he'd viewed his father as a hindrance to his attaining all of the Montague wealth, as well as a drunk and a foolish old man, but he was beginning to realize he had other, more positive feelings toward him as well. Rafe had only realized that because of the way his father looked up to Andrew; instances of his childhood had slowly surfaced in his mind, times when he'd admired Pierre for the man he had been. And in many ways still was.

Now, however, his father wasn't giving him the chance to redeem himself and his bad investments. He was relying on Andrew. Rafe had diverted their money only in order to increase the Montague fortune. His initial reasons might have been somewhat self-serving, but not entirely. Neither was Pierre ever inviting him to enjoy a drink with him as he once had. He now preferred Andrew's company.

Something *had* to be done about that man!

Rafe finished off his brandy and set the empty glass back on the liquor table. "I think I'll retire myself, Father," he said quietly, at loose ends, secretly wishing Pierre would invite him to stay.

"As you wish, boy."

"Well . . . uh, I'll see you at breakfast."

With a last nod to his father, Rafe strode out of the room, vowing that Andrew's days to live were definitely numbered.

Bright moonlight illuminated Marianne's darkened bedchamber. Lying on the beautifully appointed bed, surrounded by mosquito netting, she stared at the ceiling, her thoughts centered on Drew.

What a magnificent specimen she'd thought him tonight! And what an angry one upon discovering the length of time she'd been in residence without having once sought him out. In essence, she'd reneged on the promise she'd so desperately wanted to keep.

Of course, she hadn't meant for things to turn out that way. She'd hoped to see Drew on the first night of her arrival, but then as now, Rafe had made it impossible to escape his presence. Since Drew wasn't coming to the house, she hadn't been able to see him before tonight.

If only she could have seen him privately. Yet it seemed that such a happenstance would never occur. Her plan to gentle Rafe was working, but not in the way she'd expected. He seemed even that much more inclined to *her*. Not once had he mentioned Genevieve, which meant Marianne couldn't attempt any matchmaking between them. Just because Genevieve insinuated tender feelings toward Rafe didn't mean he returned them. Perhaps by applying herself to gentling Rafe she had succeeded in bringing out the best in him, just as Genevieve had suggested. But doing so had taken all of Marianne's energies, and she had yet to truly understand him. Because it didn't matter how kind and loving he was toward her; Rafe wasn't the man whom Marianne wanted to marry. She still hadn't fallen in love with him.

Turning onto her stomach, Marianne sighed. Perhaps, short of leaving, there was no escaping her upcoming nuptials. The time-consuming tasks that filled her days certainly suggested so.

When she'd arrived, Pierre had been more than happy to hear the reason, and had immediately insisted she set into motion the running of the house as if she were already mistress of it. Besides actually planning her wedding, she was now in charge of the vast household, which was the only thing she didn't object to, because she enjoyed having tasks to occupy her mind.

Yet everything still felt so wrong. She had no one, absolutely no one, to confide in. Clarisse would take with the vapors if Marianne mentioned she didn't want to marry Rafe. Genevieve would probably end up hurt anyway because she'd know Rafe had been hell-bent on wedding Marianne. Monsieur Pierre would be hurt that she'd spurned the family and disappointed in her breeding. Rafe would be furious.

And Drew? Drew would take her into his arms and kiss her with all the abandon she dreamed of.

Marianne sat up, the gauzy netting fluttering with her

movement. Her heart had begun to pound. Drawing her knees to her chest, she closed her eyes and rested her head on them.

Drew's image as he'd looked framed within the doorway on first sight of her this evening floated through her mind. He'd been the very embodiment of masculine sexuality. His golden hair, longer now than when she'd first met him, had flirted with the nape of his neck. Dark blue eyes had admired, devoured, promised. The straight lines of his tailored clothing had hung upon his long, muscular body with devastating exactness, shamelessly showing the perfection of his limbs.

But the moment of awareness had been ruined with his perception of her and Rafe's show of happiness.

How could she have been so foolish? The entire evening she'd pretended to ignore Drew for his and her benefit, thinking maybe Rafe would grow tedious of Drew's presence and excuse himself, leaving her, Drew, and Pierre to their own devices. Instead, Drew had tired of Rafe's insults and left.

Suddenly she had to see him. Bounding off the bed, her hair spilling about her back and shoulders, she grabbed the matching wrapper to her nightgown and hurriedly donned it. As quietly as possible, she opened the door and stepped into the dark, deserted hallway.

After reaching the *garçonnière*, Drew shed his clothes and stretched out on the bed in the small bedroom. Angry with Marianne, he was disgusted with himself for being so. Marianne belonged to Rafe, and he, Drew, didn't belong anywhere.

That had been quite evident tonight at dinner. Although Pierre acknowledged him most of the evening, there were periods when he was indeed treated like the help. Rafe had deliberately steered conversation toward things about which Drew knew nothing: the state of the city's politics, Rafe's mother's sister, some planter whose wife's brother married a woman of questionable repute.

Drew really didn't give a mosquito's balls about any of those things, but Marianne had seemed to. She was very familiar with politics and gossip, and that galled Drew. Even with an apparently prudish turd like Rafe, she was able to hold her own.

Well, Drew decided, Rafe couldn't be that prudish if he'd broached the subject of a suspected whore in Marianne's presence. But Drew thought that was a point directed at him, since Rafe had looked directly at him while belittling the merits of unvirtuous, traitorous women.

At the moment, he felt like a fool and understood fully what Rafe had been implying. He'd thought he and Marianne had something between them. But she'd proven him wrong.

Yes, he wanted to make love to her, but he wanted her friendship more. At the very least, she could have sent one of the servants to let him know she was at the mansion. It hurt him deeply to discover she thought so little of their friendship.

The open window in his room allowed the full light of the moon to illuminate it and the outside surroundings, casting wraithlike shadows from the trees. Below his bedroom, muffled steps in the small garden sounded loud in the stillness of the night. He might have been uneasy over their hesitancy, thinking it was Rafe coming to murder him, but such sounds weren't unusual.

When he'd first heard the footsteps, he'd gotten up to see where they originated and had seen house servants making their way in the dead of night from the mansion toward the cabins, probably for a romantic tryst or merely to visit a forbidden friend.

Drew didn't care, and was too tired and annoyed to lift his head for a second look. He wondered whether Pierre approved of such rendezvous. Perhaps he didn't, forcing the servants to skulk about under cover of darkness. Well, they certainly deserved some of life's pleasures.

He sighed deeply. It would be a miracle if he slept tonight. He suddenly wished he could pick up a telephone and call Teal to hear her little voice.

Knowing that he couldn't, he felt like crying, weeping with all the self-pity, loneliness, and anger in him. He'd never before felt so down and defeated. He'd begun to doubt he'd ever see his precious daughter again. But he knew he couldn't give up. He'd just have to find another watch and make another attempt.

If only he had someone to talk to. Marianne knew about him. If things were different, he could have talked to her about how he was feeling, but it seemed he'd lost her.

A door opened and closed.

Halting his thinking, Drew sat up and listened. When he didn't hear anything else right away, he frowned, sure he'd heard something downstairs. His gaze searched for a weapon, but after a few minutes of silence, he lay back down. Perhaps it had only been his imagination.

A soft sigh alerted him that it wasn't.

"Andrew?"

Marianne's whisper drifted to him from the stairway that led directly to the bedroom from the sitting room.

"Marianne!" Drew jumped out of bed, stunned to see her standing there in nothing but her nightclothes. Realizing his state of undress when his body began to respond to *her* state of undress and the soft perfume floating toward him, he pulled the top sheet off the bed and covered himself. "My God! What are you doing here?" he managed to get out.

"Andrew," Marianne began softly, walking to him like a goddess out of the pages of history, "forgive me."

Jet black hair curtained the white lace-and-cotton wrapper she wore. Her features were pale and inviting in the darkness of the room. Blood rushed through his veins, engorged his manhood, made him feel giddy.

"Forgive you?" he asked in confusion, the urge to possess her sending rushes of desire through his body. "I beg your pardon?"

Huge, vulnerable eyes nearly divested him of all reasonable thought. She glided to the only chair in the room.

"May I sit down, Drew?"

Drew swallowed, hard. "Of . . . of course you may," he said, anxious to hear why she was there, why she'd asked for forgiveness.

"I didn't mean to hurt you this evening, monsieur," she began in a soft, husky voice.

Without answering, Drew quietly lit a small gaslamp, hoping to restore some sanity to himself. The dark chamber invoked too many thoughts of passion, too much hot need. Returning to the bed, he sat on the edge and stared at Marianne, waiting for her to continue.

Marianne twirled her hands in her lap and chewed on her soft lower lip. She shifted in her chair.

"Tell me about it, sweetheart," Drew urged when the silence continued.

"It's true. I did arrive a week ago. I came to start preparations for my wedding in September." She bowed her head and twirled the ribbon at her neck. "At least that's what I told Rafe, Monsieur Pierre, and my family," she added so softly Drew had to strain to hear her.

"I don't understand," Drew said, his heart pounding, thinking that he did.

"I needed an excuse to keep the promise I made to you, Andrew," Marianne continued, "and the reasons I stated to Rafe had to be believable. I gave him no reason to accuse you, or me for that matter, of improprieties."

Relieved that he'd guessed correctly, Drew chuckled softly, ignoring the need of his body. Holding the sheet loosely about his lower half, he went to her. "Not even now?"

Not answering and avoiding his eyes, Marianne looked down at her hands, nervously entwined in her lap.

Drew reached for her hand and tugged gently. She rose from her chair. He caressed the smoothness of her cheek. "What a wonderful actress you are, darling."

Marianne's teary gaze found his. "What must you think of me?"

"You'll never know how wonderful I think you are," he said, pulling her close with his free hand, "and how you've disproved everything I've ever read about nineteenth-century women. You are as liberated as any woman I've ever known in the twenty-first century." He kissed her nose. "And just as daring."

Marianne slipped her arms around his neck, then grazed her lips across his chin. Because of the closeness of her body and the thinness of the materials covering their nudity, Drew knew she felt his hardness. Unable to stop himself, he bent and tasted the lips she'd teased his chin with.

"I couldn't bear to see the look of hurt in your eyes, Drew," she said between his kisses, not protesting as he wrapped his arms about her in a crushing embrace, lifting her off the ground in the process. Unashamed, she nibbled at his tongue. "I had to come here and tell you so."

His tongue played with hers, tasted, tested, mated. She sighed at his invasion, melting against him. The sweetness of her mouth made him crazy with desire. She clung to him, dew to a rose petal, arousing his most erotic fantasies.

"I thought you wanted nothing more to do with me," he said, trailing his mouth along her chin, her cheeks, her eyelids, her wealth of dark hair a lover's mantle falling about them.

Delicate fingertips rose between them and settled upon his cheeks. With one last kiss, she pushed away. "Perhaps I'd better start back, monsieur."

His heart was pounding, and his head was spinning. He needed to make love to her with a desperation he'd never before known. Yet Marianne seemed to have come only to tease and entice, then flee him again.

Drew ran a finger over her cheek and was rewarded with her deep intake of breath. "I was thinking about you, Marianne, before you came," he said hoarsely, his manhood throbbing, his need painful. "I know nothing of you. What I do know is that you've consented to marry a man you obviously don't love. Yet weeks ago you readily came to my aid. And tonight you've put yourself at risk for my sake."

Marianne scooted away from him and out of reach of his touch. An angry flush spread across her face, and her breasts heaved in outrage. "You offend me, monsieur," she bit out. "You have no right to question me with such impertinence."

Regretting the loss of her nearness, Drew went back to the bed and sat. "If I am wrong I apologize, Mari. But if you're offended by my observations, that means your engagement is more complicated than you want me to believe."

The mouth that had so sweetly allowed Drew's onslaught dropped open, then snapped shut. Her flush deepened. Her reaction suggested to Drew that he'd hit closer to home than she cared to admit. It didn't matter. He had to impress upon her that marrying for any reason other than love was never a wise decision. Even if the history books related that she wouldn't be the one to marry Rafe after all.

"How can you be so presumptuous, Andrew? It is as you say: You know nothing of me!"

"You're right," Drew agreed mildly as he closed the space between them. He damned the desire that this conversation was leaving unfulfilled. "So enlighten me: Why did you decide to help me?"

Marianne walked away from him, then gazed out the window and into the starry night. "Because no one else would," she said quietly, her back to him. "And because you desperately needed help."

"Even at the risk of your apparently tenuous engagement?" Drew snapped, determined to remain where he was.

Spinning about, she met his eyes, a scowl spreading across her face. He hadn't meant to sound so belligerent, but he could hardly control his rising anger. Or his desire for her. There she stood, beautiful, mysterious, desirable, and unattainable. The hair that she kept styled after the fashion of the day had been brushed out, the tips reaching midway down her back. The perfection of her body teased and tempted.

That she'd helped him because no one else would was plausible, but Drew didn't believe that had been her only reason. She intrigued him, but she obviously wasn't going to explain herself to him any more than she already had.

"Tenuous or not, Andrew, my betrothal and my other personal affairs are none of your concern," she said resentfully, her chin raised, her slim body rigid.

"I've angered you," he said, truly fascinated. He'd never seen her in this state.

"*Oui,* monsieur!" she said, all but stomping her foot. "You've managed to turn a simple act of charity into a complicated conspiracy."

Drew arched his eyebrow. "Conspiracy?" he echoed, unclear about her meaning.

Folding her arms, she nodded curtly. "A conspiracy," she reiterated, her voice cracking with her effort to conceal her inner turmoil. "You are implying that in the course of assisting you, I also plotted to cover up my true relationship with Rafe. I think it's terribly unfair of you."

Ashamed of himself, Drew took her hand into his own. She sniffled, holding back her tears, but didn't pull away. "Then I'll try to be fair, Mari. I promise I won't ask you anything more about Rafe if you answer one more question for me."

Marianne hesitated a moment before nodding. "Very well," she finally answered, her anger expended. "What is it?"

Drew leaned closer to her ear, the scent of her maddening. "Have you fallen as helplessly in love with me as I have with you?"

"Oh!" Marianne gasped, and attempted to pull away from him.

He held her quick, and the tears she'd fought so hard to keep at bay betrayed her, glistening like tiny diamonds on her cheeks in the moonlight.

Sacre bleu! she thought. Drew would know her tears

were falling for a reason, yet she dared not tell him why.
Dared not tell him she was marrying for wealth. He'd already figured out that she didn't love Rafe.

"Mari?"

The sound of his concern made her tears fall harder, but
she could no more deny him an answer than she could deny
herself this time with him. "What if I did love you, monsieur? Then you would think me no more than a . . . a har-
lot!"

He drew her closer to him, and his hard length pressed
into her belly.

"Don't cry, darling. I already know the answer to my
question."

He kissed her then, deeply and stirringly. Marianne's
arms automatically went around his neck. His warm, moist
tongue wreaked havoc with her senses, and her body, sending spirals of want curling through her, making wet heat
pool between her thighs. "*Mon monsieur, mon amour.*"

"Tell me, baby," Drew said, kissing the column of her
throat, the pulse point in her neck. "Tell me you love me."

"*Oui,* I do love you, so very much," she said before his
lips found hers again.

His tongue gliding over hers made her quiver. She felt
the heat emanating from him and wondered if he could feel
how hot she was. The intense warmth curled around her,
fanned into every fiber of her being, and melted every other
conscious thought but Drew and the havoc of his demanding kisses. She moaned, not caring about her engagement
or what Drew might think of her. She only concentrated on
her need to be in his arms. To savor his kisses. To feel his
warmth.

His mouth never leaving hers, Drew finally let go of the
sheet around his waist and undid the ribbons of her nightwrap, modestly tied at her neck. Then, with an ease borne
of experience, he slipped her nightgown over her shoulders.
The soft cotton whispered along her heated skin and slid
to the floor, ending in a heap at her feet.

For long moments they stared into each other's eyes, his

so dark with desire they appeared black. Her lips trembled, and her heart pounded.

A large hand cupped her bare breast, his thumb teasing the rosy nipple to pebble hardness. Heat coursed through her body, and she threw her head back, encouraging him to continue his sweet torture.

"You're beautiful, Mari. So perfect." His tongue glided over her nipple, and she gasped, her nerve endings rippling, burning. Heat scalded her loins when he began suckling one breast and then the other. She buried her fingers in the thickness of his hair and strained against him as he continued his ministrations.

Then abruptly his mouth found hers once again, and she clung to him, his fingertips caressing her now-sensitive breasts, touching her flat belly, gliding through the soft, silky curls at the juncture of her thighs.

His fingers lying at the entrance of her body, his thumb found the rigid bud of her sex. She opened at his touch. With methodical madness, he began massaging her wet folds, their mouths locked, her body burning white hot as she rocked against his finger. Sensations raced through her being, prickling, scalding, bringing her ever closer to the edge of insanity.

While the pressure of his thumb increased, a finger entered her, and she emitted a cry, collapsing against him, her body spasming against his hand. Drew held her firmly until her shivers ceased, then in one fluid motion lifted her up and brought her to the bed.

He lay beside her, and she felt the evidence of his passion against her thigh. A thrill of excitement danced through her—and was immediately dashed by the dread rising within her.

She was going to surrender her innocence to Drew. Since she was betrothed to marry another, she knew how wrong that was. But nothing in her life had ever felt so right as being held in his arms.

"Mari," Drew murmured, her naked flesh an erotic bea-

con, more potent than any fantasy he'd ever experienced.
"Mari, my love."

His mouth roamed over the smoothness of her body. The
skin that was like the finest silk. The long, perfect limbs
worthy of Venus. The pink cleft that was the heart-pulse
of her desire.

His arms locking her hips in place, he tasted the essence
of her, her black curls teasing, titillating. Her surprised gasp
turned into incomprehensible moans as she opened wider
for him, her need building, rising. He suckled her, his
tongue savoring her juices.

"Drew, please!" she panted, breathless, shivering, rocking against his mouth. She moved against him faster and
faster, clutching his hair, murmuring a thousand senseless,
sweet words, until her spasmodic release began again and
cries of joy escaped her throat.

For long moments after, Drew lay there, breathing heavily. He was sizzling and wanted nothing more than to make
her his own. But he would savor the moment. He had
wanted her for so long.

Slowly he lifted himself and lay flush against her. Taking
her hand in his, he guided it to his phallus. "Feel it, sweetheart."

Hesitantly her soft touch stroked the length of him, and
he gulped in an unsteady breath. Her touch grew bolder,
closing around him, gliding up and then down.

"It's . . . so *big*," Marianne whispered.

"All the better to thrill you with, my dear," he said, trying to chuckle but groaning instead as she incited his passion to a fever pitch. He moved his hips to the cadence of
her fingers and knew that if he didn't stop her, he'd shortly
embarrass himself. He wondered if she'd ever done this
before, since she was so damn good at it. This thought, he
reprimanded himself, was an irrelevant one, doubly so because she was engaged to be married to another. But she
loved *him*. The knowledge sent a surge of pleasure through
his blood.

"Ahh, Mari! Your hands are like velvet. Have you any idea what you're doing to me?"

To stop the sweet torture, he captured her hands and held them.

"Giving you as much pleasure as you gave me." Reclaiming her hands, she sat up. "I want to see you, Drew. All of you."

Drew complied by lying spread-eagle on his back. His manhood, huge and throbbing, pointed to his chin.

"*Mon Dieu!* You are *magnifique!*"

"*Merci,*" Drew said with a satisfied chortle. Watching as the moon cast its light on the paleness of her skin, seeing her face aglow with wonder, he swallowed convulsively.

Marianne leaned over him. "*Mon amour,* you are beautiful," she said, running her hands across the width of his smooth chest. She glided her tongue over his nipple, and he groaned. Continuing down to his hard stomach, she flicked her tongue into his navel and down farther over the glistening bead of wetness escaping him.

"No, darling," Drew said in a whisper, gently raising her head. "I want to get inside you, and what you have in mind will never do."

Marianne allowed herself to be flipped onto her back as Drew shifted his position, climbed atop her, and spread her thighs apart with his knees. His well-endowed maleness brushed against her slick femininity, massaging her bud, exciting her senseless. Her body was aflame, feverish, and she began gyrating her hips wildly, needing succor from this strange and demanding torment.

When she thought she would go mad, a powerful thrust pierced her maidenhead, taking her breath away. The pain stunned her momentarily, but it wasn't entirely unexpected. It was what she'd wanted, having practically initiated it by coming to Drew's quarters.

His hand slipped between them, and he found the centerpiece of her desire again. She gasped as he began moving a finger, pain turning into a distant memory. Urging him closer to her, he claimed her mouth again, and she clung to him as he drove his organ into her hot wetness. Torrid sensations shook her. She surged upward, meeting his every thrust, undulating herself to the rhythm of her heart.

He filled her, touched her womb, stretched her to capacity, igniting her like a fiery furnace. He delved into her recesses, laving her throat, kissing her eyes, reclaiming her lips.

She entwined her legs around his back. He pumped into her, deeply and swiftly. She thought he surely would cause her demise, in a most joyous way. Each of his strokes burned like cool fire and sent blood rushing through her veins. Her nails trailed across his shoulder blades and the rippling biceps in his arms, scoring a path down his back.

Bright, brilliant light exploded around her, surged through her brain, shattering, shuddering, rapturous. She screamed in sheer, unadulterated passion, driven over the brink, adrift in ecstasy.

Drew held her firmly while she violently shook with the force of her climax, aware of his deep, guttural groan, aware of a hot geyser spurting into her. He whispered words of love into her ear, caressed her damp hair, then rested his head on her shoulder.

After long moments, he withdrew from her, leaving her with a weightless, languid feeling.

He kissed her flushed cheek, her moist lips. "Mari, my sweet Mari," he said huskily. "I love you so. Stay with me tonight."

As much as she wanted to, she couldn't. There was still the issue of her betrothal, and Rafe's finding them in bed together wouldn't be a way out. Rather, it would be a way for Drew to die. Besides, he'd only asked her to stay the night. He'd said nothing about the rest of their lives. As far as she knew, he still intended to return to his time and his daughter and leave her behind. She sat up. "*Mon amour,* I cannot."

Drew stroked her thigh. "Why not?"

"Oh, Drew," she said, despondent now that their lovemaking was over. "I've never experienced such ecstasy before and I will never be sorry for what happened. But I cannot stay."

His features a mask of disbelief, Drew sat up. "You're not going back to Rafe, Mari, not after what we just shared?" he questioned in ire.

Scooting from the bed, Marianne quickly dressed herself, the soreness between her thighs and the tenderness of her breasts a vivid reminder of all that they had shared. Still, she had prayed he would say that they had a future together, that somehow they'd overcome their adversities together, and he hadn't. She drew in a shaky breath, thinking of all that she'd risked for him. "Please don't judge me too harshly, but I cannot turn my back on my obligations," she said, unsure of what else to say and refusing to put any undue burden on him by asking his intentions toward her. But she knew what she had to do, and that no longer included marrying Rafe.

She went to the bed and put her arms around his neck, kissing him with all the love and passion she felt. "I love you," she said, then turned and made her way down the steps without looking back.

Drew sat there stunned. He watched the staircase, hoping she'd change her mind and come back and throw herself into his arms, saying "gotcha!" But he knew she never would. She wouldn't have known about "gotcha" anyway.

When he heard the entrance door close downstairs, he knew he was only wishing on a star. She wouldn't return.

Going to the window, he gazed out, watching as her figure dashed across the lawn. She covered the distance between his quarters and the manor house with lightning speed.

"Good night, my love," he whispered, the taste of her haunting him, the remembered feel of her pure torture.

He turned from the window, went back to the bed, and stopped. The oil lamp had long since burned out, but the moonlight reflected dark stains on the pristine white sheet.

Drew leaned down for a closer inspection. "Blood! My

God!" His heart skipped a beat. Fumbling for another match, he quickly relit the lamp on the table next to his bed and held it over the sheet. Confirming his suspicions, he placed the lamp back on the table. "Oh, God!" he repeated, sinking down on the edge of the bed.

Marianne had been a virgin! Because she was engaged, he'd just assumed she wasn't. But this was the nineteenth century, and most people had a different spin on morals.

What had he done?

He wasn't worried about himself. In a fair fight, he was sure he could best Rafe. It was Marianne he was concerned about. Her wedding was to take place in a few short weeks, but well after the time he needed to return to his own era.

What would Rafe do to her when he discovered that she was no longer a virgin? The man was an egomaniac. He'd want to kill her for allowing herself to be ruined by another man. And if Rafe didn't kill her, Drew feared, he'd make her pay in unspeakable ways.

Well, he wouldn't let that happen. He'd persuade her to come back to the future with him. After all, it was he to whom she truly belonged, he whom she truly loved.

Christ! What would he do if she refused him? He couldn't stay to protect her. He had to get home to Teal.

Just when he began to feel helpless, a thought struck him. He'd forgotten that Genevieve, not Marianne, had married Rafe. Still, that was no guarantee that she'd return with him. Anything might happen.

He needed answers, and quickly. He needed to go to New Orleans to secure a bank loan for seed. While there, he'd pay another visit to Laurinda Toussaint.

This time he'd conquer his fear that the old harridan might turn him into the head of a chicken if he got out of line and not leave until she told him what he wanted to hear.

Chapter 24

"WELL, GOOD MORNING, Andrew," Rafe said, the ever-present smirk evident in his voice as he walked into the parlor.

Drew's attention remained focused on the pristine beauty of the gardens in the early morning. It had been only a few hours since he'd held Marianne in his arms and then watched as she left him. Sleep had eluded him the entire night, and as he'd watched the black night turn into gray dawn, he'd given up. But instead of heading toward the fields, he'd come to the mansion to await Pierre. He hadn't had to wait long. Five minutes after he'd walked into the parlor, Pierre strode in, newspaper in hand.

Drew quickly explained that he needed to go to New Orleans and try to secure a bank loan in order to buy seed and equipment. Without hesitation, Pierre agreed and went to his office to draft a letter explaining Drew's relationship to the family and giving his permission for Drew to act on his behalf.

That was when Rafe walked in. Thoughts of Marianne returned to Drew with a vengeance, but she seemed hell-bent on marrying Rafe, despite her lost innocence. What exactly did Rafe have that he didn't?

Knowing the question was unanswerable, Drew turned and met the smug features of his rotten ancestor.

An eyebrow arched, Rafe's gaze traveled down Drew's body, from his fine lawn shirt and black cravat to his burgundy topcoat and dark gray trousers, down to the highly polished boots he wore. "Surely you're not dressed in such finery to work in the fields, Cousin?"

"No, he isn't," Pierre announced proudly, ambling into the room, holding a glass of orange juice. "Andrew is making an effort to salvage the crops, Rafe. For that, he'll need cash for seed. So he's going to New Orleans to secure a modest loan."

Rafe spun on his heel. "What?" he sputtered, his eyes bulging, his fists clenching at his side. "Father, have you lost your mind?"

"Lost my mind, boy?" Pierre repeated as a fit of coughing seized him. Not wanting to spill the contents of his glass, he set it down on a table. He took the handkerchief he kept in his pocket and placed it over his mouth.

Frowning, Drew stepped closer to Pierre. "Shall I send for a doctor, Uncle?"

"No, you idiot," Rafe snapped, guiding his father to a chair and laying a hand on his shoulder. Pierre's coughing had ceased, but his face was flushed, and he seemed tired. "For the past half-year my father has suffered bouts of violent coughing at one time or another. This will pass!"

Not responding to Rafe, Drew got Pierre's orange juice and handed it to him. Pierre drank deeply from the glass, then handed it back to Drew.

"I'm fine, Andrew," he said, and glared at Rafe. "Lost my mind, huh? Explain yourself!"

Rafe shrugged, his features masked. But Drew would have sworn he saw an emotion resembling hurt glimmer in his eyes. "Father, Andrew may be your brother's son, a claim about which I have serious doubts. The fact still remains, however, that you know nothing about him. How can you trust him not to abscond with the money after he gets it?"

"Horseshit!" Pierre said, rising to his feet again. "Andrew is my nephew, and I trust him implicitly. Much more than I ever should have trusted you. He, at least, is making an effort to help put Bienvenu back on its feet."

Rafe stiffened. "Very well, Father. Don't say I didn't warn you." He started toward the dining room. "I'm going in for breakfast."

"Good idea," Pierre said. "Come along, Andrew. You can't very well leave here on an empty stomach."

Once Drew seated himself and Eve began to serve, barely a minute had passed before Marianne walked in.

She curtsied prettily. "*Bon matin,* messieurs."

His heart leaped at the smile brightening her beautiful face. He'd worried about how she was faring after their lovemaking, but he needn't have. She was positively glowing.

"Why, Marianne," Rafe said, standing along with Pierre and Drew as she approached the table, "what a pleasant surprise, my dear. It's barely six o'clock. What brings you to the breakfast table so early?" He pulled out her chair.

In one graceful movement, Marianne seated herself, not flinching when Rafe tenderly squeezed her shoulders. "I only came to see you off, Rafe. I understand from the servants that you're going to New Orleans today."

Her voice was music to Drew's ears. Though she seemed hardly to notice him, he couldn't take his eyes off her. The blue calico she wore suggested she'd spend the day at home, but the faint rosiness of her mouth and the languid sensuality in her green eyes were reminders of their night together.

"Those gossiping servants never carry a tale with accuracy," Rafe said, returning to his seat. "I have no plans to go to New Orleans today."

"Actually it's Andrew, *mon cherie,*" Pierre interjected around a mouthful of sausage and egg. "He's going on an errand for me."

Her glance flitted across Drew's face. "What a kind gesture, monsieur."

"It's the least I can do to repay my uncle's generosity."

"Marianne, my dear," Rafe said, "I am pleased and honored that you thought enough of me to see me off, even if your early rising was for naught."

"I only wanted to warn you against lingering too long in the city. Avoid spending a night there. The Yellow Fever season has started."

Too busy listening to the pounding of his heart, Drew didn't hear Rafe's response. Although Marianne was looking directly at Rafe, he knew her words were for him. He wanted to haul her into his arms and taste her sweetness again, thank her for her concern and kiss her for her daring and great acting.

Drew tossed aside his napkin, then stood. "I really have no appetite for food this morning, Uncle Pierre. So, Marianne, perhaps I'd better take your advice myself."

"You would be smart to, boy," Pierre said. "Don't even eat in the city. I'll have Hortenzia prepare something for you. Simon will bring you in the carriage. You'd best be ready to leave in about twenty minutes so you can return by sundown."

"Of course, Uncle Pierre," Drew agreed. "Oh, by the way, I injured my . . . er . . . upper leg yesterday. The evidence of that painful occurrence can be found on my bed. Please ask Hortenzia or Eve to change the sheet."

Jabbing another sausage with his fork, Pierre nodded. "You'll have a clean bed and a hot meal waiting for you when you get back this evening, son."

Rafe chuckled nastily and winked at Marianne. She didn't acknowledge the gesture but looked toward Drew as Rafe spoke.

"It's the least you can do, Father. Maybe he got his injury yesterday when I found him wallowing in the dirt with the slaves."

Refusing to let Rafe bait him, Drew smiled coldly, but remained silent. He focused his full attention on Marianne, and noticed how furiously she was blushing. Like himself, she was probably recalling the reason for the stains on his sheet. He never would have believed she was a virgin—he took Rafe for every foul creature known to man, including a consummate lech.

He pushed his chair under the table. "That's the breaks. I'll wait outside for Simon until Hortenzia brings the food basket." He looked at Marianne. "Marianne, it's been a pleasure seeing you again."

He noticed the pulse pounding in her throat. It was one of the spots of satiny skin he'd feasted upon last night.

She swallowed. "*Merci,* Andrew. Do have a safe journey. *Bonjour.*" Her perfect mouth curved into the slightest of smiles. Just for him.

He nodded. "Good day, mademoiselle." With that, he turned and left the room, wondering if he'd ever hold her in his arms again.

Chapter 25

Brightly painted cottages housing shops of all sorts populated the tree-lined Main Street in the heart of St. Francisville. Bienvenu stood on the outskirts of town, right near the banks of the Mississippi, but close enough that Marianne opted to go into town unescorted.

Then again, even if it had been fifty miles away, she would have gone on her own. Her intended destination didn't allow for company.

Instead, just after breakfast ended, an hour after Drew's departure, she encouraged Rafe to head out to the fields and Pierre to leave her to her own devices. Soon after, she asked Eve to send for a cabriolet for her.

As she pulled the horse to a stop in front of the town's only pawnshop, she bit down on her bottom lip, afraid. She wasn't as well known here as she was in Roseland or even parts of New Orleans, but still there was the chance that her plans would be discovered. And if they were, Rafe's reaction might be fearsome. Still, that was a risk she had to take.

She hadn't intended on leaving right away. She'd wanted to spend another night of passion with Drew—wanted to give him another chance to ask her to stay with him *forever*, wherever that might be.

With a deep sigh, she stepped onto the banquette, tightly holding the reticule containing a number of pieces of her jewelry. Glancing covertly up and down the street and finding it virtually deserted, she stiffened her spine and went inside. The jingling bells announced her entrance, and a short, rotund shopkeeper smiled in her direction.

"*Bienvenu,* mademoiselle!" he called to her, then nodded. "Welcome," he repeated in English.

Gliding to the counter, Marianne set her heirlooms down on the glass top. "*Bonjour,* monsieur." Falling silent, she stared at the man. She hated to think that in a few minutes she would be parting with a king's ransom in jewels, pieces that her father had gifted her with, pieces that had been handed down for four generations.

The silence stretched into a full minute before the shopkeeper finally spoke.

"Mademoiselle, are you in need of anything?"

Marianne cleared her throat and shifted her weight. "*Oui,*" she said with a nod. She opened her bag and emptied its contents on the countertop. "I-I need to know what I could get for these?"

The little man's gaze went to the jewelry. Diamonds, sapphires, pearls, and emeralds glinted beneath the light. His eyebrows flew up, his brown gaze gleaming as he refocused his attention on her.

"Er, well—"

"They are worth a small fortune, monsieur," Marianne interrupted when she saw the wheels of his avarice turning. "Do not think to swindle me."

His cheeks flushed, and he worked the muscles in his throat, seeking a reply. "Mademoiselle, are you certain you wish to part with these?"

Blinking back what felt like a hot rush of tears, Marianne nodded. She didn't want to marry Rafe, and if she didn't flee from him she surely would have to. She had no other choice. "*Oui,* monsieur."

"Very well," he said, then got a jeweler's glass and began carefully examining each piece.

Not wanting to watch, Marianne browsed the shop, her mind wandering, searching for answers to the problems that had plagued her for months. Everything had been so much less complicated before Drew came. She was happy that she'd met him, happy that she had surrendered her innocence to him. But she remained miserable all the same. They loved each other, and there wasn't a thing to be done about it except to have a few stolen days of passion—because Drew didn't belong here, and she couldn't stay here.

A display of watches and fobs, sitting on a back counter, caught her interest. As far as she knew, Drew hadn't found the watch he needed to bring him back to his own time, though she knew it hadn't been for lack of looking.

She skimmed over them before she settled on one to her liking. When she picked up the gold watch, its heaviness surprised her. The metal grew hot in her hand, and a powerful eeriness surrounded her.

Her only thought was to put it down, to rid herself of it. It frightened her, and she thought of the legends of the town. Supposedly St. Francisville had once been an Indian burial ground and spirits of all sorts roamed the streets. Today one of those spirits seemed to inhabit this watch, and she didn't think it was a very nice one.

A shiver went through her as she settled the watch back in its place. But she couldn't walk away; she was drawn to the watch's continuous ticking, which seemed to grow louder and louder, making her slightly dizzy.

"Mademoiselle?"

Spinning around on her heel, Marianne met the shopkeeper's gaze.

"I have come to a figure that I think you'll be pleased with."

He held a scrap of paper between his pudgy fingers.

"*Merci*." Unsteadily she walked to where the man stood and accepted the paper. Her heart pounding in anticipation, she gazed down at the figures. Two thousand dollars. More than enough. She looked at her jewels again. No choice, she reminded herself. "*Oui*. I accept."

"Very good." He quickly removed the jewels from the counter and went to the back of the shop. When he returned a few minutes later, he held the cash in his hands. He passed it to Marianne. "I noticed you were admiring the watches," he said as she began counting the money.

"*Oui*," she answered distractedly.

"Did you have anybody in mind to purchase one for, mademoiselle?"

She refused to answer until she finished the counting. Once she was done and the money was settled securely in her reticule, she said, "I was only browsing."

"It would make someone a fine gift," he pressed. "Your father, perhaps?"

"*Non*, monsieur," Marianne said in a small voice. "My father is deceased."

As much as she wanted to leave, she couldn't; somehow the force of the watch prevented her. But it wouldn't suit Drew. She couldn't see something so strange and threatening belonging to him. It was better suited for Rafe.

Perhaps she could leave it for Rafe as a parting gift. Maybe it would help to soothe his anger. Besides, Drew hadn't asked for any additional help from her, and although he might have been strange and out of place, he certainly wasn't *threatening*.

"As a matter of fact, monsieur, I think I *will* purchase the watch," she said, getting it from the case. She tried to ignore the heat permeating her hand, to ignore the sickening ticking, especially since the shopkeeper seemed unaffected by it. "Would you be so kind as to engrave it with the initials *RM* on the back in script. It is for my intended, and I want it to be special."

The rotund little man nodded eagerly and took the watch from her. "It shall be ready in three days. Your betrothed is a lucky man, mademoiselle."

"*Merci.*"

But as she returned to the cabriolet, she wasn't so sure Rafe was all that lucky. The watch had an unearthly presence about it that left her wondering if she should have purchased it at all.

Chapter 26

WITH DREW RIDING on the perch next to him, Simon pulled the team of grays to a stop on the outskirts of the city.

Knowing the reason for the servant's sudden halting, Drew scowled and sucked in an agitated breath. The superstitions of the black population really annoyed him. He needed to see Laurinda and he wouldn't be deterred by unfounded beliefs.

"Mr. Drew, please don't make me go there," Simon implored, staring at him with wide, frightened eyes.

"Look," he began, trying not to sound too agitated, "I intend to see Miss Toussaint this morning, Simon. If you wish, you may wait for me in Congo Square."

Simon bowed his head. "Thank you, suh. I'll wait for you."

"All right. Just tell me how to start these horses, how to make them go in the right direction, and how to get them to stop."

"Yessuh, I be glad to. Fust, to get the horses to go, you snap the reins and say, '*Giddup,* horses.' To guide them left or right, you turn the reins in the direction you be wantin' to go. And when you wants to stop, you say 'Stop' or 'Whoa.' "

"Thank you, Simon," Drew said with a laugh. "That was a mouthful. But by God I think I've got it."

Reaching Congo Square a little while later, Drew pulled on the team's reins. "Whoa, whoa," he declared with confidence. The horses obediently came to a halt, and he chuckled happily. "All right!" It was early in the morning, and evidence of rain lay in stagnant puddles of muck and water in the nearly deserted streets. The smell of tar and pitch hung in the damp air, and the sight of a wagon piled with coffins sent a strange chill through Drew. He turned to Simon. "Off you go, Simon. This shouldn't take very long. Miss Laurinda doesn't know I'm coming. She may not even see me."

"Yessuh," Simon replied timidly, climbing off the perch.

Forcing a smile, Drew wondered if he should take Simon's lead and avoid the mysterious enchantress. But in spite of his trepidation, he vowed, nothing would keep him from trying to get the answers he so desperately needed. He felt drawn to Laurinda, almost as if he had no choice but to seek her out. For that matter, it didn't seem he had much choice with a lot of things—first among them that damned watch.

"Simon, amuse yourself until I return. I still have to see the bank president." He snapped the reins. "Giddy up." When the horses began moving, he waved to Simon. "Piece of cake. I'll be back as soon as I can."

He guided the team in the direction of the clearing beyond the square, toward the now-familiar Grand Route St. John. It seemed uncomfortably cool for the time of day, especially since it was a mere week away from summer. But cool and damp weather had prevailed since his arrival. It was also a breeding ground for the mosquitoes that were so deadly in this century.

He grimaced, glad he'd come from an era in which Yellow Fever had been eradicated because city sanitation was so much better.

He urged the horses on. The animals seemed jittery as they loped along the path to Laurinda's cabin. Of course, he told himself, it was all his imagination. After all, he was from New Orleans, one of the places in the country that in modern times had a helluva lot of "haunted houses." And these "hauntings" were a direct result of what had happened in this era.

Personally he'd never experienced anything of a supernatural nature, but he decided he could easily change his thinking and become a believer, given his spooky surroundings.

Fog swirled along the ground and the trunks of trees as the horses galloped by. When the sun rose fully in the sky, the fog would burn off. Still, it created an eerie effect, and this phenomenon, he reasoned, probably played a large part in the locals' superstitions.

When Laurinda's cabin came into view a few hundred yards in the distance, Drew slowed the team's pace. Reaching her door, he pulled the horses to a stop.

His heart pounding like a drumbeat, he sat atop the perch and gazed about, the smell of sulfuric acid burning his nose. He appeared to be the only one around. The other times he'd visited, there was at least one other person with him. But now, if he stepped out of line, she could strike that cobra's-head staff against the floor and turn him into alligator meat, and no one would be the wiser.

Gathering his courage, he climbed down from the carriage and walked the few feet to the cabin. He hesitated only a moment before he raised his closed fist and knocked. He waited. And waited. And waited.

Having the sensation of being watched, he looked around again and frowned. He was still alone. Acute disappointment and unease engulfing him, he knocked again. He really didn't want to return to Bienvenu without talking to Laurinda. Maybe he'd come back here after he concluded his business with the bank.

For good measure, with a final effort he knocked again.

The door swung open so fast, Drew jumped back, startled. The sulfuric acid he'd smelled earlier hit him full force, watering his eyes and causing him to cough. He hadn't expected a response, since he'd been at the door nearly five minutes with no answer.

Clad all in black from scarfed head to shod feet, Laurinda occupied a small space in the doorway. Her pupils appeared yellow, and her leathery face showed concern and anger.

"You go!" she commanded, rapping the staff against the floor. "Leave Laurinda!"

"Miss Laurinda, please don't send me away," he begged, not moving, immobilized by an inkling of fear and the over-whelming smell of the sulfuric acid. "You said I can know only my fate, but if Marianne is to become part of that fate, I must know about hers as well."

The enchantress looked drawn and tired, her gray irises cloudy with fatigue. She tightened the black wrap around her shoulders. "There is not much Laurinda can tell you."

Drew took a hesitant step closer just as she began a bout of coughing. He needed to get past her reservations. Maybe if she knew of his and Marianne's intimacies, she might be more yielding. Suddenly something else that had occurred to him only in passing hit him hard: Marianne was a distant ancestor of his. "Miss Laurinda, my family history records Genevieve as having married Rafe. If that's true, then Marianne is my great-great aunt with whom I've committed . . . God, I can't even say it!"

For the first time since he'd met her, Laurinda's look softened, by a large measure. She clasped his shoulder. "Genevieve and your Marianne aren't related by blood, boy," she whispered. "That girl was took in by the Beauforts after her maman and papa died from the Fever when she was a newborn *bebe*."

Caught off guard by Laurinda's words, Drew straight-ened, his mouth dropping open. "Why didn't Mari tell me this?"

As Laurinda stepped back, another bout of coughing seized her, and a trickle of blood escaped the side of her mouth. Perhaps whatever she'd been doing in there with the sulfuric acid had affected her lungs, Drew mused. "Are you all right, Miss Laurinda?"

"Laurinda is fine!" She answered so sharply that Drew decided against inquiring further. She pulled a handkerchief from her pocket, wiped off the blood, and continued. "Neither girl knows about Genevieve's birth," she informed him. "And that's how it has to be. That's how the Beauforts want it."

"H-how do *you* know all this?"

"Jean-Louis Beaufort came to me when he got Genevieve. His best friend wasn't as wealthy as him, and when the man's wife died, leavin' the young *bebe,* he ask Masta Jean to take her. Mam'zelle Clarisse was sufferin' from a difficult labor at the time. She almost die, but the *bebe* wasn't alive when he came from her womb, so Masta Jean pretend Genevieve the new Beaufort *bebe.* When he fin' his friend dead two days later from the Fever, he wanted to make sure no one told her of her beginnings. So I make everybody else involved forget. Mam'zelle Clarisse don't know that girl ain't hers to this day."

"This is fantastic! Just wonderful," he said, relieved at the turn of events that excluded Marianne from being a blood relative. Baby switching received a lot of media attention in his time, but he supposed it happened all through the ages, for one reason or another. Encouraged by Laurinda's willingness to divulge this information, he said, "Please, tell me again exactly what I have to do to get back home."

Laurinda cackled. "No need to get so excited, boy. You don't have the pocket watch you need yet. If you get it before September, when you'll be doomed to stay here, then come to me. Now, leave Laurinda! She's expectin' a high-payin' customer."

"You still won't tell me Marianne's fate, huh, ma'am?" he asked, smiling, knowing he'd have to find that out for himself, and grateful for the information she had been willing to give him. As expected, she remained silent. Drew bowed. "Thank you, Miss Laurinda. You've been very helpful and very kind."

A bony hand raised to caress his cheek. "That's because

you've been kind to my great-great-great-granddaughter, boy."

Drew arched his eyebrows together, surprised that she'd know of Alaina's existence, but refusing to pretend ignorance. Laurinda's knowledge intrigued as much as it frightened. "She did speak of you on occasion," he said in awe, amazed at the fact that people he'd only heard about in discussions now actually inhabited his life. "How do you know about her?"

She drew herself up to her full height, once again the regal, dominating presence he'd first met. "There's things I just know about, C. Andrew Montague III. Things people like you best leave be. But I can tell you our Alaina will rise to become surgeon general in your century. She ain't finished her schoolin' yet," she explained, bursting with pride. The old woman's features lost their intensity and ire. Peace and contentment replaced them, then concern. "I see danger all around you, Andrew. 'Specially today. Be on your guard, my son. You shouldn't have come here. You don't know what you're in for. Now, go quickly. My customer approaches."

Looking around, Drew saw no one. With a shrug he returned his gaze to Laurinda and raised her leathery hand to his lips. Placing a kiss on the back of it, he put a double eagle gold coin in her palm. It was the entire amount of money Pierre had given him for incidental expenses he might incur while in the city. "Thank you again for your kindness, ma'am." He lingered a moment longer before making his way the few feet to the carriage.

Laurinda watched as the carriage rolled slowly away, then returned inside when it disappeared around the bend in the road.

The boy was resourceful and likable; it was no wonder Alaina valued his friendship so much. Still, Laurinda had had to take him away from everyone he knew and loved. There were too many people who needed him here, too much he never would have learned there. She'd never meant, however, to keep him away from his daughter and mother and father and brothers forever.

But he'd thrown away the watch he needed, and she had reached the end of her time. It seemed the boy was doomed after all.

For in all of her years, there was only one thing she hadn't counted on: She'd never expected to catch the Fever.

"Lawdy, Mr. Drew." Simon jumped from the crate he was sitting on when he saw Drew roll to a stop on the edges of Congo Square forty-five minutes later. Climbing next to Drew, he grabbed the reins. "I was powerful worried about you. I thought that old witch had turned you into a toady frog."

Not quite so burdened after his visit to Laurinda, Drew laughed. "Not a chance, Simon. I think the old girl likes me. Now, let's get moving. We have other business to attend to."

Making their way past the Square, Drew found the Vieux Carrè alive with activity now that it was past mid-morning and the sun was high and bright in the sky.

With the social season over, most or all of the wealthy had fled the city. Those who had no alternative made the best of their time here. Having no choice, they went about their lives as normally as possible, despite the threat of Yellow Fever hanging over them.

Evidence of the season's beginnings lay everywhere: in the smell of lime, in the smoky residue of the burning of tar and pitch from the night before; in the creaking wheels of the death wagons, all piled with five or ten coffins; in the cries of the drivers to "Bring out your dead."

Seeing this, Drew decided to take Pierre's advice and complete his business as quickly as possible, then head to the safety of the plantation. He didn't need to urge Simon at a faster pace. The man seemed to read his mind, and Drew soon found himself in front of the redbrick, green-shuttered building of the Crescent City Bank of Nouveau Orleans on Rue Chartres.

When Simon pulled the horses to a stop, Drew jumped from the conveyance. "Hold down the fort until I get back."

"Yessuh, Mr. Drew."

After an interminable length of time had passed—he had to present various papers, provide proof of ownership of Bienvenu, and sign an unbelievable amount of documents—Drew emerged from the bank.

In his topcoat pocket he had ten thousand dollars in cash for seed, equipment, and other necessities. Until now, he hadn't thought much of the warning Laurinda had given him again today, because she'd cautioned him so often, and with Marianne's new devotion to Rafe, he seemed not as intent upon murdering Drew.

Yet with the money pressing against his side, Laurinda's latest warning rang now in his mind. "Be on your guard, son." As usual, she hadn't told him from what. It occurred to him that Rafe could in some way try to rob him of the money, since the man knew of Drew's plans.

Even Rafe, however, couldn't be that low-down and dirty, Drew told himself. He wouldn't risk the plantation for the sake of revenge. But damn, there was also the belief in Rafe's mind that his honor had somehow been infringed upon, and for that a man like him would risk everything. Even his life.

"We be ready to go now, Mr. Drew?"

Drawing in a breath, Drew looked around thoughtfully. On the other side of the street, he noticed three disreputable-looking men, definitely out of their realm in the Chartres Street business section. When they saw him glance their way, Drew almost laughed at their attempt to look nonchalant and interested in the expensive merchandise in the jewelry shop they stood in front of.

"We have one . . . no, two more stops before we can start for home, Simon. Bear with me a while longer."

"Yessuh."

Drew climbed atop the seat beside Simon. "We're heading for Decatur Street for seedlings, then Peters Street."

"Yessuh."

Simon was beginning to look feeble to Drew, and he supposed the man was as hungry as he. But he needed to get his business behind him before he could even think about eating. It was useless to suggest that Simon eat without him, because Rafe would never allow the servants to eat if he hadn't, and many of them still thought Drew was like his "cousin," despite his efforts to dispel that notion.

The three characters at the jewelry display window quickly got into the one horse and buggy parked on the street in front of the jewelry store.

Drew decided to see if he was being paranoid or not. If the men showed up at the French Market on Decatur Street, his suspicions would be confirmed; it would mean they were tailing him. But in fairness he wouldn't implicate Rafe without proof. Those three men might be acting on their own and just be crooks who saw him leave the bank and head to the Montague carriage.

Stopping the carriage across from the open-air market, Drew maneuvered through the throng of shoppers. Almost anything a person wanted could be found there. After a few minutes of shoving through the crowds, he found the vendor he sought and purchased the seeds and seedlings he needed for planting.

Bringing a couple of crates of potted seeds to Simon at the carriage, Drew told the servant where to find the remainder of them. Then he fastened his gaze on the trio, who were sitting in the buggy not far from him.

Anger vibrated through him, and as much as he didn't want to, he suspected Rafe had had a hand in this. Removing the lunch basket and placing it beneath the perch, he pushed the two crates inside the carriage, then waited for Simon to return.

It wasn't long before they were back on the road again, heading for Rue Peters, the inside of the carriage filled to capacity. Drew reached the Master Weapons Shop and bought a pistol and several rounds of ammunition. Emerging from the establishment, he noticed that the buggy with the three men was parked a short distance away.

Drew still had money left over to make purchases in St. Francisville. If he was going to be robbed, however, he already had the seedlings and he wouldn't lose as much cash. If that's all they wanted.

He was an expert with a gun, but he didn't relish having to use one on a fellow human being. Still, he'd be damned if he'd let those bastards get the best of him.

Sticking the gun in his waist, the handle in plain view, he got back on the carriage. "Are you hungry, Simon?" he asked loudly, hoping his voice carried to where the three men sat in the buggy.

Simon perked up at the thought of imminent sustenance. "Yessuh!"

"Why don't you open that basket Hortenzia fixed for us."

"I'm way ahead of you, Mista Drew," Simon said, reaching under the perch and getting the basket.

Drew laughed. "Good for you. Why don't we just sit here and eat before starting out. I don't want to stop to eat once we get on the road."

Simon nodded his full agreement as he attacked a fried chicken leg.

Certain the three men had robbery or worse on their minds, Drew needed the extra time to think. He had a gun. Now what? He was one person with one gun. They were three beefy brutes, each probably carrying a weapon.

Gazing in their direction again, he blinked. One goon now stood outside the buggy, looking Drew's way, while the other two sat inside, also looking at him. What held his attention was the small *B* emblazoned on the side of the vehicle. The golden *B* stood for Bienvenu. It was the same buggy he'd gone to the ball in!

Was Rafe really that bold, or was he just the stupidest son-of-a-bitch that ever walked the earth?

"Sit tight, Simon," Drew said, climbing back down.

Constables around this part of town were very much in evidence to insure against theft of the market goods not far away. Walking to one, Drew tapped him on the shoulder.

"Pardon me, Constable"—he looked at his name tag—

"O'Steen. I have a problem that needs fixing."

"Well, ye've come to the right fella," O'Steen said. He was a big man with piercing green eyes and a coppery beard to match the hair on his head. "What is yer problem, and how can I fix it?"

"My name is Andrew Montague—," Drew began.

"Not the Montagues o' Bienvenu?"

"The very same," Drew answered with a nod. "Pierre is my uncle, and Rafe is my cousin."

The Irishman pumped his hand vigorously. "Well, well, well. 'Tis a mighty pleasure to make yer acquaintance, lad. I know Pierre like I know me own brother. I would be honored to help his kin."

"Thank you, Mr. O'Steen," Drew said, then pointed to the buggy. "You see that vehicle over there?"

"Aye."

"Well, sir, I've been searching for it most of the morning. We brought it to load up on supplies, in case the carriage wasn't big enough. But lo and behold, when we came out of a store on Toulouse Street, those three men had confiscated it, and they refuse to give it back," he finished, trying hard to keep a straight face at the lie he'd concocted. He'd beat Rafe at his own game, without a drop of blood being shed—his or anyone else's.

"Oh, they did, did they?" O'Steen growled, anger flushing his features. "Well, we'll just see about that. O'Malley!" he called to the other browsing constable, who was the size of a city bus. "I may need your assistance in making some arrests of thieves."

"Really?" The giant looked Drew up and down. "Would this be yer stealer?"

"No, O'Malley, he's the steal*ee*," O'Steen said, and pointed to the buggy. "The thieves are over there, sitting in the evidence of their foul deed. This young man is Pierre Montague's nephew—"

O'Malley raised his beefy hands. "Say no more," he flared. "Anyone who'd steal from a foine gentleman like

Pierre deserves to have his balls introduced to a nut-cracker."

Drew winced. "Ouch!" he said, laughing at their terminology.

He followed the two constables to the buggy. The man who'd been leaning against it in abject boredom quickly displayed alertness. The other two hopped down to stand next to him.

"What's the trouble, Constable?" the leaner asked.

"What's yer name?" O'Malley snarled.

"Ma name is Percy," the leaner answered. "These are ma brothers, Darson and Franklin."

"Howdy, suh," the two men chorused.

"What are ye doing here?" O'Steen asked.

The three men looked from one to the other, encompassing Drew in their gaze. "We . . . um . . . just came to git our weekly supply of food," Percy answered.

"You're a liar," Drew snapped, his anger slowly rising. Those idiots meant to harm him, probably at the direction of another idiot.

"I'll handle these lying, uncouth Kaintocks, Mr. Montague," O'Steen said. "Get yer boy to take yer buggy back or whatever arrangements ye had fer the buggy and carriage. These buggers are under arrest!"

"Hey, wait a minute!" Percy protested. "What are you arrestin' us for?"

"Number one, fer stealin' a horse," O'Malley answered, his big body rigid with anger. "And ye know what punishment that offense carries."

"I'm sure we'll find other reasons to hold ye, but fer now that won't be necessary," O'Steen added, pushing Darson forward. "Now, come along quietly."

Drew watched the three men being taken away, and, in spite of himself, he felt sorry for them. They surely would have robbed him, and perhaps even killed him. But he felt they'd been duped by Rafe into attempting such a deed. In the end, after they were caught with Bienvenu property and faced with charges of harming Drew, Rafe probably would have abandoned those poor fools and damned them to their punishments.

Great piece of work, his pretend cousin.

His adversaries secure in the arms of the law, Drew felt infinitely better about making the trip back to St. Francisville—although he wasn't sure he wouldn't be met along the way by Rafe himself. He put nothing past a pyschopath like Rafe. He'd been smart enough to choose riffraff, river scum from the other side of Canal Street, to do his dirty work, and he might have figured that Drew could outwit them.

Of course, if anything had happened to Drew at the hands of Percy, Darson, and Franklin, they would never have gotten away with accusing Rafe of setting Drew up. It would have been their word against that of a gentleman planter.

Drew decided he wouldn't dwell on those unfortunate, ignorant bastards any longer. They deserved to go to jail for what they'd tried to do, whatever it was. He only hoped the law for stealing horses was different here than out West. Had they been there, they would already be strung up.

Allowing—no, *preferring*, that Simon handle the larger carriage, Drew took the buggy and started back home, satisfied with the way things had turned out for him today. He'd outwitted Rafe and had had a rather interesting visit with Laurinda.

Now as he covered the miles back to Bienvenu, he could reflect on his day . . . and his night. He'd tried to avoid that until now. Thoughts of Mari and their lovemaking would only arouse him and leave him hungry for her.

He ached to see Teal again but felt trapped between a rock and a hard place. He was deeply in love with Marianne but still didn't know what had become of her, didn't know her true fate.

He couldn't wait to see Rafe's face when he showed up at Bienvenu driving the buggy. If the cell phone had been invented in this time, he would have called ahead so everyone could be waiting for him on the veranda.

That bastard would know that Drew was on to him, know that it would be harder to ambush him now.

Drew sighed, thinking of Marianne again. What were her plans? Would she still be at Bienvenu? Or had she fled?

He wanted to feel her body joined with his again and to ask her to return with him to the future. Maybe it was best if she'd left the plantation already, he decided. It would be hard to look at her and accept not ever kissing her again because she still intended to marry Rafe.

Suddenly his day didn't seem so triumphant after all.

Chapter 27

TIRED AND EXHAUSTED from the tedious ride back to Bienvenu, Drew finally arrived at the mansion at dusk. Wearily he climbed down from the buggy, then instructed Simon, who'd ridden up behind him, to take care of the horses and vehicles.

Going into the house, he found the interior ablaze with light. Garbled voices emanating from the parlor alerted Drew to visitors, and he cursed, in no mood to see anyone tonight. He thought about bypassing the parlor altogether but wanted to give an account of his day to Pierre. The man was probably waiting to hear if Drew's plans for the plantation had fallen through.

His decision made, he walked to the chamber and stopped in the doorway. Clarisse and Genevieve sat in a settee facing Rafe and Marianne, who sat next to each other. Pierre relaxed in a Queen Anne chair, his back to the door. Drew frowned as he realized they were debating his whereabouts and were taking no notice of him.

"I warned you, Father," Rafe gritted, his face a mask of outrage and sympathy. "You know nothing of the man, yet you allowed him to secure a cash loan against our property."

"Shut up, Rafe!" Pierre snapped. "You should learn to trust."

"I do, Father," Rafe replied, calmer. He brought Marianne's hand to his lips and placed a gentle kiss there, then smiled at his father. "I have every confidence that Cousin Andrew has absconded with our money." He gazed into Marianne's eyes. "Would *you* so readily give such blind trust to a virtual stranger, *ma cherie*?"

"Moi?" Marianne answered, as if she hadn't been paying the slightest bit of attention to the debate.

"Oui, Marianne," Rafe said, scowling. *"You."*

She smiled serenely. "Well, if Monsieur Andrew is a virtual stranger, Rafe, in effect he's ceased to be an actual stranger." Her gaze focused in Drew's direction, and her smile deepened, a passionate promise entering her jade eyes.

He'd never felt more male, more sexually desired than in that moment. Winking at her, he put his fingers to his lips, silently asking her not to give his presence away, just as Pierre spoke again.

"Added to that, Marianne, is the fact that the boy is kin. It's a matter of honor to give trust!"

Rafe stiffened and narrowed his eyes, his gaze never leaving Marianne's face. "So you agree with Father?" he asked, bristling.

"Stop this bickering," Clarisse scolded with a firm clap of her hands. "Monsieur Andrew will explain himself when he returns."

"Oui, Monsieur Rafe," Genevieve put in softly, capturing Rafe's attention. "Maman's right—"

Having heard enough, Drew employed his favorite gesture—he cleared his throat—then stepped into the room.

Clarisse and Genevieve craned their necks to see who the newcomer was, while Pierre rose to his feet. A blush spread across Genevieve's cheeks, and a grin lit Pierre's face when they saw his cavalier bow. Drew sort of liked bowing and did it so well it seemed as if he'd been born to it.

"Monsieur Andrew!" Genevieve gasped.

"*Bonsoir,* everyone," Drew said, comfortable with the little French he'd learned.

Pierre went to him with open arms and hugged him affectionately. "Am I glad to see you, son! I thought you'd come to harm."

"Not a chance, Uncle Pierre." Drew sent an icy look in Rafe's direction. His mottled red complexion let Drew know that Rafe was angry at this turn of events. His smug knowledge of Drew's supposed dishonor was coming back to haunt him. "Had I not been on my guard, however, I might have."

A muscle ticked in Rafe's jaw as Pierre clasped Drew's shoulder.

"What do you mean, Andrew?" Almost as an afterthought, he indicated a vacant chair. "Sit down, son. I'm sure you're acquainted with Clarisse and Genevieve?"

"Yes, sir, I am," Drew confirmed.

Genevieve scooted closer to her mother, making room for him to sit, which he did immediately. Marianne's annoyance wasn't quite as shocking as Rafe's, who gritted his teeth and sent Genevieve and Drew a dark look.

"Eve, bring Master Andrew a brandy."

Eve had been standing on the opposite side of the room, almost blending in with the furniture, she'd been so silent and still. But at Pierre's order, she curtsied. "Yes, sir."

After she handed him the drink and returned to her post, Drew focused his attention on Pierre. Tiredly he passed his hand over his eyes, then stroked his chin. "Uncle Pierre, I caught three criminals in a Bienvenu buggy today," he said, glancing in Rafe's direction. He sat as still as stone, his face as white as a sheet. As tired as he was, Drew was enjoying this and wouldn't have missed it for anything. Except maybe a trip back to the future.

Pierre's eyes widened, then narrowed as he gazed at Rafe and back to Drew. He stood next to his chair, his fists clenched. "What! Someone stole property from here?"

Drew nodded. "Apparently so," he answered mildly.

Pierre wasn't a fool, and it was obvious that he was as suspicious of Rafe as Drew had been. Drew smiled coldly in Rafe's direction as his "cousin" squirmed in his seat, removing his hand from Marianne's.

"D-did . . . ," Rafe began, stopping to clear his throat.

I know the feeling, Great-Great-Granddaddy. Drew chuckled to himself. But his laughter died as he took in Marianne's worry. A frown creasing her perfect brow, her gaze traveled the length of him. He read the questioning concern in her eyes and answered with the barest of nods and the hint of a smile.

"Did they say how they got the buggy?" Rafe got out, in control of his dismay.

"As a matter of fact, they didn't," Drew answered, and glared at Rafe as Rafe's shoulders sagged with relief. A pulse pounded furiously at the base of Marianne's long neck, and she shifted away from Rafe. She had figured it out as well. "They had obviously planned to add robbery to their theft."

"How's that?" Pierre asked, seating himself.

"The senseless fools tailed me from the bank. *In* the Bienvenu buggy! Now, I would have to be as witless as they are if I hadn't recognized Montague property."

Marianne's hand flew to her breast. "*Mon Dieu!* How lucky you are to have escaped harm."

"Just in case luck had deserted me, Marianne, I bought a pistol to use in my defense against such occurrences." Once again, Drew locked his chilling, unforgiving gaze with Rafe's hard one. "I can shoot an acorn off an oak at sixty yards. I'm an expert shot and rarely, if ever, miss what I aim to hit." He kept his voice low, calm, and precise, hinting at a deadly promise: vengeance against his ancestor.

Yet if it ever came to such a pass, he had to keep both himself and Rafe alive—an almost insurmountable task given their now-mutual hate. Judging by the paleness of Rafe's countenance, Drew knew he'd struck a chord in him. Rafe would never forgive Drew for this night. Drew also knew that by his thwarting Rafe's plans, however, the bastard was aware of his determination to defend himself.

"Luckily it didn't come to that, Marianne," Drew continued, his own fury percolating. "The constables carted them off to jail before we left the city."

"Mon Dieu!" Genevieve said, echoing Marianne's earlier sentiments and patting his leg. "You are a very brave man, monsieur."

"Oui, it seems so," Clarisse said, frowning at Genevieve's gesture. "Monsieur Andrew appears to be a man of many talents. And so handsome, too."

Drew noticed that the black widow's weeds she'd favored upon his arrival had been replaced by a deep burgundy gown that was the height of fashion. He smiled at her compliment. "Thank you, ma'am."

"I agree, Maman," Genevieve stated, batting her eyelashes flirtatiously at him, giving his leg the barest caress.

Arching an eyebrow at Genevieve, Drew noticed the change in Marianne's posture. She sat more erect, straightening herself in jealous pique. Didn't she know she had nothing to worry about where he was concerned? He only wished he could say the same about his worry for her. Nonetheless, her reaction to Genevieve's actions warmed him. And he was relieved to see that no one else except Clarisse had seemed to notice the sisters' actions. With a smile that was teasingly wicked, he said, "You ladies are most generous with your compliments."

"Really, Clarisse!" Rafe scolded. "My cousin is in no position to pursue matrimony at this time, if that's what you're hinting at. . . ." Noticing Pierre's frown, his words trailed off. "I-I mean no offense to anyone," he added quickly, looking at his father with uncertainty. "Genevieve is quite an attractive young woman, Clarisse. As her mother, you should urge her to seek a man of means. Such as myself."

Drew burst out laughing. "And you are quite a prize, Cousin."

Rafe scowled at him.

Pierre joined Drew in laughter, the anger in his features

dissolving. Since Drew hadn't directly accused Rafe, Pierre seemed reluctant to do so as well.

"You brought it on yourself, son," Pierre said to Rafe. "Andrew's a fine young man. Genevieve could do worse."

"Perhaps, Father, but not much worse."

"But better than you," Drew retorted.

"Besides, as far as I know, messieurs, polygamy is not legal," Marianne stated sweetly, her green eyes like shards of stone as she glared at Rafe. "Which means, *cheri,* since you hinted that you'd be better suited to Gen than Andrew is, you'd have to make a choice."

Rafe's smile froze. "You are blowing this out of proportion, my sweet. There is no other for me but you." He looked at Drew, his nostrils flaring. "And no other man for you but me."

"Am I missing something?" Pierre asked, the sudden tension in the room hard to ignore. He looked at Rafe and pointed to Drew. "Is the feud between you two more than just Andrew's Montague heritage?"

Piercing Rafe with a blue glacier gaze, Drew's grin was positively villainous. "Cousin Rafe's the man," he said in modern slang. "*And* kin. Which, in spite of his doubt, has been accepted as fact. So what could there possibly be for us to feud over?" Pointedly he transferred his gaze to Marianne.

"What indeed?" Rafe responded with a smirk of his own as he slipped his hand into Marianne's.

Fighting down jealousy, Drew felt vindicated, after a fashion. Without accusing Rafe, he'd let him know he was on to his robbery scheme. Although he might have roused Marianne's and Pierre's suspicions, he'd allayed their concerns about his well-being and never accused Rafe outright. A gracious, honorable act, indeed, when he only wanted to pound the bastard into the floor.

He stood. "Madame, mesdemoiselles," he said to the three women, chivalrously kissing their hands, "your presence here is a pleasant surprise, but I am road-weary and very tired."

"We understand, Andrew," Pierre said. "But you never did say, son. Did you get the loan?"

"Yes, Uncle Pierre, and I've already purchased the seedlings. We can begin planting as soon as tomorrow."

"Wonderful!" Pierre said, laughing. "I do believe the fates sent you here just for this purpose."

Just for this purpose? Could that really be the reason for my being here? It was grasping at straws to think that somehow Marianne might have needed him as well, despite the fact that on his second visit to Laurinda, she'd said Marianne was planning something that only he could prevent her from doing. He was trying to prevent her wedding to Rafe, but she seemed intent on going through with the plans.

"Maybe you're right, Uncle Pierre. Good night, everyone." He paused at the door and focused on Rafe. "I know how grateful you are that I recovered the buggy, Cousin, but thanks isn't necessary. I know you'll think of ways to make the culprits pay for their stupidity. Have a pleasant evening, all, and you especially, Rafe." With that, Drew departed the room.

When he got on the path to the *garçonnière,* he was tired and quite hungry. He'd be damned, however, if he'd spend an evening with Rafe fawning over Marianne and Genevieve flirting with *him.* Some evening that would be, with Drew being jealous of Rafe's attention to Mari and Mari upset over Genevieve's attention to him. Of course, if he had a sister like Genevieve, who constantly vacillated between love and envy, he'd be upset, too. And how easy the girl's envy was to read.

The stillness and beauty of the grounds as night stole the light annoyed him tonight. There was nothing like the sound of the huge engines of a passing jet or the whirring of sirens to jar you back to reality. A little jarring after the events of the day was just what he needed. But, unfortunately, such progress was decades away, and his restless anger only underscored that.

As he reached his quarters, the light of the rising moon

shone bright enough to outline shadows and shapes. Drew clearly saw the shape of a man going toward the stables. Further study revealed the man to be Rafe.

A few minutes passed before Rafe emerged riding his palomino. If Drew had had any doubts that the figure was Rafe, the sight of the horse confirmed his suspicions. Rafe's horse was the showiest in the region, and he'd forbidden anyone else to ride him.

Knowing the furtive figure bode ill will, Drew watched until Rafe disappeared. Entering his rooms and closing the door, he reminded himself to be wary of his relative.

Chapter 28

"ANDREW?" MARIANNE STOOD on the top step of the staircase in Drew's bedchamber, waiting for his reply, knowing she couldn't stay very long. On the heels of Drew's departure, Rafe had announced an important meeting that he'd forgotten with the Elders of St. Francisville. Excusing himself, he'd promised to return as soon as possible and rushed out. She'd waited only ten minutes before doing the same and heading for the *garçonnière*, careful of every shadow she crossed.

Now it seemed she'd come for naught. A gaslamp burned low, outlining Drew's long figure as he lay in the big half-tester. He appeared to be sleeping. She hated to wake him, but hated to leave as well without being in his arms one last time. As soon as she received the watch to give to Rafe, she was going to leave for Paris.

She walked to the bed. "Drew?" she called, louder this time.

He opened his eyes and stared at her. The yearning in his blue gaze sent a wave of desire through her. He waited, not speaking. But she didn't want words tonight.

The silent standoff went on for a few minutes before Drew sat up. "You came."

"I couldn't stay away."

His seductive look slid downward, and her whole being danced with anticipation. He held out his hand, which she eagerly accepted.

Lying beside him on the bed, she wrapped her arms around his neck and cried out with joy when his tongue plundered her mouth. There was no shyness, no hesitation, only urgency driving them to completion, and she soon found herself as naked as he was beneath the covers.

His hot kisses trailed her throat, found her breasts, teased her nipple.

Impatient for him, she sat up and gently pushed him back. Straddling him, she impaled herself upon his manhood. She threw her head back and started slow, delicious movements. His hands clutched her buttocks as she slid down upon him, and she doubted that anything was ever going to ruin the memory of this night.

"Hortenzia! Quick, girl, let me in!" Simon's frantic cries and pounding on the door pierced the stillness of the night. "I's gotta see Masta Pierre."

From her place in the small chamber connected to the outside kitchen, Hortenzia scrambled to her feet. Bent on giving Simon a piece of her mind for disturbing her sleep, she rushed to the door and yanked it open. "Is you done lost your min', Simon?" she asked angrily. "You's about to wake the whole house—"

"Quit yo' gabbin', woman!" Simon snapped, brushing past her. "There's men out in the carriage house fixin' to steal Mista Drew's seedlin's. Rouse Masta Pierre! He gotta stop 'em."

"Oh, Lawdy," Hortenzia exclaimed, making the sign of the cross. "Wait here, Simon." Grabbing her thread-thin wrapper and quickly putting it on, she turned and ran into the house, yelling at the top of her lungs for Masta Pierre.

He hurried down the stairs, a pair of hastily donned breeches beneath his nightshirt, his feet bare. Eve and Ralph and Genevieve and Clarisse, in various forms of night garments, came as well from all over the place.

"What the hell's wrong with you?" Pierre blustered, sounding more like Rafe than the kind man he was. "What's going on?"

Swallowing past the lump in her throat, Hortenzia curtsied. "Masta Pierre, Simon say mens is in the carriage house, tryin' to steal Masta Drew's seeds."

"Where is Simon?" Pierre snarled.

Hortenzia pointed in the direction of the outside kitchen just as Marianne came down the hallway.

He frowned at her. "What are you doing up and about, Marianne? It's close to midnight."

"Monsieur—"

"Pardon me, Masta Pierre," Hortenzia interrupted, frantic that all of Masta Drew's hard work would be stolen away. "Please come!"

"Calm yourself," Clarisse ordered. "Hortenzia, take Pierre to find Simon so he can figure out what's going on. I'll deal with Marianne."

"Maman," Marianne said, not in the least worried by her mother's words, "let's all go into the study. Hortenzia will instruct Simon to go there."

"Very well," Pierre said. "And bring some brandy with you, Hortenzia."

"Yessuh." Hortenzia hurried to her quarters and got Simon, then grabbed a bottle of brandy from the storehouse. Only a few minutes had passed before she and Simon got to the study.

"Masta Pierre," Simon said, as excited as ever, "some mens is in the carriage house fixin' to steal the seedlin's Mista Drew done bought for plantin'. I thought I done seed Masta Rafe, too." At the narrowing of the old man's eyes, Simon stepped back and said, " 'Course, I could be mistaken."

"You're not!" Masta Pierre gritted, rising to his feet. He was as angry as a bull on a charge. "Simon, get my goddamn shotgun from the gun cabinet. Then arouse Master Drew. Tell him to meet me at the carriage house. Tell him don't forget his gun and to shoot anything that moves there. Hortenzia, get back to your quarters!" Quickly he followed Simon out of the room.

"*Mon Dieu!*" Marianne gasped, watching as Hortenzia followed in the men's wake. Thoughts of Drew's lovemaking replayed in her mind, and she was grateful that she'd decided to leave him when she had. Imagine if she had been caught in his arms!

Clarisse clutched her chest and sank into the nearest chair.

"Maman, I cannot believe that Monsieur Pierre would shoot his own son!" Genevieve said, her voice trembling.

"Don't be ridiculous, Gen," Marianne said crossly. "Monsieur Pierre loves his son. He would never shoot Rafe." Even if he *did* deserve it, she wanted to add, and even if that *would* be a way out of marrying Rafe and her not having to leave her family and go to Paris.

But was Rafe really so despicable? Could he possibly be out there defending Bienvenu against the thieves? She suddenly felt guilty for being so judgmental when she didn't know all the facts. Or maybe it was the censure in her mother's eyes. Whatever it was, for the sake of fairness she decided to hold her judgment in reserve.

"Would you care if Monsieur Pierre did shoot Rafe?" Genevieve huffed.

Heat rushed into her cheeks. "I would not like to see anyone hurt, Genevieve," she replied with ire.

"That is not what I asked you, Marianne," Genevieve bit out. "You are absolutely too indifferent to Rafe and not indifferent enough toward Monsieur Andrew."

"How dare you! Because of your own tendresse toward Rafe, you presume to tell me how I should feel and act," Marianne snapped.

"Enough!" Clarisse yelled. "You are sisters. The messieurs Montague appear to be in deep trouble. They will need our sympathy at the outcome. Whatever the outcome, your bickering will cease."

Marianne bowed her head. "You're right, of course, Ma-man."

Raising her chin, Genevieve folded her arms but relented at Clarisse's glare. "*Oui*, Maman," she agreed. "I should not have provoked Mari." She smiled. "I'm sorry, *mon chou.*"

Marianne nodded, the pleasure she'd experienced in Drew's arms evaporating under the strain of these new and dire developments. "It was a silly argument, Gen," she said quietly. "Please, let's just wait for their return."

It was a wait that turned out to be interminable. An hour went by, then two and three. The three women sat alone before Eve and Hortenzia dressed and prepared coffee for them, then joined the tense vigil.

Finally, at close to four in the morning, the sound of the front door bursting open reached them. Hurrying to the foyer, they watched as a bruised and bloodied Rafe stumbled into the room. A livid Pierre followed close behind, shotgun in hand.

"You will leave this place, Rafe, at first light. Bienvenu is no longer your home. You goddamn bastard, how could you try to sabotage Drew's plans?" he roared, his voice cracking.

Drew charged through the open door, and Rafe managed a scowl in his direction as he answered his father. "Bienvenu will always be my home, old man," he spat around swollen lips. "I wouldn't try to change that fact if I were you. I vow Andrew will not benefit from this."

Pierre leveled the shotgun at Rafe's head. "Don't threaten me, boy. I'll send you to your maker in a heartbeat!"

"Uncle Pierre, no!" Drew said frantically. "It's not worth it. Put down that gun before it goes off accidentally!"

His eyes wild with anger, his hair disheveled, his clothes as unkempt as Drew's and Rafe's, Pierre hesitated. It was obvious the three of them had been involved in quite a scuffle.

"*Please!* You don't want to kill your own son, Uncle."

Rafe shoved Drew aside, not in the least frightened that his father was contemplating pulling the trigger. "I don't need defending from you against my own father, you meddling bastard!"

In a split second, Pierre raised the shotgun above Rafe's head and fired. Plaster and mortar flew everywhere as pellets landed in the wall. Marianne screamed; Clarisse and Genevieve clutched each other.

Drew and Rafe merely stared at Pierre in shock.

"Get out!" he snarled. "Get out *now,* Rafe!"

Rafe drew in a deep breath. "My pleasure, Pa Pa *cheri,*" he said with scorn. He looked at Marianne, hardly noticing her trembling, not caring that Genevieve was weeping piteously. "Prepare to leave immediately, Marianne. I will escort you and your family back to Baywood. The wedding plans can go on there."

Speechless, Marianne looked from her mother to her sister and then at Drew. Imploring eyes begged her to stay with him. She wanted to stay, could have easily done so. But she wanted to prevent any further bloodshed. If she refused Rafe's request—no, demand—he'd surely attack Drew. As angry as Pierre was, he'd shoot Rafe on the spot.

But Pierre loved Rafe, she told herself. Before a fortnight passed, he'd summon him back to Bienvenu. They were both just too angry to see reason at the moment.

She'd go with Rafe and her family to Baywood until things settled down.

Marianne walked to where Pierre stood. She gingerly took the shotgun from him without any resistance and passed it to Drew, then touched his arm. "Monsieur?"

"You'd best prepare to leave, Marianne," Pierre said quietly. He stared at her, his glance registering hurt and confusion. "The sooner he's out of here the better."

Her heart went out to him, because he looked suddenly tired and older than his years.

Holding her tears at bay, Marianne hugged him tightly. But it was like clutching a granite statue, for he remained still and unmoving. "*Au revoir,* monsieur," she whispered.

"Come along, Maman, Genevieve," she said briskly, letting him go. "There's much to be done and not long to do it." Without glancing at Drew, she hurried to the stairs, not caring one way or the other if her mother and sister followed.

Chapter 29

A CARDINAL LANDED on the black wrought-iron banister and gazed at Marianne through beady eyes as she leaned against one of the Doric columns surrounding the veranda at Baywood. The bird seemed to sense her disquiet, its brilliant red color a vivid reminder of nature's perfection. A torrential downpour yesterday had cleansed the air and left cloudless blue skies and moist green foliage.

Contemplating the events of the past two days, Marianne sat on the swing and rested her hands against her belly. The cardinal flew away, and she closed her eyes, tired and exhausted from another sleepless night as she tried to comprehend the makeup of Rafe's character.

She marveled at how content he'd become the past two days, never once mentioning the terrible rift between him and his father. Or the terrible deed he'd been accused of. Surely he loved his father, yet he'd destroy with one fell swoop everything his father loved. All because of his hatred of Andrew, which in essence was because of her.

Yet she wasn't in the least sorry that she'd met Andrew. She wasn't in the least sorry that she'd allowed him to make love to her. But the sorrow that she'd never see him again when she left reached deep down to the very marrow of her bones.

With a weary sigh, she opened her eyes and rubbed them. Yawning, she allowed her gaze to meander as far as her eyes could see. The cotton in the not-too-distant fields was not yet ripe enough for picking, so the few slaves out there were cleaning the weeds away.

Along the pathway, she saw Rafe and Genevieve on horseback. He sat astride his beautiful palomino, while Gen rode sidesaddle on a gray gelding. They looked fine together, as right as she and Drew did. She'd try to help her sister get her heart's desire, but she herself would have to live with but a memory of Drew for the rest of her life. Too many complications stood in the way of their finding lasting happiness.

"Are your thoughts troubling you, *ma cherie*?"

Clarisse's voice drifted to Marianne through her misery. She transferred her gaze in the direction of the sound and gave her mother a half-smile of her own. Clarisse had walked noiselessly onto the gallery and stood there watching Marianne through all-knowing eyes. The striped dark green gown she wore was a refreshing change from the widow's weeds she'd favored until a couple weeks ago. Suddenly Marianne had the inkling that her mother would be fine, with or without her. The thought cheered her, because Clarisse had been terribly sad and crippled with grief for the past year.

"Mari?"

Marianne giggled nervously, afraid she might let slip some clue about her intention to leave on a ship bound for Paris. "*Non,* Maman, nothing is troubling me. Not at all."

Settling next to her, Clarisse patted her arm, then looked to where Rafe and Genevieve sat atop their horses. "I cannot help but see the difference in this situation, Marianne."

"How so, Maman?" Marianne asked, frowning, unsure what her mother meant.

Clarisse nodded toward the couple. "Shouldn't you be the one riding with Monsieur Rafe?"

"Oh, Maman, you make too much out of nothing," Marianne said with a laugh, waving a dismissing hand. "I was feeling unwell today, so Gen volunteered to ride with him, that's all."

Arching her eyebrows, Clarisse pursed her lips. "Is it, indeed?" she asked. Then she indicated the two figures with a gesture of her hand as Rafe leaned from his horse toward Genevieve. He caressed her bosom before their faces came close to one another in what could only be a kiss.

Shocked at their boldness, Marianne gasped and straightened in her seat. "*Sacre bleu!* Genevieve is stealing Rafe from me, Maman!"

Clarisse frowned at her. "I'll have none of your theatrics, Marianne Beaufort," she snapped, narrowing her eyes. "If you cared about Rafe, he would be kissing you out there instead of Genevieve!"

Leaning back in her seat, Marianne sighed. She had never been any good at theatrics. "I do not want Rafe Montague's kisses."

Now it was Clarisse's turn to sigh. She rubbed her temples. "So I've noticed, *cherie,*" she said softly, without any rancor. "Not since Andrew came into your life." She smiled tenderly. "I think he's the man who owns your heart."

Her bottom lip trembling at her mother's perception, Marianne fixed a tortured gaze on Clarisse, but turned at the sound of horses' hooves. Their hair blowing in the wind, Rafe and Genevieve rode toward them.

"*Bonjour*, Maman, Mari," Genevieve greeted happily upon reaching them, her gloved hands holding tightly to the reins.

Rafe jumped off his horse and went to assist Genevieve off hers. "*Bonjour,* mesdames," he said once his task was complete, still holding Genevieve's hand in his as Henry hurried to where they stood and took the horses away.

Beside Marianne, Clarisse stiffened. She gave the two a tight smile. "I trust your ride was satisfactory?"

Tucking her riding crop under her arm, Genevieve bounced up the steps, pulling Rafe along with her. For a man who'd nearly lost his life at his father's hands because of his vicious scheming, he seemed entirely too content, Marianne thought with irritation.

"*Oui*, Maman, the ride was *magnifique!*" Genevieve said, then focused her smug attention on Marianne. "Really, Mari. You should ride with your fiancé. Someone could steal him from you."

Hands on hips, Rafe widened his eyes, then released a very masculine chuckle. "There's not a chance of that happening, Gen," he announced, going to place a kiss on Marianne's cheek.

Her cheeks reddening, Genevieve cracked the side of the banister with her riding crop and flounced inside.

Clarisse sniffed as the big entrance door slammed shut. "What do you suppose is her problem?" she asked, looking at Rafe with annoyance.

"I don't know, Maman," Marianne answered, barely able to stand Rafe's presence. The quicker she got away, the better. Early this morning, she'd sent for the watch she'd bought for Rafe in St. Francisville. "Maybe we should ask her."

"*Non, mon petites,*" Rafe quickly answered, seating himself at the small wicker table. "She will work out her own problems. Do not invade her private thoughts."

Rafe would condemn and scorn her for loving Andrew and giving herself to him when—there was little doubt of it in Marianne's mind—he had already bedded Genevieve. Yet he still sought to marry her, instead of doing the honorable thing, the *best* thing, for all concerned and severing their betrothal. It made her decision seem all the more wise and increased her disgust toward Rafe tenfold.

She smiled demurely at him. "We have no secrets between us, Rafe. Her private thoughts are ours. You may be right, however, in this instance. We will leave her to her privacy for the moment." She sent him a cool glance. After the display Rafe and Genevieve had just put on, she didn't care what Rafe thought. As much as possible, she had always shown Rafe the utmost respect during her dealings with Drew. Even if most of that respect had been due to ulterior motives—to insure her mother and sister's future well-being—she expected no less from him. "She will eventually, and without a doubt, tell us what's troubling her."

Rafe threaded his hand through his hair. "Really?" he said, sprawling his legs carelessly before him, the gesture so like Drew's that it was easy to see the family resemblance. "That's interesting. But as long as she's truthful in what she says . . ." His voice trailing off, he shrugged his shoulders.

Clarisse and Marianne exchanged glances before her mother turned on him.

"Truthful?" Clarisse flared. "Neither of my girls ever lie, monsieur!"

"But of course not, madame," Rafe agreed, folding his arms and smiling with uncertainty. "I would be less than a gentleman if I even suggested such. I am merely trying to point out that some things can be misconstrued. Taken out of context."

"I see," Marianne said, choosing to answer when Clarisse drew in a great intake of breath, ready to lambaste him. Quickly she changed the subject. "Tell me, Rafe, did something happen on your outing with Gen that I should know about?"

If Rafe had realized she was out on the veranda observing her surroundings, Marianne figured, he never would have been bold enough to kiss her sister. If she was able to see them, however, they'd have been able to see her as well—except that they hadn't been paying attention. They'd been too focused on one another.

"Nothing that I can think of, *cherie,*" Rafe answered with another insolent shrug. Then he laughed bitterly. "Of course, the news of that old witch's death could have upset her."

Marianne stared at Rafe, a cold dread engulfing her. There was only one witch whom she knew of, only one whom Gen ever associated with. She refused to believe that Laurinda was dead. She seemed immortal, as if she'd live forever. Her heart pounding, she scooted to the edge of her seat. "What old witch?" she croaked, her voice cracking with fear and disbelief.

"But I don't think the woman's death affected her," Rafe went on as though he hadn't heard Marianne. "It's probably the fact that she was amongst the first to die this year of Yellow Jack. Gen is probably upset because it brings back unwanted memories."

"D-do you know her n-name?" Marianne stammered, a shiver going through her.

Rafe shifted in his seat and drummed his fingers on the table. "I believe everyone has heard of her," he said. "Laurinda Toussaint. She's supposedly an enchantress. To me that's just a proper name for 'witch.' "

Marianne clutched her chest. *"Mon Dieu!"* she blurted. "Laurinda Toussaint is dead? When?"

"Three days ago," Rafe replied with cold nonchalance. The discussion of the death of a fine thoroughbred would've garnered more sympathy from him. "But I know how you feel, *cherie*. One could almost believe the old hag would never die," he said, chuckling. "But she most certainly proved us wrong."

Marianne's mouth felt dry, and her head pounded. Laurinda had been Drew's window back to his world and his daughter. Without her, he might be stuck here forever, as she'd predicted. What if he needed Laurinda to get home? Suppose he was depending on her for some additional knowledge? Marianne knew no one else as wise as Laurinda. Who would help Drew now?

"Well," Rafe was saying, "this is just a warning for all of us to stay out of New Orleans. The black population is rarely visited by Yellow Fever, and if Laurinda and a few others of my acquaintance got it, then it is quite an ill omen."

"And so early in the season," Clarisse put in quietly. "It is virtually unheard of for the disease to strike before August. What do the editorialists have to say about this?"

"Nothing, madame. Supposedly the reports of deaths

from the Fever are nothing more than hysterics, though they could very well destroy the city's commerce if these early cases are proven as fact." He cleared his throat to dispel the solemn pall that had fallen around them, then stood. "I am most appreciative of my lodgings here, mesdames. I wouldn't want to be stuck in the city at this time."

"Who would?" Marianne asked absently, thinking of Drew. Did he know of Laurinda's death? And if he didn't, how would he ever find out unless the news came from her? She wanted to stay near him until she was certain things worked out for him, but couldn't. The longer she remained, the closer her wedding day to Rafe would come, and the more difficult it would be to bow out gracefully. "But Baywood in a sense is already yours, Rafe."

"I have no intention of claiming Baywood, Marianne, until after the nuptials."

"How gallant you are, monsieur," Clarisse remarked with a smile. "And generous."

Rafe bowed. "*Merci*, madame. I do try. Now *pardonnez-moi, s'il vous plaît,* mesdames. There are things at Baywood that need tending."

"Of course," Marianne responded. She watched him descend the steps and head in the direction of the stables.

A few minutes of silence passed before Clarisse spoke again. "Marianne, what are your plans?"

Marianne stilled, her mother's question catching her off guard. There was something poignant in the query, as if Clarisse had an inkling of Marianne's intentions. Or maybe it was only her guilt. Though her mother was much stronger these past weeks, she was still depending on Marianne for much. Too much.

"I don't understand, Maman. My plans?"

"I think you do, *petite fleur*. Surely you must be curious about other possible intimate moments between your sister and Rafe."

"I suppose I am," Marianne admitted calmly. "But what can I do?"

"The question, *ma petite,* is what *will* you do?"

Marianne leaned back in her seat, tension creeping into her. "Why, marry Rafe, Maman. What else?"

Her choices were few. But they didn't include marrying Rafe Montague. He himself had given her the perfect out when she'd discovered him kissing her sister. Marianne could never become part of his two-woman harem, and besides, she was convinced that Genevieve was best for him. From the looks of things, Rafe didn't seem opposed to Gen's attentions. Therefore, her sister would get her wish and wed Rafe.

In a strange way, Marianne envied Genevieve. By marrying Rafe, Gen would capture the man she loved.

Marianne's heart tightened in her chest. She loved Drew but had to accept that he would never be hers. She really wasn't losing him by going to Paris, since he'd never really been hers to begin with. But she knew she had to see him one last time before she boarded the ship that would whisk her across the Atlantic.

She would abide the separation from her mother and sister; one day she'd return for a visit. *Non*, she amended, after some years went by she could return for good. But she could almost feel her heart shattering into tiny pieces at the thought of never seeing Drew again.

Their fates were sealed, and she was powerless to intervene except on her own behalf. As soon as the household was asleep tonight, she'd set her plan in motion.

She thought of how great Rafe's fury would be. Maybe she shouldn't envy Gen after all, she mused. Only God knew what unsavory acts Rafe was truly capable of.

"Marianne?"

"Maman, please, let's drop the subject," Marianne answered tiredly.

"Very well, *cherie*," Clarisse agreed without hesitation. "Would you like some cool lemonade, Mari?"

"*Non,* Maman," Marianne said, rising from her chair. "What I would like is a rest before dinner. I would like to look refreshed when Rafe returns." In truth, she wanted to pack a few things in a valise to have ready when she departed later, and to make sure her money was there.

Clarisse rose. "I suppose I will rest, too, *cherie,*" she said, looking around. "Baywood is quite nice, don't you think?"

Marianne smiled sadly. "Very nice," she agreed wistfully, nearly choking on her heartbreak. Impulsively she flung her arms around Clarisse's neck. "I love you, Maman," she whispered, unable to hold back her tears.

How would her mother accept losing her? Clarisse had almost lost her senses upon Jean-Louis's death. Marianne consoled herself with the thought their separation would only last for a short while. She intended to stay away for two or three years, long enough for Rafe and Gen to get comfortable in their marriage.

That is, assuming they *did* wed.

Clarisse kissed Marianne's cheek, and her arms tightened around her. "I love you, too, *enfante cherie.* I will always be here for you."

When they broke apart, Marianne saw the tears glistening in her mother's eyes. She saw the worry—and the understanding. She knew Clarisse had guessed her intentions.

She smiled, unable to do anything more. "*Merci,* Maman. I'll remember that. Always. Now I must seek out Tomas."

"I'll see you at supper, *cherie,*" Clarisse said.

"Of course, Maman."

With that, Marianne made her way to the stables. She patted the gray gelding Gen had ridden earlier, his nose cold and wet, his face velvety. "Would you like to take me to Bienvenu tonight, Mack?"

"Miz Mari?" Tomas said, alerting her to his presence as he raised his head from the stall he was cleaning.

"Tomas, I must speak to you," she said without hesitation.

Tomas pushed his way out of the stall and closed the door behind him. "What's wrong, mam'zelle?"

"I can trust you, *oui, ami*?"

"Sho' you can, Miz Mari. What's the trouble?"

"I'm going to Bienvenu tonight to visit Monsieur Pierre—"

Frowning, Tomas scratched his head. "Tonight, mam'zelle?"

"*Oui,* Tomas," Marianne answered impatiently. "Tonight. But I must go under the cover of darkness, because Monsieur Rafe would forbid me to go."

"I understand, Miz Mari," Tomas said, nodding. "I heard 'bout what happened at Bienvenu. I'll take you there."

"*Non,* Tomas, I can find my way alone. I am not afraid. Monsieur Rafe might get angry if you help me, and this is his plantation. He can do with you as he pleases. Just see to it that Mack is saddled. He's surefooted and fast."

"Sho' will, Miz Mari."

"Don't tell anyone we've spoken or where I've gone."

"You can sho' count on me, Miz Mari. I won't say nuthin'. Not even after you returns."

Marianne didn't have the heart to tell him she wouldn't be returning to Baywood. That would alarm him, and, in fear for her safety, he'd probably let her secret slip. She embraced him, and he jumped back in surprise, not returning the hug. "*Merci,* Tomas."

Everything was set. Now all she had to do was wait.

Nearing three the next morning, Marianne inched her way downstairs. All was silent and still as she reached the front door and quietly opened it. The hinges creaked, and her breath caught in her throat.

When no one rushed down the stairs, she slipped out into the pitch-black night. Clouds threatening rain covered the moon, and the night mist rolling from the river swirled amongst the trees.

She paused on the veranda, daunted for a second. She had no time to gainsay her decision, however. She could be discovered at any minute. If not by Rafe, then by a servant.

Quickly recovering her nerve, she started toward the stables, surprised and grateful to see Tomas walking in her direction.

"I got him ready for you, Miz Mari," the servant whispered. "It look like rain, though. You sho' you can make it alone?"

"*Oui,* Tomas. I'm sure." With Tomas's assistance, Marianne climbed into the saddle and sat astride the horse. "Hurry back indoors before you are discovered."

"Yes'm."

As Tomas disappeared from sight, she took a last look at her childhood home and swallowed the lump rising in her throat. Tears stinging her eyes, she galloped away.

Chapter 30

HOURS LATER, AS a light, steady rain plagued the day, a stunned Rafe held a letter from Marianne. She'd left it in the dining chamber, weighted down by an exquisite gold watch and fob. But her generosity paled in the light of her betrayal. She was leaving him, bowing out of the wedding that was supposed to seal Baywood in her family. Instead, she'd shocked him and fled. With her went his dreams of having her for his own. She'd run away and deprived him of the magnetic personality that drew everyone to her.

She had stolen the contentment he'd experienced in her company these past weeks. Never in his wildest dreams did he think she'd ever do such a thing. He hadn't thought her that bold.

He glanced at her words again, then looked at Clarisse and Genevieve. Ten minutes ago, just after he'd found the letter, they'd come rushing in. Luella had informed the women of Marianne's absence, and now the entire household was in disarray, worried about his fiancée.

Clarisse touched his arm. "Please, Rafe, what does she say?" she asked, her voice trembling.

Taking pity upon her, Rafe looked at the letter again, the

weight of the watch heavy in his hand. " '*Monsieur*,' " he
began, swallowing hard. He had never felt so lost before,
not in the long years of lacking a mother's presence, not
in the turbulent times with his father. " 'I know you won't
find it easy to forgive me. That will not deter my decision,
however, one that I thought over very precisely. . . .' " He
clenched his jaw, the next line branded into his memory.
Sitting, he indicated for Clarisse and Genevieve to do the
same. "I think you'd better," he said, and waited until they
complied before he continued. " 'By the time you read this,
I will be on a ship bound for Paris.' "

"Oh, *mon Dieu!* Paris?" Clarisse cried out, clutching her
chest. "*Non, non!* You must be mistaken. Paris!"

"Maman, please let him finish," Genevieve implored,
taking her mother's hand. She nodded to Rafe, her look
grave. "Go ahead, monsieur."

" 'I implore you not to take your anger toward me out
on Maman and Gen,' " he went on, wondering where indeed his anger had gone. He should have been raging, vowing vengeance upon her. Instead, he clutched the watch
she'd left for him as if it was a lifeline. He cleared his
throat. " 'Do not throw them off Baywood lands. If the
affection, the kiss, I witnessed between you and Gen means
anything—and I forgive you that indiscretion—you will for
once do what is required of you.' "

The kiss! God in heaven, she'd seen the kiss! Was it any
wonder she'd fled him? If only he could turn back the hands
of time, he would have sent Genevieve on her way after
the rendezvous in the carriage house and returned to the
manor alone. What had he done? His own lust had cost him
Marianne.

"Is that all?" Clarisse asked tearfully.

He sighed and stared at Gen, who was close to tears and
pale. "No, madame." Focusing on the letter again, he read,
" 'Unlike myself, Maman and Genevieve need masculine
presence in their existence. Do not abandon them, I beg
you. Please relay my love to them. There was no affection
between you and me, Rafe,' " he continued, starting the last

paragraph, " 'only a business arrangement. I do not want to be locked in such a marriage. I have much regret for the loss I will bear by leaving. *Merci beaucoup* for your consideration of the Beaufort women. *Adieu,* monsieur. Remorsefully, Marianne.' "

Crumpling it in a tight fist, he let the letter fall to the floor.

"Oh, Maman," Genevieve wailed. "How could she?"

"Hush, Genevieve!" Clarisse snapped. "How could *we*? We had no right to burden her so. I am glad she did not allow herself to become a sacrificial lamb for us." She looked at Rafe as she stood. But the scorn he expected from her for his indiscriminate kiss with Genevieve didn't come. Instead, she said, "Monsieur, we will be out of here as soon as possible."

Rafe sniffed in irritation. He needed time to think, time to get his spiraling emotions under control. "There's no need for such haste, madame. I am due in Atlanta by week's end and will be away for a month. We will discuss this and reach a decision upon my return."

Clarisse curtsied. "You're very gracious, monsieur. If we can assist you in any way—"

"That won't be necessary," Rafe interrupted impatiently, the first vestiges of anger hitting him. "I'll have Tomas assist me, madame. Now, if you'll both excuse me?"

"But, of course, monsieur. Come along, Genevieve." Waiting until her daughter preceded her out, Clarisse departed with grace and style, her chin raised and pride in every move.

Long after the women had left him alone, Rafe sat in the parlor, turning the watch over and over. The curlicued initials were an extra-special touch, no doubt meant to soothe his rage. But Marianne had made a misstep, for it only served to fuel his darker emotions. His shock and hurt were disintegrating, for which he was grateful. Such emotions were for weaklings, and he definitely couldn't afford to be weak in this situation. He had too many scores to settle.

Marianne! The bitch! He'd known all along she didn't

love him, but he thought she'd held him in some small regard. He was the best catch in all of southern Louisiana, and he thought she'd finally come to realize that. But the act she'd put on for him was just to gain his confidence.

His fist closed around the watch, and a jolt went through him. The piece of jewelry seemed alive, vibrating, seething with an unseen force. Yet it didn't frighten him. It fascinated him, and he stared at it, thinking of Marianne.

She had caught him off guard and fled without warning, while he foolishly thought she would marry him.

Well, good riddance. He didn't need her. Rafe smiled wickedly, the gold filigree on the watch gleaming in the sunlight. The knowledge that if he couldn't have her, dear Cousin Andrew wouldn't either consoled him. He still had a grievance with his cousin, however.

Maybe Pierre had been right. Rafe should never have tried to sabotage Andrew's work at the plantation when his plan to have him buried in the river by those three fools failed. But he'd been so worried that Drew would succeed when he hadn't been able to find a way to do so. He'd only needed a little more time to come up with another plan to save Bienvenu. As a result, he'd acted in haste. And gotten caught for his efforts.

He'd never seen his father quite so angry. Or hurt. He'd heard it said that his father had been grief-stricken over Rafe's mother's death when he was just a boy, too young even to remember her existence. But Pierre had always been a jovial, robust figure whom Rafe admired as much as he resented.

Then along came Drew, the son of the brother who'd disappeared years ago. Perfect, mysterious, uncouth Andrew. All Pierre saw in Rafe from that point on were his flaws. Rafe could do no right, and Drew could do no wrong.

Well, he'd let Cousin Andrew raise Bienvenu back to its former glory, then see him run off the plantation. The bastard had stolen his father's affections from him; Rafe vowed not to let him steal his inheritance as well. He'd see Andrew dead first.

Standing in the doorway, Tomas cleared his throat, and Rafe looked up from his contemplation.

"Miz Clarisse said you be wantin' to see me, suh."

"Yes, Tomas," Rafe said wearily, getting up from his seat. He deposited the watch and fob into his topcoat pocket and crushed the crumpled letter beneath his boot heel. "I am departing these premises at once. I will need your aid in starting me on my way."

"Yessuh," Tomas said.

Rafe followed the slave through the door, intent on biding his time in exacting revenge on Andrew, the man who'd caused such upheaval in his life.

Soaked from riding through a persistent light rain, Marianne gratefully steered Mack toward the *garçonnière* at Bienvenu later that afternoon. Exhausted and bedraggled, she unhooked her valise from the saddle horn and slid down the side of the horse. She looked over the dreary lands and saw figures walking along the levee, heading for the fields, oblivious to the drizzle.

Knowing Drew as well as she did, she figured he was probably already in the fields, working furiously. Hesitating momentarily, she decided against making her presence known to anyone just yet. With her valise firmly in hand, she trod to the entrance door of Drew's bachelor quarters. When she walked into the dry, brightly lit interior, she heaved a sigh of relief to be out of the elements.

She went up the steps to his bedchamber, where a delightful surprise greeted her: the brass tub was filled with water.

Walking to the tub, she leaned down and rippled the water to test it. It was pleasantly warm. That meant Drew would return soon. The servants wouldn't have filled the tub otherwise.

She released a squeal of delight, her joy boundless. Her limbs were stiff, and her inner thighs were sore from riding for hours. Fatigue had forced her to seek shelter twice along the way, lengthening the journey and adding to the danger for her as a woman alone.

Knowing that Drew expected to make use of the bath, which he'd probably ordered, Marianne stalled her intention to soak away her tiredness—but only for a brief moment. She'd be out of the bath so quickly, Drew would be none the wiser.

Without further ado, she stripped off her wet clothes and climbed into the tub. Sinking deep into the soothing water, she sighed in contentment. She lathered herself with the spicy soap on the iron stand next to the tub. She used it to wash her hair, then reached for the pitcher of water on the floor beside the tub.

When she poured the water over her head, she gasped loudly. It was freezing cold! It had probably been left for Drew's use to cool his bath, if he'd taken immediate use of it. But the heavy brass held the heat in, and steaming-hot water would cool slowly over the course of an hour.

Goose bumps raising her skin because of the cold water she'd poured into her hair, she wrung the excess water from her tresses, climbed out of the tub, then wrapped a towel around herself. There were only two towels there, but her hair was wet, so she secured the other one around her head.

After drying her hair as much as possible with the second towel, she draped it over a chair, hoping it would at least reach the damp stage before Drew attempted to use it.

The bath was more draining than she'd have thought. Fatigue hit her full force. It taxed her even to extract a nightgown from her valise and don it before sprawling on Drew's bed.

Chapter 31

"Nat," DREW SAID, stretching his arms to the cloudy, rainy sky. Dizziness was now accompanying the persistent headache and body pains he'd awakened with. But it was probably due to exhaustion from staying out in the fields for hours on end these past several days. "Let's all call it a day. We've made great progress today."

"Yessuh, Mista Drew," Nat said proudly. "And the Lawd done answered our prayers for rain."

Like Drew and the others out there, Nat was soaked to the skin and didn't seem to mind at all. Drew only wished this was the twenty-first century, when payment accompanied praise to such hard workers.

"It certainly looks like He has," Drew agreed with a laugh. "We can do this again tomorrow. I must be getting old, my friend—my muscles are aching like hell." He stretched his neck, then squeezed his temples. "On top of that, I have the damnedest headache."

"Ain't nothin' Hortenzia can't cure, Mista Drew," Nat reassured him. "She'll make you a herb soup. Less'n you want chicken soup?"

"Let's see." Drew laid a finger on his chin, pretending deep thought. "Herb or chicken? Tell you what, Nat. Why don't you tell her to make them both. That way, I can make my own choice by taste."

"All right, suh," Nat said with a nod. "Soon's she makes it, I'll bring it. I 'speck your bath must be cold 'bout now—you done ordered it over a hour ago. Do you wants me to bring you some hot water to put in your tub?"

"No thanks, Nat. I'll only be in long enough to wash the grime off myself. Tell Hortenzia I'll be waiting for her. I'll see you and the others tomorrow."

"All right, suh. I'll git the buckboard and take you to your gent'min's quarters."

"Just what I need, my friend," Drew said tiredly, walking with Nat to the pathway where the wagon stood hitched to the mule.

A short while later, Drew arrived at his quarters. He frowned when he saw the horse grazing near the garden surrounding the structure. Rafe! What had he come to do now, using a Beaufort horse no less? The bastard was really a numb-brain, leaving his calling card out in plain view.

For the past few hours, a strange weakness had seized Drew, but at the moment anger fueled a measure of strength in him. Not only was he going to beat his ancestor sense-less, but he'd personally escort him off the plantation. His great-great-grandpappy or not, Rafe needed to be taught a lesson.

"Thanks for the lift, Nat." Drew jumped off the wagon with renewed vigor. Thunder rumbled across the heavens, and lightning flashed a wide arc in the distance. Big, fat raindrops came streaming down suddenly. He pointed to the gray. "Hitch that horse to the back of the buckboard, Nat, and bring him to the stable. Then get out of this weather yourself."

He caught Nat's "Yessuh, Mista Drew," as he went cau-tiously to his door, the rain pounding him. He really didn't need to develop pneumonia in the here and now, given the medical knowledge of the time. He didn't need to develop *any* diseases. Surely he'd be a dead man and never get back to his daughter.

Walking as quickly and as quietly as possible, he made his way up the steps and to his bedroom. Suddenly he stopped in his tracks, afraid his eyes deceived him.

Jet black hair blanketed his pristine white pillow and the side of her face. Endlessly long eyelashes fanned her smooth cheeks as she lay on her side in restful repose. A cotton-and-lace nightgown covered her slender body and added a tender innocence to her exquisite beauty.

Marianne!

It couldn't be. She was just a mirage, born out of the terrible dizziness seizing him. Swaying on his feet, he moved closer to the bed.

"Marianne?" he whispered as he became steady once more. "Marianne?"

He received no response. Sitting on the edge of the bed, he perused his surroundings, making sure no one else stood in the shadows.

Finding them alone, he turned his full attention to her. He leaned over and kissed her cheek, then took one of her delicate hands into his own.

"Mari, darling?" he whispered in her ear, gently shaking her. "What are you doing here?"

Stretching luxuriously, Marianne turned from her side to her back. When she opened her sleep-filled eyes, her green gaze mesmerized him. "Umm," she murmured, smiling sensually. "I ran away, Drew." Her heavy lids closed over her beautiful eyes.

The implications of her statement ran through his mind. Rafe was probably hightailing it here at this very minute. It would be wise, Drew knew, to get her out of Rafe's reach as soon as possible. Maybe he could secure a room for Marianne in Baton Rouge. Drew hoped Rafe wouldn't think to look for her there until way after Drew had gotten her safely away. *He* had to return, because he still had about a week's work left to do to set everything on the road to prosperity again. After that, the rest was up to Mother Nature.

After he was done here, he'd return to wherever he'd

deposited Marianne, take her with him to Laurinda, and see what else could be done to get him and Marianne back to the future. Maybe Laurinda could do something for him without needing that elusive watch.

It was two days into August, which meant his time to make a successful return to 2000 was running out. He shuddered at the thought, his insides churning with tension and uncertainty. But it was up to him to pull Bienvenu out of the mire Rafe had managed to dig, which meant Drew was bound to the plantation for another few days, in spite of the perilous urgency of his own situation. Now Marianne's current predicament took precedence because she had run away.

"You ran away?" Drew echoed, considering that statement further and deciding he was being hasty to want to remove her. Marianne had never put him in any danger where Rafe was concerned, and she wouldn't do so now. He was suddenly secure in the knowledge that if she believed Rafe was after her, she definitely wouldn't have come to Bienvenu. "You ran away!" he repeated, the ramifications of that startling him. She'd run away from Rafe and come to him. He shook her gently. "Mari?"

"I'm tired, Drew," she said. As if to emphasize her point, she yawned.

"I know, my love," Drew whispered, seeing two of Marianne as his vision blurred again. He swallowed hard, his heart beating fast and furious, his mouth dry. "Marianne, have you broken your engagement?"

"I ran away."

"But you came to me," he answered, her simple answer tempering the excitement he felt at thinking she'd forsaken Rafe to be with him. "Why?"

"Because I wanted to tell you goodbye," she whispered groggily. "The end of summer is drawing near and—"

"The end of summer is six weeks away," Drew stated succinctly. "Are you telling me you didn't come so we could return to my time together?"

"No, Drew. I can't say that I haven't considered return-ing with you, but . . ."

Her voice trailed off. In frustration, Drew finished for her. "But you have your own agenda. You have your family and your rotten engagement!"

A soft snore was her only response. He cursed viciously and released her hand, watching as she turned onto her stomach, fast asleep.

Stunned by his unexpected guest, Drew didn't know what to make of her appearance. Whatever her reasons, she had come to *him* when she could have gone anywhere else in the world. There would be time enough to hear the full details, but he was as tired as she was at the moment and could wait to hear the whole story. Or point out the reasons why she should consider returning with him, he thought grimly, the sudden intensity of his aching muscles hard to ignore. A bath would hopefully soak away the aches and pains, even if he should have been accustomed to the hard labor by now, he told himself.

Noticing the soggy mess on the floor and her wet heap of clothes near the tub, Drew chuckled. The cheeky little witch had made use of *his* bathwater! Well, he was about to add his grime to hers, not that the water looked partic-ularly dirty.

Drew wearily got to his feet, shed his clothes, and climbed into the tub. He found it completely cold, but strangely soothing to his tired body. Using the spicy soap bar, he quickly bathed, then got out and put on a nightshirt.

With a sigh he lay down beside Marianne. Light-headedness nearly blinded him, and sharp pains in his mus-cles felt as if someone were driving pins into his body. He couldn't imagine what was happening to him.

Perhaps the myriad problems he'd acquired were stress-ing him to the limit. He'd heard that stress caused a range of illnesses, and he seemed to be finally succumbing to them.

Pierre hadn't been sober in the days since he'd ordered Rafe away. The man was hardly aware of Drew's presence.

Drew looked in on the old man at least once a day, but left Pierre's care to the servants, while doing as much as he could to help out in the fields. He couldn't fight Pierre's demons for him, however; that was something he needed to do for himself. At the present time, that didn't seem to be his top priority.

Drew pulled the sleeping Marianne into his arms and kissed the top of her head. She snuggled closer to him, moving sensuously against his body, stirring him to passion. Blood erected his manhood. He groaned, and his skin heated.

"Mari, how tired are you, darling?" he whispered, skimming his hand over one of her long legs and raising her nightgown in the process. His fingers brushed the curls at the vee of her thigh.

"Mista Drew!" Hortenzia's voice floated up the stairs. "I got your food, suh."

"Damn!" he whispered under his breath, pulling down Marianne's gown so that it once again modestly covered her lower body. Not only had he forgotten to lock the door against Rafe, but he'd also forgotten about the food Nat had promised him. He wasn't even hungry anymore.

"Mista Drew, suh!" Hortenzia called again, halfway up the stairs, her voice closer.

"Wait one minute, Hortenzia!" Reluctantly Drew got out of bed and started for the staircase. He wobbled like a drunk, dizziness once again nearly toppling him over. "Leave the tray on the table downstairs," he called when he realized he wouldn't make it any farther.

"Yessuh!"

With supreme effort, he made it back to the bed and collapsed beside Marianne, darkness engulfing him.

Chapter 32

STRETCHING CONTENTEDLY, MARIANNE stirred, and her eyelids fluttered open. Sunlight streaming through the open drapes flooded the bedchamber. Even so, it felt uncommonly warm for early summer, registering a marked change from just yesterday. It seemed as if she were lying next to a flaming furnace.

Focusing her sleepy regard around the room, realization struck her, and she bolted upright.

Mon Dieu! Recollections of her boldness of the day before assaulted her senses. She'd run away from Rafe Montague, leaving her mother and sister with him, so she could rendezvous with Drew before going to Paris!

Andrew! She was in his bedchamber, and the hard, heated figure next to her belonged to the man in question. Turning toward him, she stared at his back. Golden-blond hair touched his nape and fell onto his pillow. Lean muscles corded the planes of his back and broad shoulders. The covers falling low around him revealed a narrow waist and slim hips. A firm buttock and hard thigh peeked from under the bedspread.

Drew was sound asleep, and judging from the position of the sun outside, Marianne figured it was at least mid-morning, maybe even later. He really had to be tired to remain abed so late, she thought. Yet there was something strange about this situation. The deep tan of his skin held a slightly yellow undertone that she'd never seen there before.

Sick dread welling inside her, she scooted closer to him and laid a hand on his shoulder. She found his skin hot and dry, and she gasped, her heart sinking.

Gently pulling him onto his back, she cried out at the sallowness of his complexion.

"Non! Non! Non!" she wailed. "The Fever! Yellow Jack! It cannot be so! Not Andrew!"

Her cries awakened him, and he opened his eyes. A glazed, dark-blue gaze found hers, the yellow around his irises bringing horrible recollections of her father's demise back to haunt her.

"Marianne?" Drew's voice was low and hoarse. He reached out and caressed her cheek, his fingers as hot as a brazier, warming her skin. "I thought I was dreaming last night when I came and found you asleep in my bed." He drew in a deep breath and groaned. Closing his eyes, he rubbed his forehead with his free hand. "I wonder what's wrong with me, my love. I feel rotten."

Marianne clasped his hand tighter and leaned her cheek into it. She swallowed hard, knowing she must pull herself together for Andrew's sake. He needed her. He needed her to make him well again.

"Andrew," she whispered, wiping away the tears rolling down her cheeks. "You have the Fever, *cheri*."

Opaque eyes fastened onto her as Drew struggled to sit up. "What? Yellow Fever?"

"Non," Marianne scolded, pushing him back down, her temples pounding over how easily he succumbed to her efforts. He was very weak, too weak to attempt to sit up and too weak to resist her orders. She needed to get a basin filled with cool water and rub him down. "You mustn't, *mon amour*."

"Teal," he whispered, the word filled with anguish. Sinking back on the pillow, Drew closed his eyes. "I'll die without ever seeing my baby again."

Shuddering at his defeat, Marianne moistened her suddenly dry lips. Images of Jean-Louis crying out deliriously for Clarisse, of him clutching Marianne's hand as though she possessed the knowledge to heal him, assailed her. He'd fought for his life valiantly, but it hadn't been enough.

Yet Drew seemed to have given up. Then she remembered something he'd told her upon their first meeting, something that had scared the wits out of her upon hearing it—1853 was the year that eleven thousand people died of Yellow Jack.

She sagged on the bed, despair filling her. Had he come here merely to die? She surmised that his statement was motivated more by fear of the knowledge he possessed than by his actually waiting to die.

Glancing at him, she found him staring at the ceiling. For long moments she watched the rise and fall of his chest, saw the pulse point at the base of his neck, recalled the vital, sensual man that she knew him to be.

"*Non,* Andrew," she said, suddenly angry at the injustice of it all and determined to make him better. As long as delirium didn't set in, he would be safe. Once he became incoherent, he'd be a hairsbreadth away from falling into a coma. If he fell into a coma, she'd lose him. "I will not let you die, monsieur! We must find out how you got infected here at Bienvenu. Someone must have brought it from New Orleans—"

"Oh, God," he interrupted, stricken. He was still quite lucid, yet the look in his eyes remained as it had been since he'd awakened. "I did, Mari."

"But how? When?"

He frowned in concentration. "Three or four days ago, I went to New Orleans to secure that loan for my uncle. Remember?"

"*Oui,*" Marianne said slowly, wondering how she could have forgotten. That was the day he'd almost been robbed.

"But the people you saw were apparently free of the disease."

Drew coughed. "God, it hurts to do that."

Marianne laid a hand on his arm, barely able to watch him as he sagged with fatigue after the coughing bout ended. She caressed him. "I know it hurts."

"You can't stay here, Marianne," Drew told her. "You might get it."

She smiled at his bossy tone. "I've already had it, Andrew. I thought you were told about that. Once a person contracts the disease and recovers, he or she is immune for life. Remember?"

"No."

"It does not matter, *cheri*," she said softly, getting off the bed. "I must find out if Simon has it. He went with you to the city."

"I hope he's all right, Mari. He spent a longer time in the city than I did."

"But wasn't Simon with you all day?"

"No, sweetheart. I paid Laurinda a visit, and Simon waited for me in Congo Square. He was too frightened to go with me."

Marianne clutched the frame that held the mosquito netting, the blood draining from her face. Seeing her obvious distress, Drew paused.

"What's the matter, Mari?" he asked in alarm.

"Oh, Andrew," she said, her voice trembling. "Laurinda died two days ago of the Fever."

Drew passed his hands over his eyes. "Oh, my God!" he whispered. "She told me to come back when I'd found the watch. I assume it was for whatever final instructions I needed to get back home." He tried to raise up again.

Marianne placed a restraining hand on him and pushed him gently but firmly back down. "Listen to me, Andrew. We must get you well. Afterward, I promise we will sort out Laurinda's plans together so you can get back to your little Teal."

She wanted to say "so *we* can get back to your little

Teal," but Drew had his plans. Because of that, she hadn't altered hers. But she'd abandon them in a heartbeat, she knew, if he as much as hinted that he wanted her at his side in his world.

Not wanting an encounter with Rafe, she had planned to stay away from the manor house in case he returned for any reason. But now that was a chance she'd have to take. She needed to give the servants instructions about a menu for Drew. She also needed clean bed linen and to have the ones that he now lay on burned.

After that she'd find Monsieur Pierre. He seemed fond of the man he thought his nephew. She hoped she could count on his aid, even if he might elect to stay away from Drew's chamber if he hadn't already had the disease. And although the black population rarely contracted the disease, she still worried about Simon. She also worried that the servants might refuse to go near Drew. Though they didn't get it as much, they were as frightened of the disease as anyone else.

She hurried to the window and looked outdoors. In the distance, field hands lumbered along the levee, going to their tasks of sowing and planting. White, fluffy clouds rose in the blue sky, partially covering the sun. It was a pretty day, belying the illness raging in Drew. Everyone went about their tasks as usual. And so must she.

Moving away from the window, she peeked in Drew's direction, and paused. He'd fallen asleep. As long as his fever didn't rise, sleep was best. Quickly checking his temperature and satisfied that he didn't feel any hotter—although no cooler, either—she went to her valise and found a simple day gown. Knowing that time was of the utmost importance, she dressed in record time, then hurried down the stairs and out the front door. She soon found herself on the pathway to the mansion.

"Miss Mari!" Nat called out as he raced toward her from across the lawn, having spotted her as he headed for the levee.

Marianne stopped, then turned and waited for him, hoping he wasn't going to tell her someone else had fallen sick.

"*Bonjour,* Nat," she said when he reached her side. "What can I do for you?"

"Nuthin', Miss Mari. I's just tryin' to save you some steps. Yonder come Simon and Hortenzia with Mista Drew's lunch now."

"Lunch?" Marianne echoed, surprised. "Is it really that late?"

"Sho'ly is, Miz Mari," Simon said as he and Hortenzia came upon her and Nat. He was carrying a huge tray, laden down with silver platters and fine china, while Hortenzia held a pitcher of lemonade and a glass.

"We done fixed Mista Drew's food for him," Hortenzia volunteered. "But we 'speck he truly must be wore out, since he ain't even come out for breakfast this morning."

"Do you wants us to take him his lunch, Miss Mari?" Nat asked eagerly.

Marianne looked from one to the other. She suspected their eagerness was due more to the fact that they wanted to see Drew than to any particular desire to bring him his lunch. He treated them with respect, as equals, which, when she really thought about it, was as it should be. It seemed inbred in Drew to consider them men and women, just as it seemed a matter of course for people of her time to consider them property.

"Miss Mari?"

She bowed her head at Nat's uncertain inquiry. With a deep sigh, she looked at them again. "Drew is still asleep," she said quietly. "I need to ask you something, Nat."

"Yes'm?" Nat said, his caramel features registering confusion.

"Have you noticed if anyone is sick?"

Nat shook his head. "No, ma'am, Miss Mari."

"Simon? How about you?"

"Ain't nobody been sick, 'ceptin' Mista Drew," Simon volunteered, shifting the weight of the tray. "He been complainin' 'bout muscle pain."

"I see," Marianne said, then hesitated. She didn't want

to cause a furor amongst the slaves. Yellow Fever cases were usually confined to the city proper of New Orleans. People fled to escape the disease, and Drew could very well have brought it here from Laurinda Toussaint, the enchantress most feared by all and sundry. But she knew she might as well get it out in the open so the slaves could rebel and be done with it. She certainly couldn't stop it. She wondered if Monsieur Pierre could. Bracing herself for the panic, she said, "Mr. Drew is very ill. He has contracted Yellow Fever."

The pitcher in Hortenzia's hand shook. "Lawdy, not Mista Drew," she said almost reverently, her voice trembling.

Nat scratched his head and stepped closer to her. "How bad is it, Miss Mari?"

Marianne swallowed at their concern. "Not very bad, Nat," she whispered. "If we keep it from blossoming, he'll make it."

"Then we's got to keep it from blossomin'," Simon vowed.

"Aren't you the least bit afraid that you'll get it?" she asked, stunned at how deeply their concern and affection for Drew went. It was almost as deep as her love.

"Yes, ma'am, we is," Hortenzia told her. "But Mista Drew is the kindiss man whoever came to Bienvenu. We don't min' helpin' him."

Marianne held back her tears, determined not to fall apart. Drew had really made an impression on the slaves. What a comparison between him and Rafe. They probably would have ignored Rafe totally, perhaps even wished for his demise.

"First, we shouldn't tell anyone else about this," she instructed. "We don't want to frighten anybody."

"Ever'one else loves him like we do, ma'am," Hortenzia said. "We's all gonna help."

"*Merci*. Now, I've got to inform Monsieur Pierre about Mr. Drew."

"Won't do no good," Hortenzia said. "That man been

liquored up drunk ever since Masta Rafe done left."

"Mais non!"

"Go and see for yo'self," Simon said, turning in the direction of the kitchen and starting toward it, with Hortenzia trailing behind him.

"I will," she called after him. After giving instructions to Nat for Simon and Hortenzia, Marianne went to the manor.

She found Pierre in his study, in an appalling condition. Disheveled and unshaven, he sat with his head resting on his desk. An empty gin bottle lay in the circle of his arms, and the fumes of stale alcohol and acrid cigar smoke hung heavy in the confines of the chamber. She crept forward and laid a hand on his back.

"Monsieur?" she whispered, shaking him. "Monsieur Pierre?"

He raised his head, the tips of his hair standing on edge. Bleary, bloodshot eyes tried to focus but couldn't. He blinked. "Rafe?" he asked, his voice thick and unsteady. "You came back, boy? Thank God I didn't shoot you! You know I didn't mean what I said, son."

The piteously ragged tones tore at Marianne's heart, and she touched his arm again, drawing his attention. *"Non,* monsieur. It is me, Marianne."

"Marianne?" Pierre asked, surprised, turning his head sideways to look at her. "Marianne Beaufort?"

The smell of gin clung to him, nearly overpowering her, but Marianne wouldn't turn away from him. He needed her. *"Oui,* monsieur."

"You've come to see me?" he said, sounding surprised at the mere thought of such an occurrence.

She smiled. *"Oui,* monsieur, I have." She tugged at his shoulders, and he straightened in his seat.

Pierre clasped her hand and rested his stubbled cheek there before kissing the back of it. *"Merci,* child. My son's gone, Mari. He's gone! I didn't know he had such malevolence inside him."

"Don't, monsieur—"

"Yet he *is* my son," Pierre interrupted, ignoring her words. "And Andrew is my nephew. He's the person I wish Rafe was. He's my *nephew*, Marianne, Emory's boy. I couldn't turn him away, despite how my son felt."

He wasn't Emory's boy at all, she knew, but Pierre's great-great-great grandson. Nonetheless, she believed that if Drew had been able to tell his true story, Pierre undoubtedly would have been proud to realize that the Montague blood still glowed, 150 years in the future, in the generous, loving spirit of the man Drew was.

"Of course you couldn't turn him away, monsieur," Marianne whispered with sympathy. He was clearly anguished over the loss of his son. "Now you must pull yourself together and think of a way to bring Rafe back."

"He won't come back unless *I* send for him, Marianne. And he won't come back as long as Andrew is here."

"Then give him some time, at least a few weeks to get over his anger and humiliation at being ordered to leave here." A few weeks, she reasoned, might be enough time for Drew to get back home. Then Rafe could have Bienvenu and his father all to himself. Sharp, profound sadness seized her at the thought of Drew's leaving, but she pushed it aside. She'd deal with it later—if it took place at all. For now, more important things took precedent. "You must take care of yourself, monsieur. You will put yourself to rights, and I will have Eve prepare a nourishing meal for you."

Pierre sighed. "*Merci*. You are very kind, Marianne." He rubbed his hand over his eyes. "Please ask my nephew to stop in and see me."

Marianne considered before replying. Pierre's emotions were so fragile. Losing both Rafe and Drew—Drew to the Fever—might send him into permanent despair. Yet he had to be informed about Drew's illness. Indeed, it might very well sober him enough to realize that he could end up having to run Bienvenu alone for the first time since Rafe had reached adulthood. For that Pierre would need all his wits.

She put her hand on his shoulder again. "Andrew is quite ill."

His bushy eyebrows drawing together in a frown, he rose unsteadily from his chair. "He is? What ails him?"

Before changing her mind about telling him, Marianne blurted, "He has the Fever, monsieur!"

"The Fever?" Pierre's eyes widened as comprehension dawned. "You mean Yellow Jack?"

Her gaze unwavering, Marianne nodded. "*Oui,* monsieur. He contracted it when he went to New Orleans to borrow the money for the seeds."

"*Mon Dieu!*" Pierre made the sign of the cross, his posture straightening. "Send Simon in here, Marianne," he said briskly, a semblance of the robust man she'd always known returning. "I'd best go see Andrew, but I want to clean up first."

Smiling at his abrupt change, Marianne curtsied. "Of course, monsieur."

Much later, she sat next to Drew's bed, holding his parched hand. His quarters had been scrupulously cleaned and the bed linen changed. It now smelled like a fresh spring morning inside, especially since Drew wouldn't allow any sulfur or tar to be burned in the brazier in his room, telling her it had absolutely no medicinal value, except maybe to suffocate the mosquitoes that caused the Fever. When he added that many people had probably choked on the very concoctions that were supposed to heal them, Marianne giggled at his light tone.

She felt so right there with him. Instinct told her he'd survive the disease as she had. Although his complexion was far from normal, he wasn't as jaundiced as many other cases she'd witnessed. Drew was also still quite lucid, which greatly decreased her fear. Even his fever seemed to have abated, once he'd drunk the marigold syrup and fence grass tea Hortenzia brought up to him.

Monsieur Pierre came and sat most of the afternoon with Drew. But Drew slept for the most part, oblivious to his visitors.

She smiled to herself when she recalled Pierre's rapid turnaround for Drew's sake. His love for Drew was obvious. Of course, that wasn't surprising. Drew was very easy to love.

A gurgling sound snapped Marianne out of her reverie. Before she was out of her chair, next to the bed, and leaning over Drew, the gurgling had become choking.

"Oh!" she exclaimed, horrified when blood dribbled down the sides of Drew's mouth.

Chapter 33

"OH, *MON DIEU!*" With all the strength she could muster, Marianne pulled Drew up to a sitting position. "Drew! Wake up."

"Ohhh," he moaned, sagging.

Leaning him back against the headboard, Marianne got a dampened towel from the iron stand, then hurriedly went and pressed it to his mouth, cleaning away the blood.

"God, Marianne," Drew managed weakly, not bothering to open his eyes. "The taste of blood is in my mouth."

"*Oui, amour.* It is caused by the Fever. Are you in much pain?"

"My muscles are aching," Drew replied. "I know about the bleeding, Mari. The gums, then the stomach lining, then—"

"*Non, non,* Andrew! Do not think such thoughts. You are a healthy man. You can fight this." She paused, smiling encouragement at him in spite of her rising desperation. "You have a lot to live for, don't you?"

"Yes. I have Teal. I must win this battle for her sake."

And mine, Marianne added to herself. It took the few resources that hadn't been drained by her worry over his condition not to let him see how his words affected her.

She wanted to be part of his reason for living. But it wasn't going to be.

Even if he had become her reason for breathing. Drew had helped to change her values completely. Wealth, she now knew, couldn't replace love, especially the love she'd developed for him.

She'd been so foolish, pretending she could live in a loveless marriage for the sake of money, even if it was to help her mother and sister. Her mother wasn't as dependent as Marianne had believed. During their last moments together, Clarisse had understood completely Marianne's new self-awareness, and she hadn't held it against her. Nor had she fallen to pieces.

What of Genevieve's appreciation for the sacrifice Marianne was going to make? Her sister had undoubtedly made love to Rafe, and would likely have continued to do so long after Marianne married him.

For Drew and the love she bore him, she'd gladly live in squalor and cross the barriers of time. But the watch he needed had yet to be found, and she couldn't remain anywhere near Rafe, who wouldn't easily dismiss her injustices against him. That meant she couldn't stick around to help Drew—if he recovered!—find the watch.

If she and Drew parted, she was certain, her heart would no longer beat for love. Its main function would be to keep her alive. To help her exist in a dreary world.

"Andrew," she said, pushing her troubling thoughts aside when he shifted restlessly, "Hortenzia is going to bring you a new mixture of herb medicine she concocted, and you must drink it. When she departed after bringing you the other tea and syrup, she said that your condition might get worse before it improves. So she was brewing something else. Her secret recipe."

That dark, deep blue gaze finally rested upon her. She saw the pain, the fear, which he'd tried to shield from her. Wordlessly she tried to convey her own feelings to him, her need to be with him, her understanding of what he was going through.

He forced a laugh, breaking the spell. "Anything at this juncture, Mari. Bring on the miracle concoction."

The bitter black liquid was like nothing Drew had ever tasted before, but it stopped his gums from bleeding and relieved the tenderness there.

Four days later—four days of muscle aches, dizziness, high fever, and intermittent bleeding—Drew finally noticed his condition improving. He began to feel better. The aches were disappearing, the fever had broken and had yet to return, his equilibrium was once again restored, and the bleeding had completely stopped.

Day and night Marianne had been there, and he wondered if she *had* left Rafe for him. He hoped so. In feeling better, his passion had returned, and he barely kept his desire for her in check.

Yesterday Pierre had visited with reports of how the planting was progressing. He'd told Drew how well the field hands were working under Nat's direction. Everything was going as smoothly as it would have had Drew been out there on the job himself. The old man exuded pride in both himself and in Drew. He seemed genuinely relieved to see Bienvenu on the road to restoration.

With his own recuperation, Drew became restless. He wondered what Pierre thought of Marianne's solicitations toward him, when she was engaged to his son. Perhaps she'd told him a convincing story of why she'd come to Bienvenu in the first place. He only wished she'd enlighten *him*.

In any case, Pierre didn't seem concerned, didn't even seem to care. Yesterday he'd even invited Drew to move into the manor, since Rafe was absent. Taken by surprise, Drew replied he'd think about it when he fully recovered. He didn't want the old man getting overly attached to him, because he had every intention of finding a way home before summer's end.

Marianne had run away. But what did that mean for him and her? Had she broken her engagement as well?

Getting up from the bed, Drew walked to the window.

Seeing the place all but deserted, he wondered where Marianne was. Earlier, when the servants came to clean his quarters, she'd left, saying she'd return when they finished. But that had been hours ago.

Dammit, he missed her! And he loved her. How could he ever leave without her? But he had to, for Teal's sake. According to Laurinda, Marianne had her own destiny, in her own time, to fulfill. Laurinda had told him he could stop her, however.

But stop her from what?

Pacing the length of the room and chewing on mint leaves to freshen his mouth, he again stopped at the window when he could find no answers to his questions. The scenery, as beautiful as it was, was beginning to bore him.

Directing his gaze toward the mansion, he saw Marianne moving toward the *garçonnière,* carrying a picnic basket. The simplest of gowns framed her slim body, and judging from the way it hung on her, he guessed she wasn't wearing much beneath it. A simple ribbon tamed her luxurious ink black hair. Her step was light and carefree, and more than once she glanced toward his quarters.

His heart skipped a beat, and with the exuberance of a child he hurried down the stairs to meet her.

By the time he reached the door, she was already entering.

"Sacre bleu!" she declared, clutching her chest. "You gave me a fright."

"Sacre bleu?" Drew repeated, arching his eyebrows. "Not again? Should a lady of your standing use such language?"

Marianne giggled and closed the door. "Never mind my language, monsieur. You must stay abed until you're well enough to venture outdoors."

Taking the basket from her, Drew placed it on the sideboard and pulled her into his arms. "In modern times, it's been discovered that the bed saps a person's strength."

"Andrew . . ."

He ignored her warning tone and nuzzled her neck.

"Since you suggested that I might be a weakling, I mean to prove you wrong." He planted a feathery-light kiss on her lips.

"Umm," she murmured, placing her arms around his neck and returning his kiss. "Nice." She moved against him. "But no proof of your strength as a man. Perhaps if you were a butterfly."

Drew chuckled. "Ahh, a tease, are you?" he said huskily, capturing her firm buttocks and holding her close to his growing erection. "My love, my body might not be up to par, but only you can put strength in a certain part of my anatomy."

One hand still around his neck, Marianne brought her other to his arousal and caressed it through his trousers. He was near to bursting with need from the gossamer-like massage. "I want to feel that strength inside me," she whispered, stroking him slowly, showing him by touch the tempo she wanted him to use with her.

Groaning, Drew kissed her passionately, tasting her warm recesses, exploring her mouth with his tongue. She moaned, kissing him wildly in return. Unbuttoning his nightshirt, she began kissing his chest, his nipples, his shoulders.

"Andrew, you're still so *hot!*"

Drew unfastened the buttons on her bodice, his fingers brushing each part of velvety skin he bared. "Believe me, my love," he said as he went about his tender task, "the heat I am emanating at the moment has nothing to do with my fever."

With swift precision, he lifted the nightshirt over his head and flung it aside. His nakedness revealed, his manhood stood erect and throbbing. Grabbing her again, he kissed Marianne hungrily, stopping only long enough to aid her in shedding her clothes.

With their mouths locked together in a fiery kiss, Drew lifted her up onto the console table against the wall.

"Mari, my sweet love," he murmured, blazing a trail to her luscious breasts. He kissed each smooth globe, then gently caressed them with his hands. "So perfect," he whispered, closing his mouth over one.

"Mon amour!" Marianne gasped as he suckled her, shivers racking her, heat licking at her body. Loving the feel of his warm, wet tongue upon her, she threw her head back, grasping his shoulders, wild with excitement. Slowly he slid his hands down her body with practiced expertise, touching, exploring, caressing, inciting. His fingers tangled in the silken triangle of hair between her thighs. She opened at his touch and unashamedly rocked against his hand. He glided into her wet center and massaged her pleasure point, teasing and titillating, taking her mouth in a demanding kiss as his hand continued its assault.

Clinging to him, kissing him with a force that matched his, Marianne tried to comprehend the depths of such maddening pleasure. His hands left her center and caressed her buttocks. She groaned at the loss.

Lifting her slightly, he thrust his phallus fully into her woman's place, filling her completely. She shuddered, scalding sensations rippling through her and stirring her emotions.

Drew moved within her, his strokes powerful. She wrapped her legs around his back, her buttocks bouncing against the unyielding surface of the table.

Abruptly withdrawing from her without a word, he lifted her off the table and laid her on the Persian rug. He mounted her, then slid into her slick heat and cried out as he raised her hips to his rhythm. Deliberately slow and furiously exciting, he inflamed her being with his appetite, his feverish thrusts.

She entwined her legs with his and fisted her hands to keep from tearing the flesh on his back. Pleasure engulfed her, surrounded her. With one final gasp, she clung to him in glowing surrender.

Feeling her trembles of release, hearing her cries of exultation, Drew felt her tug at his heart more than ever. Each stroke inside her magnified his love for her. Thrilling surges rushed to his brain, and he tightened his arms around her.

Fierce tremors racked him as his release came in a swift torrent, nearly overwhelming him. His body shook, and his breath came in short pants as he collapsed on top of her.

He loved her and had to find a way to take her with him to the future. "Mari," he said, withdrawing from her ever so slowly and feeling—though he wouldn't let her know it—as weak as a newborn babe.

"*Oui*, my strong and perfect man?"

Smiling at her words, Drew rolled off her. "And don't you forget it, woman," he teased.

Marianne sat up and kissed his cheek. "How could I? Not when you can provide such proof of your strength and virility."

Drew's smile deepened, then he, too, sat up. He was immediately sorry that he did. Damn! He hadn't realized how weak he still was. He hoped Marianne wouldn't ask him to lift her picnic basket, or even to get dressed to eat, for that matter. He was too weak to chew gum, if he'd had any, let alone to eat a meal. Maybe he'd just take a quick snooze right on the rug.

He looked at Marianne and frowned. While he'd been debating his options, she'd dressed, and now stood before him fully clothed.

"Sooo," he said, forcing a light tone, "we couldn't take it, could we?"

"What do you mean?"

"You were afraid I'd ask for seconds, so you took temptation out of my view." *God! Don't let her call my bluff and start disrobing!*

Marianne chuckled. "You were so very thorough, Andrew, I fear I am fully drained."

Drew released a great sigh of relief. "Thank heaven," he mumbled.

"*Pardonnez-moi?*" Marianne asked, her voice cracking with laughter.

"What?" Drew asked innocently.

"You said 'Thank heaven.' "

"Er . . . yeah . . . um—"

Marianne burst out laughing. *"Mon amour,* you do not have to prove anything to me. I know your weaknesses as well as your strengths."

"Mari, my love," Drew began contentedly, "I am most grateful for your perception of me."

"I'm glad, Andrew."

In no hurry to get up, he entwined his hands and placed them behind his head. He groaned as Marianne's gaze traveled the length of his nude body. His manhood stirred, but he ignored the feeling. They were both worn out. Instead, he asked, "Why did you really come to Bienvenu, Mari?"

Her movements stilled. "Why, to see you, of course, monsieur. But you mustn't tell Monsieur Pierre. He believes it was for his benefit, and as ... as his f-future daughter-in-law, I'll take care of him while I remain on the premises. Just the same as I would if Rafe was around."

Drew heard the tremor in her voice and knew she hadn't stated the full reason that she'd come. But his heart sank. It sounded as if she still intended to marry Rafe.

"Now," she continued before he'd fully formed a response, "you must get back to bed so that I can feed you and nurse you back to your full health."

"That'll work." Drew picked up his nightshirt and managed to slip it over his head. He decided to ask for answers later. Grinning mischievously, he allowed Marianne to take his hand and lead him back to bed. The little boy in him rejoiced, for he knew that she'd provide him with care as gentle as she'd have offered a child.

As Drew completed his recovery, the passing days grew into weeks. He was happier than he'd ever been in his life, with the exception of the birth of his little Teal.

The crops were thriving, showing signs of a substantial yield in the coming harvest, and Marianne never once left his side. She'd even begun to show curiosity in his world, and every night he shared some new tidbit about what it was like to live in modern-day New Orleans. Her interest sparked hope within him. Certainly she wouldn't ask about such things if she wasn't considering a future with him. He looked forward to their time spent together, away from everyone and everything.

So that they could continue to be alone, he declined Pierre's request to move into the family mansion. His clever Marianne, on the other hand, created the illusion that *she* was living in the house, a deception that was aided by the servants. They brought phantom breakfasts to her bedroom, pretended to tidy up, and even changed her bed linen.

All this, while she would sleep snugly in his arms in his bachelor digs. Thoroughly confused over her destiny, Drew made the best of this time, all the while wondering when Rafe would put in an appearance, if not to search for Marianne, then to try and make amends with Pierre. Surely he wouldn't give up on either so easily. But when Drew questioned Marianne on when she intended to return to Rafe and attempted to discover exactly *why* she'd run away in the first place, she always steered the conversation elsewhere.

Drew was beginning to believe that when Marianne ran away, she'd led Rafe to assume she wouldn't ever return. If that was the case, he wanted to know where she intended to go. Yet no matter how he tried to coax the truth from her, she never told him what really happened. He couldn't save her from a mistake if he had no idea about her future plans.

Reluctantly he gave up questioning her, knowing he was at a critical stage. He had to discover the means to get back to his daughter without delay.

Because he now shared the common bond of being a Yellow Fever survivor with Marianne, they ventured back to New Orleans on a desperate search for the watch. Staying at the St. Louis Hotel for three days, they visited every pawnshop and jewelry shop they could find. They returned to Roudin's store. On a chance that it might be there, they even searched the place where Drew had first materialized. All to no avail.

That was the only dark spot in his existence. He needed that damned watch!

He wanted Teal. He wanted television. He wanted the Bulls and the Knicks. He wanted the Saints and the Cowboys. He wanted all the things he told Marianne about.

He wanted his own life back!

As the summer's end neared, Drew became more nostalgic. He believed he'd conquered his demons regarding Bienvenu and his father; his boundless satisfaction at pulling his ancestral heritage out of near ruin proved that. Of course, if his father had come to him for such help, Drew would have laughed in Cranneck's face. But because of his backbreaking labor, because of his successful negotiations, he'd earned Pierre's everlasting respect, and Bienvenu had earned his.

Drew had no doubt the crop would continue to flourish, even after he found a way home and returned to Teal. But what dreams and regrets would haunt him by leaving Mari behind?

If he found the watch in time, he wanted to convince her to return with him, despite her unwavering determination to marry Rafe, despite the words she'd uttered so long ago that she could never leave all that she knew behind.

He loved her, and she loved him.

Drew walked outside into the late-summer evening, needing to give some perspective to his ceaseless thinking. Warm breezes carried the scents of the flowers blooming in profusion all around him. The cicadas whirred their nightly song. Above, in the leafy branch of a tree, the song of a robin touched him.

He thought of Pierre, thought of how fond he'd become of him. He wouldn't have made it without him, without the man's kindness and unwavering belief in him. Well, without him and Marianne.

"Mista Drew! Mista Drew!" Simon shouted, bounding down the lane toward him.

Frowning, Drew hurried to meet him. "Calm down,

Simon," he admonished. "I can hear you. What the hell are you shouting for?"

Panic widened Simon's eyes, creased his brow. "Mista Drew, Miz Mari wants you to come to the house, suh," he said, his voice quivering.

Seeing the sweat beading Simon's brow and the tears stinging his eyes, Drew was gripped by apprehension. His first thought was Marianne. Something had happened to her! Rafe was there and—

"It's Masta Pierre, suh," Simon went on before Drew could question him further. "He's done fell dead in the parlor."

Simon's words struck Drew like a mallet in the gut. Pierre dead? That couldn't possibly be true. He'd seen him just yesterday, as hearty as he'd been when he'd met him. He hadn't taken a drink in weeks, or even smoked a cigar. The cough that had once plagued him had all but disappeared.

No, Pierre couldn't be dead.

With Rafe gone, who would run Bienvenu if Pierre was truly dead? *He* couldn't stay—yet how could he abandon the lifeblood of the Montague family with no one else there to oversee things? How could he leave, when it was his fault Rafe was gone?

A picture of bouncing red curls and sparkling green eyes entered his mind. Teal. He would leave, no matter what, because of Teal.

But Pierre couldn't be dead.

Bombarded by unanswerable questions, he took off for the mansion. What seemed like insurmountable obstacles in his path would certainly be cleared away when he got there and took charge and discovered that Pierre had merely fallen ill.

Chapter 34

A COUPLE OF days later, Drew laid Pierre to rest in the family plot without much fanfare and with only the servants, himself, and Marianne in attendance.

In shock, he stood at graveside, listening to the minister give last rites over the coffin. Just over a day and a half had gone by since he'd rushed into the study and found Marianne leaning over an unmoving Pierre. He hadn't believed Simon. He hadn't *wanted* to believe him. But the fact was Pierre was already dead when Drew arrived.

He suspected it was from a massive heart attack. Marianne told him the old man had been talking one minute, then clutching his chest and dropping to the floor the next.

Drew only wished he had been there with him. He only wished he'd had a chance to tell him how much he'd come to love him as a second father. But that chance was now being buried with Pierre.

Of course, he'd known his great-great-great-grandfather would die. In his time, he'd paid scant attention to when his death had taken place; Rafe had consumed Cranneck's and therefore his own attention. Yet even Rafe had only been a figure of history, a legend passed down through the ages.

Drew, however, had actually come to know Pierre as a living, breathing human being. That's how he wished his memory of Pierre had remained. He shouldn't have been watching Marianne lay a solitary white rose on the casket, her cheeks tearstained, her eyes red. He shouldn't have had to listen to the miserable wails of the grieving servants.

Such desolate grief shouldn't have been sweeping through him and erasing all else. He bowed his head, tears stinging his eyes.

Whatever else his reasons for being here were, he'd learned some valuable lessons—the importance of life and the need to cherish those you loved.

When he returned home, *if* he returned home, one of his first priorities would be to tell his father how very much he loved him.

Two days after the burial, Drew took up residence in the mansion. He was sorry he hadn't done it before, but he'd thought having Marianne in his arms was more important than humoring an old man.

He missed Pierre terribly. His presence was everywhere, and Drew wanted things to remain that way.

Sitting in Pierre's favorite wingback chair, Drew gazed at Marianne. She sat at the big desk, bent over the distasteful task of penning notices of Pierre's death, to be sent to the neighboring plantations.

Efficiently she folded yet another piece of parchment and put it in an envelope, then sealed it with the Montague stamp. Having lost her own father the year before, she was taking this loss hard. Yet she'd been a rock throughout this entire tragedy. Other than her initial reaction of going into screaming hysterics when Pierre had first dropped dead, she had been right at Drew's side.

Laying her pen aside, she rubbed her temples, then looked up from the desk. "I've sent missives to Baywood for Rafe and Maman. I've added a few lines to my mother's explaining certain things to her. But I thought it was only fair they be informed of Monsieur Pierre's death. You know when Rafe hears of his father's passing, *amour*," she said quietly, "he'll return to Bienvenu, and you will be in mortal danger."

Drew merely nodded. He hadn't given Rafe much thought these past days; he'd been preoccupied with Pierre. But he knew Marianne was right. Only the presence of his father had prevented Rafe from openly trying to slaughter Drew. Now that the man was dead, he wouldn't be safe.

He smiled sadly over Marianne's concern for his safety. She had become as loving as a wife to him. She had become his everything. But he would leave her. Her words constantly rang in his ears: She wouldn't leave with him under any circumstances. And how could he expect her to? Everything she knew would be abruptly changed. One hundred forty-seven years of progress would be as hard to adapt to as his own one-hundred-forty-seven-year regression had been for him. But then Marainne was smart, well read, and charming—as well as sexy and beautiful. He had no doubt she could adapt to his world.

Still, he wouldn't pressure her to come with him. Her decision was made. If Rafe returned before he discovered the watch he needed, Drew would leave Bienvenu and hide out until the day he could finally depart. Then, if the end of summer arrived without any luck, he'd try to breach the time barrier without the watch. But he knew this was only wishful thinking. Without the watch, his attempts would be futile.

Restless, he stood and walked over to the desk. He massaged Marianne's shoulders. "Are you almost finished, darling?"

"*Oui, mon amour.* I have only one more, then you may have all my attention."

Drew lowered his head and kissed her on her lips. "May I depend on that?"

Without responding, Marianne hurriedly scribbled a few words on the monogrammed writing paper in her beautiful, flowing penmanship. Then she folded it, as she had the others, stuffed it into an envelope, sealed it, and placed it on the stack of completed notices.

"There," she said, standing. "All finished."

Drew pulled her into his arms. "Thank you, Marianne, for all you've done to help. I don't know what I would have done without you." He kissed her then, with all the anguish and love in him. "I love you," he murmured, and hugged her tightly to him before releasing her. She remained silent, and he shifted his weight uncomfortably. "Would you like to accompany me to the city for one more try at finding the watch?"

"*Oui*, Andrew," she replied, her expression unfathomable. "This time we will leave no stone unturned." She walked to the window, out of his reach. Leaning against the sill, she faced him. "If I were not going to marry Rafe, what would you foresee for our future, Andrew?"

The question caught him off guard, and the hope that she was considering attempting the return with him increased. She had never expressed an interest in their future before. It had always been her and Rafe. He shrugged, unsure how to answer. "I can't say, Marianne, because I could never remain here."

Staring at him a moment longer, she nodded, an odd look on her face. She seemed almost hurt by his answer. But Drew knew it was the best one he could give, without begging her to return with him.

"Are you ready to head for the city?" he asked.

"*Oui.*"

Before leaving, Marianne made sure the missives were sent on to their various destinations by one of the servants. Slowly but surely, her heart was breaking. She would never know how she'd managed her calm demeanor over the last few weeks. She loved Drew with an aching fierceness, and he'd repeatedly told her how much he loved her.

He had yet to utter the words that would bind them to each other, however, and after his answer today, she knew he wouldn't. He still thought her engaged to Rafe. She should have told him the truth long ago, but she'd just started to realize the importance of fulfilling her own needs, after Drew had fallen so terribly ill and after Pierre's sudden death.

Now, not only wasn't Drew aware she'd broken her engagement, but also he still believed she wouldn't return with him under any circumstances. How could she tell him any differently when he sounded uninterested in having her return to his own time with him?

Maybe she should just tell him that she no longer thought it necessary to sacrifice her happiness for the sake of her family and judge his reaction then.

Rafe and Genevieve seemed suited to one another. Her mother was much stronger. And Rafe was bound and determined to kill Andrew on general principle. Her leaving, with or without Drew, wouldn't deter Rafe.

She had never intended to stay at Bienvenu this long when she'd fled Baywood. She had come to tell Drew good-bye and then get on the first steamer bound for Paris. Only Drew had fallen ill, and Pierre had come to depend upon her. Once again, she'd pushed aside her own plans for the sake of others.

Now everything had changed again, and she worried about what she would do when Rafe came back. In the meantime, she'd have Drew for as long as she could, in any way that she could. But Rafe *would* return. Of that she had no doubt.

Until that time came, she'd remain with Drew. The day Rafe arrived, she would leave. Then, and only then, would she follow through with her plans to go to Paris. For now, she'd push those thoughts aside.

Marianne made the sign of the cross as she followed Drew through the door. Only a miracle could help them now.

An urgent knock sounded upon the door. Cursing violently, Rafe untangled the woman's arms from around his neck and pushed her nude body aside as she remained fast asleep. Not bothering to cover his own nakedness, he stumbled to the door, his head pounding from the large amount of alcohol he'd consumed last night before taking Darlene to his bed.

He cracked the door and scowled at the young servant who stood there.

"Yes?"

"Mr. Rafe, sir," the boy began, his Adam's apple bobbing nervously. "Sorry to disturb you, sir, but this just came for you." He held an envelope out to him, the wine-colored Montague seal immediately recognizable. "The messenger said it's urgent. Madame Beaufort had this forwarded from your father's plantation."

Satisfaction ran through him as he grabbed the letter and slammed the door. Undoubtedly his father was asking for his return. Rafe wouldn't hesitate to return, but when he did he'd demand that Andrew depart. If Pierre had gone to these lengths to bring him back, then he certainly would do as Rafe asked.

Once back at Bienvenu, he'd work to make his father proud of him. Unbelievably, he'd missed the old man, more so now that he was four hundred miles away.

He'd also press his suit for Genevieve. She'd made a very enticing bedmate and she was quite biddable. Besides, marrying one of the Beaufort girls would give him access to the dowry he'd needed to help put Bienvenu's resources back to right—before Andrew's schemes had beaten him to the punch. But Rafe craved the marriage portion anyway. It might have been small compared with others, but now that the very fertile Baywood was in his possession, he needed all the cash he could get.

Disappointment surged through him. He'd wanted Marianne along with everything else. That's why he'd taken part of the money he'd mortgaged for Bienvenu to purchase Baywood when Clarisse had enticed him with marriage to Marianne.

Eventually she'd tire of Paris and return home, he reassured himself. Then he'd deal with her.

Smiling at the thought of all the ways he'd make her suffer, he tore open the letter and read it.

With a howl of rage and anguish, he dropped to his knees.

Perhaps she should have prayed for more than a miracle ten days ago, Marianne thought as she lay beside Drew at Bienvenu.

The watch continued to elude Andrew. Clarisse had sent a return missive to Marianne after receiving her note of Pierre's death, expressing her shock that Marianne hadn't yet left for Paris, but swearing to adhere to her daughter's plea that she not reveal her whereabouts, not even to Genevieve. Clarisse also informed Marianne that Rafe had departed Baywood for Atlanta the day he'd found her note and that she'd forwarded it to him. Word had come from him that he was en route from Atlanta to Bienvenu. Clarisse wished her well and begged her to leave before Rafe arrived.

It was advice she'd heed. Before Rafe returned, she had to set her own plans in motion.

Marianne drew in an unsteady breath and rubbed her finger across Drew's washboard-hard stomach.

"Mari?" Drew croaked, sliding her into his embrace. "Are you all right?"

"*Oui,*" she lied, and turned toward him. Stretching the length of her body to his, she kissed the hollow of his neck.

His response was immediate. He nibbled at her earlobe, tracing the curve of her ear with his tongue, then forged a trail of hot kisses along her throat.

"Mari—"

The fingertips she placed over his lips quieted him. Tonight she wanted no words. This would be her last night with him, and she wanted to know all of him. She wanted to explore him with her lips, her tongue, her fingertips, before making love to him.

Raising herself across his bare chest, she kissed his

shoulders and then his nipples, her fingers massaging his hardness, stiff and massive in her hand.

"Marianne," Drew whispered. "Stop before—"

Ignoring Drew's protests, Marianne probed farther, moving her tongue to the flat plane of his stomach and the indentation of his navel, her hand still moving rhythmically, her own desire heightening as he began to move his hips.

She brought her lips to his rigid shaft and kissed the smooth, hot length shyly. He had taught her about pleasure, and she was determined to show what an apt student she was. Instead of discouraging her, he whispered her name, the sound husky and seemingly drawn from the core of him.

Her mouth worked around him, his groans and heated murmurs exciting her. She shivered, wanting, needing more. Lifting herself on top of him, she slid her heated slickness down onto his velvet-steel maleness. Drew touched her heated skin, stroked her peaked nipples. She rocked back and forth upon him, their groans of pleasure mingling. Tangling his hands in her hair, he locked his mouth to hers and kissed her feverishly, deeply, their tongues mating.

"Oh, Andrew!" Marianne cried.

"Mari, my Mari," Drew croaked in a hoarse whisper, pumping into her with urgency.

He held on to her hips, lifting up her up and down, filling her, rapidly, swiftly, until her being tingled, rippled with rapture, until her breath was all but stolen. Her woman's place shuddered and throbbed, the fire there intense and hot, the relentless friction of Drew's manhood sending a tizzy of emotions through her. Volcanic heat surged low in her belly and in her nether region, and erupted. The explosion flashed brilliantly around her, reaching her very soul. She felt one final thrust before his embrace tightened and he released his seed inside her.

She collapsed on Drew's chest, and for long moments he held her without saying a word. Marianne felt the strength in his arms, heard the strong, furious beats of his heart. It was as if he knew she would be leaving him.

What Marianne knew was that this night was special. Not because it was their last night together, but because of how she felt, of *what* she felt during their lovemaking. When she and Drew parted for the last time, he would leave a portion of him behind with her. She wouldn't have felt such ecstasy if their mutual love hadn't created a new life within her. With such knowledge, perhaps now she could bear the separation.

Snuggling closer to him, she settled in his arms. Sleep would elude her tonight. More to the point, she didn't *want* to sleep tonight. She wanted to be awake and spend time with Drew. She would treasure it for the rest of her life.

The next morning, while Drew inspected the fields, Marianne stole away from Bienvenu. When she arrived in New Orleans, hours later, she went straightaway to book passage on the next steamer bound for Paris.

"The next ship ain't leavin' 'til the twentieth mum," the man behind the desk in the dingy office told her. "Take it or leave it."

"I'll take it, monsieur," she said numbly. How ironic it was that the same day she would depart, Drew's fate would be decided. The 20th of September, the day after tomorrow. The end of summer, the final day for Drew to leave or be stranded forever.

Chapter 35

Drew READ THE note, penned in Marianne's fancy handwriting. So she'd really left him. He'd always known it would happen, but he hadn't wanted to believe it. He should have been more hurt, or even angry, but he wanted her happiness. If their separation made her happy, then so be it.

In her note she explained it was best for her to be gone when Rafe arrived. Drew understood her reasoning, but had a hard time telling that to his heart. Where had she run to anyway? Had she returned to Baywood? Or had she run away from Rafe in the first place?

Perhaps the suggestion from Laurinda that he was to save Marianne from making a mistake had helped her to see that she didn't belong with Rafe.

He needed answers, but had to remain here. According to the servants' rumor mill, today was the day Rafe was expected back. He had to stay and face his maddened ancestor once and for all.

Since Drew hadn't found the watch, he seemed doomed to live out his life in this century. Yet, how could he without Marianne at his side? If he could never see his daughter again, at least he could have the woman he loved there to help assuage that loss.

But Rafe was coming, so he'd dwell upon Marianne later. He didn't think Rafe would barge in like gangbusters. After all, he'd just lost his father, a man whom, despite Rafe's show of disinterest, he truly loved. So Drew would probably have a small reprieve from his vile temper.

The hours ticked slowly away. He missed Marianne terribly and couldn't even console himself with the thought of seeing Teal. Now it looked as if his great-great-grandfather would be a no-show.

Just as that thought ran through his mind, the sound of a horse's hooves reached him, followed by neighing. With a sigh, Drew left the parlor and went to meet Rafe. When he reached the foyer, the door swung open.

They stood facing each other. Rafe was unshaven and had dark circles beneath his eyes—eyes that were wide with anguish. Drew couldn't believe the sight before him. If ever a man was stricken with grief, it was Rafe. Grime covered his usually impeccable attire and indicated he'd ridden his prized horse hard to get home.

"Hello, Rafe."

Rafe blinked, then glanced around as if searching for someone else—Pierre, no doubt, coming out and blustering that the news of his death had all been a cruel joke. "Where's my father?" he asked hoarsely.

Drew shifted his weight, pity toward Rafe welling deep within him. "Buried next to your mother," he said quietly.

"You had no right!" Rafe yelled, pushing past him. He stalked to the parlor.

"I had every right," Drew countered, following behind him. "Apparently Clarisse Beaufort knew of your whereabouts, but I didn't. I was his next of kin on the premises and therefore had to make the decision to bury him immediately."

"Why? So that you could steal my inheritance, too?"

"What the hell are you talking about, jerk?" Drew snapped.

"You know damn well what I am talking about, you bastard! You stole my father's affections. Without a second thought, he threw me off the place where I was born. Because of you."

"Me?" Drew retorted. "Get a grip, Rafe. You hired men to vandalize the seed your father needed to put Bienvenu back on its feet. Don't you think he had a right to get pissed off?"

"Get a grip of what, half-wit? Your throat, perhaps? And lucky for you I choose to ignore your crude insinuations about my father's bodily functions. But, your ruffian talk aside, there's *no* excuse for a man to turn his only son out. Unless he's influenced by scum like you! My father was fond of you, *Cousin,*" he said, stressing the word with scathing sarcasm. "Out of the love I yet bear for him, for his sake, I will allow you to remain on the premises tonight." He pushed aside his torn topcoat and looked at the immaculate gold watch and chain attached to his stained waistcoat. "It's seven o'clock. I want you long gone by this time tomorrow. Or you will rue the day you ever set foot on Bienvenu soil."

Drew stood mesmerized, staring at the watch. In an instant, he knew. Rafe had the watch he needed to return him home! The watch he and Marianne had been searching for all these weeks.

God! *Rafe* had the watch? How would he ever get it back?

"Why, Cousin, you're as pale as a cotton ball," Rafe smirked. "You should be. My father isn't here to protect you anymore. *I'm* master of Bienvenu now, and *my* word is law. So you would be wise not to provoke me during the rest of your short stay here. Now, I'd like to be alone." Without another word, he went out the door.

Knowing he must be continuously aware of Rafe's whereabouts at this crucial point, Drew didn't want him far from his sight. Leaving the parlor, he started down the hall very quietly, hoping to catch Rafe before he got too far away. As Drew passed Pierre's study, he stopped at the muffled sounds coming from the other side of the door.

He put his ear to the door and listened. Racking sobs that

only profound grief generates pierced the quietness. Rafe was weeping for Pierre. He'd obviously loved his father the only way he knew how. But Rafe's brand of love had caused Pierre untold misery and probably hastened his demise. Ever since Rafe's departure, he'd been only a shell of his former self.

His heart already broken for so many reasons, Drew felt tears well in his own eyes. In spite of his and Rafe's mutual dislike, Drew deeply sympathized with the man. If he'd loved his father so much, he couldn't be all bad.

A chair slid across the floor, followed by footsteps heading in the direction of the door to the hallway. Drew hurried to the parlor. If Rafe thought he'd been eavesdropping, he would only use it as something else against him. When Rafe didn't appear, Drew decided to remain where he was; at least in the parlor he could see when Rafe retired to his bedroom. Drew would keep vigil until Rafe went to sleep. Then he would somehow get the watch and be on his way.

The wait proved interminable. Several hours passed before Rafe finally emerged from the study. Without glancing right or left, he headed for the stairs, a silent, angry man in deep mourning.

Knowing the folly of rushing too quickly behind Rafe, Drew decided to err on the side of discretion and allowed several more hours to pass before he ventured into Rafe's bedchamber. He opened the door with stealth, cursing under his breath at the creaking hinges: Didn't these people oil them periodically? Why were they so loud tonight?

He paused briefly, half expecting Rafe to jump out of his bed and attempt to strangle him. When that didn't happen, he stepped fully into the room, wishing he could have lit his way. A flashlight would have come in handy, or at least a book of matches. If not for Rafe's presence, that is.

Adjusting to the gloom, he stood without moving. Rafe lay prone on the bed, the bedspread rising and falling with his even breathing. A slight glint emanated from the chest against the wall near the door, and he breathed a sigh of relief. The watch!

Feeling as if Divine Providence were protecting him, Drew inched noiselessly to the chest. He touched the surface, and his hand fell right on the watch.

Immediately that strange ticking began, the metal pulsing to life in his palm, as if some other force possessed it. Holding it tightly, he rushed out the door.

Chapter 36

A COLD OBJECT nuzzled Drew's cheek. Through the fog of sleep, he brushed it aside again and again, but his hand kept hitting an obstacle. He turned on his side, not wanting to awaken from the dream he was having of him, Marianne, and Teal enjoying a day at City Park.

"Get up!"

The snarl broke into his reverie. His lids flew open, and he sat up abruptly, focusing his eyes on Rafe. All semblance of sleep disappeared at the sight of the gun aimed at his head.

"Have you lost your goddamn mind, Rafe?" Drew demanded in a show of bravado. The barrel pressed into his jaw, and bile rose in his throat. "Put that gun away!"

Rafe's wild expression made Drew nervous. At any minute he expected blood and bone and skin to fly. His own.

He hadn't thought that Rafe would mind if he'd slept in the parlor last night, since he'd given Drew twenty-four hours to remain. He'd just been too damned tired and weary to get to the *garçonnière* after taking the watch. Every emotion seemed to have converged upon him at once—anticipation, apprehension, elation, and grief—and leaving in the dead of night hadn't appealed to him. But he'd remained the extra hours for other reasons as well.

As much as he wanted his daughter and as much as he despised Rafe, he hadn't been able to walk away just then. He'd needed the additional time to realize he'd truly have to depart without the woman he loved; he truly had to place his grief for Pierre aside and once again relegate him to the pages of history as if he hadn't shared many evenings with him.

Now it seemed he was done for because he hadn't fled immediately.

"You've just earned yourself a duel, Cousin," Rafe said, fuming, the gun pressing even farther into his skin. One wrong move, Drew knew, might set the trigger off.

He swallowed. "What the hell for?"

"For the theft of the watch Marianne gave me."

"W-what?" Drew asked, confusion now vying for the spot his fear occupied. Marianne had had the watch he needed, and gave it to Rafe? How could that be?

"Don't pretend ignorance," Rafe snapped. "I didn't miss how interested you were in the watch yesterday."

"Looking is not a crime, Rafe!" Drew protested, not daring to move a muscle other than to speak, and questioning the wisdom of even that.

"No, Cousin, looking isn't a crime. But stealing is. I always suspected you held a tendresse for Marianne."

"What the hell does that have to do with anything?"

"She gave me the watch you stole," Rafe accused, his skin a mottled red, the veins standing out in his neck. "That's the reason you want it—because Marianne gave it to me."

"You're a fool, Rafe!" Drew charged, angry over his helplessness, fearful that if Rafe decided to search him he'd discover the watch in his pocket. "How would I know she gave you a watch?" *My watch!*

"That doesn't matter," Rafe spat. "She left for Paris weeks ago and gave it to me as a parting gift."

God! Never having seen the original watch, Marianne hadn't known she had it in her possession. Drew breathed in a great draft of air, sweat beading his brow. "I don't have your watch, Rafe," he lied.

Rafe laughed, ruthless and maniacal. "That doesn't matter either, Cousin. You need killing for more reasons than just stealing my watch."

"People are in and out of here all the time," Drew offered in desperation. "Maybe someone picked it up by accident."

"The servants never take things, especially by accident. They know better," Rafe added ominously. He lifted his other hand. It held the mate to the pistol still pressed to Drew's jaw. "You once bragged about what a good shot you are." His gaze boring into Drew's, he held him hostage one final moment before backing away and putting the pistols down on the table. "Now's your chance to prove it."

"You can't be serious!" His dilemma was the same as it always had been: He couldn't kill his great-great-grandfather. As a direct descendant, Rafe was the reason his family existed. But neither could Drew allow himself to be killed.

"If you have any intention of defending yourself, you had better pick up that pistol," Rafe demanded.

Swallowing convulsively, Drew stood and went to the table. He stared down at the weapon, hating it. Rafe thumped him on the back. Slowly Drew picked up one of the guns and tested it for weight.

"No seconds, Rafe?" he asked, buying time. He wanted Rafe to remember the vaunted honor of the time. That honor wouldn't permit Rafe to deviate from the traditional way of dueling. First shot at twenty paces, the second one fired at ten paces.

"This won't take long, Andrew. Seconds won't be necessary."

"Suppose I get lucky and get you with the first shot, Rafe?"

"Then you'll be a very rich man, Cousin." Rafe indicated their surroundings with a sweep of his hand. "All this will be yours."

"Much obliged, Cousin." With lightning speed, Drew

slammed the butt of the gun into Rafe's head. He watched as his great-great-grandfather dropped to the floor like a brick. "But my family already owns Bienvenu."

Standing over Rafe, Drew felt a strange pull toward him. He had caused Drew untold problems, but they were alike in many ways. Wanting to make sure he hadn't hurt Rafe too badly, he knelt beside him and touched his head. Rafe moaned, and Drew breathed in, relieved. The hard-as-a-rock skull hadn't been fractured.

Calling for Hortenzia to look after Rafe, Drew rushed out the door to the stables.

His destiny at a hitching post awaited him.

Chapter 37

HOLDING ON FOR dear life, Simon sat in the buggy beside Drew as the horse galloped across the countryside at full speed twenty minutes later. It was a rough ride, fraught with the dangers of overturning because of rough terrain or of becoming mired in swampy muck. It was a risk Drew had to take. Once Rafe awakened, there'd be hell to pay.

"I didn't mean to gainsay you, Mista Drew." Simon's voice trembled with the rhythm of the buggy.

"I know you didn't, Simon," Drew called back, raising his voice in order to be heard over the creaking wheels and galloping hooves. Adrenaline surged through him at the high rate of speed, the type of rush he always experienced on his Harley.

When he'd asked Simon to hitch up the buggy for New Orleans, the servant had happily agreed. Upon finding out that Drew wouldn't be returning, however, Simon had insisted on accompanying him in order to bring the horse and carriage back to the plantation.

Not wanting to argue with him and waste time, Drew had allowed Simon to come. He'd also reasoned that such a conscientious gesture on Simon's part might win the servant points with Rafe.

"Mista Drew, suh," Simon began, clutching the seat as Drew urged the horse on at an even faster speed, "why's you runnin' the horse so fast?"

Drew chuckled at Simon's worry and pulled on the reins to slow the horse's pace a little. He wouldn't tell Simon he was running for his life. Rafe was probably nursing a huge headache at the moment, so he presumed he still had a far enough advantage to decrease his speed to a more moderate rate. But he wasn't deluded into thinking his ancestor wouldn't come after him, in pain or not, in his quest for revenge.

Noticing Simon's peaked look and pitying him for it, Drew handed the reins to him. He suspected he would have seen the same look had they been riding on the back of Drew's motorcycle.

"Here, pal. You take over for a spell," he said, knowing that not everyone was cut out for speed.

A visibly relieved Simon eagerly grabbed the reins. "I wasn't scairt, you understand, Mista Drew?" he asked with bravado, settling comfortably into controlling the horse.

"I'm sure you weren't," Drew agreed without cracking a smile.

"It's like I done tol' Miss Mari—"

"Miss Mari?" Drew interrupted. "When did you see her?"

"Why, day 'fore yesterday I took her to New Orleans to her maman's on Rue Dumaine." His eyes on the road, Simon shook his head. "Don't know why she wants to be there by herse'f. Ain't nobody else there yet."

Drew's mind whirled, another rush of excitement speeding his heartbeat. Marianne was in New Orleans! He closed his eyes, thinking of their time together and all that they had shared.

He'd promised himself he wouldn't attempt to talk her into doing something she hesitated to do. But she was the woman he loved, he told himself now, and he'd be less than a man if he *didn't* try. Just because he would invite her back with him wouldn't mean he was disrespecting her plans. He realized that's why he'd never really talked to her about it. He hadn't wanted to seem like an insensitive jerk whose own plans and dreams took precedence over hers. But he at least deserved one chance, and if she still resisted the idea, then he'd leave without her.

He cleared his throat. "Why did she go to New Orleans, Simon?" he asked mildly. "Do you know?"

"Well, suh, I done took her to the docks to catch a boat, so's I can bring the buggy back." He glanced sideways at Drew and grinned. "Jus' like I'm doin' for you. But she done miss her boat and asked to go to her maman's. Like I said, I don't know why she stay there by herse'f."

"She won't be there by herself for long, my friend," Drew said. He took the reins from Simon and grabbed the whip. "Giddy up, horse!" he shouted, snapping the whip. The carriage shot away like a bullet.

"Lawdy, Mista Drew!" Simon wailed. "Is you awright?"

Drew laughed, feeling the weight of the watch in his pocket, hearing the drone of the constant ticking, and knowing Marianne's whereabouts. "I've never been better."

The miles dissolved, and the scenery flew by; soon they neared the outskirts of the city. As Drew went around a sharp curve, Simon leaned over the side of the buggy, nearly falling off.

"Hold on, friend."

Righting himself, Simon took another shocked look over his shoulder. "Lawdy, Mista Drew! Yonder come Masta Rafe and three more mens!"

"What?" Drew asked, incredulous. Chancing a look back, he saw three riders being led by Rafe and his showy horse. He couldn't see any of their faces, but he'd have known that palomino anywhere. It was Rafe and his minions, all right, and they were coming fast. Hell-bent on revenge.

Damn, he'd underestimated that spawn. Rafe's headache hadn't been as huge as Drew had hoped.

"Like I said, Simon, hold on!"

He hated that he was running the horse at such a furious

pace, but his life was in jeopardy. Rafe was making up the distance between them, not having a cumbersome buggy to slow him down.

The outskirts of the city finally loomed before him. Once there, where could he go? Not to the authorities. Rafe would accuse him of stealing the watch he carried in his pocket, the watch with Rafe's initials engraved on it, and Drew would be arrested on the spot.

There was only one other place he could think of, and that was the Beaufort cottage on Rue Dumaine.

Minutes later they sprinted into the city, and Drew reined the panting horse to a stop. His stomach roiled as the heat of the sun heightened the repulsive stench of lime, tar, gunpowder, death, and decay.

"Simon, say nothing to Rafe about Miss Mari. He thinks she has already left for Paris," Drew said, jumping off the buggy.

"Awright, suh," Simon agreed with a nod. "I can bring you to her house before Masta Rafe gits here, Mista Drew."

"I won't be going there," Drew lied, not wanting to put Simon in a precarious position when Rafe questioned him; if Simon lied for Drew and Rafe ever found out, he wouldn't show the servant any mercy. It was better that Simon be kept in the dark. "I'm going down to the docks to hire on as a seaman. Without Pierre to stop him, Rafe would make my life a living hell—if both of us survived *this* confrontation." He clasped the man's hand in a quick handshake. "Good-bye, Simon. Take care of yourself."

With that, he turned and lost himself in the throng of people scurrying about the French Market.

Which wouldn't do at all. Rafe was well known, and any number of people in the crowd could be acquaintances. Despite his fierce temper, or maybe because of it, Rafe elicited extreme loyalty from a lot of people. All Rafe would have to do would be incite them against Drew, and it would be all over.

Catching sight of Rafe and his henchmen entering the marketplace, Drew sauntered away in an attempt to be inconspicuous. Seeing a stack of wooden crates, he quickly concealed himself behind them.

Rafe pushed through the crowd and swaggered up to the nearest constable. While he was preoccupied with the officer, Drew made his getaway. He slipped out of the open-air market and onto a side street.

He kept to the back streets and alleys and, after an interminable amount of time, found himself on Rue Dumaine. He glanced about cautiously. There wasn't a lot of activity. Unlit tar pots stood on the corners, but the thick, oppressive smell lingered in the light of day, clogging the air.

This section of the city was still pretty deserted because the Yellow Fever epidemic kept the rich away. Those at the French Market were probably the poor and the immigrants who'd had to remain behind, not having the means or the sense to escape the city's summers and the scourge they brought.

Starting forward, he quickly reached the Beaufort house. He opened the iron gate, went to the door, and banged the knocker. He waited. After a few minutes, he banged again.

The curtain on the window moved ever so slightly.

"Marianne?" he called.

Another minute passed before the door opened.

Jade eyes stared at him; the delectable pink mouth formed an *O* in surprise. She wore a plaid housedress, her hair a silken-mass around her shoulders and down her back.

Her hand flew to her breast. "Andrew?" she whispered in disbelief. "What are you doing here?"

Drew pushed his way inside and closed the door, encouraged by the softening of her gaze, the melting smile creasing her lips. Darkness surrounding them, he pulled her into his arms and kissed her fervently. He touched her hair, her eyelids, her cheeks, loving the feel of her. "Marianne, I thought I'd lost you," he said, choking with emotion.

Wrapping her arms around his waist and laying her head on his chest, she hugged him tightly. "Have you come to take me back with you, monsieur? Wherever that might be."

"If you'll go, yes."

She flung her arms around his neck and rewarded him with short kisses all over his face, preventing him from sharing the news about the watch with her. "Oh, Drew, that's all I've ever wanted to hear from you. I stupidly thought to sacrifice my happiness for that of my family's. Why did you wait until now to ask me back with you?" she continued in a rush.

"I didn't want to put undue pressure on you, Mari." He kissed her pert little nose, then settled on her mouth again. "And I thought you knew I wanted you to go with me, sweetheart. I didn't think I had to say anything else."

Would he ever learn? he wondered. His apathy had almost cost him Marianne, just as his stubbornness had cost him his father's love and understanding. He hoped it wasn't too late for him and Cranneck, as it had been for Rafe and Pierre. He hoped he could smooth out his relationship with his father as smoothly as he had with Marianne.

"Oh, Drew, I'm so glad you came. Just in time, too. I—"

The knocker slammed against the door with impatient urgency, and she jumped, startled. Drew cursed as Rafe's voice drifted through the closed door.

"The mesdames Beauforts have not yet returned, monsieur," he said to someone, banging the knocker again. "I do not believe my worthless cousin is aware of this place. Nevertheless, we will leave no stone unturned. The house is as secured as I thought it would be, but I want you to scale the courtyard walls and search the slave quarters."

"Sacre bleu!" Marianne exclaimed, her eyes widening in alarm as the sounds of Rafe's and the other man's voice faded. "Rafe is pursuing you?"

At Drew's sheepish nod, she hugged him again.

"What does he want, *amour*?"

"Calm down, darling," Drew said, brushing a heavy lock of hair behind her ear. "It isn't as bad as it seems. All Rafe wants to do is kill me in the worst way possible. I took—"

"Oh, *mon Dieu*! What will we do, Andrew? The man wants to kill you, and you are indifferent," she accused.

"As long as he doesn't have a key to this house, it's all right. And you'll have to remain quiet. If we can hear them through the door, they'll also be able to hear us."

"Oh, *oui*," Marianne said, softer.

The doorknob rattled, and Drew raised his finger to his lips for silence. Marianne made the sign of the cross. Minutes passed as they stood motionless, barely daring to breathe.

"Let's go, Monsieur Montague. Your cousin isn't here," an unfamiliar voice said.

"Just watch the place to make sure he doesn't slip past us, in case he does know of the cottage," Rafe ordered briskly.

Retreating footsteps followed the tense conversation.

Drew beckoned Marianne forward. "Come," he said, taking her hand and leading her to the parlor. There, she lit one lamp. Drew took out the watch and chain, which gleamed brightly in the gloom of the house. Because of their need for stealth, all the curtains remained drawn.

"Oh, Drew!" Marianne whispered, touching the jewelry in awe. "You found the watch!"

"Only after you did."

"*Moi?* I do not understand."

"The watch and chain you gifted Rafe with are the same ones that brought me here," Drew told her. "Where did you get it, and why did you give it to Rafe?"

Marianne gasped. "*Mais non!* It cannot be!" She explained why she'd given the watch to Rafe and where she'd purchased it. She told him of the strange eeriness that had surrounded her when she'd held it. "Since it was Rafe's watch to begin with, how did it end up in twenty-first-century New Orleans?"

"I'm sure Laurinda had something to do with that," Drew said wryly. "She as much as told me I needed to learn a lesson in humility and family values and pride. She was right. I understand my father's pride in Bienvenu much better now that I've been a part of these early years."

"I'm glad, *amour*." She frowned. "How will we ever get away from the house with Rafe lurking about?"

He sat on the delicate settee and ran his hand through his hair. The flow of adrenaline that had jetted through him during his escape was leaving him, and, as opposed to the euphoria he'd experience after a wild motorcycle ride, he felt drained. His life was still in danger; with Marianne's decision, so was hers.

Knowing Rafe's persistence, he had no idea how to answer her question. How indeed would they get to the hitching post? By now Rafe probably had the entire city on his trail. Yet tomorrow was the last day of summer, which meant he had a little over twenty-four hours to figure a way out of his dilemma here and get back to the the twenty-first century and home as well. Not wanting Marianne to worry, he said, "We'll manage."

She smiled, trusting him.

"What made you change your mind about marrying Rafe?" he asked, rubbing a hand over his chin.

Marianne drew in a breath and perched beside him. "I could cite many reasons. The fact that I didn't love him wouldn't have mattered. Despite my indecision, I would have married him to save Baywood."

"Why didn't you stay and marry him?" Drew pressed.

Marianne clutched his hand. "Because he isn't you, Andrew. You, whom I love with all my heart."

Upon hearing her words, Drew pulled her into his arms and kissed her with all the love inside him. Marianne returned his kisses with the same passion. With a bright future in the twenty-first century beckoning them, they made love on the parlor floor.

Later, Drew reiterated the wonders of the time he'd come from. Airplanes. Automobiles. Motorcycles. Refrigerators. Telephones. Televisions. Everything that he'd taken for granted and missed fiercely.

"Oh, Andrew, it sounds like a miracle! I do not know what new thing I want to experience first."

"You'll want to experience television first, my love," he

said, thinking of the football games that would be underway by now. "TV for short."

"I will?"

"Yes. Though women are allowed to watch only during the week," he said mischievously.

"Really? No other time? Why is that?"

"That's so they can bring their guys beer and pizza on weekends while the men watch the games," Drew teased, chuckling.

Marianne's excited confusion deepened. "What kind of games? What is pizza and beer? Will I like telephones?"

Drew laughed. "Ahh, yes, most women like telephones." He threaded his fingers through her wealth of beautiful hair. "There are many things that will amaze and enchant you, Mari. But the only thing that will astound you is the complexion of the country."

"I do not understand. 'Complexion'?"

"Years from now, Mari, slavery will be abolished. Men like Simon and Tomas and Henry will be free. In my time, America is the most hyphenated country in the world."

" 'Hyphenated'?" Marianne raised up and looked at him. "What does that mean?"

"It means most people place their nationality in front of 'American.' 'Irish-American,' 'Italian-American,' 'African-American,' and so forth."

"How odd. Is this a political rule of the time?"

"No, love, it's cultural pride."

Marianne clapped her hands. "How wonderful! I will like the twenty-first century, *amour*."

"One other important thing, Mari. My daughter. Teal is a wonderful little girl. I'm sure you'll love her. She has had a lot of adjustments to make in her short life, and I can't wait to hold her in my arms again."

"I already love her, Andrew," Marianne reassured him. Snuggling in his arms again, she patted her stomach. "Would you object to giving her a playmate?"

Drew stared at her in disbelief. "You mean you're . . . ?"

"I'm not at all sure yet, Drew, but I have this feeling—"

He cut off her words with a searing kiss. "Then we'll just have to work on that prospect until sunup." With a wolfish grin, he rolled over and buried himself inside her.

Chapter 38

ARTILLERY FIRE ROCKED the early-morning hours. The blazing tar pots on almost every corner of the city flared so intensely that the dark of night shone as brightly as the middle of day. Thick clouds of smoke suspended over the city choked the atmosphere, eclipsing the predawn blackness.

A makeshift hearse paused on the corner as Drew and Marianne melted into the shadows of the cottage. He held tightly to her hand and clutched the watch in his other one.

"Bring out your dead!" the driver yelled to no one in particular, seemingly undisturbed by the acrid combination of tar and gunpowder that was supposed to clarify the air and chase away the Fever still ravaging the city. When no doors to the houses of the privileged swung open, the death wagon rattled on.

Despite the morbid activity going on around him, Drew thought this to be the best time to try to escape. Once darkness descended and the city turned once more into an awful spectacle of gloom, his pursuers would have secured a hotel room. But Rafe would rise with the end of the artillery-fire at dawn and lead the search for Drew again.

"Come on, darling."

Hurrying forward, he held on to Marianne. They had a few blocks to go before they reached the place on Orleans Avenue where he'd first landed. He assumed that by leaving from the place he'd arrived at, he'd return to the spot he left from. Yet when they reached the St. Louis Hotel, he realized there were no hitching posts with horses' heads in front of the building.

"Hey, you! Montague!" It was Fred, the guy from the ball who'd supplied Rafe with the swords, bringing Drew's worst fears to life. "Hey, Sam! Go get Rafe. I found the thief."

"Okay," Sam agreed, waddling off. "Make sure you don't kill him, Fred," he called over his shoulder. "Rafe said he wants that pleasure hisself."

"Marianne," Drew said, pulling her forward as Fred started in their direction. "Lift up that long dress, darling, and hold it up."

"*Oui,* monsieur," she said, yawning because of the little rest she'd gotten, but complying with the utmost haste.

She held her dress in her free hand, and they took off running, Fred hot on their trail. The goon was quickly joined by others. To Drew's dismay, Rafe was amongst them, riding his palomino and bearing down on them at breakneck speed.

Just before them stood a line of hitching posts topped with horses' heads. Drew didn't know whether the watch worked with just any old hitching post or a particular one, but figured he'd soon find out. Remembering his attempt with the watch from Roudin's, he had a feeling the post and watch worked in conjunction.

He made a mad dash for the post, Marianne's hand securely in his, then hung the watch from its chain on the ear of the horse. Holding the pendulum, he recited the chant.

The watch vibrated violently in his hand. His body trembled, and his hand slipped out of Marianne's. Lights danced before his eyes as her terrified shout not to leave her behind reached him.

He reached out, pressure around his waist, nausea curling

in his stomach. Blindly he reached out for her, grasping at nothingness, his head pounding, dizziness careening through him.

He felt as if he were being pulled in two, fighting two worlds, torn asunder by his need to return for Marianne and his desperation to see his daughter.

Darkness surrounded him as he was propelled forward, the floating that had seized him before weighted down now with the grief already assailing him. After all they'd been through, he'd lost her. She'd been left behind, pregnant with his child.

He opened his eyes. Immediately he blinked against the bright sunlight overhead as he lay flat on his back, his heart beating fast and furious. His emotional distress was as great as any physical pain he'd ever experienced. Once he'd checked on Teal, he'd just have to go back. He and Marianne belonged together.

Coolness washing over him, he breathed in the fresh, clean air, rose unsteadily to his feet, and realized he was standing at the bus stop on North Rampart Street, the very one he'd walked Alaina to. A newspaper vending box stood not far away. A girl leaned against it, while a teenaged boy sat on top of it. The stop was crowded with people waiting for the bus's arrival.

A hand brushed his shoulder. With a sigh he turned and met an awestruck jade gaze.

"Marianne?" he whispered. "How did you . . . ? I thought I'd lost you."

She hugged him. "Never, Andrew. My arms were around your waist." She pointed to the patch of grass behind them. "Somehow I awakened over there instead of right beside you."

Drew was so elated, he was momentarily speechless. He whooped with joy, and one of the waiting passengers turned around.

"Where y'all from?" he asked, mildly curious.

"Around the corner," Drew responded lightly. This being New Orleans, costumes such as the ones they wore were not all that unusual. In and around the French Quarter, movies were frequently being filmed. From Drew's answer, he and Marianne might have been movie extras.

Accepting the answer, the stranger shrugged and walked away. No one else paid much attention to their nineteenth-century attire.

"I want to check something. Come on." Grabbing her hand, Drew led Marianne to the newspaper box and leaned down. He firmly believed he'd breached the time barrier, but he wanted to be sure.

Leaning down, he checked the date and heaved a great sigh of relief. Under the newspaper's title, it read: Monday, November 20, 2000.

Chapter 39

"MARI, ARE YOU all right?" he asked half an hour later, seeing her features rapt with wonder. He'd all but forgotten this was her first time viewing twenty-first-century marvels.

They'd just left his old apartment and found it rented, which didn't surprise him. He'd been gone four months. By now his family probably thought the worst.

By now, Teal had adjusted to what everyone believed would be a life without her father.

Standing in front of his former residence, he pushed that thought aside. He was back, and he would see to it that he was at his daughter's side for any other transition she had to make in life.

"I'm fine," Marianne answered, drawing his attention back to her. "Drew?"

"Yes, darling?"

"Will your maman like me?"

"My mother will love you!" Drew assured her, guiding her to Mrs. Watts's front door and knocking.

When the door swung open, the talkative woman stared, speechless for the first time since he'd known her. The color dropping from her face, she held on to the door for support.

Drew rushed forward and put a supporting arm around her ample girth. "Easy, Mrs. Watts."

"Oh, Drew! Drew!" she said, clutching his neck. "Where have you been?" She kissed him with motherly affection and then slapped his arm. "How could you do this to us!"

He hugged Mrs. Watts. "Please forgive me. I didn't mean to worry you, I promise. I'll explain later," he said, releasing her and pulling Marianne forward. "In the meantime, I'd like you to meet Marianne Beaufort, my soon-to-be wife."

Tears in her eyes, Mrs. Watts pulled Marianne into her embrace. "It's a pleasure to meet you, child. When Drew turned up missing, I just hoped wherever he was he was well cared for, and it seems I got my wish."

Marianne smiled at Mrs. Watts. "Thank you," she said.

"Come on." Mrs. Watts tugged her forward. "You have to tell me where you've been, Drew, and where you met this wonderful girl. What did Teal do when she saw you? And your folks?"

"I haven't been there yet," Drew said, "which is the reason we can't remain here. I came hoping against hope that I could change into my own clothes and get cleaned up before I saw my daughter and parents again, but my house has been rented out."

Mrs. Watts frowned at their clothes. "Where have you been, Drew? You and Marianne look like you've stepped out of a compilation at the Historic New Orleans Collection."

"I know, Mrs. Watts," Drew said with an indulgent sigh. "I'll explain, I swear, but I need you to lend me some money. I don't have any right now." At least not any that was currently accepted. "I can't walk into my parents' house like this—they're going to receive enough of a shock. So, please, with the money you loan me, would you go and buy us some decent clothes and give us a little extra for pocket change? I feel strange going into a store looking like this."

Her lips thinning in displeasure at not being able to hear

the full story just then, Mrs. Watts nodded. After getting their sizes, she went and bought jeans, T-shirts, socks, underwear, and sneakers for them, returning within the hour, since Canal Place wasn't that far away.

When he saw Marianne in the new clothes, he choked. She had the figure of a goddess. High, round breasts strained against the T-shirt. Slim hips flared out from a flat stomach and small waistline and, along with a firm derriere and long legs, filled the jeans.

Smoothing a crease from the middle of the T-shirt, smelling of new clothes and Mrs. Watts's perfume, Marianne glowed. The effect of leaving her own time would slowly sink in, Drew realized, and with the love she bore Clarisse and Genevieve, the impact would overwhelm her. But he'd make up for their loss with all the love in him.

He thought the watch would probably work again, but didn't feel that risking another breach of time would be wise. The next time they mightn't be as lucky as they had this time in ending up together after it had seemed she'd been left behind.

"You look great in modern clothes, Mari," he whispered lustfully. "Now, let's go get Teal."

"Yes, child. You look like a supermodel."

Marianne frowned at Mrs. Watts, having no idea what she was talking about, and not asking. "Why, it's indecent!" she protested instead, gazing at herself in the bedroom mirror, and turning this way and that. "I cannot go out there like this!"

"Believe me, Marianne," Mrs. Watts interjected, putting one of her sweaters around Marianne's shoulders. "Some women show much more than a modest view of their figures."

Drew tugged at her arm. "Come on, darling." When they got outside, he waved to his former neighbor. "We'll see you later, Mrs. Watts."

"You'd better," the kind woman called. "Don't go losing yourself again, and if you need any more money to tide you over, be sure and let me know."

After waving a final good-bye to Mrs. Watts, Marianne hesitated as Drew started forward. "Are you sure it's all right . . . ?" she asked, pointing at herself in her strange new clothes.

"I'm positive."

Wanting Marianne to experience a ride in a car and needing to see Teal as soon as possible, Drew had told Marianne he was going to "hail" something called a "cab," which he now did. Within minutes, he was paying the "fare" and pulling Marianne out of the vehicle.

He breathed in deeply. He was actually home in one piece, with Marianne at his side. Gazing at the stately old mansion with reverence and briefly wondering what it had looked like in its infancy, he hurried down the pathway. He ran onto the porch and rang the doorbell.

The butler opened the door. Receiving much the same reaction from Webster as he had from Mrs. Watts, Drew ignored it. He rushed forward and hauled the butler into his arms for a big bear hug.

"Webster, my good man, wonderful to see you," he said, releasing him. "Where are my parents?"

An unintelligible sound fell from Webster's lips.

"Never mind. I'll find them," Drew went on, urging Marianne forward. "This is Marianne, Webster," he said as they walked farther into the house. "Mother!" he called.

"Dadee!"

Teal's call from down the hall prevented him from going back to aid Webster, who had just hit the floor in a dead faint. So much for imperturbable Englishmen, Drew mused.

"Dadee!" Riotous curls bouncing and tiny arms flailing, Teal raced into Drew's arms.

"God!" he murmured, picking her up and holding her tightly to him. He kissed her hair and her little cheeks over and over, tears streaming down his cheeks. Teal hugged him as tightly, her little fingers tousling his hair.

"You went from me," she pouted.

"I know, princess, but I came back to you," he told her hoarsely, just as his mother's voice reached him.

"Andrew?" Ursula barely whispered, throwing her arms around him and Teal. "Drew! Where have you been?"

"Mother, it's a long story—"

"Cranneck!"

His father's voice reached him, and he stiffened at the rough tone. His hold around Teal tightening, he gazed at Marianne as his mother moved aside so he could better see his father.

It shocked him to see Alaina standing next to Cranneck, who stood silent, his ruddy cheeks pale, looking more like Rafe at that moment than at any time Drew could remember.

"Where the hell have you been, boy?" Cranneck blustered.

But the slight crack in Cranneck's voice told Drew of his worry and pain at thinking he'd lost his son. He swallowed hard and walked over to his father.

"Hello, Dad," he said quietly, feeling everyone's gazes on them, enjoying the weight of Teal in his arms. Securing Teal on his hip, he put an arm around his father's neck. "I've missed you. We have a lot to talk about. First, I want to apologize for being such a disappointment to you all these years. I apologize for the way I behaved. I know everything you did was because you love me. I love you, too—"

Cranneck grabbed him in a fierce hug. "It doesn't matter what you've done, Andrew," he said, using the name he preferred for the first time in years. Silent tears wet Drew's shirt. "What matters most is that I have you back, and so does that beautiful little girl."

That beautiful little girl squirmed. "Put me down!" she yelled.

In four months' time, she had progressed remarkably. Of course, she was only two months away from her third birthday, so those changes were expected.

Drew watched in shock as Teal went to her grandfather and held out her arms to him. Without hesitating, Cranneck released Drew and took Teal into his arms. It seemed as if

Cranneck had taken Teal into his heart as well.

His father released him as Alaina stepped forward. She eyed Marianne, who was standing silently as Drew reacquainted himself with his daughter and parents. Alaina's look wasn't one of jealousy, Drew recognized. It seemed, rather, one of recognition.

Impossible, he thought as he kissed her on the cheek and hugged her tightly.

"Hi, Drew."

"Hi, honey."

"We missed you."

"We certainly did," Ursula interjected, hugging him again. "Let's retire to the parlor and hear where you've been, and then meet this beautiful woman at your side."

When they reached the parlor, his family smothered him yet again with hugs and kisses. This time they included Marianne in their affections, after Drew introduced her and said they planned to marry. Their questions were endless, and everyone shed more tears. Teal played happily, brushing off the emotional reunion with a child's resiliency.

For a brief moment, Drew considered telling a wild, but more plausible tale to explain his long absence. Having learned to appreciate the family plantation, however, and having just witness his father's profound relief that Drew was back, he knew that Cranneck only wanted what was best for him. Though they might believe he'd lost his mind and think an insane asylum was best for him, Drew decided to take the chance and tell his parents the truth. If he wanted a clean slate with his father, he had to start off honestly.

With Marianne helping, he related the tale of his exploits, then waited for their disbelief. It never came. Instead, Ursula gave him an understanding look.

"So that's what it was?" Ursula said, almost relieved.

"Yes, Mother," Drew answered, not quite believing her ready acceptance.

Cranneck laughed. "I see the legacy continues."

"What!" Drew shouted, surprised. "What legacy? You mean this has happened before? To you two?"

"Enough, Drew," Ursula said.

"Listen, Andrew," Cranneck went on, ignoring Drew's demands for an explanation. "Your love for me goes without saying. I *know* you love me, just as I've always loved you. I just didn't know how much until I thought I'd lost you. As you said, we have a lot to talk about." He stood and grabbed Drew in another bear hug. "Welcome home, and just in time for Thanksgiving, too. It's three days away, and we have a lot to be thankful for this year. Now, enough of this," he grumbled. "This calls for a celebration. A drink of some kind. Where the hell is that butler?"

"I almost forgot," Drew said with a mischievous laugh, putting the issue of the mysterious legacy to the side for the moment. "He passed out when he opened the door for Marianne and me. That was twenty minutes ago. I guess he's dragged himself up by now."

After a fashion, things settled down. Ursula called Nolan and Sebastian, and the brothers expressed their relief and happiness that Drew was safe. They also promised to beat the shit out of him for worrying the family when they saw him at Thanksgiving.

Relishing the challenge from his brothers, Drew soon learned that Alaina had visited Teal at his parents' house on a regular basis. After Drew's disappearance, she was concerned for the girl's well-being. But she was glad he'd returned, because she'd won a scholarship to Xavier University to continue her education there.

Her visits would have become infrequent as she concentrated on her studies at the highly competitive school.

"I'm very happy for you, Alaina," Drew said, smiling as he saw Teal, carrying a Barbie doll, walk over to where Marianne sat talking to Ursula.

"I'm happy, too. For you especially." She hugged him fiercely, then stood on tiptoe to whisper in his ear, "Your Marianne is exquisite. Make sure you keep that watch in a revered place, C. Andrew Montague III. It opened your father's heart and mind and brought you the woman you love."

Drew's blood ran cold at her words. "Laurinda?" he croaked, staring at her.

Alaina smiled, her beautiful caramel face animated, her gray eyes sparkling. Gray? Weren't they light brown?

"You're Laurinda, aren't you?"

"I must go," she said, her smile deepening, her long, straight hair fluttering about her shoulders. "I won't need your escort, Drew—it's still daylight. Oh, I almost forgot: I've misplaced my contact lenses. You know, the ones that turn my eyes light brown? They could be anywhere. If you find them, just give me a call." She went to Teal and kissed her. "Bye, sweetie. Bye, all." Winking at Marianne, she strolled from the room.

"Mon Dieu!" Marianne gasped, her face chalk white. "It's . . . it's *her*. It's Laurinda!"

"No," Drew told her. "The resemblance is just coincidence."

"Who are you two talking about?" Ursula asked, sipping her sherry.

"Just an enchantress Mari and I met way back when."

His parents had the same enigmatic expression they'd had earlier. "I see," Cranneck said as Webster wobbled into the room. "Webster, bring in something to drink and ignore everything else. We're living in strange times."

"Yes, Mr. Cranneck, sir."

"You mentioned a legacy earlier," Drew said, deciding to try again. "Dammit, what legacy, Mother?"

Ursula waved her hand in dismissal. "Never mind, dear," she said breezily. "Just reacquaint yourself with your daughter while we acquaint ourselves with our intended daughter-in-law. She saved your life after Rafe tried to slice you in half, and for that we're forever grateful."

The hours slipped by too quickly. Drew found his father to be a different person from the one he'd left behind. Cranneck promised to release Drew's inheritance, and to pay for his tuition at law school as well. Drew happily accepted, but told his father he wanted to work at Bienvenu first, and that he'd be proud to do so.

Drew read Teal a bedtime story and held her long after she'd fallen asleep. Finally, seeing Marianne's exhaustion, he laid his daughter in her frilly bed.

Now, with the occupants of the house slumbering, he held Marianne in his arms, in the "spoon" position.

"Forgive me, my love?" he asked softly.

She turned and looked at him. "For what?"

"For practically ignoring you all evening."

"Non, mon amour," she said, caressing his cheek and raising up to kiss his lips. "It was as it should be. Your family is important. Teal is important. And everyone made it clear that so am I. I received as much attention as you did. And your mother was most gracious to me."

"That's my mom," Drew said.

"I like her, Drew."

"Let's talk about us, darling. Are you having any regrets?"

"Only that I will never see my maman again. But it would have been far more devastating for me if I'd lost *you.*"

"We've found each other, my love, and nothing will ever come between us. I love you." He brushed his lips over hers.

"Andrew?" Marianne said when the kiss ended. "Do you think we'll ever see Alaina again?"

Drew remained silent for a moment, thinking of his friend. He shook his head. "No, sweetheart. I can't explain it, but Laurinda's powers breached the centuries. I think Laurinda brought Alaina into my life for the same purpose she took me back in time: to bring me closer to my family and meet the woman I love with all my soul."

"Now you'll have more family to get close to," she murmured, nuzzling his neck, her hand going to his manhood. "So get close."

"Umm," Drew groaned, "you wanton wench, I wholeheartedly accept your invitation." He rolled on top of her, and she opened to him. "Is this close enough?" he whispered, before closing his mouth over hers.

Author's Note

In 1853, it is believed, forty thousand people contracted Yellow Fever. Of that number, the estimate of those who succumbed ranges from eight thousand to eleven thousand.

It was rare that the disease struck before August, but it was unseasonably cool and damp in 1853. The city's unsanitary conditions proved a breeding ground for the *Aedes Aegypti* mosquito, whose bite spread the disease. That fact wouldn't be discovered until the early twentieth century, and in the six years following the 1853 epidemic, twelve thousand more would lose their lives to Yellow Fever.

Ironically it was the Civil War that brought temporary relief from the yearly menace. The Union blockade of the Mississippi River didn't allow any vessel to come onto that body of water from May 1862 on. General Benjamin "Beast" Butler's sanitation measures controlled the disease in New Orleans, virtually eradicating Yellow Fever there until the year after Reconstruction ended. In that year, 1878, the illness struck twenty-seven thousand and killed forty-four hundred.

We love hearing from readers!
Write to us:
Christine Holden
P.O. Box 8815
New Orleans, LA 70182
Or visit our website:
http://www.tlt.com/authors/christineholden.htm

TIME PASSAGES

FRIENDS ROMANCE

Can a man come between friends?

❏ **A TASTE OF HONEY**
by DeWanna Pace   0-515-12387-0

❏ **WHERE THE HEART IS**
by Sheridon Smythe   0-515-12412-5

❏ **LONG WAY HOME**
by Wendy Corsi Staub   0-515-12440-0

All books $5.99

A Quilting Romance

True love, like a beautiful handmade quilt, pieces together the many patterns and colors of two hearts...

☐ **Patterns of Love**

      by Christine Holden   0-515-12481-8/$5.99

☐ **Pieces of Yesterday**

      by Carol Card Otten   0-515-12524-5/$5.99

☐ **The Coming home Quilt**

      by Joanna Hampton   0-515-12552-0/$5.99

☐ **Mended hearts**

      by Linda Shertzer   0-515-12611-X/$5.99